W9-BAQ-750

*Only death can keep you from the
finish line—in the ultimate competition
of the all-too-near future. . . .*

THE LONG WALK

Every year, on the first day of May, one hundred
teenage boys meet for an event known through-
out the country as "The Long Walk." Among this
year's chosen crop is sixteen-year-old Ray Garraty. He knows the rules: that warnings are issued
if you fall under speed, stumble, sit down. That
after three warnings . . . you get your ticket. And
what happens then serves as a chilling reminder
that there can be only one winner in the Walk—
the one that survives. . . .

WORKS BY STEPHEN KING

NOVELS

Carrie
'Salem's Lot
The Shining
The Stand
The Dead Zone
Firestarter
Cujo
THE DARK TOWER I:
The Gunslinger
Christine
Pet Sematary
Cycle of the Werewolf
The Talisman
(with Peter Straub)
It
The Eyes of the Dragon
Misery
The Tommyknockers
THE DARK TOWER II:
*The Drawing
of the Three*
THE DARK TOWER III:
The Waste Lands

The Dark Half
Needful Things
Gerald's Game
Dolores Claiborne
Insomnia
Rose Madder
Desperation
The Green Mile
THE DARK TOWER IV:
Wizard and Glass
Bag of Bones
The Girl Who Loved Tom
Gordon
Dreamcatcher
Black House
(with Peter Straub)
From a Buick 8
THE DARK TOWER V:
Wolves of the Calla
THE DARK TOWER VI:
Song of Susannah
THE DARK TOWER VII:
The Dark Tower

AS RICHARD BACHMAN

Rage
The Long Walk
Roadwork
The Running Man
Thinner
The Regulators

COLLECTIONS

Night Shift
Different Seasons
Skeleton Crew
Four Past Midnight
Nightmares and
Dreamscapes
Hearts in Atlantis
Everything's Eventual

SCREENPLAYS

Creepshow
Cat's Eye
Silver Bullet
Maximum Overdrive
Pet Sematary
Golden Years
Sleepwalkers
The Stand
The Shining
Rose Red
Storm of the Century

NONFICTION

Danse Macabre
On Writing

THE
LONG
WALK

Stephen King

writing as Richard Bachman

With an introduction by the author,
"The Importance of Being Bachman"

Ⓞ

A SIGNET BOOK

SIGNET
Published by New American Library, a division of
Penguin Group (USA) Inc., 375 Hudson Street,
New York, New York 10014, USA
Penguin Group (Canada), 90 Eglinton Avenue East, Suite 700, Toronto,
Ontario M4P 2Y3, Canada (a division of Pearson Penguin Canada Inc.)
Penguin Books Ltd., 80 Strand, London WC2R 0RL, England
Penguin Ireland, 25 St. Stephen's Green, Dublin 2,
Ireland (a division of Penguin Books Ltd.)
Penguin Group (Australia), 250 Camberwell Road, Camberwell, Victoria 3124,
Australia (a division of Pearson Australia Group Pty. Ltd.)
Penguin Books India Pvt. Ltd., 11 Community Centre, Panchsheel Park,
New Delhi - 110 017, India
Penguin Group (NZ), 67 Apollo Drive, Rosedale, North Shore 0632,
New Zealand (a division of Pearson New Zealand Ltd.)
Penguin Books (South Africa) (Pty.) Ltd., 24 Sturdee Avenue,
Rosebank, Johannesburg 2196, South Africa

Penguin Books Ltd., Registered Offices:
80 Strand, London WC2R 0RL, England

The Long Walk was first published in a Signet edition under the name Richard
Bachman, and later appeared in NAL hardcover and Plume trade paperback omnibus editions titled *The Bachman Books* under the name Stephen King. "The Importance of Being Bachman" appeared in slightly different form in the 1996 Plume
edition of *The Bachman Books*.

First Printing, July 1979
First Printing (King Introduction), April 1999

30 29

Copyright © Richard Bachman, 1979
Introduction copyright © Stephen King, 1996
All rights reserved

 REGISTERED TRADEMARK—MARCA REGISTRADA

Printed in the United States of America

The Importance of Being Bachman

by Stephen King

This is my second introduction to the so-called Bachman Books—a phrase which has come to mean (in my mind, at least) the first few novels published with the Richard Bachman name, the ones which appeared as unheralded paperback originals under the Signet imprint. My first introduction wasn't very good; to me it reads like a textbook case of author obfuscation. But that is not surprising. When it was written, Bachman's alter ego (me, in other words) wasn't in what I'd call a contemplative or analytical mood; I was, in fact, feeling robbed. Bachman was never created as a short-term alias; he was supposed to be there for the long haul, and when my name came out in connection with his, I was surprised, upset, and pissed off. That's not a state conducive to good essay-writing. This time I may do a little better.

Probably the most important thing I can say about Richard Bachman is that *he became real*. Not entirely, of course (he said with a nervous smile); I am not writing this in a delusive state. Except . . . well . . . maybe I am. Delusion is, after all, something writers of fiction try to encourage in their readers, at least during the time that the book or story is open before them, and the writer is hardly immune from this state of . . . what shall I call it? How does "directed delusion" sound?

At any rate, Richard Bachman began his career not as a delusion but as a sheltered place where I could publish a few early works which I felt readers might like. Then he began to grow and come alive, as the creatures of a writer's imagination so frequently do. I began to imagine his life as a dairy farmer . . . his wife, the beautiful Claudia Inez Bachman . . . his solitary New Hampshire mornings, spent milking the cows, getting in the wood, and thinking about his stories . . . his evenings spent writing, always with a glass of whiskey beside his Olivetti typewriter. I once knew a writer who would say his current story or novel was "putting on weight" if it was going well. In much the same way, my pen-name began to put on weight.

Then, when his cover was blown, Richard Bachman died. I made light of this in the few interviews I felt required to give on the subject, saying that he'd died of cancer of the pseudonym, but it was actually shock that killed him: the realization that sometimes people just won't let you alone. To put it in more fulsome (but not at all inaccurate) terms, Bachman was the vampire side of my existence, killed by the sunlight of disclosure. My feelings about all this were confused enough (and *fertile* enough) to bring on a book (a Stephen King book, that is), *The Dark Half*. It was about a writer whose pseudonym, George Stark, actually comes to life. It's a novel my wife has always detested, perhaps because, for Thad Beaumont, the dream of being a writer overwhelms the reality of being a man; for Thad, delusive thinking overtakes rationality completely, with horrific consequences.

I didn't have that problem, though. Really. I put Bachman aside, and although I was sorry that he had to die, I would be lying if I didn't say I felt some relief as well.

The books in this omnibus were written by a young man who was angry, energetic, and deeply infatuated with the art and craft of writing. They weren't written as Bachman books per se (Bachman hadn't been invented yet, after all), but in a Bachman state of mind: low rage, sexual frustration, crazy good humor, and simmering despair. Ben Richards, the scrawny, pre-tubercular protagonist of *The Running Man* (he is about as far from the Arnold Schwarzenegger character in the movie as you can get), crashes his hijacked plane into the Network Games skyscraper, killing himself but taking hundreds (maybe thousands) of Free-Vee executives with him; this is the Richard Bachman version of a happy ending. The conclusions of the other Bachman novels are even more grim. Stephen King has always understood that the good guys don't always win (see *Cujo*, *Pet Sematary*, and—perhaps—*Christine*), but he has also understood that mostly they do. Every day, in real life, the good guys win. Mostly these victories go unheralded (MAN ARRIVES HOME SAFE FROM WORK YET AGAIN wouldn't sell many papers), but they are nonetheless real for all that . . . and fiction should reflect reality.

And yet . . .

In the first draft of *The Dark Half*, I had Thad Beaumont quote Donald E. Westlake, a very funny writer who has penned a series of very grim crime novels under the name Richard Stark. Once asked to explain the dichotomy between Westlake and Stark, the writer in question said, "I write Westlake stories on sunny days. When it rains, I'm Stark." I don't think that made it into the final version of *The Dark Half*, but I have always loved it (and *related* to it, as it has become fashionable to say). Bachman—a fictional creation who became more real to me with each published book which bore his byline—was a rainy-day sort of guy if ever there was one.

The good folks mostly win, courage usually triumphs over fear, the family dog hardly ever contracts rabies: these are things I knew at twenty-five, and things I still know now, at the age of 25 X 2. But I know something else as well: there's a place in most of us where the rain is pretty much constant, the shadows are always long, and the woods are full of monsters. It is good to have a voice in which the terrors of such a place can be articulated and its geography partially described, without denying the sunshine and clarity that fill so much of our ordinary lives.

In *Thinner*, Bachman spoke for the first time on his own—it was the only one of the early Bachman novels that had his name on the first draft instead of mine—and it struck me as really unfair that, just as he was starting to talk with his own voice, he should have been mistaken for me. And a mistake was just what it felt like, because by then Bachman had become a kind of id for me; he said the things I couldn't, and the thought of him out there on his New Hampshire dairy farm—not a best-selling writer who gets his name in some stupid *Forbes* list of entertainers too rich for their own good or his face on the *Today* show or doing cameos in movies— quietly writing his books gave him permission to think in ways I could not think and speak in ways I could not speak. And then these news stories came out saying "Bachman is really King," and there was no one—not even me—to defend the dead man, or to point out the obvious: that King was also really Bachman, at least some of the time.

Unfair I thought then and unfair I think now, but sometimes life bites you a little, that's all. I determined to put Bachman out of my thoughts and my life, and so I did, for a number of years. Then, while I was writing a novel (a *Stephen King* novel) called *Desperation*, Richard Bachman suddenly appeared in my life again.

I was working on a Wang dedicated word processor at that time; it looked like the visiphone in an old Flash Gordon serial. This was paired with a marginally more state-of-the-art laser printer, and from time to time, when an idea occurred to me, I would write down a phrase or a putative title on a scrap of paper and Scotch-tape it to the side of the printer. As I neared the three-quarter mark on *Desperation*, I had a scrap with a single word printed on it: REGULATORS. I had had a great idea for a novel, something that had to do with toys, guns, TV, and suburbia. I didn't know if I would ever write it—lots of those "printer notes" never came to anything—but it was certainly cool to think about.

Then, one rainy day (a Richard Stark sort of day), as I was pulling into my driveway, I had an idea. I don't know where it came from; it was totally unconnected to any of the trivia tumbling through my head at the time. The idea was to take the characters from *Desperation* and put them into *The Regulators*. In some cases, I thought, they could play the same people; in others, they would change; in neither case would they do the same things or react in the same ways, because the different stories would dictate different courses of action. It would be, I thought, like the members of a repertory company acting in two different plays.

Then an even more exciting idea struck me. If I could use the rep company concept with the *characters*, I could use it with the plot itself as well—I could stack a good many of the *Desperation* elements in a brand-new configuration, and create a kind of mirror world. I knew even before setting out that plenty of critics would call this twinning a stunt . . . and they would not be wrong, exactly. But, I thought, it could be a good stunt. Maybe even an illuminating stunt, one which showcased the muscularity and versatility of story, its all but limitless ability to adapt a few basic elements into endlessly pleasing variations, its prankish charm.

But the two books couldn't *sound* exactly the same, and they couldn't *mean* the same, any more than an Edward Albee play and one by William Inge can sound and mean the same, even if they are performed on successive nights by the same company of actors. How could I possibly create a different voice?

At first I thought I couldn't, and that it would be best to consign the idea to the Rube Goldberg bin I keep in the bottom of my mind—the one marked INTERESTING BUT UNWORKABLE CONTRAPTIONS. Then it occurred to me that I had had the answer all along: Richard Bachman could write *The Regulators*. His voice sounded superficially the same as mine, but underneath there was a world of difference— all the difference between sunshine and rain, let us say. And his view of people was always different from mine, simultaneously funnier and more cold-hearted (Bart Dawes in *Roadwork*, my favorite of the early Bachman books, is an excellent example).

Of course Bachman was dead, I had announced that myself, but death is actually a minor problem for a novelist—just ask Paul Sheldon, who brought Misery Chastain back for Annie Wilkes, or Arthur Conan Doyle, who brought Sherlock Holmes back from Reichenbach Falls when fans all over the British Empire clamored for him. I didn't actually bring Richard Bachman back from the dead, anyway; I just visualized a box of neglected manuscripts in his basement, with *The Regulators* on top. Then I transcribed the book Bachman had already written.

That transcription was a little tougher . . . but it was also immensely exhilarating. It was wonderful to hear Bachman's voice again, and what I had hoped might happen *did* happen: a book rolled out that was a kind of fraternal twin to the one I had written under my own name (and the two books were quite literally written back-to-back, the King book finished on one day and the Bachman book commenced on the very next). They were no more alike than King and Bachman themselves. *Desperation* is about God; *The Regulators* is about TV. I guess that makes them both about higher powers, but very different ones just the same.

The importance of being Bachman was always the importance of finding a good voice and a valid point of view that were a little different from my own. Not *really* different; I am not schizo enough to believe that. But I do believe that there are tricks all of us use to change our perspectives and our perceptions—to see ourselves new by dressing up in different clothes and doing our hair in different styles—and that such tricks can be very useful, a way of revitalizing and refreshing old strategies for living life, observing life, and creating art. None of these comments are intended to suggest that I have done anything great in the Bachman books, and they are surely not made as arguments for artistic merit. But I love what I do too much to want to go stale if I can help it. Bachman has been one way in which I have tried to refresh my craft, and to keep from being too comfy and well-padded.

These early books show some progression of the Bachman *persona*, I hope, and I hope they also show the essence of that *persona*. Dark-toned, despairing even when he is laughing (despairing *most* when he's laughing, in fact), Richard Bachman isn't a fellow I'd want to be all the time, even if he *were* still alive . . . but it's good to have that option, that window on the world, polarized though it may be. Still, as the reader works his or her way through these stories, he/she may discover that Dick Bachman has one thing in common with Thad Beaumont's alter ego, George Stark: he's not a very nice guy.

And I wonder if there are any other good manuscripts, at or near completion, in that box found by the widowed Mrs. Bachman in the cellar of their New Hampshire farmhouse.

Sometimes I wonder about that *a lot*.

—Stephen King

Lovell, Maine
April 16, 1996

THE
LONG
WALK

This is for Jim Bishop
and Burt Hatlen and Ted Holmes.

"To me the Universe was all void of Life, or Purpose, of Volition, even of Hostility; it was one huge, dead, immeasurable Steam-engine, rolling on, in its dead indifference, to grind me limb from limb. O vast, gloomy, solitary Golgotha, and Mill of Death! Why was the Living banished thither companionless, conscious? Why, if there is no Devil; nay, unless the Devil is your God?"

—Thomas Carlyle

"I would encourage every American to walk as often as possible. It's more than healthy; it's fun."

—John F. Kennedy (1962)

"The pump don't work
'Cause the vandals took the handle."

—Bob Dylan

Part One

STARTING OUT

Chapter I

"Say the secret word and win a hundred dollars.
George, who are our first contestants?
George . . . ? Are you there, George?"

—Groucho Marx
You Bet Your Life

An old blue Ford pulled into the guarded parking
lot that morning, looking like a small, tired dog
after a hard run. One of the guards, an expressionless young man in a khaki uniform and a Sam
Browne belt, asked to see the blue plastic ID card.
The boy in the back seat handed it to his mother.
His mother handed it to the guard. The guard took
it to a computer terminal that looked strange and
out of place in the rural stillness. The computer
terminal ate the card and flashed this on its screen:

>GARRATY RAYMOND DAVIS
>RD 1 POWNAL MAINE
>ANDROSCOGGIN COUNTY
>ID NUMBER 49-801-89
>OK-OK-OK

The guard punched another button and all
of this disappeared, leaving the terminal screen

smooth and green and blank again. He waved them forward.

"Don't they give the card back?" Mrs. Garraty asked. "Don't they—"

"No, Mom," Garraty said patiently.

"Well, I don't like it," she said, pulling forward into an empty space. She had been saying it ever since they set out in the dark of two in the morning. She had been moaning it, actually.

"Don't worry," he said without hearing himself. He was occupied with looking and with his own confusion of anticipation and fear. He was out of the car almost before the engine's last asthmatic wheeze—a tall, well-built boy wearing a faded army fatigue jacket against the eight o'clock spring chill.

His mother was also tall, but too thin. Her breasts were almost nonexistent: token nubs. Her eyes were wandering and unsure, somehow shocked. Her face was an invalid's face. Her iron-colored hair had gone awry under the complication of clips that was supposed to hold it in place. Her dress hung badly on her body as if she had recently lost a lot of weight.

"Ray," she said in that whispery conspirator's voice that he had come to dread. "Ray, listen—"

He ducked his head and pretended to tuck in his shirt. One of the guards was eating C rations from a can and reading a comic book. Garraty watched the guard eating and reading and thought for the ten thousandth time: It's all *real*. And now, at last, the thought began to swing some weight.

"There's still time to change your mind—"

The fear and anticipation cranked up a notch.

"No, there's no time for that," he said. "The back-out date was yesterday."

Still in that low conspirator's voice that he hated: "They'd understand, I know they would. The Major—"

"The Major would—" Garraty began, and saw his mother wince. "You know what the Major would do, Mom."

Another car had finished the small ritual at the gate and had parked. A boy with dark hair got out. His parents followed and for a moment the three of them stood in conference like worried baseball players. He, like some of the other boys, was wearing a light packsack. Garraty wondered if he hadn't been a little stupid not to bring one himself.

"You won't change your mind?"

It was guilt, guilt taking the face of anxiety. Although he was only sixteen, Ray Garraty knew something about guilt. She felt that she had been too dry, too tired, or maybe just too taken up with her older sorrows to halt her son's madness in its seedling stage—to halt it before the cumbersome machinery of the State with its guards in khaki and its computer terminals had taken over, binding himself more tightly to its insensate self with each passing day, until yesterday, when the lid had come down with a final bang.

He put a hand on her shoulder. "This is my idea, Mom. I know it wasn't yours. I—" He glanced around. No one was paying the slightest attention to them. "I love you, but this way is best, one way or the other."

"It's not," she said, now verging on tears. "Ray, it's not, if your father was here, he'd put a stop to—"

"Well, he's not, is he?" He was brutal, hoping to stave off her tears . . . what if they had to drag her off? He had heard that sometimes that happened. The thought made him feel cold. In a softer voice he said, "Let it go now, Mom. Okay?" He forced a grin. "Okay," he answered for her.

Her chin was still trembling, but she nodded. Not all right, but too late. There was nothing anyone could do.

A light wind soughed through the pines. The sky was pure blue. The road was just ahead and the simple stone post that marked the border between America and Canada. Suddenly his anticipation was greater than his fear, and he wanted to get going, get the show on the road.

"I made these. You can take them, can't you? They're not too heavy, are they?" She thrust a foil-wrapped package of cookies at him.

"Yeah." He took them and then clutched her awkwardly, trying to give her what she needed to have. He kissed her cheek. Her skin was like old silk. For a moment he could have cried himself. Then he thought of the smiling, mustachioed face of the Major and stepped back, stuffing the cookies into the pocket of his fatigue jacket.

"G'bye, Mom."

"Goodbye, Ray. Be a good boy."

She stood there for a moment and he had a

sense of her being very light, as if even the light puffs of breeze blowing this morning might send her sailing away like a dandelion gone to seed. Then she got back into the car and started the engine. Garraty stood there. She raised her hand and waved. The tears were flowing now. He could see them. He waved back and then as she pulled out he just stood there with his arms at his sides, conscious of how fine and brave and alone he must look. But when the car had passed back through the gate, forlornness struck him and he was only a sixteen-year-old boy again, alone in a strange place.

He turned back toward the road. The other boy, the dark-haired one, was watching his folks pull out. He had a bad scar along one cheek. Garraty walked over to him and said hello.

The dark-haired boy gave him a glance. "Hi."

"I'm Ray Garraty," he said, feeling mildly like an asshole.

"I'm Peter McVries."

"You are ready?" Garraty asked.

McVries shrugged. "I feel jumpy. That's the worst."

Garraty nodded.

The two of them walked toward the road and the stone marker. Behind them, other cars were pulling out. A woman began screaming abruptly. Unconsciously, Garraty and McVries drew closer together. Neither of them looked back. Ahead of them was the road, wide and black.

"That composition surface will be hot by noon,"

McVries said abruptly. "I'm going to stick to the shoulder."

Garraty nodded. McVries looked at him thoughtfully.

"What do you weigh?"

"Hundred and sixty."

"I'm one-sixty-seven. They say the heavier guys get tired quicker, but I think I'm in pretty good shape."

To Garraty, Peter McVries looked rather more than that—he looked awesomely fit. He wondered who *they* were that said the heavier guys got tired quicker, almost asked, and decided not to. The Walk was one of those things that existed on apocrypha, talismans, legend.

McVries sat down in the shade near a couple of other boys, and after a moment, Garraty sat beside him. McVries seemed to have dismissed him entirely. Garraty looked at his watch. It was five after eight. Fifty-five minutes to go. Impatience and anticipation came back, and he did his best to squash them, telling himself to enjoy sitting while he could.

All of the boys were sitting. Sitting in groups and sitting alone; one boy had climbed onto the lowest branch of a pine overlooking the road and was eating what looked like a jelly sandwich. He was skinny and blond, wearing purple pants and a blue chambray shirt under an old green zip sweater with holes in the elbows. Garraty wondered if the skinny ones would last or burn out quickly.

The boys he and McVries had sat down next to were talking.

"I'm not hurrying," one of them said. "Why should I? If I get warned, so what? You just adjust, that's all. Adjustment is the key word here. Remember where you heard that first."

He looked around and discovered Garraty and McVries.

"More lambs to the slaughter. Hank Olson's the name. Walking is my game." He said this with no trace of a smile at all.

Garraty offered his own name. McVries spoke his own absently, still looking off toward the road.

"I'm Art Baker," the other said quietly. He spoke with a very slight Southern accent. The four of them shook hands all around.

There was a moment's silence, and McVries said, "Kind of scary, isn't it?"

They all nodded except Hank Olson, who shrugged and grinned. Garraty watched the boy in the pine tree finish his sandwich, ball up the waxed paper it had been in, and toss it onto the soft shoulder. He'll burn out early, he decided. That made him feel a little better.

"You see that spot right by the marker post?" Olson said suddenly.

They all looked. The breeze made moving shadow-patterns across the road. Garraty didn't know if he saw anything or not.

"That's from the Long Walk the year before last," Olson said with grim satisfaction. "Kid was so scared he just froze up at nine o'clock."

They considered the horror of it silently.

"Just couldn't move. He took his three warnings

and then at 9:02 AM they gave him his ticket. Right there by the starting post."

Garraty wondered if his own legs would freeze. He didn't think so, but it was a thing you wouldn't know for sure until the time came, and it was a terrible thought. He wondered why Hank Olson wanted to bring up such a terrible thing.

Suddenly Art Baker sat up straight. "Here he comes."

A dun-colored jeep drove up to the stone marker and stopped. It was followed by a strange, tread-equipped vehicle that moved much more slowly. There were toy-sized radar dishes mounted on the front and back of this halftrack. Two soldiers lounged on its upper deck, and Garraty felt a chill in his belly when he looked at them. They were carrying army-type heavy-caliber carbine rifles.

Some of the boys got up, but Garraty did not. Neither did Olson or Baker, and after his initial look, McVries seemed to have fallen back into his own thoughts. The skinny kid in the pine tree was swinging his feet idly.

The Major got out of the jeep. He was a tall, straight man with a deep desert tan that went well with his simple khakis. A pistol was strapped to his Sam Browne belt, and he was wearing reflector sunglasses. It was rumored that the Major's eyes were extremely light-sensitive, and he was never seen in public without his sunglasses.

"Sit down, boys," he said. "Keep Hint Thirteen in mind." Hint Thirteen was "Conserve energy whenever possible."

Those who had stood sat down. Garraty looked at his watch again. It said 8:16, and he decided it was a minute fast. The Major always showed up on time. He thought momentarily of setting it back a minute and then forgot it.

"I'm not going to make a speech," the Major said, sweeping them with the blank lenses that covered his eyes. "I give my congratulations to the winner among your number, and my acknowledgments of valor to the losers."

He turned to the back of the jeep. There was a living silence. Garraty breathed deep of the spring air. It would be warm. A good day to walk.

The Major turned back to them. He was holding a clipboard. "When I call your name, please step forward and take your number. Then go back to your place until it is time to begin. Do this smartly, please."

"You're in the army now," Olson whispered with a grin, but Garraty ignored it. You couldn't help admiring the Major. Garraty's father, before the Squads took him away, had been fond of calling the Major the rarest and most dangerous monster any nation can produce, a society-supported sociopath. But he had never seen the Major in person.

"Aaronson."

A short, chunky farmboy with a sunburned neck gangled forward, obviously awed by the Major's presence, and took his large plastic 1. He fixed it to his shirt by the pressure strip and the Major clapped him on the back.

"Abraham."

A tall boy with reddish hair in jeans and a T-shirt. His jacket was tied about his waist schoolboy style and flapped wildly around his knees. Olson sniggered.

"Baker, Arthur."

"That's me," Baker said, and got to his feet. He moved with deceptive leisure, and he made Garraty nervous. Baker was going to be tough. Baker was going to last a long time.

Baker came back. He had pressed his number 3 onto the right breast of his shirt.

"Did he say anything to you?" Garraty asked.

"He asked me if it was commencing to come off hot down home," Baker said shyly. "Yeah, he . . . the Major talked to me."

"Not as hot as it's gonna commence getting up here," Olson cracked.

"Baker, James," the Major said.

It went on until 8:40, and it came out right. No one had ducked out. Back in the parking lot, engines started and a number of cars began pulling out—boys from the backup list who would now go home and watch the Long Walk coverage on TV. It's on, Garraty thought, it's really on.

When his turn came, the Major gave him number 47 and told him "Good luck." Up close he smelled very masculine and somehow overpowering. Garraty had an almost insatiable urge to touch the man's leg and make sure he was real.

Peter McVries was 61. Hank Olson was 70. He was with the Major longer than the rest. The Major laughed at something Olson said and clapped him on the back. "I told him to keep a lot of money on short call," Olson said when he came back. "And he told me to give 'em hell. Said he liked to see someone who was raring to rip. Give 'em hell, boy, he said."

"Pretty good," McVries said, and then winked at Garraty. Garraty wondered what McVries had meant, winking like that. Was he making fun of Olson?

The skinny boy in the tree was named Stebbins. He got his number with his head down, not speaking to the Major at all, and then sat back at the base of his tree. Garraty was somehow fascinated with the boy.

Number 100 was a red-headed fellow with a volcanic complexion. His name was Zuck. He got his number and then they all sat and waited for what would come next.

Then three soldiers from the halftrack passed out wide belts with snap pockets. The pockets were filled with tubes of high-energy concentrate pastes. More soldiers came around with canteens. They buckled on the belts and slung the canteens. Olson slung his belt low on his hips like a gunslinger, found a Waifa chocolate bar, and began to eat it. "Not bad," he said, grinning. He swigged from his canteen, washing down the chocolate, and Garraty wondered if Olson was just fronting, or if he knew something Garraty did not.

The Major looked them over soberly. Garraty's wristwatch said 8:56—how had it gotten so late? His stomach lurched painfully.

"All right, fellows, line up by tens, please. No particular order. Stay with your friends, if you like."

Garraty got up. He felt numb and unreal. It was as if his body now belonged to someone else.

"Well here we go," McVries said at his elbow. "Good luck, everyone."

"Good luck to you," Garraty said, surprised.

McVries said: "I need my fucking head examined." He looked suddenly pale and sweaty, not so awesomely fit as he had earlier. He was trying to smile and not making it. The scar stood out on his cheek like a wild punctuation mark.

Stebbins got up and ambled to the rear of the ten wide, ten deep queue. Olson, Baker, McVries, and Garraty were in the third row. Garraty's mouth was dry. He wondered if he should drink some water. He decided against it. He had never in his life been so aware of his feet. He wondered if he might freeze and get his ticket on the starting line. He wondered if Stebbins would fold early—Stebbins with his jelly sandwich and his purple pants. He wondered if *he* would fold up first. He wondered what it would feel like if—

His wristwatch said 8:59.

The Major was studying a stainless steel pocket chronometer. He raised his fingers slowly, and everything hung suspended with his hand. The hundred boys watched it carefully, and the silence was awful and immense. The silence was everything.

Garraty's watch said 9:00, but the poised hand did not fall.

Do it! Why doesn't he *do* it?

He felt like screaming it out.

Then he remembered that his watch was a minute fast—you could set your watch by the Major, only he hadn't, he had forgotten.

The Major's fingers dropped. "Luck to all," he said. His face was expressionless and the reflector sunglasses hid his eyes. They began to walk smoothly, with no jostling.

Garraty walked with them. He hadn't frozen. Nobody froze. His feet passed beyond the stone marker, in parade-step with McVries on his left and Olson on his right. The sound of feet was very loud.

This is it, this is it, this is it.

A sudden insane urge to stop came to him. Just to see if they really meant business. He rejected the thought indignantly and a little fearfully.

They came out of the shade and into the sun, the warm spring sun. It felt good. Garraty relaxed, put his hands in his pockets, and kept step with McVries. The group began to spread out, each person finding his own stride and speed. The half-track clanked along the soft shoulder, throwing thin dust. The tiny radar dishes turned busily, monitoring each Walker's speed with a sophisticated on-board computer. Low speed cutoff was exactly four miles an hour.

"Warning! Warning 88!"

Garraty started and looked around. It was Stebbins. Stebbins was 88. Suddenly he was sure Stebbins was going to get his ticket right here, still in sight of the starting post.

"Smart." It was Olson.

"What?" Garraty asked. He had to make a conscious effort to move his tongue.

"The guy takes a warning while he's still fresh and gets an idea of where the limit is. And he can sluff it easy enough—you walk an hour without getting a fresh warning, you lose one of the old ones. You know that."

"Sure I know it," Garraty said. It was in the rule book. They gave you three warnings. The fourth time you fell below four miles an hour you were . . . well, you were out of the Walk. But if you had three warnings and could manage to walk for three hours, you were back in the sun again.

"So now he knows," Olson said. "And at 10:02, he's in the clear again."

Garraty walked on at a good clip. He was feeling fine. The starting post dropped from sight as they breasted a hill and began descending into a long, pine-studded valley. Here and there were rectangular fields with the earth just freshly turned.

"Potatoes, they tell me," McVries said.

"Best in the world," Garraty answered automatically.

"You from Maine?" Baker asked.

"Yeah, downstate." He looked up ahead. Several boys had drawn away from the main group, making perhaps six miles an hour. Two of them were wearing identical leather jackets, with what looked like eagles on the back. It was a temptation to speed up, but Garraty refused to be hurried. "Conserve energy whenever possible"—Hint 13.

"Does the road go anywhere near your home-town?" McVries asked.

"About seven miles to one side. I guess my mother and my girlfriend will come to see me." He paused and added carefully: "If I'm still walk-ing, of course."

"Hell, there won't be twenty-five gone when we get downstate," Olson said.

A silence fell among them at that. Garraty knew it wasn't so, and he thought Olson did, too.

Two other boys received warnings, and in spite of what Olson had said, Garraty's heart lurched each time. He checked back on Stebbins. He was still at the rear, and eating another jelly sandwich. There was a third sandwich jutting from the pocket of his ragged green sweater. Garraty wondered if his mother had made them, and he thought of the cookies his own mother had given him—pressed on him, as if warding off evil spirits.

"Why don't they let people watch the start of a Long Walk?" Garraty asked.

"Spoils the Walkers' concentration," a sharp voice said.

Garraty turned his head. It was a small dark, intense-looking boy with the number 5 pressed to the collar of his jacket. Garraty couldn't remember his name. "Concentration?" he said.

"Yes." The boy moved up beside Garraty. "The Major has said it is very important to concentrate on calmness at the beginning of a Long Walk." He pressed his thumb reflectively against the end of his rather sharp nose. There was a bright red pimple there. "I agree. Excitement, crowds, TV later. Right now all we need to do is focus." He stared at Garraty with his hooded dark brown eyes and said it again. "Focus."

"All I'm focusing on is pickin' 'em up and layin' 'em down." Olson said.

5 looked insulted. "You have to pace yourself. You have to focus on yourself. You have to have a Plan. I'm Gary Barkovitch, by the way. My home is Washington, D.C."

"I'm John Carter," Olson said. "My home is Barsoom, Mars."

Barkovitch curled his lip in contempt and dropped back.

"There's one cuckoo in every clock, I guess," Olson said.

But Garraty thought Barkovitch was thinking pretty clearly—at least until one of the guards called out "Warning! Warning 5!" about five minutes later.

"I've got a stone in my shoe!" Barkovitch said waspishly.

The soldier didn't reply. He dropped off the halftrack and stood on the shoulder of the road opposite Barkovitch. In his hand he held a stainless steel chronometer just like the Major's. Barkovitch stopped completely and took off his shoe. He shook a tiny pebble out of it. Dark, intense, his olive-sallow face shiny with sweat, he paid no attention when the soldier called out, "Second warning, 5." Instead, he smoothed his sock carefully over the arch of his foot.

"Oh-oh," Olson said. They had all turned around and were walking backward.

Stebbins, still at the tag end, walked past Barkovitch without looking at him. Now Barkovitch was all alone, slightly to the right of the white line, re-tying his shoe.

"Third warning, 5. Final warning."

There was something in Garraty's belly that felt like a sticky ball of mucus. He didn't want to look, but he couldn't look away. He wasn't conserving energy whenever possible by walking backward, but he couldn't help that, either. He could almost feel Barkovitch's seconds shriveling away to nothing.

"Oh, boy," Olson said. "That dumb shit, he's gonna get his ticket."

But then Barkovitch was up. He paused to brush some road dirt from the knees of his pants. Then he broke into a trot, caught up with the group, and settled back into his walking pace. He passed Stebbins, who still didn't look at him, and caught up with Olson.

He grinned, brown eyes glittering. "See? I just got myself a rest. It's all in my Plan."

"Maybe you think so," Olson said, his voice higher than usual. "All I see that you got is three warnings. For your lousy minute and a half you got to walk three . . . fucking . . . *hours*. And why in hell did you need a rest? We just started, for Chrissake!"

Barkovitch looked insulted. His eyes burned at Olson. "We'll see who gets his ticket first, you or me," he said. "It's all in my Plan."

"Your Plan and the stuff that comes out of my asshole bear a suspicious resemblance to each other," Olson said, and Baker chuckled.

With a snort, Barkovitch strode past them.

Olson couldn't resist a parting shot. "Just don't stumble, buddy. They don't warn you again. They just . . ."

Barkovitch didn't even look back and Olson gave up, disgusted.

At thirteen past nine by Garraty's watch (he had taken the trouble to set it back the one minute), the Major's jeep breasted the hill they had just started down. He came past them on the shoulder opposite the pacing halftrack and raised a battery-powered loudhailer to his lips.

"I'm pleased to announce that you have finished the first mile of your journey, boys. I'd also like to remind you that the longest distance a full complement of Walkers has ever covered is seven and three-quarters miles. I'm hoping you'll better that."

The jeep spurted ahead. Olson appeared to be considering this news with startled, even fearful, wonder. Not even eight miles, Garraty thought. It wasn't nearly as far as he would have guessed. He hadn't expected anyone—not even Stebbins—to get a ticket until late afternoon at least. He thought of Barkovitch. All he had to do was fall below speed once in the next hour.

"Ray?" It was Art Baker. He had taken off his

coat and slung it over one arm. "Any particular reason you came on the Long Walk?"

Garraty unclipped his canteen and had a quick swallow of water. It was cool and good. It left beads of moisture on his upper lip and he licked them off. It was good, good to feel things like that.

"I don't really know," he said truthfully.

"Me either." Baker thought for a moment. "Did you go out for track or anything? In school?"

"No."

"Me either. But I guess it don't matter, does it? Not now."

"No, not now," Garraty asked.

Conversation lulled. They passed through a small village with a country store and a gas station. Two old men sat on folding lawn-chairs outside the gas station, watching them with hooded and reptilian old men's eyes. On the steps of the country store, a young woman held up her tiny son so he could see them. And a couple of older kids, around twelve, Garraty judged, watched them out of sight wistfully.

Some of the boys began to speculate about how much ground they had covered. The word came back that a second pacer halftrack had been dispatched to cover the half a dozen boys in the vanguard . . . they were now completely out of sight. Someone said they were doing seven miles an hour. Someone else said it was ten. Someone told them authoritatively that a guy up ahead was flagging and had been warned twice. Garraty wondered why they weren't catching up to him if that was true.

Olson finished the Waifa chocolate bar he had started back at the border and drank some water. Some of the others were also eating, but Garraty decided to wait until he was really hungry. He had heard the concentrates were quite good. The astronauts got them when they went into space.

A little after ten o'clock, they passed a sign that said LIMESTONE 10 MI. Garraty thought about the only Long Walk his father had ever let him go to. They went to Freeport and watched them walk through. His mother had been with them. The Walkers were tired and hollow-eyed and barely conscious of the cheering and the waving signs and the constant hoorah as people cheered on their favorites and those on whom they had wagered. His father told him later that day that people lined the roads from Bangor on. Up-country it wasn't so interesting, and the road was strictly cordoned off—maybe so they could concentrate on being calm, as Barkovitch had said. But as time passed, it got better, of course.

When the Walkers passed through Freeport that year they had been on the road over seventy-two hours. Garraty had been ten and overwhelmed by everything. The Major had made a speech to the crowd while the boys were still five miles out of town. He began with Competition, progressed to Patriotism, and finished with something called the Gross National Product—Garraty had laughed at that, because to him gross meant something nasty, like boogers. He had eaten six hotdogs and when he finally saw the Walkers coming he had wet his pants.

One boy had been screaming. That was his most vivid memory. Every time he put his foot down he had screamed: *I can't. I CAN'T. I can't. I CAN'T.* But he went on walking. They all did, and pretty soon the last of them had gone past L.L. Bean's on U.S. 1 and out of sight. Garraty had been mildly disappointed at not seeing anyone get a ticket. They had never gone to another Long Walk. Later that night Garraty had heard his father shouting thickly at someone into the telephone, the way he did when he was being drunk or political, and his mother in the background, her conspiratorial whisper, begging him to stop, please stop, before someone picked up the party line.

Garraty drank some more water and wondered how Barkovitch was making it.

They were passing more houses now. Families sat out on their front lawns, smiling, waving, drinking Coca-Colas.

"Garraty," McVries said. "My, my, look what you got."

A pretty girl of about sixteen in a white blouse and red-checked pedal pushers was holding up a big Magic Marker sign: GO-GO-GARRATY NUMBER 47 *We Love You Ray* "Maine's Own."

Garraty felt his heart swell. He suddenly knew he was going to win. The unnamed girl proved it.

Olson whistled wetly, and began to slide his stiff index finger rapidly in and out of his loosely curled fist. Garraty thought that was a pretty goddam sick thing to be doing.

To hell with Hint 13. Garraty ran over to the side of the road. The girl saw his number and squealed. She threw herself at him and kissed him hard. Garraty was suddenly, sweatily aroused. He kissed back vigorously. The girl poked her tongue into his mouth twice, delicately. Hardly aware of what he was doing, he put one hand on a round buttock and squeezed gently.

"Warning! Warning 47!"

Garraty stepped back and grinned. "Thanks."

"Oh . . . oh . . . oh sure!" Her eyes were starry.

He tried to think of something else to say, but he could see the soldier opening his mouth to give him the second warning. He trotted back to his place, panting a little and grinning. He felt a little guilty after Hint 13 just the same, though.

Olson was also grinning. "For that I would have taken three warnings."

Garraty didn't answer, but he turned around and walked backward and waved to the girl. When she was out of sight he turned around and began to walk firmly. An hour before his warning would be gone. He must be careful not to get another one. But he felt good. He felt fit. He felt like he could walk all the way to Florida. He started to walk faster.

"Ray." McVries was still smiling. "What's your hurry?"

Yeah, that was right. Hint 6: Slow and easy does it. "Thanks."

McVries went on smiling. "Don't thank me too much. I'm out to win, too."

Garraty stared at him, disconcerted.

"I mean, let's not put this on a Three Muske- teers basis. I like you and it's obvious you're a big hit with the pretty girls. But if you fall over I won't pick you up."

"Yeah." He smiled back, but his smile felt lame.

"On the other hand," Baker drawled softly, "we're all in this together and we might as well keep each other amused."

McVries smiled. "Why not?"

They came to an upslope and saved their breath for walking. Halfway up, Garraty took off his jacket and slung it over his shoulder. A few moments later they passed someone's discarded sweater ly- ing on the road. Someone, Garraty thought, is go- ing to wish they had that tonight. Up ahead, a couple of the point Walkers were losing ground.

Garraty concentrated on picking them up and putting them down. He still felt good. He felt strong.

Chapter 2

"Now you have the money, Ellen, and
that's yours to keep. Unless, of course,
you'd like to trade it for what's behind the curtain."
                                    —Monty Hall
                                    Let's Make a Deal

"I'm Harkness. Number 49. You're Garraty. Number 47. Right?"

Garraty looked at Harkness, who wore glasses and had a crewcut. Harkness's face was red and sweaty. "That's right."

Harkness had a notebook. He wrote Garraty's name and number in it. The script was strange and jerky, bumping up and down as he walked. He ran into a fellow named Collie Parker who told him to watch where the fuck he was going. Garraty suppressed a smile.

"I'm taking down everyone's name and number," Harkness said. When he looked up, the mid-morning sun sparkled on the lenses of his glasses, and Garraty had to squint to see his face. It was 10:30, and they were 8 miles out of Limestone, and they had only 1.75 miles to go to beat the record of the farthest distance traveled by a complete Long Walk group.

"I suppose you're wondering why I'm writing down everyone's name and number," Harkness said.

"You're with the Squads," Olson cracked over his shoulder.

"No, I'm going to write a book," Harkness said pleasantly. "When this is all over, I'm going to write a book."

Garraty grinned. "If you win you're going to write a book, you mean."

Harkness shrugged. "Yes, I suppose. But look at this: a book about the Long Walk from an insider's point of view could make me a rich man."

McVries burst out laughing. "If you win, you won't need a book to make you a rich man, will you?"

Harkness frowned. "Well . . . I suppose not. But it would still make one heck of an interesting book, I think."

They walked on, and Harkness continued taking names and numbers. Most gave them willingly enough, joshing him about the great book.

Now they had come six miles. The word came back that it looked good for breaking the record. Garraty speculated briefly on why they should want to break the record anyhow. The quicker the competition dropped out, the better the odds became for those remaining. He supposed it was a matter of pride. The word also came back that thunder showers were forecast for the afternoon—someone had a transistor radio, Garraty supposed.

If it was true, it was bad news. Early May thunder-showers weren't the warmest.

They kept walking.

McVries walked firmly, keeping his head up and swinging his arms slightly. He had tried the shoulder, but fighting the loose soil there had made him give it up. He hadn't been warned, and if the knapsack was giving him any trouble or chafing, he showed no sign. His eyes were always searching the horizon. When they passed small clusters of people, he waved and smiled his thin-lipped smile. He showed no signs of tiring.

Baker ambled along, moving in a kind of knee-bent shuffle that seemed to cover the ground when you weren't looking. He swung his coat idly, smiled at the pointing people, and sometimes whistled a low snatch of some tune or other. Garraty thought he looked like he could go on forever.

Olson wasn't talking so much anymore, and every few moments he would bend one knee swiftly. Each time Garraty could hear the joint pop. Olson was stiffening up a little, Garraty thought, beginning to show six miles of walking. Garraty judged that one of his canteens must be almost empty. Olson would have to pee before too long.

Barkovitch kept up the same jerky pace, now ahead of the main group as if to catch up with the vanguard Walkers, now dropping back toward Stebbins's position on drag. He lost one of his three warnings and gained it back five minutes later. Garraty decided he must like it there on the edge of nothing.

Stebbins just kept on walking off by himself. Garraty hadn't seen him speak to anybody. He wondered if Stebbins was lonely or tired. He still thought Stebbins would fold up early—maybe first—although he didn't know why he thought so. Stebbins had taken off the old green sweater, and he carried the last jelly sandwich in his hand. He looked at no one. His face was a mask.

They walked on.

The road was crossed by another, and policemen were holding up traffic as the Walkers passed. They saluted each Walker, and a couple of the boys, secure in their immunity, thumbed their noses. Garraty didn't approve. He smiled and nodded to acknowledge the police and wondered if the police thought they were all crazy.

The cars honked, and then some woman yelled out to her son. She had parked beside the road, apparently waiting to make sure her boy was still along for the Walk.

"Percy! *Percy!*"

It was 31. He blushed, then waved a little, and then hurried on with his head slightly bent. The woman tried to run out into the road. The guards on the top deck of the halftrack stiffened, but one of the policemen caught her arm and restrained her gently. Then the road curved and the intersection was out of sight.

They passed across a wooden-slatted bridge. A small brook gurgled its way underneath. Garraty walked close to the railing, and looking over he could see, for just a moment, a distorted image of his own face.

They passed a sign which read LIMESTONE 7 MI. and then under a rippling banner which said LIMESTONE IS PROUD TO WELCOME THE LONG WALKERS. Garraty figured they had to be less than a mile from breaking the record.

Then the word came back, and this time the word was about a boy named Curley, number 7. Curley had a charley horse and had already picked up his first warning. Garraty put on some speed and came even with McVries and Olson. "Where is he?"

Olson jerked his thumb at a skinny, gangling boy in bluejeans. Curley had been trying to cultivate sideburns. The sideburns had failed. His lean and earnest face was now set in lines of terrific concentration, and he was staring at his right leg. He was favoring it. He was losing ground and his face showed it.

"Warning! Warning 7!"

Curley began to force himself faster. He was panting a little. As much from fear as from his exertions, Garraty thought. Garraty lost all track of time. He forgot everything but Curley. He watched him struggle, realizing in a numb sort of way that this might be his struggle an hour from now or a day from now.

It was the most fascinating thing he had ever seen.

Curley fell back slowly, and several warnings were issued to others before the group realized they were adjusting to his speed in their fascination. Which meant Curley was very close to the edge.

"Warning! Warning 7! Third warning, 7!"

"I've got a charley horse!" Curley shouted hoarsely. "It ain't no fair if you've got a charley horse!"

He was almost beside Garraty now. Garraty could see Curley's adam's apple going up and down. Curley was massaging his leg frantically. And Garraty could smell panic coming off Curley in waves, and it was like the smell of a ripe, freshly cut lemon.

Garraty began to pull ahead of him, and the next moment Curley exclaimed: "Thank God! She's loosening!"

No one said anything. Garraty felt a grudging disappointment. It was mean, and unsporting, he supposed, but he wanted to be sure someone got a ticket before he did. Who wants to bow out first?

Garraty's watch said five past eleven now. He supposed that meant they had beaten the record, figuring two hours times four miles an hour. They would be in Limestone soon. He saw Olson flex first one knee, then the other, again. Curious, he tried it himself. His knee joints popped audibly, and he was surprised to find how much stiffness had settled into them. Still, his feet didn't hurt. That was something.

They passed a milk truck parked at the head of a small dirt feeder road. The milkman was sitting on the hood. He waved good-naturedly. "Go to it, boys!"

Garraty felt suddenly angry. Felt like yelling. *Why don't you just get up off your fat ass and go to it with us?* But the milkman was past eighteen. In fact, he looked well past thirty. He was old.

"Okay, everybody, take five," Olson cracked suddenly, and got some laughs.

The milk truck was out of sight. There were more roads now, more policemen and people honking and waving. Someone threw confetti. Garraty began to feel important. He was, after all, "Maine's Own."

Suddenly Curley screamed. Garraty looked back over his shoulder. Curley was doubled over, holding his leg and screaming. Somehow, incredibly, he was still walking, but very slowly. Much too slowly.

Everything went slowly then, as if to match the way Curley was walking. The soldiers on the back of the slow-moving halftrack raised their guns. The crowd gasped, as if they hadn't known this was the way it was, and the Walkers gasped, as if they hadn't known, and Garraty gasped with them, but of course he had known, of course they had all known, it was very simple, Curley was going to get his ticket.

The safeties clicked off. Boys scattered from around Curley like quail. He was suddenly alone on the sunwashed road.

"It isn't fair!" he screamed. "It just isn't *fair!*"

The walking boys entered a leafy glade of shadow, some of them looking back, some of them looking straight ahead, afraid to see. Garraty was looking. He had to look. The scatter of waving spectators had fallen silent as if someone had simply clicked them all off.

"It isn't—"

Four carbines fired. They were very loud. The noise traveled away like bowling balls, struck the hills, and rolled back.

Curley's angular, pimply head disappeared in a hammersmash of blood and brains and flying skull-fragments. The rest of him fell forward on the white line like a sack of mail.

99 now, Garraty thought sickly. 99 bottles of beer on the wall and if one of those bottles should happen to fall . . . oh Jesus . . . oh Jesus . . .

Stebbins stepped over the body. His foot slid a little in some of the blood, and his next step with that foot left a bloody track, like a photograph in an *Official Detective* magazine. Stebbins didn't look down at what was left of Curley. His face didn't change expression. Stebbins, you bastard, Garraty thought, you were supposed to get your ticket first, didn't you know? Then Garraty looked away. He didn't want to be sick. He didn't want to vomit.

A woman beside a Volkswagen bus put her face in her hands. She made odd noises in her throat, and Garraty found he could look right up her dress to her underpants. Her blue underpants. Inexplicably, he found himself aroused again. A fat man with a bald head was staring at Curley and rubbing frantically at a wart beside his ear. He wet his large, thick lips and went on looking and rubbing the wart. He was still looking when Garraty passed him by.

They walked on. Garraty found himself walking with Olson, Baker, and McVries again. They were almost protectively bunched up. All of them were looking straight ahead now, their faces carefully expressionless. The echoes of the carbines seemed to hang in the air still. Garraty kept thinking about the bloody footprint that Stebbins's tennis shoe had left. He wondered if it was still tracking red, almost turned his head to look, then told himself not to be a fool. But he couldn't help wondering. He wondered if it had hurt Curley. He wondered if Curley had felt the gas-tipped slugs hitting home or if he had just been alive one second and dead the next.

But of course it had hurt. It had hurt before, in the worst, rupturing way, knowing there would be no more you but the universe would roll on just the same, unharmed and unhampered.

The word came back that they had made almost nine miles before Curley bought his ticket. The Major was said to be as pleased as punch. Garraty wondered how anyone could know where the hell the Major was.

He looked back suddenly, wanting to know what was being done with Curley's body, but they had already rounded another curve. Curley was out of sight.

"What have you got in that packsack?" Baker asked McVries suddenly. He was making an effort to be strictly conversational, but his voice was high and reedy, near to cracking.

"A fresh shirt," McVries said. "And some raw hamburger."

"Raw hamburger—" Olson made a sick face.

"Good fast energy in raw hamburger," McVries said.

"You're off your trolley. You'll puke all over the place."

McVries only smiled.

Garraty kind of wished he had brought some raw hamburger himself. He didn't know about fast energy, but he liked raw hamburger. It beat chocolate bars and concentrates. Suddenly he thought of his cookies, but after Curley he wasn't very hungry. After Curley, could he really have been thinking about eating raw hamburger?

The word that one of the Walkers had been ticketed out ran through the spectators, and for some reason they began to cheer even more loudly. Thin applause crackled like popcorn. Garraty wondered if it was embarrassing, being shot in front of people, and guessed by the time you got to that you probably didn't give a tin whistle. Curley hadn't looked as if he gave a tin whistle, certainly. Having to relieve yourself, though. That would be bad. Garraty decided not to think about that.

The hands on his watch now stood firmly straight up at noon. They crossed a rusty iron bridge spanning a high, dry gorge, and on the other side was a sign reading: ENTERING LIMESTONE CITY LIMITS—WELCOME, LONG WALKERS!

Some of the boys cheered, but Garraty saved his breath.

The road widened and the Walkers spread across it comfortably, the groups loosening up a little. After all, Curley was three miles back now.

Garraty took out his cookies, and for a moment turned the foil package over in his hands. He thought homesickly of his mother, then stuffed the feeling aside. He would see Mom and Jan in Freeport. That was a promise. He ate a cookie and felt a little better.

"You know something?" McVries said.

Garraty shook his head. He took a swig from his canteen and waved at an elderly couple sitting beside the road with a small cardboard GARRATY sign.

"I have no idea what I'll want if I do win this," McVries said. "There's nothing that I really need. I mean, I don't have a sick old mother sitting home or a father on a kidney machine, or anything. I don't even have a little brother dying gamely of leukemia." He laughed and unstrapped his canteen.

"You've got a point there," Garraty agreed.

"You mean I *don't* have a point there. The whole thing is pointless."

"You don't really mean that," Garraty said confidently. "If you had it to do all over again—"

"Yeah, yeah, I'd still do it, but—"

"Hey!" The boy ahead of them, Pearson, pointed. "Sidewalks!"

They were finally coming into the town proper. Handsome houses set back from the road looked down at them from the vantage of ascending green lawns. The lawns were crowded with people, waving and cheering. It seemed to Garraty that almost all of them were sitting down. Sitting on the ground, on lawn chairs like the old men back at the gas station, sitting on picnic tables. Even sitting on swings and porch gliders. He felt a touch of jealous anger.

Go ahead and wave your asses off. I'll be damned if I'll wave back anymore. Hint 13. Conserve energy whenever possible.

But finally he decided he was being foolish. People might decide he was getting snotty. He was, after all, "Maine's Own." He decided he would wave to all the people with GARRATY signs. And to all the pretty girls.

Sidestreets and cross-streets moved steadily past. Sycamore Street and Clark Avenue, Exchange Street and Juniper Lane. They passed a corner grocery with a Narragansett beer sign in the window, and a five-and-dime plastered with pictures of the Major.

The sidewalks were lined with people, but thinly lined. On the whole, Garraty was disappointed. He knew the real crowds would come further down the line, but it was still something of a wet firecracker. And poor old Curley had missed even this.

The Major's jeep suddenly spurted out of a sidestreet and began pacing the main group. The vanguard was still some distance ahead.

A tremendous cheer went up. The Major nodded and smiled and waved to the crowd. Then he made a neat left-face and saluted the boys. Garraty felt a thrill go straight up his back. The Major's sun-glasses glinted in the early afternoon sunlight.

The Major raised the battery-powered loudhailer to his lips. "I'm proud of you, boys. Proud!"

From somewhere behind Garraty a voice said softly but clearly: "Diddly shit."

Garraty turned his head, but there was no one back there but four or five boys watching the Major intently (one of them realized he was saluting and dropped his hand sheepishly), and Stebbins. Stebbins did not even seem to be looking at the Major.

The jeep roared ahead. A moment later the Major was gone again.

They reached downtown Limestone around twelve-thirty. Garraty was disappointed. It was pretty much of a one-hydrant town. There was a business section and three used-car lots and a Mc-Donalds and a Burger King and a Pizza Hut and an industrial park and that was Limestone.

"It isn't very big, is it?" Baker said.

Olson laughed.

"It's probably a nice place to live," Garraty said defensively.

"God spare me from nice places to live," McVries said, but he was smiling.

"Well, what turns you on," Garraty said lamely.

By one o'clock, Limestone was a memory. A small swaggering boy in patched denim overalls walked along with them for almost a mile, then sat down and watched them go by.

The country grew hillier. Garraty felt the first

real sweat of the day coming out on him. His shirt was patched to his back. On his right, thunderheads were forming, but they were still far away. There was a light, circulating breeze, and that helped a little.

"What's the next big town, Garraty?" McVries asked.

"Caribou, I guess." He was wondering if Stebbins had eaten his last sandwich yet. Stebbins had gotten into his head like a snatch of pop music that goes around and around until you think you're going to go crazy with it. It was one-thirty. The Long Walk had progressed through eighteen miles.

"How far's that?" Garraty wondered what the record was for miles walked with only one Walker punched out. Eighteen miles seemed pretty good to him. Eighteen miles was a figure a man could be proud of. I walked eighteen miles. Eighteen.

"I said—" McVries began patiently.

"Maybe thirty miles from here."

"Thirty," Pearson said. "Jesus."

"It's a bigger town than Limestone," Garraty said. He was still feeling defensive, God knew why. Maybe because so many of these boys would die here, maybe all of them. Probably all of them. Only six Long Walks in history had ended over the state line in New Hampshire, and only one had gotten into Massachusetts, and the experts said that was like Hank Aaron hitting seven hundred and thirty home runs, or whatever it was . . . a record that would never be equaled. Maybe he would die here, too. Maybe he would. But that was different.

Native soil. He had an idea the Major would like that. "He died on his native soil."

He tipped his canteen up and found it was empty. "Canteen!" he called. "47 calling for a canteen!"

One of the soldiers jumped off the halftrack and brought over a fresh canteen. When he turned away, Garraty touched the carbine slung over the soldier's back. He did it furtively. But McVries saw him.

"Why'd you do that?"

Garraty grinned and felt confused. "I don't know. Like knocking on wood, maybe."

"You're a dear boy, Ray," McVries said, and then put on some speed and caught up with Olson, leaving Garraty to walk alone, feeling more confused than ever.

Number 93—Garraty didn't know his name—walked past him on Garraty's right. He was staring down at his feet and his lips moved soundlessly as he counted his paces. He was weaving slightly.

"Hi," Garraty said.

93 cringed. There was a blankness in his eyes, the same blankness that had been in Curley's eyes while he was losing his fight with the charley horse. He's tired, Garraty thought. He knows it, and he's scared. Garraty suddenly felt his stomach tip over and right itself slowly.

Their shadows walked alongside them now. It was quarter of two. Nine in the morning, cool, sitting on the grass in the shade, was a month back.

At just before two, the word came back again. Garraty was getting a firsthand lesson in the psy-

chology of the grapevine. Someone found something out, and suddenly it was all over. Rumors
were created by mouth-to-mouth respiration. It
looks like rain. Chances are it's going to rain. It's
gonna rain pretty soon. The guy with the radio
says it's gonna shit potatoes pretty quick. But it
was funny how often the grapevine was right. And
when the word came back that someone was slowing up, that someone was in trouble, the grapevine
was always right.

This time the word was that number 9, Ewing,
had developed blisters and had been warned twice.
Lots of boys had been warned, but that was normal. The word was that things looked bad for
Ewing.

He passed the word to Baker, and Baker looked
surprised. "The black fella?" Baker said. "So black
he looks sorta blue?"

Garraty said he didn't know if Ewing was black
or white.

"Yeah, he's black," Pearson said. He pointed to
Ewing. Garraty could see tiny jewels of perspira-
tion gleaming in Ewing's natural. With something
like horror, Garraty observed that Ewing was wearing sneakers.

Hint 3: Do not, repeat, *do not* wear sneakers.
Nothing will give you blisters faster than sneakers
on a Long Walk.

"He rode up with us," Baker said. "He's from
Texas."

Baker picked up his pace until he was walking
with Ewing. He talked with Ewing for quite a

while. Then he dropped back slowly to avoid getting warned himself. His face was bleak. "He started to blister up two miles out. They started to break back in Limestone. He's walkin' in pus from broken blisters."

They all listened silently. Garraty thought of Stebbins again. Stebbins was wearing tennis shoes. Maybe Stebbins was fighting blisters right now.

"Warning! Warning 9! This is your third warning, 9!"

The soldiers were watching Ewing carefully now. So were the Walkers. Ewing was in the spotlight. The back of his T-shirt, startlingly white against his black skin, was sweat-stained gray straight down the middle. Garraty could see the big muscles in his back ripple as he walked. Muscles enough to last for days, and Baker said he was walking in pus. Blisters and charley horses. Garraty shivered. Sudden death. All those muscles, all the training, couldn't stop blisters and charley horses. What in the name of God had Ewing been thinking about when he put on those P.F. Flyers?

Barkovitch joined them. Barkovitch was looking at Ewing, too. "Blisters!" He made it sound like Ewing's mother was a whore. "What the hell can you expect from a dumb nigger? Now I ask you."

"Move away," Baker said evenly, "or I'll poke you."

"It's against the rules," Barkovitch said with a smirk. "Keep it in mind, cracker." But he moved away. It was as if he took a small poison cloud with him.

Two o'clock became two-thirty. Their shadows got longer. They walked up a long hill, and at the crest Garraty could see low mountains, hazy and blue, in the distance. The encroaching thunderheads to the west were darker now, and the breeze had stiffened, making his flesh goosebump as the sweat dried on him.

A group of men clustered around a Ford pickup truck with a camper on the back cheered them crazily. The men were all very drunk. They all waved back at the men, even Ewing. They were the first spectators they had seen since the swaggering little boy in the patched overalls.

Garraty broke open a concentrate tube without reading the label and ate it. It tasted slightly porky. He thought about McVries's hamburger. He thought about a great big chocolate cake with a cherry on the top. He thought about flapjacks. For some crazy reason he wanted a cold flapjack full of apple jelly. The cold lunch his mother always made when he and his father went hunting in November.

Ewing bought a hole about ten minutes later.

He was clustered in with a group of boys when he fell below speed for the last time. Maybe he thought the boys would protect him. The soldiers did their job well. The soldiers were experts. They pushed the other boys aside. They dragged Ewing over to the shoulder. Ewing tried to fight, but not much. One of the soldiers pinned Ewing's arms behind him while the other put his carbine up to Ewing's head and shot him. One leg kicked convulsively.

"He bleeds the same color as anyone else," McVries said suddenly. It was very loud in the stillness after the single shot. His adam's apple bobbed, and something clicked in his throat.

Two of them gone now. The odds infinitesimally adjusted in favor of those remaining. There was some subdued talk, and Garraty wondered again what they did with the bodies.

You wonder too goddam much! he shouted at himself suddenly.

And realized he was tired.

Part Two

GOING
DOWN
THE ROAD

Chapter 3

"You will have thirty seconds, and
   please remember that your answer must
   be in the form of a question."
                                    —Art Fleming
                                       Jeopardy

It was three o'clock when the first drops of rain
fell on the road, big and dark and round. The sky
overhead was tattered and black, wild and fascinating. Thunder clapped hands somewhere above
the clouds. A blue fork of lightning went to earth
somewhere up ahead.

Garraty had donned his coat shortly after Ewing had gotten his ticket, and now he zipped it and
turned up his collar. Harkness, the potential author, had carefully stowed his notebook in a Bag-
gie. Barkovitch had put on a yellow vinyl rainhat.
There was something incredible about what it did
to his face, but you would have been hard put to
say just what. He peered out from beneath it like a
truculent lighthouse keeper.

There was a stupendous crack of thunder. "Here
it comes!" Olson cried.

The rain came pouring down. For a few moments it was so heavy that Garraty found himself

totally isolated inside an undulating shower curtain. He was immediately soaked to the skin. His hair became a dripping pelt. He turned his face up into the rain, grinning. He wondered if the soldiers could see them. He wondered if a person might conceivably—

While he was still wondering, the first vicious onslaught let up a little and he could see again. He looked over his shoulder at Stebbins. Stebbins was walking hunched over, his hands hooked against his belly, and at first Garraty thought he had a cramp. For a moment Garraty was in the grip of a strong panicky feeling, nothing at all like he had felt when Curley and Ewing bought it. He didn't want Stebbins to fold up early anymore.

Then he saw Stebbins was only protecting the last half of his jelly sandwich, and he faced forward again, feeling relieved. He decided Stebbins must have a pretty stupid mother not to wrap his goddam sandwiches in foil, just in case of rain.

Thunder cracked stridently, artillery practice in the sky. Garraty felt exhilarated, and some of his tiredness seemed to wash away with the sweat from his body. The rain came again, hard and pelting, and finally let off into a steady drizzle. Overhead, the clouds began to tatter.

Pearson was now walking beside him. He hitched up his pants. He was wearing jeans that were too big for him and he hitched up his pants often. He wore horn-rimmed glasses with lenses like the bottoms of Coke bottles, and now he whipped them off and began to clean them on the tail of his shirt. He goggled in that myopic, defenseless way that people with very poor eyesight have when their glasses are off. "Enjoy your shower, Garraty?"

Garraty nodded. Up ahead, McVries was urinating. He was walking backward while he did it, spraying the shoulder considerately away from the others.

Garraty looked up at the soldiers. They were wet, too, of course, but if they were uncomfortable, they didn't show it. Their faces were perfectly wooden. I wonder what it feels like, he thought, just to shoot someone down. I wonder if it makes them feel powerful. He remembered the girl with the sign, kissing her, feeling her ass. Feeling her smooth underpants under her pedal pushers. That had made him feel powerful.

"That guy back there sure doesn't say much, does he?" Baker said suddenly. He jerked a thumb at Stebbins. Stebbins's purple pants were almost black now that they were soaked through.

"No. No, he doesn't."

McVries pulled a warning for slowing down too much to zip up his fly. They pulled even with him, and Baker repeated what he had said about Stebbins.

"He's a loner, so what?" McVries said, and shrugged. "I think—"

"Hey," Olson broke in. It was the first thing he had said in some time, and he sounded queer. "My legs feel funny."

Garraty looked at Olson closely and saw the

seedling panic in his eyes already. The look of bravado was gone. "How funny?" he asked.

"Like the muscles are all turning . . . baggy."

"Relax," McVries said. "It happened to me a couple of hours ago. It passes off."

Relief showed in Olson's eyes. "Does it?"

"Yeah, sure it does."

Olson didn't say anything, but his lips moved. Garraty thought for a moment he was praying, but then he realized he was just counting his paces.

Two shots rang out suddenly. There was a cry, then a third shot.

They looked and saw a boy in a blue sweater and dirty white clamdiggers lying facedown in a puddle of water. One of his shoes had come off. Garraty saw he had been wearing white athletic socks. Hint 12 recommended them.

Garraty stepped over him, not looking too closely for holes. The word came back that this boy had died of slowing down. Not blisters or a charley horse, he had just slowed down once too often and got a ticket.

Garraty didn't know his name or number. He thought the word would come back on that, but it never did. Maybe nobody knew. Maybe he had been a loner like Stebbins.

Now they were twenty-five miles into the Long Walk. The scenery blended into a continuous mural of woods and fields, broken by an occasional house or a crossroads where waving, cheering people stood in spite of the dying drizzle. One old lady stood frozenly beneath a black umbrella, neither waving nor speaking nor smiling. She watched them go by with gimlet eyes. There was not a sign of life or movement about her except for the wind-twitched hem of her black dress. On the middle finger of her right hand she wore a large ring with a purple stone. There was a tarnished cameo at her throat.

They crossed a railroad track that had been abandoned long ago—the rails were rusty and witch-grass was growing in the cinders between the ties. Somebody stumbled and fell and was warned and got up and went on walking with a bleeding knee.

It was only nineteen miles to Caribou, but dark would come before that. No rest for the wicked, Garraty thought and that struck him funny. He laughed.

McVries looked at him closely. "Getting tired?"

"No," Garraty said. "I've been tired for quite a while now." He looked at McVries with something like animosity. "You mean you're not?"

McVries said, "Just go on dancing with me like this forever, Garraty, and I'll never tire. We'll scrape our shoe on the stars and hang upside down from the moon."

He blew Garraty a kiss and walked away.

Garraty looked after him. He didn't know what to make of McVries.

By quarter of four the sky had cleared and there was a rainbow in the west, where the sun was sitting below gold-edged clouds. Slanting rays of the late afternoon sunlight colored the newly turned fields they were passing, making the furrows sharp and black where they contoured around the long, sloping hills.

The sound of the halftrack was quiet, almost soothing. Garraty let his head drop forward and semi-dozed as he walked. Somewhere up ahead was Freeport. Not tonight or tomorrow though. Lot of steps. Long way to go. He found himself still with too many questions and not enough answers. The whole Walk seemed nothing but one looming question mark. He told himself that a thing like this must have some deep meaning. Surely it was so. A thing like this must provide an answer to every question; it was just a matter of keeping your foot on the throttle. Now if he could only—

He put his foot down in a puddle of water and started fully awake again. Pearson looked at him quizzically and pushed his glasses up on his nose. "You know that guy that fell down and cut himself when we were crossing the tracks?"

"Yeah. It was Zuck, wasn't it?"

"Yeah. I just heard he's still bleeding."

"How far to Caribou, Maniac?" somebody asked him. Garraty looked around. It was Barkovitch. He had tucked his rainhat into his back pocket where it flapped obscenely.

"How the hell should I know?"

"You live here, don't you?"

"It's about seventeen miles," McVries told him. "Now go peddle your papers, little man."

Barkovitch put on his insulted look and moved away.

"He's some hot ticket," Garraty said.

"Don't let him get under your skin," McVries replied. "Just concentrate on walking him into the ground."

"Okay, coach."

McVries patted Garraty on the shoulder. "You're going to win this one for the Gipper, my boy."

"It seems like we've been walking forever, doesn't it?"

"Yeah."

Garraty licked his lips, wanting to express himself and not knowing just how. "Did you ever hear that bit about a drowning man's life passing before his eyes?"

"I think I read it once. Or heard someone say it in a movie."

"Have you ever thought that might happen to us? On the Walk?"

McVries pretended to shudder. "Christ, I hope not."

Garraty was silent for a moment and then said, "Do you think . . . never mind. The hell with it."

"No, go on. Do I think what?"

"Do you think we could live the rest of our lives on this road? That's what I meant. The part we would have had if we hadn't . . . you know."

McVries fumbled in his pocket and came up with a package of Mellow cigarettes. "Smoke?"

"I don't."

"Neither do I," McVries said, and then put a cigarette into his mouth. He found a book of matches with a tomato sauce recipe on it. He lit the cigarette, drew smoke in, and coughed it out. Garraty thought of Hint 10: Save your wind. If you smoke ordinarily, try not to smoke on the Long Walk.

"I thought I'd learn," McVries said defiantly.

"It's crap, isn't it?" Garraty said sadly.

McVries looked at him, surprised, and then threw the cigarette away. "Yeah," he said. "I think it is."

The rainbow was gone by four o'clock. Davidson, 8, dropped back with them. He was a good-looking boy except for the rash of acne on his forehead. "That guy Zuck's really hurting," Davidson said. He had had a packsack the last time Garraty saw him, but he noticed that at some point Davidson had cast it away.

"Still bleeding?" McVries asked.

"Like a stuck pig." Davidson shook his head. "It's funny the way things turn out, isn't it? You fall down any other time, you get a little scrape. He needs stitches." He pointed to the road. "Look at that."

Garraty looked and saw tiny dark spots on the drying hardtop. "Blood?"

"It ain't molasses," Davidson said grimly.

"Is he scared?" Olson asked in a dry voice.

"He says he doesn't give a damn," Davidson said. "But *I'm* scared." His eyes were wide and gray. "I'm scared for all of us."

They kept on walking. Baker pointed out another Garraty sign.

"Hot shit," Garraty said without looking up. He

was following the trail of Zuck's blood, like Dan'l Boone tracking a wounded Indian. It weaved slowly back and forth across the white line.

"McVries," Olson said. His voice had gotten softer in the last couple of hours. Garraty had decided he liked Olson in spite of Olson's brass-balls outer face. He didn't like to see Olson getting scared, but there could be no doubt that he was.

"What?" McVries said.

"It isn't going away. That baggy feeling I told you about. It isn't going away."

McVries didn't say anything. The scar on his face looked very white in the light of the setting sun.

"It feels like my legs could just collapse. Like a bad foundation. That won't happen, will it? Will it?" Olson's voice had gotten a little shrill.

McVries didn't say anything.

"Could I have a cigarette?" Olson asked. His voice was low again.

"Yeah. You can keep the pack."

Olson lit one of the Mellows with practiced ease, cupping the match, and thumbed his nose at one of the soldiers watching him from the halftrack. "They've been giving me the old hairy eyeball for the last hour or so. They've got a sixth sense about it." He raised his voice again. "You like it, don't you, fellas? You like it, right? That goddam right, is it?"

Several of the Walkers looked around at him and then looked away quickly. Garraty wanted to look away too. There was hysteria in Olson's voice. The soldiers looked at Olson impassively. Garraty wondered if the word would go back on Olson pretty quick, and couldn't repress a shudder.

By four-thirty they had covered thirty miles. The sun was half-gone, and it had turned blood red on the horizon. The thunderheads had moved east, and overhead the sky was a darkening blue. Garraty thought about his hypothetical drowning man again. Not so hypothetical at that. The coming night was like water that would soon cover them.

A feeling of panic rose in his gullet. He was suddenly and terribly sure that he was looking at the last daylight in his life. He wanted it to stretch out. He wanted it to last. He wanted the dusk to go on for hours.

"Warning! Warning 100! Your third warning, 100!"

Zuck looked around. There was a dazed, uncomprehending look in his eyes. His right pantsleg was caked with dried blood. And then, suddenly, he began to sprint. He weaved through the Walkers like a broken-field runner carrying a football. He ran with that same dazed expression on his face.

The halftrack picked up speed. Zuck heard it coming and ran faster. It was a queer, shambling, limping run. The wound on his knee broke open again, and as he burst into the open ahead of the main pack, Garraty could see the drops of fresh blood splashing and flying from the cuff of his pants. Zuck ran up the next rise, and for a moment he was starkly silhouetted against the red sky, a galvanic black shape, frozen for a moment in midstride like a scarecrow in full flight. Then he was gone and the halftrack followed. The two soldiers that had dropped off it trudged along with the boys, their faces empty.

Nobody said a word. They only listened. There was no sound for a long time. An incredibly, unbelievably long time. Only a bird, and a few early May crickets, and somewhere behind them, the drone of a plane.

Then there was a single sharp report, a pause, then a second.

"Making sure," someone said sickly.

When they got up over the rise they saw the halftrack sitting on the shoulder half a mile away. Blue smoke was coming from its dual exhaust pipes. Of Zuck there was no sign. No sign at all.

"Where's the Major?" someone screamed. The voice was on the raw edge of panic. It belonged to a bulletheaded boy named Gribble number 48. "I want to see the Major, goddammit! Where is he?"

The soldiers walking along the verge of the road did not answer. No one answered.

"Is he making another speech?" Gribble stormed. "Is that what he's doing? Well, he's a *murderer*! That's what he is, a *murderer*! I . . . I'll tell him! You think I won't? I'll tell him to his face! I'll tell him *right to his face*!" In his excitement he had fallen below the pace, almost stopping, and the soldiers became interested for the first time.

"Warning! Warning 48!"

Gribble faltered to a stop, and then his legs picked up speed. He looked down at his feet as he walked.

Soon they were up to where the halftrack waited. It began to crawl along beside them again.

At about 4:45, Garraty had supper—a tube of processed tuna fish, a few Snappy Crackers with cheese spread, and a lot of water. He had to force himself to stop there. You could get a canteen anytime but there would be no fresh concentrates until tomorrow morning at nine o'clock ... and he might want a midnight snack. Hell, he might *need* a midnight snack.

"It may be a matter of life and death," Baker said, "but it sure isn't hurtin' your appetite any."

"Can't afford to let it," Garraty answered. "I don't like the idea of fainting about two o'clock tomorrow morning."

Now there was a genuinely unpleasant thought. You wouldn't know anything, probably. Wouldn't feel anything. You'd just wake up in eternity.

"Makes you think, doesn't it?" Baker said softly.

Garraty looked at him. In the fading daylight, Baker's face was soft and young and beautiful. "Yeah. I've been thinking about a whole hell of a lot of things."

"Such as?"

"Him, for one," Garraty said, and jerked his head toward Stebbins, who was still walking along at the same pace he had been walking at when they started out. His pants were drying on him. His face was shadowy. He was still saving his last half-sandwich.

"What about him?"

"I wonder why he's here, why he doesn't say anything. And whether he'll live or die."

"Garraty, we're all going to die."

"But hopefully not tonight," Garraty said. He kept his voice light, but a shudder suddenly wracked him. He didn't know if Baker saw it or not. His kidneys contracted. He turned around, unzipped his fly, and began walking backward.

"What do you think about the Prize?" Baker asked.

"I don't see much sense thinking about it," Garraty said, and began to urinate. He finished, zipped his fly, and turned around again, mildly pleased that he had accomplished the operation without drawing a warning.

"I think about it," Baker said dreamily. "Not so much the Prize itself as the money. All that money."

"Rich men don't enter the Kingdom of Heaven," Garraty said. He watched his feet, the only things that were keeping him from finding out if there really was a Kingdom of Heaven or not.

"Hallelujah," Olson said. "There'll be refreshments after the meetin'."

"You a religious fella?" Baker asked Garraty.

"No, not particularly. But I'm no money freak."

"You might be if you grew up on potato soup and collards," Baker sid. "Sidemeat only when your daddy could afford the ammunition."

"Might make a difference," Garraty agreed, and then paused, wondering whether to say anything else. "But it's never really the important thing."

He saw Baker looking at him uncomprehendingly and a little scornfully.

"You can't take it with you, that's your next line," McVries said.

Garraty glanced at him. McVries was wearing that irritating, slanted smile again. "It's true, isn't it?" he said. "We don't bring anything into the world and we sure as shit don't take anything out."

"Yes, but the period in between those two events is more pleasant in comfort, don't you think?" McVries said.

"Oh, comfort, shit," Garraty said. "If one of those goons riding that overgrown Tonka toy over there shot you, no doctor in the world could revive you with a transfusion of twenties or fifties."

"I ain't dead," Baker said softly.

"Yeah, but you could be." Suddenly it was very important to Garraty that he put this across. "What if you won? What if you spent the next six weeks planning what you were going to do with the cash—never mind the Prize, just the cash—and what if the first time you went out to buy something, you got flattened by a taxicab?"

Harkness had come over and was now walking beside Olson. "Not me, babe," he said. "First thing I'd do is buy a whole fleet of Checkers. If I win this, I may never walk again."

"You don't understand," Garraty said, more exasperated than ever. "Potato soup or sirloin tips, a mansion or a hovel, once you're dead that's it, they put you on a cooling board like Zuck or Ewing and that's it. You're better to take it a day at a time, is all I'm saying. If people just took it a day at a time, they'd be a lot happier."

"Oh, such a golden flood of bullshit," McVries said.

"Is that so?" Garraty cried. "How much planning are you doing?"

"Well, right now I've sort of adjusted my horizons, that's true—"

"You bet it is," Garraty said grimly. "The only difference is we're involved in dying right now."

Total silence followed that. Harkness took off his glasses and began to polish them. Olson looked a shade paler. Garraty wished he hadn't said it; he had gone too far.

Then someone in back said quite clearly: "Hear, hear!"

Garraty looked around, sure it was Stebbins even though he had never heard Stebbins's voice. But Stebbins gave no sign. He was looking down at the road.

"I guess I got carried away," Garraty muttered, even though he wasn't the one who had gotten carried away. That had been Zuck. "Anyone want a cookie?"

He handed the cookies around, and it got to be five o'clock. The sun seemed to hang suspended halfway over the horizon. The earth might have stopped turning. The three or four eager beavers who were still ahead of the pack had dropped back until they were less than fifty yards ahead of the main group.

It seemed to Garraty that the road had become a sly combination of upgrades with no corresponding downs. He was thinking that if that were true they'd all end up breathing through oxygen faceplates before long when his foot came down on a discarded belt of food concentrates. Surprised, he looked up. It had been Olson's. His hands were twitching at his waist. There was a look of frowning surprise on his face.

"I dropped it," he said. "I wanted something to eat and I dropped it." He laughed, as if to show what a silly thing that had been. The laugh stopped abruptly. "I'm hungry," he said.

No one answered. By that time everyone had gone by and there was no chance to pick it up. Garraty looked back and saw Olson's food belt lying across the broken white passing line.

"I'm hungry," Olson repeated patiently.

The Major likes to see someone who's raring to rip, wasn't that what Olson had said when he came back from getting his number? Olson didn't look quite so raring to rip anymore. Garraty looked at the pockets of his own belt. He had three tubes of concentrate left, plus the Snappy Crackers and the cheese. The cheese was pretty cruddy, though.

"Here," he said, and gave Olson the cheese.

Olson didn't say anything, but he ate the cheese.

"Musketeer," McVries said, with that same slanted grin.

By five-thirty the air was smoky with twilight. A few early lightning bugs flitted aimlessly through the air. A groundfog had curdled milkily in the ditches and lower gullies of the fields. Up ahead someone asked what happened if it got so foggy you walked off the road by mistake.

Barkovitch's unmistakable voice came back quickly and nastily: "What do you think, Dumbo?"

Four gone, Garraty thought. Eight and a half hours on the road and only four gone. There was a small, pinched feeling in his stomach. I'll never outlast all of them, he thought. Not *all* of them. But on the other hand, why not. Someone had to.

Talk had faded with the daylight. The silence that set in was oppressive. The encroaching dark, the groundmist collecting into small, curdled pools . . . for the first time it seemed perfectly real and totally unnatural, and he wanted either Jan or his mother, some woman, and he wondered what in the hell he was doing and how he ever could have gotten involved. He could not even kid himself that everything had not been up front, because it had been. And he hadn't even done it alone. There were currently ninety-five other fools in this parade.

The mucus ball was in his throat again, making it hard to swallow. He realized that someone up ahead was sobbing softly. He had not heard the sound begin, and no one had called his attention to it; it was as if it had been there all along.

Ten miles to Caribou now, and at least there would be lights. The thought cheered Garraty a little. It was okay after all, wasn't it? He was alive, and there was no sense thinking ahead to a time when he might not be. As McVries had said, it was all a matter of adjusting your horizons.

At quarter of six the word came back on a boy named Travin, one of the early leaders who was now falling slowly back through the main group. Travin had diarrhea. Garraty heard it and couldn't believe it was true, but when he saw Travin he knew that it was. The boy was walking and holding his pants up at the same time. Every time he squatted he picked up a warning, and Garraty wondered sickly why Travin didn't just let it roll down his legs. Better to be dirty than dead.

Travin was bent over, walking like Stebbins with his sandwich, and every time he shuddered Garraty knew that another stomach cramp was ripping through him. Garraty felt disgusted. There was no fascination in this, no mystery. It was a boy with a bellyache, that was all, and it was impossible to feel anything but disgust and a kind of animal terror. His own stomach rolled queasily.

The soldiers were watching Travin very carefully. Watching and waiting. Finally Travin half-squatted, half-fell, and the soldiers shot him with his pants down. Travin rolled over and grimaced at the sky, ugly and pitiful. Someone retched noisily and was warned. It sounded to Garraty as if he was spewing his belly up whole.

"He'll go next," Harkness said in a business-like way.

"Shut up," Garraty choked thickly. "Can't you just shut up?"

No one replied. Harkness looked ashamed and began to polish his glasses again. The boy who vomited was not shot.

They passed a group of cheering teenagers sitting on a blanket and drinking Cokes. They recognized Garraty and gave him a standing ovation. It made him feel uncomfortable. One of the girls had very large breasts. Her boyfriend was watching them jiggle as she jumped up and down. Garraty decided that he was turning in to a sex maniac.

"Look at them jahoobies," Pearson said. "Dear, dear me."

Garraty wondered if she was a virgin, like he was.

They passed by a still, almost perfectly circular pond, faintly misted over. It looked like a gently clouded mirror, and in the mysterious tangle of water plants growing around the edge, a bullfrog croaked hoarsely. Garraty thought the pond was one of the most beautiful things he had ever seen.

"This is one hell of a big state," Barkovitch said someplace up ahead.

"That guy gives me a royal pain in the ass," McVries said solemnly. "Right now my one goal in life is to outlast him."

Olson was saying a Hail Mary.

Garraty looked at him, alarmed.

"How many warnings has he got?" Pearson asked.

"None that I know of," Baker said.

"Yeah, but he don't look so good."

"At this point, none of us do," McVries said.

Another silence fell. Garraty was aware for the first time that his feet hurt. Not just his legs, which had been troubling him for some time, but his feet.

He noticed that he had been unconsciously walking on the outside of the soles, but every now and then he put a foot down flat and winced. He zipped his jacket all the way up and turned the collar against his neck. The air was still damp and raw.

"Hey! Over there!" McVries said cheerfully.

Garraty and the others looked to the left. They were passing a graveyard situated atop a small grassy knoll. A fieldstone wall surrounded it, and now the mist was creeping slowly around the leaning gravestones. An angel with a broken wing stared at them with empty eyes. A nuthatch perched atop a rust flaking flagholder left over from some patriotic holiday and looked them over perkily.

"Our first boneyard," McVries said. "It's on your side. Ray, you lose all your points. Remember that game?"

"You talk too goddam much," Olson said suddenly.

"What's wrong with graveyards, Henry, old buddy? A fine and private place, as the poet said. A nice watertight casket—"

"Just shut up!"

"Oh, pickles," McVries said. His scar flashed very white in the dying daylight. "You don't really mind the thought of dying, do you, Olson? Like the poet also said, it ain't the dying, it's laying in the grave so long. Is that what's bugging you, booby?" McVries began to trumpet. "Well, cheer up, Charlie! There's a brighter day com—"

"Leave him alone," Baker said quietly.

"Why should I? He's busy convincing himself

he can crap out any time he feels like it. That if he just lays down and dies, it won't be as bad as everyone makes out. Well, I'm not going to let him get away with it."

"If he doesn't die, you will," Garraty said.

"Yeah, I'm remembering," McVries said, and gave Garraty his tight, slanted smile . . . only this time there was absolutely no humor in it at all. Suddenly McVries looked furious, and Garraty was almost afraid of him. "He's the one that's forgetting. This turkey here."

"I don't want to do it anymore," Olson said hollowly, "I'm sick of it."

"Raring to rip," McVries said, turning on him. "Isn't that what you said? Fuck it, then. Why don't you just fall down and die then?"

"Leave him alone," Garraty said.

"Listen, Ray—"

"No, you listen. One Barkovitch is enough. Let him do it his own way. No musketeers, remember."

McVries smiled again. "Okay, Garraty. You win."

Olson didn't say anything. He just kept picking them up and laying them down.

Full dark had come by six-thirty. Caribou, now only six miles away, could be seen on the horizon as a dim glow. There were few people along the road to see them into town. They seemed to have all gone home to supper. The mist was chilly around Ray Garraty's feet. It hung over the hills in ghostly limp banners. The stars were coming brighter overhead, Venus glowing steadily, the Dipper in its accustomed place. He had always been good at the constellations. He pointed out Cassiopeia to Pearson, who only grunted.

He thought about Jan, his girl, and felt a twinge of guilt about the girl he had kissed earlier. He couldn't remember exactly what that girl had looked like anymore, but she had excited him. Putting his hand on her ass like that had excited him—what would have happened if he had tried to put his hand between her legs? He felt a clockspring of pressure in his groin that made him wince a little as he walked.

Jan had long hair, almost to her waist. She was sixteen. Her breasts were not as big as those of the girl who had kissed him. He had played with her breasts a lot. It drove him crazy. She wouldn't let him make love to her, and he didn't know how to make her. She wanted to, but she wouldn't. Garraty knew that some boys could do that, could get a girl to go along, but he didn't seem to have quite enough personality—or maybe not quite enough *will*—to convince her. He wondered how many of the others here were virgins. Gribble had called the Major a murderer. He wondered if Gribble was a virgin. He decided Gribble probably was.

They passed the Caribou city limits. There was a large crowd there, and a news truck from one of the networks. A battery of lights bathed the road in a warm white glare. It was like walking into a sudden warm lagoon of sunlight, wading through it, and then emerging again.

A fat newspaperman in a three-piece suit trotted along with them, poking his long-reach microphone at different Walkers. Behind him, two technicians busily unreeled a drum of electric cable.

"How do you feel?"

"Okay. I guess I feel okay."

"Feeling tired?"

"Yeah, well, you know. Yeah. But I'm still okay."

"What do you think your chances are now?"

"I dunno ... okay, I guess. I still feel pretty strong."

He asked a big bull of a fellow, Scramm, what he thought of the Long Walk. Scramm grinned, said he thought it was the biggest fucking thing he'd ever seen, and the reporter made snipping motions with his fingers at the two technicians. One of them nodded back wearily.

Shortly afterward he ran out of microphone cable and began wending his way back toward the mobile unit, trying to avoid the tangles of unreeled cord. The crowd, drawn as much by the TV crew as by the Long Walkers themselves, cheered enthusiastically. Posters of the Major were raised and lowered rhythmically on sticks so raw and new they were still bleeding sap. When the cameras panned over them, they cheered more frantically than ever and waved to Aunt Betty and Uncle Fred

They rounded a bend and passed a small shop where the owner, a little man wearing stained white, had set up a soft drink cooler with a sign over it which read: ON THE HOUSE FOR THE LONG WALKERS!! COURTESY OF "EV'S" MARKET! A police cruiser was parked close by, and two policemen were patiently explaining to Ev, as they undoubtedly did every year, that it was against the rules for spectators to offer any kind of aid or assistance—including soft drinks—to the Walkers.

They passed by the Caribou Paper Mills, Inc., a huge, soot-blackened building on a dirty river. The workers were lined up against the cyclone fences, cheering good-naturedly and waving. A whistle blew as the last of the Walkers—Stebbins—passed by, and Garraty, looking back over his shoulder, saw them trooping inside again.

"Did he ask you?" a strident voice inquired of Garraty. With a feeling of great weariness, Garraty looked down at Gary Barkovitch.

"Did who ask me what?"

"The reporter, Dumbo. Did he ask you how you felt?"

"No, he didn't get to me." He wished Barkovitch would go away. He wished the throbbing pain in the soles of his feet would go away.

"They asked me," Barkovitch said. "You know what I told them?"

"Huh-uh."

"I told them I felt great," Barkovitch said aggressively. The rainhat was still flopping in his back pocket. "I told them I felt real strong. I told them I felt prepared to go on forever. And do you know what else I told them?"

"Oh, shut up," Pearson said.

"Who asked you, long, tall and ugly?" Barkovitch said.

"Go away," McVries said. "You give me a headache."

Insulted once more, Barkovitch moved on up the line and grabbed Collie Parker. "Did he ask you what—"

"Get out of here before I pull your fucking nose off and make you eat it," Collie Parker snarled. Barkovitch moved on quickly. The word on Collie Parker was that he was one mean son of a bitch.

"That guy drives me up the wall," Pearson said.

"He'd be glad to hear it," McVries said. "He likes it. He also told that reporter that he planned to dance on a lot of graves. He means it, too. That's what keeps him going."

"Next time he comes around I think I'll trip him," Olson said. His voice sounded dull and drained.

"Tut-tut," McVries said. "Rule 8, no interference with your fellow Walkers."

"You know what you can do with Rule 8," Olson said with a pallid smile.

"Watch out," McVries grinned, "you're starting to sound pretty lively again."

By 7 PM the pace, which had been lagging very close to the minimum limit, began to pick up a little. It was cool and if you walked faster you kept warmer. They passed beneath a turnpike overpass, and several people cheered them around mouthfuls of Dunkin' Donuts from the glass-walled shop situated near the base of the exit ramp.

"We join up with the turnpike someplace, don't we?" Baker asked.

"In Oldtown," Garraty said. "Approximately one hundred and twenty miles."

Harkness whistled through his teeth.

Not long after that, they walked into downtown Caribou. They were forty-four miles from their starting point.

Chapter 4

"The ultimate game show would be one
where the losing contestant was killed."
—Chuck Barris
Game show creator
MC of *The Gong Show*

Everyone was disappointed with Caribou.

It was just like Limestone.

The crowds were bigger, but otherwise it was
just another mill-pulp-and-service town with a
scattering of stores and gas stations, one shopping
center that was having, according to the signs
plastered everywhere, OUR ANNUAL WALK-IN
FOR VALUES SALE!, and a park with a war memorial in it. A small, evil-sounding high school
band struck up the National Anthem, then a med-
ley of Sousa marches, and then, with taste so bad it
was almost grisly, *Marching to Pretoria*.

The same woman who had made a fuss at the
crossroads so far back turned up again. She was
still looking for Percy. This time she made it through
the police cordon and right onto the road. She
pawed through the boys, unintentionally tripping
one of them up. She was yelling for her Percy to
come home now. The soldiers went for their guns,

and for a moment it looked very much as if Percy's mom was going to buy herself an interference ticket. Then a cop got an armlock on her and dragged her away. A small boy sat on a KEEP MAINE TIDY barrel and ate a hotdog and watched the cops put Percy's mom in a police cruiser. Percy's mom was the high point of going through Caribou.

"What comes after Oldtown, Ray?" McVries asked.

"I'm not a walking roadmap," Garraty said irritably. "Bangor, I guess. Then Augusta. Then Kittery and the state line, about three hundred and thirty miles from here. Give or take. Okay? I'm picked clean."

Somebody whistled. "Three hundred and thirty miles."

"It's unbelievable," Harkness said gloomily.

"The whole damn thing is unbelievable," McVries said. "I wonder where the Major is?"

"Shacked up in Augusta," Olson said.

They all grinned, and Garraty reflected how strange it was about the Major, who had gone from God to Mammon in just ten hours.

Ninety-five left. But that wasn't even the worst anymore. The worst was trying to visualize McVries buying it, or Baker. Or Harkness with his silly book idea. His mind shied away from the thought.

Once Caribou was behind them, the road became all but deserted. They walked through a country crossroads with a single lightpole rearing high above, spotlighting them and making crisp black shadows as they passed through the glare. Far away a train whistle hooted. The moon cast a dubious light on the groundfog, leaving it pearly and opalescent in the fields.

Garraty took a drink of water.

"Warning! Warning 12! This is your final warning, 12!"

12 was a boy named Fenter who was wearing a souvenir T-shirt which read I RODE THE MT. WASHINGTON COG RAILWAY. Fenter was licking his lips. The word was that his foot had stiffened up on him badly. When he was shot ten minutes later, Garraty didn't feel much. He was too tired. He walked around Fenter. Looking down he saw something glittering in Fenter's hand. A St. Christopher's medal.

"If I get out of this," McVries said abruptly, "you know what I'm going to do?"

"What?" Baker asked.

"Fornicate until my cock turns blue. I've never been so horny in my life as I am right this minute, at quarter of eight on May first."

"You mean it?" Garraty asked.

"I do," McVries assured. "I could even get horny for you, Ray, if you didn't need a shave."

Garraty laughed.

"Prince Charming, that's who I am," McVries said. His hand went to the scar on his cheek and touched it. "Now all I need is a Sleeping Beauty. I could awake her with a biggy sloppy soul kiss and the two of us would ride away into the sunset. At least as far as the nearest Holiday Inn."

"Walk," Olson said listlessly.

"Huh?"

"Walk into the sunset."

"Walk into the sunset, okay," McVries said. "True love either way. Do you believe in true love, Hank dear?"

"I believe in a good screw," Olson said, and Art Baker burst out laughing.

"I believe in true love," Garraty said, and then felt sorry he had said it. It sounded naive.

"You want to know why I don't?" Olson said. He looked up at Garraty and grinned a scary, furtive grin. "Ask Fenter. Ask Zuck. They know."

"That's a hell of an attitude," Pearson said. He had come out of the dark from someplace and was walking with them again. Pearson was limping, not badly, but very obviously limping.

"No, it's not," McVries said, and then, after a moment, he added cryptically: "Nobody loves a deader."

"Edgar Allan Poe did," Baker said. "I did a report on him in school and it said he had tendencies that were ne-necro—"

"Necrophiliac," Garraty said.

"Yeah, that's right."

"What's that?" Pearson asked.

"It means you got an urge to sleep with a dead woman," Baker said. "Or a dead man, if you're a woman."

"Or if you're a fruit," McVries put in.

"How the hell did we get on this?" Olson croaked. "Just how in the hell did we get on the subject of screwing dead people? It's fucking repulsive."

"Why not?" A deep, somber voice said. It was Abraham, 2. He was tall and disjointed-looking; he walked in a perpetual shamble. "I think we all might take a moment or two to stop and think about whatever kind of sex life there may be in the next world."

"I get Marilyn Monroe," McVries said. "You can have Eleanor Roosevelt, Abe old buddy."

Abraham gave him the finger. Up ahead, one of the soldiers droned out a warning.

"Just a second now. Just one motherfucking second here." Olson spoke slowly, as if he wrestled with a tremendous problem in expression. "You're all off the subject. All off."

"The Transcendental Quality of Love, a lecture by the noted philosopher and Ethiopian jug-rammer Henry Olson," McVries said. "Author of *A Peach Is Not a Peach without a Pit* and other works of—"

"Wait!" Olson cried out. His voice was as shrill as broken glass. "You wait just one goddam second! Love is a put-on! It's nothing! One big fat el zilcho! You got it?"

No one replied. Garraty looked out ahead of him, where the dark charcoal hills met the star-punched darkness of the sky. He wondered if he couldn't feel the first faint twinges of a charley horse in the arch of his left foot. I want to sit down, he thought irritably. Damn it all, I want to sit down.

"Love is a fake!" Olson was blaring. "There are three great truths in the world and they are a good meal, a good screw, and a good shit, and that's *all*! And when you get like Fenter and Zuck—"

"Shut up," a bored voice said, and Garraty knew it was Stebbins. But when he looked back, Stebbins was only looking at the road and walking along near the left-hand edge.

A jet passed overhead, trailing the sound of its engines behind it and chalking a feathery line across the night sky. It passed low enough for them to be able to see its running lights, pulsing yellow and green. Baker was whistling again. Garraty let his eyelids drop mostly shut. His feet moved on their own.

His half-dozing mind began to slip away from him. Random thoughts began to chase each other lazily across its field. He remembered his mother singing him an Irish lullaby when he was very small . . . something about cockles and mussels, alive, alive-o. And her face, so huge and beautiful, like the face of an actress on a movie screen. Wanting to kiss her and be in love with her for always. When he grew up, he would marry her.

This was replaced by Jan's good-humored Polish face and her dark hair that streamed nearly to her waist. She was wearing a two-piece bathing suit beneath a short beach coat because they were going to Reid Beach. Garraty himself was wearing a ragged pair of denim shorts and his zoris.

Jan was gone. Her face became that of Jimmy Owens, the kid down the block from them. He had been five and Jimmy had been five and Jimmy's mother had caught them playing Doctor's Office in the sandpit behind Jimmy's house. They both had boners. That's what they called them—boners. Jimmy's mother had called his mother and his mother had come to get him and had sat him down in her bedroom and had asked him how he would like it if she made him go out and walk down the street with no clothes on. His dozing body contracted with the groveling embarrassment of it, the deep shame. He had cried and begged, not to make him walk down the street with no clothes on . . . and not to tell his father.

Seven years old now. He and Jimmy Owens peering through the dirt-grimed window of the Burr's Building Materials office at the naked lady calendars, knowing what they were looking at but not really knowing, feeling a crawling shameful exciting pang of something. Of something. There had been one blond lady with a piece of blue silk draped across her hips and they had stared at it for a long, long time. They argued about what might be down there under the cloth. Jimmy said he had seen his mother naked. Jimmy said he knew. Jimmy said it was hairy and cut open. He had refused to believe Jimmy, because what Jimmy said was disgusting.

Still he was sure that ladies must be different from men down there and they had spent a long purple summer dusk discussing it, swatting mosquitoes and watching a scratch baseball game in the lot of the moving van company across the street from Burr's. He could feel, actually *feel* in the half-waking dream the sensation of the hard curb beneath his fanny.

The next year he had hit Jimmy Owens in the mouth with the barrel of his Daisy air rifle while they were playing guns and Jimmy had to have four stitches in his upper lip. A year after that they had moved away. He hadn't meant to hit Jimmy in the mouth. It had been an accident. Of that he was quite sure, even though by then he had known Jimmy was right because he had seen his own mother naked (he had not meant to see her naked— it had been an accident). They were hairy down there. Hairy and cut open.

Shhh, it isn't a tiger, love, only your teddy bear, see? . . . Cockles and mussels, alive, alive-o . . . Mother loves her boy . . . Shhh . . . Go to sleep . . .

"Warning! Warning 47!"

An elbow poked him rudely in the ribs. "That's you, boy. Rise and shine." McVries was grinning at him.

"What time is it?" Garraty asked thickly.

"Eight thirty-five."

"But I've been—"

"—dozing for hours," McVries said. "I know the feeling."

"Well, it sure seemed that way."

"It's your mind," McVries said, "using the old escape hatch. Don't you wish your feet could?"

"I use Dial," Pearson said, pulling an idiotic face. "Don't you wish everybody did?"

Garraty thought that memories were like a line drawn in the dirt. The further back you went the scuffier and harder to see that line got. Until finally there was nothing but smooth sand and the black hole of nothingness that you came out of. The memories were in a way like the road. Here it was real and hard and tangible. But that early road, that nine in the morning road, was far back and meaningless.

They were almost fifty miles into the Walk. The word came back that the Major would be by in his jeep to review them and make a short speech when they actually got to the fifty-mile point. Garraty thought that was most probably horseshit.

They breasted a long, steep rise, and Garraty was tempted to take his jacket off again. He didn't. He unzipped it, though, and then walked backward for a minute. The lights of Caribou twinkled at him, and he thought about Lot's wife, who had looked back and turned into a pillar of salt.

"Warning! Warning 47! Second warning, 47!"

It took Garraty a moment to realize it was him. His second warning in ten minutes. He started to feel afraid again. He thought of the unnamed boy who had died because he had slowed down once too often. Was that what he was doing?

He looked around. McVries, Harkness, Baker and Olson were all staring at him. Olson was having a particularly good look. He could make out the intent expression on Olson's face even in the dark. Olson had outlasted six. He wanted to make Garraty lucky seven. He wanted Garraty to die.

"See anything green?" Garraty asked irritably.

"No," Olson said, his eyes sliding away. "Course not."

Garraty walked with determination now, his arms swinging aggressively. It was twenty to nine. At twenty to eleven—eight miles down the road—he would be free again. He felt an hysterical urge to proclaim he could do it, they needn't send the word back on him, they weren't going to watch him get a ticket . . . at least not yet.

The groundfog spread across the road in thin ribbons, like smoke. The shapes of the boys moved through it like dark islands somehow set adrift. At fifty miles into the Walk they passed a small, shut-up garage with a rusted-out gas pump in front. It was little more than an ominous, leaning shape in the fog. The clear fluorescent light from a telephone booth cast the only glow. The Major didn't come. No one came.

The road dipped gently around a curve, and then there was a yellow road sign ahead. The word came back, but before it got to Garraty he could read the sign for himself:

STEEP GRADE TRUCKS USE LOW GEAR

Groans and moans. Somewhere up ahead Barkovitch called out merrily: "Step into it, brothers! Who wants to race me to the top?"

"Shut your goddam mouth, you little freak," someone said quietly.

"Make me, Dumbo!" Barkovitch shrilled. "Come on up here and make me!"

"He's crackin'," Baker said.

"No," McVries replied. "He's just stretching. Guys like him have an awful lot of stretch."

Olson's voice was deadly quiet. "I don't think I can climb that hill. Not at four miles an hour."

The hill stretched above them. They were almost to it now. With the fog it was impossible to see the top. For all we know, it might just go up forever, Garraty thought.

They started up.

It wasn't as bad, Garraty discovered, if you stared down at your feet as you walked and leaned forward a little. You stared strictly down at the tiny patch of pavement between your feet and it gave you the impression that you were walking on level ground. Of course, you couldn't kid yourself that your lungs and the breath in your throat weren't heating up, because they were.

Somehow, the word started coming back—some people still had breath to spare, apparently. The word was that this hill was a quarter of a mile long. The word was it was two miles long. The word was that no Walker had ever gotten a ticket on this hill. The word was that three boys had gotten tickets here just last year. And after that, the word stopped coming back.

"I can't do it," Olson was saying monotonously. "I can't do it anymore." His breath was coming in doglike pants. But he kept on walking and they all kept on walking. Little grunting noises and soft, plosive breathing became audible. The only other sounds were Olson's chant, the scuff of many feet, and the grinding, ratcheting sound of the half-track's engine as it chugged along beside them.

Garraty felt the bewildered fear in his stomach grow. He could actually die here. It wouldn't be hard at all. He had screwed around and had gotten two warnings on him already. He couldn't be much over the limit right now. All he had to do was slip his pace a little and he'd have number three—final warning. And then . . .

"Warning! Warning 70!"

"They're playing your song, Olson," McVries said between pants. "Pick up your feet. I want to see you dance up this hill like Fred Astaire."

"What do you care?" Olson asked fiercely.

McVries didn't answer. Olson found a little more inside himself and managed to pick it up. Garraty wondered morbidly if the little more Olson had found was his last legs. He also wondered about Stebbins, back there tailing the group. How are you, Stebbins? Getting tired?

Up ahead, a boy named Larson, 60, suddenly sat down on the road. He got a warning. The other boys split and passed around him, like the Red Sea around the Children of Israel.

"I'm just going to rest for a while, okay?" Larson said with a trusting, shellshocked smile. "I can't walk anymore right now, okay?" His smile stretched wider, and he turned it on the soldier who had jumped down from the halftrack with his rifle unslung and the stainless steel chronometer in his hand.

"Warning, 60," the soldier said. "Second warning."

"Listen, I'll catch up," Larson hastened to assure him. "I'm just resting. A guy can't walk all the time. Not *all* the time. Can he, fellas?" Olson made a little moaning noise as he passed Larson, and shied away when Larson tried to touch his pants cuffs.

Garraty felt his pulse beating warmly in his temples. Larson got his third warning . . . now he'll understand, Garraty thought, now he'll get up and start flogging it.

And at the end, Larson did realize, apparently. Reality came crashing back in. "Hey!" Larson said behind them. His voice was high and alarmed. "Hey, just a second, don't do that, I'll get up. Hey, don't! D—"

The shot. They walked on up the hill.

"Ninety-three bottles of beer left on the shelf," McVries said softly.

Garraty made no reply. He stared at his feet and walked and focused all of his concentration on getting to the top without that third warning. It couldn't go on much longer, this monster hill. Surely not.

Up ahead someone uttered a high, gobbling scream, and then the rifles crashed in unison.

"Barkovitch," Baker said hoarsely. "That was Barkovitch, I'm sure it was."

"Wrong, redneck!" Barkovitch yelled out of the darkness. "One hundred per cent dead wrong!"

They never did see the boy who had been shot

after Larson. He had been part of the vanguard and he was dragged off the road before they got there. Garraty ventured a look up from the pavement, and was immediately sorry. He could see the top of the hill—just barely. They still had the length of a football field to go. It looked like a hundred miles. No one said anything else. Each of them had retreated into his own private world of pain and effort. Seconds seemed to telescope into hours.

Near the top of the hill, a rutted dirt road branched off the main drag, and a farmer and his family stood there. They watched the Walkers go past—an old man with a deeply seamed brow, a hatchet-faced woman in a bulky cloth coat, three teenaged children who all looked half-witted.

"All he needs . . . is a pitchfork," McVries told Garraty breathlessly. Sweat was streaming down McVries's face. "And . . . Grant Wood . . . to paint him."

Someone called out: "Hiya, Daddy!"

The farmer and the farmer's wife and the farmer's children said nothing. The cheese stands alone, Garraty thought crazily. Hi-ho the dairy-o, the cheese stands alone. The farmer and his family did not smile. They did not frown. They held no signs. They did not wave. They watched. Garraty was reminded of the Western movies he had seen on all the Saturday afternoons of his youth, where the hero was left to die in the desert and the buzzards came and circled overhead. They were left behind, and Garraty was glad. He supposed the farmer and his wife and the three half-witted children would be out there around nine o'clock next May first . . . and the next . . . and the next. How many boys had they seen shot? A dozen? Two? Garraty didn't like to think of it. He took a pull at his canteen, sloshed the water around in his mouth, trying to cut through the caked saliva. He spit the mouthful out.

The hill went on. Up ahead Toland fainted and was shot after the soldier left beside him had warned his unconscious body three times. It seemed to Garraty that they had been climbing the hill for at least a month now. Yes, it had to be a month at least, and that was a conservative estimate because they had been walking for just over three years. He giggled a little, took another mouthful of water, sloshed it around in his mouth, and then swallowed it. No cramps. A cramp would finish him now. But it could happen. It could happen because someone had dipped his shoes in liquid lead while he wasn't looking.

Nine gone, and a third of them had gotten it right here on this hill. The Major had told Olson to give them hell, and if this wasn't hell, it was a pretty good approximation. A pretty good . . .

Oh boy—

Garraty was suddenly aware that he felt quite giddy, as if he might faint himself. He brought one hand up and slapped himself across the face, backward and forward, hard.

"You all right?" McVries asked.

"Feel faint."

"Pour your . . ." Quick, whistling breath, ". . . canteen over your head."

Garraty did it. I christen thee Raymond Davis Garraty, pax vobiscum. The water was very cold. He stopped feeling faint. Some of the water trickled down inside his shirt in freezing cold rivulets. "Canteen! 47!" he shouted. The effort of the shout left him feeling drained all over again. He wished he had waited awhile.

One of the soldiers jog-trotted over to him and handed him a fresh canteen. Garraty could feel the soldier's expressionless marble eyes sizing him up. "Get away," he said rudely, taking the canteen. "You get paid to shoot me, not to look at me."

The soldier went away with no change of expression. Garraty made himself walk a little faster.

They kept climbing and no one else got it and then they were at the top. It was nine o'clock. They had been on the road twelve hours. It didn't mean anything. The only thing that mattered was the cool breeze blowing over the top of the hill. And the sound of a bird. And the feel of his damp shirt against his skin. And the memories in his head. Those things mattered, and Garraty clung to them with desperate awareness. They were his things and he still had them.

"Pete?"

"Yeah."

"Man, I'm glad to be alive."

McVries didn't answer. They were on the downslope now. Walking was easy.

"I'm going to try hard to stay alive," Garraty said, almost apologetically.

The road curved gently downward. They were still a hundred and fifteen miles from Oldtown and the comparative levelness of the turnpike.

"That's the idea, isn't it?" McVries asked finally. His voice sounded cracked and cobwebby, as if it had issued from a dusty cellar.

Neither of them said anything for a while. No one was talking. Baker ambled steadily along—he hadn't drawn a warning yet—with his hands in his pockets, his head nodding slightly with the flat-footed rhythm of his walk. Olson had gone back to Hail Mary, full of grace. His face was a white splotch in the darkness. Harkness was eating.

"Garraty," McVries said.

"I'm here."

"You ever see the end of a Long Walk?"

"No, you?"

"Hell, no. I just thought, you being close to it and all—"

"My father hated them. He took me to one as a what-do-you-call-it, object lesson. But that was the only time."

"I saw."

Garraty jumped at the sound of that voice. It was Stebbins. He had pulled almost even with them, his head still bent forward, his blond hair flapping around his ears like a sickly halo.

"What was it like?" McVries asked. His voice was younger somehow.

"You don't want to know," Stebbins said.

"I asked, didn't I?"

Stebbins made no reply, Garraty's curiosity about him was stronger than ever. Stebbins hadn't folded up. He showed no signs of folding up. He went on without complaint and hadn't been warned since the starting line.

"Yeah, what's it like?" he heard himself asking.

"I saw the end four years ago," Stebbins said. "I was thirteen. It ended about sixteen miles over the New Hampshire border. They had the National Guard out and Sixteen Federal Squads to augment the State Police. They had to. The people were packed sixty deep on both sides of the road for fifty miles. Over twenty people were trampled to death before it was all over. It happened because people were trying to move with the Walkers, trying to see the end of it. I had a front-row seat. My dad got it for me."

"What does your dad do?" Garraty asked.

"He's in the Squads. And he had it figured just right. I didn't even have to move. The Walk ended practically in front of me."

"What happened?" Olson asked softly.

"I could hear them coming before I could see them. We all could. It was one big soundwave, getting closer and closer. And it was still an hour before they got close enough to see. They weren't looking at the crowd, either of the two that were left. It was like they didn't even know the crowd was there. What they were looking at was the road. They were hobbling along, both of them. Like they had been crucified and then taken down and made to walk with the nails still through their feet."

They were all listening to Stebbins now. A horrified silence had fallen like a rubber sheet.

"The crowd was yelling at them, almost as if they could still hear. Some were yelling one guy's name, and some were yelling the other guy's, but the only thing that really came through was this *Go . . . Go . . . Go* chant. I was getting shoved around like a beanbag. The guy next to me either pissed himself or jacked off in his pants, you couldn't tell which.

"They walked right past me. One of them was a big blond with his shirt open. One of his shoe soles had come unglued or unstitched or whatever, and it was flapping. The other guy wasn't even wearing his shoes anymore. He was in his stocking feet. His socks ended at his ankles. The rest of them . . . why, he'd just walked them away, hadn't he? His feet were purple. You could see the broken blood vessels in his feet. I don't think he really felt it anymore. Maybe they were able to do something with his feet later, I don't know. Maybe they were."

"Stop. For God's sake, stop it." It was McVries. He sounded dazed and sick.

"You wanted to know," Stebbins said, almost genially. "Didn't you say that?"

No answer. The halftrack whined and clattered and spurted along the shoulder, and somewhere farther up someone drew a warning.

"It was the big blond that lost. I saw it all. They were just a little past me. He threw both of his arms up, like he was Superman. But instead of flying he just fell flat on his face and they gave him his ticket after thirty seconds because he was walking with three. They were both walking with three.

"Then the crowd started to cheer. They cheered and they cheered and then they could see that the kid that won was trying to say something. So they shut up. He had fallen on his knees, you know, like he was going to pray, only he was just crying. And then he crawled over to the other boy and put his face in that big blond kid's shirt. Then he started to say whatever it was he had to say, but we couldn't hear it. He was talking into the dead kid's shirt. He was telling the dead kid. Then the soldiers rushed out and told him he had won the Prize, and asked him how he wanted to start."

"What did he say?" Garraty asked. It seemed to him that with the question he had laid his whole life on the line.

"He didn't say anything to them, not then," Stebbins said. "He was talking to the dead kid. He was telling the dead kid something, but we couldn't hear it."

"What happened then?" Pearson asked.

"I don't remember," Stebbins said remotely.

No one said anything. Garraty felt a panicked, trapped sensation, as if someone had stuffed him into an underground pipe that was too small to get out of. Up ahead a third warning was given out and a boy made a croaking, despairing sound, like a dying crow. Please God, don't let them shoot anyone now, Garraty thought. I'll go crazy if I hear the guns now. Please God, please God.

A few minutes later the guns rammed their steel-death sound into the night. This time it was a short boy in a flapping red and white football jersey. For a moment Garraty thought Percy's mom would not have to wonder or worry anymore, but it wasn't Percy—it was a boy named Quincy or Quentin or something like that.

Garraty didn't go crazy. He turned around to say angry words at Stebbins—to ask him, perhaps, how it felt to inflict a boy's last minutes with such a horror—but Stebbins had dropped back to his usual position and Garraty was alone again.

They walked on, the ninety of them.

Chapter 5

"You did not tell the truth and so
you will have to pay the consequences."
—Bob Barker
Truth or Consequences

At twenty minutes of ten on that endless May first, Garraty sluffed one of his two warnings. Two more Walkers had bought it since the boy in the football jersey. Garraty barely noticed. He was taking a careful inventory of himself.

One head, a little confused and crazied up, but basically okay. Two eyes, grainy. One neck, pretty stiff. Two arms, no problem there. One torso, okay except for a gnawing in his gut that concentrates couldn't satisfy. Two damn tired legs. Muscles aching. He wondered how far his legs would carry him on their own—how long before his brain took them over and began punishing them, making them work past any sane limit, to keep a bullet from crashing into its own bony cradle. How long before the legs began to kink and then to bind up, to protest and finally to seize up and stop.

His legs were tired, but so far as he could tell, still pretty much okay.

And two feet. Aching. They were tender, no use denying it. He was a big boy. Those feet were shifting a hundred and sixty pounds back and forth. The soles ached. There were occasional strange shooting pains in them. His left great toe had poked through his sock (he thought of Stebbins's tale and felt a kind of creeping horror at that), and had begun to rub uncomfortably against his shoe. But his feet were working, there were still no blisters on them, and he felt his feet were still pretty much okay, too.

Garraty, he pep-talked himself, you're in good shape. Twelve guys dead, twice that many maybe hurting bad by now, but you're okay. You're going good. You're great. You're alive.

Conversation, which had died violently at the end of Stebbins's story, picked up again. Talking was what living people did. Yannick, 98, was discussing the ancestry of the soldiers on the halftrack in an overloud voice with Wyman, 97. Both agreed that it was mixed, colorful, hirsute, and bastardized.

Pearson, meanwhile, abruptly asked Garraty: "Ever have an enema?"

"Enema?" Garraty repeated. He thought about it. "No. I don't think so."

"Any of you guys?" Pearson asked. "Tell the truth, now."

"I did," Harkness said, and chuckled a little. "My mother gave me one after Halloween once when I was little. I ate pretty near a whole shopping bag of candy."

"Did you like it?" Pearson pressed.

"Hell, no! Who in *hell* would like a half a quart of warm soapsuds up your—"

"My little brother," Pearson said sadly. "I asked the little snot if he was sorry I was going and he said no because Ma said he could have an enema if he was good and didn't cry. He loves 'em."

"That's sickening," Harkness said loudly.

Pearson looked glum. "I thought so, too."

A few minutes later Davidson joined the group and told them about the times he got drunk at the Steubenville State Fair and crawled into the hoochie-kooch tent and got biffed in the head by a big fat momma wearing nothing but a G-string. When Davidson told her (so he said) that he was drunk and thought it was the tattooing tent he was crawling into, the red hot big fat momma let him feel her up for a while (so he said). He had told her he wanted to get a Stars and Bars tattooed on his stomach.

Art Baker told them about a contest they'd had back home, to see who could light the biggest fart, and this hairy-assed old boy named Davey Popham had managed to burn off almost all the hair on his ass and the small of his back as well. Smelled like a grassfire, Baker said. This got Harkness laughing so hard he drew a warning.

After that, the race was on. Tall story followed tall story until the whole shaky structure came tumbling down. Someone else was warned, and not long after, the other Baker (James) bought a ticket. The good humor went out of the group. Some of them began to talk about their girlfriends, and the conversation became stumbling and maudlin. Garraty said nothing about Jan, but as tired ten o'clock came rolling in, a black coalsack splattered with milky groundmist, it seemed to him that she was the best thing he had ever known.

They passed under a short string of mercury streetlights, through a closed and shuttered town, all of them subdued now, speaking in low murmurs. In front of the Shopwell near the far end of this wide place in the road a young couple sat asleep on a sidewalk bench with their heads leaning together. A sign that could not be read dangled between them. The girl was very young—she looked no more than fourteen—and her boyfriend was wearing a sport shirt that had been washed too many times to ever look very sporty again. Their shadows in the street made a merge that the Walkers passed quietly over.

Garraty glanced back over his shoulder, quite sure that the rumble of the halftrack must have awakened them. But they still slept, unaware that the Event had come and passed them by. He wondered if the girl would catch what-for from her old man. She looked awfully young. He wondered if their sign was for Go-Go Garraty, "Maine's Own." Somehow he hoped not. Somehow the idea was a little repulsive.

He ate the last of his concentrates and felt a little better. There was nothing left for Olson to cadge off him now. It was funny about Olson. Garraty would have bet six hours ago that Olson was pretty well done in. But he was still walking, and now without warnings. Garraty supposed a person could do a lot of things when his life was at stake. They had come about fifty-four miles now.

The last of the talk died with the nameless town. They marched in silence for an hour or so, and the chill began to seep into Garraty again. He ate the last of his mom's cookies, balled up the foil, and pitched it into the brush at the side of the road. Just another litterbug on the great tomato plant of life.

McVries had produced a toothbrush of all things from his small packsack and was busy dry-brushing his teeth. It all goes on, Garraty thought wonderingly. You burp, you say excuse me. You wave back at the people who wave to you because that's the polite thing to do. No one argues very much with anyone else (except for Barkovitch) because that's also the polite thing to do. It all goes on.

Or did it? He thought of McVries sobbing at Stebbins to shut up. Of Olson taking his cheese with the dumb humility of a whipped dog. It all seemed to have a heightened intensity about it, a sharper contrast of colors and light and shadow.

At eleven o'clock, several things happened almost at once. The word came back that a small plank bridge up ahead had been washed out by a heavy afternoon thunderstorm. With the bridge out, the Walk would have to be temporarily stopped. A weak cheer went up through the ragged ranks, and Olson, in a very soft voice, muttered "Thank God."

A moment later Barkovitch began to scream a

flood of profanity at the boy next to him, a squat, ugly boy with the unfortunate name of Rank. Rank took a swing at him—something expressly forbidden by the rules—and was warned for it. Barkovitch didn't even break stride. He simply lowered his head and ducked under the punch and went on yelling.

"Come on, you sonofabitch! I'll dance on your goddam grave! Come on, Dumbo, pick up your feet! Don't make it too easy for me!"

Rank threw another punch. Barkovitch nimbly stepped around it, but tripped over the boy walking next to him. They were both warned by the soldiers, who were now watching the developments carefully but emotionlessly—like men watching a couple of ants squabbling over a crumb of bread, Garraty thought bitterly.

Rank started to walk faster, not looking at Barkovitch. Barkovitch himself, furious at being warned (the boy he had tripped over was Gribble, who had wanted to tell the Major he was a murderer), yelled at him: "Your mother sucks cock on 42nd Street, Rank!"

With that, Rank suddenly turned around and charged Barkovitch.

Cries of "Break it up!" and "Cut the shit!" filled the air, but Rank took no notice. He went for Barkovitch with his head down, bellowing.

Barkovitch sidestepped him. Rank went stumbling and pinwheeling across the soft shoulder, skidded in the sand, and sat down with his feet splayed out. He was given a third warning.

"Come on, Dumbo!" Barkovitch goaded. "Get up!"

Rank did get up. Then he slipped somehow and fell over on his back. He seemed dazed and woozy.

The third thing that happened around eleven o'clock was Rank's death. There was a moment of silence when the carbines sighted in, and Baker's voice was loud and clearly audible: "There, Barkovitch, you're not a pest anymore. Now you're a murderer."

The guns roared. Rank's body was thrown into the air by the force of the bullets. Then it lay still and sprawled, one arm on the road.

"It was his own fault!" Barkovitch yelled. "You saw him, he swung first! Rule 8! Rule 8!"

No one said anything.

"Go fuck yourselves! All of you!"

McVries said easily: "Go on back and dance on him a little, Barkovitch. Go entertain us. Boogie on him a little bit, Barkovitch."

"Your mother sucks cock on 42nd Street too, scarface," Barkovitch said hoarsely.

"Can't wait to see your brains all over the road," McVries said quietly. His hand had gone to the scar and was rubbing, rubbing, rubbing. "I'll cheer when it happens, you murdering little bastard."

Barkovitch muttered something else under his breath. The others had shied away from him as if he had the plague and he was walking by himself.

They hit sixty miles at about ten past eleven, with no sign of a bridge of any kind. Garraty was beginning to think the grapevine had been wrong this time when they cleared a small hill and looked down into a pool of light where a small crowd of hustling, bustling men moved.

The lights were the beams of several trucks, directed at a plank bridge spanning a fast-running rill of water. "Truly I love that bridge," Olson said, and helped himself to one of McVries's cigarettes. "Truly."

But as they drew closer, Olson made a soft, ugly sound in his throat and pitched the cigarette away into the weeds. One of the bridge's supports and two of the heavy butt planks had been washed away, but the Squad up ahead had been working diligently. A sawed-off telephone pole had been planted in the bed of the stream, anchored in what looked like a gigantic cement plug. They hadn't had a chance to replace the butts, so they had put down a big convoy-truck tailgate in their place. Makeshift, but it would serve.

"The Bridge of San Loois Ray," Abraham said. "Maybe if the ones up front stomp a little, it'll collapse again."

"Small chance," Pearson said, and then added in a breaking, weepy voice, "Aw, *shit!*"

The vanguard, down to three or four boys, was on the bridge now. Their feet clumped hollowly as they crossed. Then they were on the other side, walking without looking back. The halftrack stopped. Two soldiers jumped out and kept pace with the boys. On the other side of the bridge, two more fell in with the vanguard. The boards rumbled steadily now.

Two men in corduroy coats leaned against a big asphalt-spattered truck marked HIGHWAY REPAIR. They were smoking. They wore green gum-rubber boots. They watched the Walkers go by. As Davidson, McVries, Olson, Pearson, Harkness, Baker, and Garraty passed in a loose sort of group one of them flicked his cigarette end over end into the stream and said: "That's him. That's Garraty."

"Keep goin', boy!" the other yelled. "I got ten bucks on you at twelve-to-one!"

Garraty noticed a few sawdusty lengths of telephone pole in the back of the truck. They were the ones who had made sure he was going to keep going, whether he liked it or not. He raised one hand to them and crossed the bridge. The tailgate that had replaced the butt planks clunked under his shoes and then the bridge was behind them. The road doglegged, and the only reminder of the rest they'd almost had was a wedge-shaped swath of light on the trees at the side of the road. Soon that was gone, too.

"Has a Long Walk ever been stopped for anything?" Harkness asked.

"I don't think so," Garraty said. "More material for the book?"

"No," Harkness said. He sounded tired. "Just personal information."

"It stops every year," Stebbins said from behind them. "Once."

There was no reply to that.

About half an hour later, McVries came up beside Garraty and walked with him in silence for a little while. Then, very quietly, he said: "Do you think you'll win, Ray?"

Garraty considered it for a long, long time.

"No," he said finally. "No, I . . . no."

The stark admission frightened him. He thought again about buying a ticket, no, buying a *bullet*, of the final frozen half-second of total knowledge, seeing the bottomless bores of the carbines swing toward him. Legs frozen. Guts crawling and clawing. Muscles, genitals, brain all cowering away from the oblivion a bloodbeat away.

He swallowed dryly. "How about yourself?"

"I guess not," McVries said. "I stopped thinking I had any real chance around nine tonight. You see, I . . ." He cleared his throat. "It's hard to say, but . . . I went into it with my eyes open, you know?" He gestured around himself at the other boys. "Lots of these guys didn't, you know? I knew the odds. But I didn't figure on *people*. And I don't think I ever realized the real gut truth of what this is. I think I had the idea that when the first guy got so he couldn't cut it anymore they'd aim the guns at him and pull the triggers and little pieces of paper with the word BANG printed on them would . . . would . . . and the Major would say April Fool and we'd all go home. Do you get what I'm saying at all?"

Garraty thought of his own rending shock when Curley had gone down in a spray of blood and brains like oatmeal, brains on the pavement and the white line. "Yes," he said. "I know what you're saying."

"It took me a while to figure it out, but it was faster after I got around that mental block. Walk or die, that's the moral of this story. Simple as that. It's not survival of the physically fittest, that's where I went wrong when I let myself get into this. If it was, I'd have a fair chance. But there are weak men who can lift cars if their wives are pinned underneath. The brain, Garraty." McVries's voice had dropped to a hoarse whisper. "It isn't man or God. It's something . . . in the brain."

A whippoorwill called once in the darkness. The groundfog was lifting.

"Some of these guys will go on walking long after the laws of biochemistry and handicapping have gone by the boards. There was a guy last year that crawled for two miles at four miles an hour after both of his feet cramped up at the same time, you remember reading about that? Look at Olson, he's worn out but he keeps going. That goddam Barkovitch is running on high-octane hate and he just keeps going and he's as fresh as a daisy. I don't think I can do that. I'm not tired—not really tired—yet. But I will be." The scar stood out on the side of his haggard face as he looked ahead into the darkness. "And I think . . . when I get tired enough . . . I think I'll just sit down."

Garraty was silent, but he felt alarmed. Very alarmed.

"I'll outlast Barkovitch, though," McVries said, almost to himself. "I can do that, by Christ."

Garraty glanced at his watch and saw it was 11:30. They passed through a deserted crossroads where a sleepy-looking constable was parked. The possible traffic he had been sent out to halt was nonexistent. They walked past him, out of the bright circle of light thrown by the single mercury lamp. Darkness fell over them like a coalsack again.

"We could slip into the woods now and they'd never see us," Garraty said thoughtfully.

"Try it," Olson said. "They've got infrared sweep-scopes, along with forty other kinds of monitoring gear, including high-intensity microphones. They hear everything we're saying. They can almost pick up your heartbeat. And they see you like daylight, Ray."

As if to emphasize his point, a boy behind them was given second warning.

"You take all the fun outta livin'," Baker said softly. His faint Southern drawl sounded out of place and foreign to Garraty's ears.

McVries had walked away. The darkness seemed to isolate each of them, and Garraty felt a shaft of intense loneliness. There were mutters and half-yelps every time something crashed through the woods they were going past, and Garraty realized with some amusement that a late evening stroll through the Maine woods could be no picnic for the city boys in the crew. An owl made a mysterious noise somewhere to their left. On the other side something rustled, was still, rustled again, was still, and then made a crashing break for less populated acreage. There was another nervous cry of "What was that?"

Overhead, capricious spring clouds began to scud across the sky in mackerel shapes, promising more rain. Garraty turned up his collar and listened to the sound of his feet pounding the pavement. There was a trick to that, a subtle mental adjustment, like having better night vision the longer you were in the dark. This morning the sound of his feet had been lost to him. They had been lost in the tramp of ninety-nine other pairs, not to mention the rumble of the halftrack. But now he heard them easily. His own particular stride, and the way his left foot scraped the pavement every now and then. It seemed to him that the sound of his footfalls had become as loud to his ears as the sound of his own heartbeat. Vital, life and death sound.

His eyes felt grainy, trapped in their sockets. The lids were heavy. His energy seemed to be draining down some sinkhole in the middle of him. Warnings were droned out with monotonous regularity, but no one was shot. Barkovitch had shut up. Stebbins was a ghost again, not even visible in back of them.

The hands on his watch read 11:40.

On up toward the hour of witches, he thought. When churchyards yawn and give up their moldy dead. When all good little boys are sacked out. When wives and lovers have given up the carnal pillowfight for the evening. When passengers sleep uneasy on the Greyhound to New York. When Glenn Miller plays uninterrupted on the radio and bartenders think about putting the chairs up on the tables, and—

Jan's face came into his mind again. He thought of kissing her at Christmas, almost half a year ago, under the plastic mistletoe his mother always hung from the big light globe in the kitchen. Stupid kid stuff. Look where you're standing. Her lips had been surprised and soft, not resisting. A nice kiss. One to dream on. His first real kiss. He did it again when he took her home. They had been standing in her driveway, standing in the silent grayness of falling Christmas snow. That had been something more than a nice kiss. His arms around her waist. Her arms around his neck, locked there, her eyes closed (he had peeked), the soft feel of her breasts— muffled up in her coat, of course—against him. He had almost told her he loved her then, but no . . . that would have been too quick.

After that, they taught each other. She taught him that books were sometimes just to be read and discarded, not studied (he was something of a grind, which amused Jan, and her amusement first exasperated him and then he also saw the funny side of it). He taught her to knit. That had been a funny thing. His father, of all people, had taught him how to knit . . . before the Squads got him. His father had taught Garraty's father, as well. It was something of a male tradition in the clan Garraty, it seemed. Jan had been fascinated by the pattern of the increases and decreases, and she left him behind soon enough, overstepping his laborious scarves and mittens to sweaters, cableknits, and finally to crocheting and even the tatting of doilies, which she gave up as ridiculous as soon as the skill was mastered.

He had also taught her how to rhumba and cha-cha, skills he had learned on endless Saturday mornings at Mrs. Amelia Dorgens's School for Modern Dance . . . that had been his mother's idea, one he had objected to strenuously. His mother had stuck to her guns, thank God.

He thought now of the patterns of light and shadow on the nearly perfect oval of her face, the way she walked, the lift and fall of her voice, the easy, desirable swing of one hip, and he wondered in terror what he was doing here, walking down this dark road. He wanted her now. He wanted to do it all over again, but differently. Now, when he thought of the Major's tanned face, the salt-and-pepper mustache, the mirrored sunglasses, he felt a horror so deep it made his legs feel rubbery and weak. Why am I here? he asked himself desperately, and there was no answer, so he asked the question again: Why am—

The guns crashed in the darkness, and there was the unmistakable mailsack thud of a body falling on the concrete. The fear was on him again, the hot, throat-choking fear that made him want to run blindly, to dive into the bushes and just keep on running until he found Jan and safety.

McVries had Barkovitch to keep him going. He would concentrate on Jan. He would walk to Jan. They reserved space for Long Walkers' relatives and loved ones in the front lines. He would see her.

He thought about kissing that other girl and was ashamed.

How do you know you'll make it? A cramp . . . blisters . . . a bad cut or a nosebleed that just won't quit . . . a big hill that was just too big and too long. How do you know you'll make it?

I'll make it, I'll make it.

"Congratulations," McVries said at his shoulder, making him jump.

"Huh?"

"It's midnight. We live to fight another day, Garraty."

"And many of 'em," Abraham added. "For me, that is. Not that I begrudge you, you understand."

"A hundred and five miles to Oldtown, if you care," Olson put in tiredly.

"Who gives a shit about Oldtown?" McVries demanded. "You ever been there, Garraty?"

"No."

"How about Augusta? Christ, I thought that was in Georgia."

"Yeah, I've been in Augusta. It's the state capital—"

"Regional," Abraham said.

"And the Corporate Governor's mansion, and a couple of traffic circles, and a couple of movies—"

"You have those in Maine?" McVries asked.

"Well, it's a small state capital, okay?" Garraty said, smiling.

"Wait'll we hit Boston," McVries said.

There were groans.

From up ahead there came cheers, shouts, and

catcalls. Garraty was alarmed to hear his own name called out. Up ahead, about half a mile away, was a ramshackle farmhouse, deserted and fallen down. But a battered Klieg light had been plugged in somewhere, and a huge sign, lettered with pine boughs across the front of the house, read:

GARRATY'S OUR MAN!!!
Aroostook County Parents' Association

"Hey, Garraty, where's the parents?" someone yelled.

"Back home making kids," Garraty said, embarrassed. There could be no doubt that Maine was Garraty country, but he found the signs and cheers and the gibes of the others all a little mortifying. He had found—among other things—in the last fifteen hours that he didn't much crave the limelight. The thought of a million people all over the state rooting for him and laying bets on him (at twelve-to-one, the highway worker had said . . . was that good or bad?) was a little scary.

"You'd think they would have left a few plump, juicy parents lying around somewhere," Davidson said.

"Poontang from the PTA?" Abraham asked.

The ribbing was halfhearted and didn't last very long. The road killed most ribbing very quickly. They crossed another bridge, this time a cement one that spanned a good-sized river. The water rippled below them like black silk. A few crickets chirred cautiously, and around fifteen past midnight, a spatter of light, cold rain fell.

Up ahead, someone began to play a harmonica. It didn't last long (Hint 6: Conserve Wind), but it was pretty for the moment it lasted. It sounded a little like *Old Black Joe*, Garraty thought. Down in de cornfiel', here dat mournful soun'. All de darkies am aweeping, Ewing's in de cole, cole groun'.

No, that wasn't *Old Black Joe*, that tune was some other Stephen Foster racist classic. Good old Stephen Foster. Drank himself to death. So did Poe, it had been reputed. Poe the necrophiliac, the one who had married his fourteen-year-old cousin. That made him a pedophile as well. All-around depraved fellows, he and Stephen Foster both. If only they could have lived to see the Long Walk, Garraty thought. They could have collaborated on the world's first Morbid Musical. *Massa's on De Cold, Cold Road*, or *The Tell-Tale Stride*, or—

Up ahead someone began to scream, and Garraty felt his blood go cold. It was a very young voice. It was not screaming words. It was only screaming. A dark figure broke from the pack, pelted across the shoulder of the road in front of the halftrack (Garraty could not even remember when the halftrack had rejoined their march after the repaired bridge), and dived for the woods. The guns roared. There was a rending crash as a dead weight fell through the juniper bushes and underbrush to the ground. One of the soldiers jumped down and dragged the inert form up by the hands. Garraty watched apathetically and thought, even the horror wears thin. There's a surfeit even of death.

The harmonica player started in satirically on *Taps* and somebody—Collie Parker, by the sound—told him angrily to shut the fuck up. Stebbins laughed. Garraty felt suddenly furious with Stebbins, and wanted to turn to him and ask him how he'd like someone laughing at his death. It was something you'd expect of Barkovitch. Barkovitch had said he'd dance on a lot of graves, and there were sixteen he could dance on already.

I doubt that he'll have much left of his feet to dance with, Garraty thought. A sharp twinge of pain went through the arch of his right foot. The muscle there tightened heart-stoppingly, then loosened. Garraty waited with his heart in his mouth for it to happen again. It would hit harder. It would turn his foot into a block of useless wood. But it didn't happen.

"I can't walk much further," Olson croaked. His face was a white blur in the darkness. No one answered him.

The darkness. Goddam the darkness. It seemed to Garraty they had been buried alive in it. Immured in it. Dawn was a century away. Many of them would never see the dawn. Or the sun. They were buried six feet deep in the darkness. All they needed was the monotonous chanting of the priest, his voice muffled but not entirely obscured by the new-packed darkness, above which the mourners stood. The mourners were not even aware that they were *here*, they were *alive*, they were screaming and scratching and clawing at the coffin-lid darkness, the air was flaking and rusting away, the air was turning into poison gas, hope fading until hope itself was a darkness, and above all of it the nodding chapel-bell voice of the priest and the impatient, shuffling feet of mourners anxious to be off into the warm May sunshine. Then, over-mastering that, the sighing, shuffling chorus of the bugs and the beetles, squirming their way through the earth, come for the feast.

I could go crazy, Garraty thought. I could go right the fuck off my rocker.

A little breeze soughed through the pines.

Garraty turned around and urinated. Stebbins moved over a little, and Harkness made a cough-ing, snoring sound. He was walking half-asleep.

Garraty became acutely conscious of all the little sounds of life: someone hawked and spat, someone else sneezed, someone ahead and to the left was chewing something noisily. Someone asked some-one else softly how he felt. There was a murmured answer. Yannick was singing at a whisper level, soft and very much off-key.

Awareness. It was all a function of awareness. But it wasn't forever.

"Why did I get into this?" Olson suddenly asked hopelessly, echoing Garraty's thoughts not so many minutes ago. "Why did I let myself in for this?"

No one answered him. No one had answered him for a long time now. Garraty thought it was as if Olson were already dead.

Another light spatter of rain fell. They passed

another ancient graveyard, a church next door, a
tiny shopfront, and then they were walking through
a small New England community of small, neat
homes. The road crosshatched a miniature business section where perhaps a dozen people had
gathered to watch them pass. They cheered, but it
was a subdued sound, as if they were afraid they
might wake their neighbors. None of them was
young, Garraty saw. The youngest was an intense-
eyed man of about thirty-five. He was wearing
rimless glasses and a shabby sport coat, pulled
against him to protect against the chill. His hair
stuck up in back, and Garraty noted with amusement that his fly was half-unzipped.

"Go! Great! Go! Go! Oh, great!" he chanted
softly. He waved one soft plump hand ceaselessly,
and his eyes seemed to burn over each of them as
they passed.

On the far side of the village a sleepy-eyed
policeman held up a rumbling trailer truck until
they had passed. There were four more streetlights,
an abandoned, crumbling building with EUREKA
GRANGE NO. 81 written over the big double doors
at the front, and then the town was gone. For no
reason Garraty could put a finger on, he felt as if
he had just walked through a Shirley Jackson short
story.

McVries nudged him. "Look at that dude,"
he said.

"That dude" was a tall boy in a ridiculous loden-
green trenchcoat. It flapped around his knees. He
was walking with his arms wrapped around his

head like a gigantic poultice. He was weaving unsteadily back and forth. Garraty watched him closely, with a kind of academic interest. He couldn't recall ever having seen this particular Walker before . . . but of course the darkness changed faces.

The boy stumbled over one of his own feet and almost fell down. Then he went on walking. Garraty and McVries watched him in fascinated silence for perhaps ten minutes, losing their own aches and tiredness in the trenchcoated boy's struggle. The boy in the trenchcoat didn't make a sound, not a groan or a moan.

Finally he did fall over and was warned. Garraty didn't think the boy would be able to get up, but he did. Now he was walking almost with Garraty and the boys around him. He was an extremely ugly boy, with the number 45 pressure-taped to his coat.

Olson whispered, "What's the matter with you?" but the boy seemed not to hear. They got that way, Garraty had noticed. Complete withdrawal from everything and everyone around them. Everything but the road. They stared at the road with a kind of horrid fascination, as if it were a tightrope they had to walk over an endless, bottomless chasm.

"What's your name?" he asked the boy, but there was no answer. And he found himself suddenly spitting the question at the boy over and over, like an idiot litany that would save him from whatever fate was coming for him out of the darkness like a black express freight. "What's your name, huh? What's your name, what's your name, what's—"

"Ray." McVries was tugging at his sleeve.

"He won't tell me, Pete, make him tell me, make him say his name—"

"Don't bother him," McVries said. "He's dying, don't bother him."

The boy with 45 on his trenchcoat fell over again, this time on his face. When he got up, there were scratches on his forehead, slowly welling blood. He was behind Garraty's group now, but they heard it when he got his final warning.

They passed through a hollow of deeper darkness that was a railroad overpass. Rain dripped somewhere, hollow and mysterious in this stone throat. It was very damp. Then they were out again, and Garraty saw with gratitude that there was a long, straight, flat stretch ahead.

45 fell down again. Footsteps quickened as boys scattered. Not long after, the guns roared. Garraty decided the boy's name must not have been important anyway.

Chapter 6

"And now our contestants are in the isolation booths."
—Jack Barry
Twenty-One

Three-thirty in the morning.

To Ray Garraty it seemed the longest minute of the longest night of his entire life. It was low tide, dead ebb, the time when the sea washes back, leaving slick mudflats covered with straggled weed, rusty beer cans, rotted prophylactics, broken bottles, smashed buoys, and green-mossed skeletons in tattered bathing trunks. It was dead ebb.

Seven more had gotten tickets since the boy in the trenchcoat. At one time, around two in the morning, three had gone down almost together, like dried cornshocks in the first hard autumn wind. They were seventy-five miles into the Walk, and there were twenty-four gone.

But none of that mattered. All that mattered was dead ebb. Three-thirty and the dead ebb. Another warning was given, and shortly after, the guns crashed once more. This time the face was a familiar one. It was 8, Davidson, who claimed he had once sneaked into the hoochie-kooch tent at the Steubenville State Fair.

Garraty looked at Davidson's white, blood-spattered face for just a moment and then he looked back at the road. He looked at the road quite a lot now. Sometimes the white line was solid, sometimes it was broken, and sometimes it was double, like streetcar tracks. He wondered how people could ride over this road all the other days of the year and not see the pattern of life and death in that white paint. Or did they see, after all?

The pavement fascinated him. How good and easy it would be to sit on that pavement. You'd start by squatting, and your stiff knee-joints would pop like toy air-pistols. Then you'd put bracing hands back on the cool, pebbled surface and snuggle your buttocks down, you'd feel the screaming pressure of your one hundred and sixty pounds leave your feet . . . and then to lie down, just fall backward and lie there, spread-eagled, feeling your tired spine stretch . . . looking up at the encircling trees and the majestic wheel of the stars . . . not hearing the warnings, just watching the sky and waiting . . . waiting . . .

Yeah.

Hearing the scatter of footsteps as Walkers moved out of the line of fire, leaving him alone, like a sacrificial offering. Hearing the whispers. It's Garraty, hey, it's Garraty getting a ticket! Perhaps there would be time to hear Barkovitch laugh as he strapped on his metaphorical dancing shoes one more time. The swing of the carbines zeroing in, then—

He tore his glance forcibly from the road and stared blearily at the moving shadows around him, then looked up at the horizon, hunting for even a trace of dawn light. There was none, of course. The night was still dark.

They had passed through two or three more small towns, all of them dark and closed. Since midnight they had passed maybe three dozen sleepy spectators, the die-hard type who grimly watch in the New Year each December 31st, come hell or high water. The rest of the last three and a half hours was nothing but a dream montage, an insomniac's half-sleeping wakemare.

Garraty looked more closely at the faces around him, but none seemed familiar. An irrational panic stole over him. He tapped the shoulder of the Walker in front of him. "Pete? Pete, that you?"

The figure slipped away from him with an irritated grunt and didn't look back. Olson had been on his left, Baker on his right, but now there was no one at all on his left side and the boy to his right was much chubbier than Art Baker.

Somehow he had wandered off the road and fallen in with a bunch of late-hiking Boy Scouts. They would be looking for him. Hunting for him. Guns and dogs and Squads with radar and heat-tracers and—

Relief washed over him. That was Abraham, up ahead and at four o'clock. All he'd had to do was

turn his head a little. The gangling form was unmistakable.

"Abraham!" he stage-whispered. "Abraham, you
awake?"

Abraham muttered something.

"I said, you awake?"

"Yes goddammit Garraty lea'me alone."

At least he was still with them. That feeling of
total disorientation passed away.

Someone up ahead was given a third warning
and Garraty thought, I don't have any! I could sit
down for a minute or a minute and a half. I could—

But he'd never get up.

Yes I would, he answered himself. Sure I would.
I'd just—

Just die. He remembered promising his mother
that he would see her and Jan in Freeport. He had
made the promise lightheartedly, almost carelessly.
At nine o'clock yesterday morning, his arrival in
Freeport had been a foregone conclusion. But it
wasn't a game anymore, it was a three-dimensional
reality, and the possibility of walking into Freeport
on nothing but a pair of bloody stumps seemed a
horribly possible possibility.

Someone else was shot down . . . behind him,
this time. The aim was bad, and the unlucky ticket-
holder screamed hoarsely for what seemed a very
long time before another bullet cut off the sound.
For no reason at all Garraty thought of bacon, and
heavy, sour spit came into his mouth and made him
feel like gagging. Garraty wondered if twenty-six

down was an unusually high or an unusually low number for seventy-five miles into a Long Walk.

His head dropped slowly between his shoulders, and his feet carried them forward on their own. He thought about a funeral he had gone to as a boy. It had been Freaky D'Allessio's funeral. Not that his real name had been Freaky, his real name had been George, but all the kids in the neighborhood called him Freaky because his eyes didn't quite jibe . . .

He could remember Freaky waiting to be picked up for baseball games, always coming in dead last, his out-of-kilter eyes switching hopefully from one team captain to the other like a spectator at a tennis match. He always stayed deep center field, where not too many balls were hit and he couldn't do much damage; one of his eyes was almost blind, and he didn't have enough depth perception to judge any balls hit to him. Once he got under one and jabbed his glove at a hunk of thin air while the ball landed on his forehead with an audible *bonk!* like a cantaloupe being whocked with the handle of a kitchen knife. The threads on the ball left an imprint dead square on his forehead for a week, like a brand.

Freaky was killed by a car on U.S. 1 outside of Freeport. One of Garraty's friends, Eddie Klipstein, saw it happen. He held kids in thrall for six weeks, Eddie Klipstein did, telling them about how the car hit Freaky D'Allessio's bike and Freaky went up over the handlebars, knocked spang out of his shitkicker boots by the impact, both of his legs flailing out behind him in crippled splendor as his body flew its short, wingless flight from the seat of his Schwinn to a stone wall where Freaky landed and spread his head like a dollop of wet glue on the rocks.

He went to Freaky's funeral, and before they got there he almost lost his lunch wondering if he would see Freaky's head spread in the coffin like a glob of Elmer's Glue, but Freaky was all fixed up in his sport coat and tie and his Cub Scouts attendance pin, and he looked ready to step out of his coffin the moment someone said baseball. The eyes that didn't jibe were closed, and in general Garraty felt pretty relieved.

That had been the only dead person he had ever seen before all of this, and it had been a clean, neat dead person. Nothing like Ewing, or the boy in the loden trenchcoat, or Davidson with blood on his livid, tired face.

It's sick, Garraty thought with dismal realization. It's just sick.

At quarter to four he was given first warning, and he slapped himself twice smartly across the face, trying to make himself wake up. His body felt chilled clear through. His kidneys dragged at him, but at the same time he felt that he didn't quite have to pee yet. It might have been his imagination, but the stars in the east seemed a trifle paler. With real amazement it occurred to him that at this time yesterday he had been asleep in the back of the car as they drove up toward the stone marking post at the border. He could almost see himself stretched out on his back, *sprawling* there, not even *moving*. He felt an intense longing to be back there. Just to bring back yesterday morning.

Ten of four now.

He looked around himself, getting a superior, lonely kind of gratification from knowing he was one of the few fully awake and aware. It was definitely lighter now, light enough to make out snatches of features in the walking silhouettes. Baker was up ahead—he could tell it was him by the flapping red-striped shirt—and McVries was behind him. He saw Olson was off to the left, keeping pace with the halftrack, and was surprised. He was sure that Olson had been one of those to get tickets during the small hours of the morning, and had been relieved that he hadn't had to see Hank go down. It was too dark even now to see how he looked, but Olson's head was bouncing up and down in time to his stride like the head of a rag doll.

Percy, whose mom kept showing up, was back by Stebbins now. Percy was walking with a kind of lopsided roll, like a long-time sailor on his first day ashore. He also spotted Gribble, Harkness, Wyman, and Collie Parker. Most of the people he knew were still in it.

By four o'clock there was a brightening band on the horizon, and Garraty felt his spirits lift. He stared back at the long tunnel of the night in actual horror, and wondered how he ever could have gotten through it.

He stepped up his pace a little, approaching McVries, who was walking with his chin against his breast, his eyes half-open but glazed and vacant, more asleep than awake. A thin, delicate cord of saliva hung from the corner of his mouth, picking up the first tremulous touch of dawn with pearly, beautiful fidelity. Garraty stared at this strange phenomenon, fascinated. He didn't want to wake McVries out of his doze. For the time being it was enough to be close to someone he liked, someone else who had made it through the night.

They passed a rocky, steeply slanting meadow where five cows stood gravely at a bark-peeled pole fence, staring out at the Walkers and chewing thoughtfully. A small dog tore out of a farmyard and barked at them ratchetingly. The soldiers on the halftrack raised their guns to high post, ready to shoot the animal if he interfered with any Walker's progress, but the dog only chased back and forth along the shoulder, bravely voicing defiance and territoriality from a safe distance. Someone yelled thickly at him to shut up, goddammit.

Garraty became entranced with the coming dawn. He watched as the sky and the land lightened by degrees. He watched the white band on the horizon deepen a delicate pink, then red, then gold. The guns roared once more before the last of the night was finally banished, but Garraty barely heard. The first red arc of sun was peering over the horizon, faded behind a fluff of cloud, then came again in an onslaught. It looked to be a perfect day, and Garraty greeted it only half-coherently by thinking: Thank God I can die in the daylight.

A bird twitted sleepily. They passed another farmhouse where a man with a beard waved at them after putting down a wheelbarrow filled with hoes, rakes, and planting-seed.

A crow cawed raucously off in the shadowy woods. The first heat of the day touched Garraty's face gently, and he welcomed it. He grinned and yelled loudly for a canteen.

McVries twitched his head oddly, like a dog interrupted in a dream of cat-chasing, and then looked around with muddy eyes. "My God, daylight. Daylight, Garraty. What time?"

Garraty looked at his watch and was surprised to find it was quarter of five. He showed McVries the dial.

"How many miles? Any idea?"

"About eighty, I make it. And twenty-seven down. We're a quarter of the way home, Pete."

"Yeah." McVries smiled. "That's right, isn't it?"

"Damn right."

"You feel better?" Garraty asked.

"About one thousand per cent."

"So do I. I think it's the daylight."

"My God, I bet we see some people today. Did you read that article in *World's Week* about the Long Walk?"

"Skimmed it," Garraty said. "Mostly to see my name in print."

"Said that over two billion dollars gets bet on the Long Walk every year. Two *billion*!"

Baker had awakened from his own doze and had joined them. "We used to have a pool in my high school," he said. "Everybody'd kick in a quarter, and then we'd each pick a three-digit number out of a hat. And the guy holding the number closest to the last mile of the Walk, he got the money."

"Olson!" McVries yelled over cheerily. "Just think of all the cash riding on you, boy! Think of the people with a bundle resting right on your skinny ass!"

Olson told him in a tired, washed-out voice that the people with a bundle wagered on his skinny ass could perform two obscene acts upon themselves, the second proceeding directly from the first. McVries, Baker, and Garraty laughed.

"Be a lotta pretty girls on the road today," Baker said, eyeing Garraty roguishly.

"I'm all done with that stuff," Garraty said. "I got a girl up ahead. I'm going to be a good boy from now on."

"Sinless in thought, word, and deed," McVries said sententiously.

Garraty shrugged. "See it any way you like," he said.

"Chances are a hundred to one against you ever having a chance to do more than wave to her again," McVries said flatly.

"Seventy-three to one now."

"Still pretty high."

But Garraty's good humor was solid. "I feel like I could walk forever," he said blandly. A couple of the Walkers around him grimaced.

They passed an all-night gas station and the attendant came out to wave. Just about everyone waved back. The attendant was calling encouragement to Wayne, 94, in particular.

"Garraty," McVries said quietly.

"What?"

"I couldn't tell all the guys that bought it. Could you?"

"No."

"Barkovitch?"

"No. Up ahead. In front of Scramm. See him?"

McVries looked. "Oh. Yeah, I think I do."

"Stebbins is still back there, too."

"Not surprised. Funny guy, isn't he?"

"Yeah."

There was silence between them. McVries sighed deeply, and unshouldered his knapsack and pulled out some macaroons. He offered one to Garraty, who took one. "I wish this was over," he said. "One way or the other."

They ate their macaroons in silence.

"We must be halfway to Oldtown, huh?" McVries said. "Eighty down, eighty to go?"

"I guess so," Garraty said.

"Won't get there until tonight, then."

The mention of night made Garraty's flesh crawl. "No," he said. Then, abruptly: "How'd you get that scar, Pete?"

McVries's hand went involuntarily to his cheek and the scar. "It's a long story," he said briefly.

Garraty took a closer look at him. His hair was rumpled and clotty with dust and sweat. His clothes were limp and wrinkled. His face was pallid and his eyes were deeply circled in their bloodshot orbs.

"You look like shit," he said, and suddenly burst out laughing.

McVries grinned. "You don't exactly look like a deodorant ad yourself, Ray."

They both laughed then, long and hysterically, clutching each other and trying to keep walking at the same time. It was as good a way as any to put an end to the night once and for all. It went on until Garraty and McVries were both warned. They stopped laughing and talking then, and settled into the day's business.

Thinking, Garraty thought. That's the day's business. Thinking. Thinking and isolation, because it doesn't matter if you pass the time of day with someone or not; in the end, you're alone. He seemed to have put in as many miles in his brain as he had with his feet. The thoughts kept coming and there was no way to deny them. It was enough to make you wonder what Socrates had thought about right after he had tossed off his hemlock cocktail.

At a little past five o'clock they passed their first clump of bona fide spectators, four little boys sitting crosslegged like Indians outside a pup tent in a dewy field. One was still wrapped up in his sleeping bag, as solemn as an Eskimo. Their hands went back and forth like timed metronomes. None of them smiled.

Shortly afterward, the road forked into another, larger road. This one was a smooth, wide expanse of asphalt, three lanes wide. They passed a truck-stop restaurant, and everyone whistled and waved at the three young waitresses sitting on the steps, just to show them they were still starchy. The only one who sounded halfway serious was Collie Parker.

"Friday night," Collie yelled loudly. "Keep it in mind. You and me, Friday night."

Garraty thought they were all acting a little immature, but he waved politely and the waitresses seemed not to mind. The Walkers spread out across the wider road as more of them came fully awake to the May 2nd morning sunshine. Garraty caught sight of Barkovitch again and wondered if Barkovitch wasn't really one of the smart ones. With no friends you had no grief.

A few minutes later the word came back, and this time the word was a knock-knock joke. Bruce Pastor, the boy just in front of Garraty, turned around to Garraty and said, "Knock, knock, Garraty."

"Who's there?"

"Major."

"Major who?"

"Major buggers his mother before breakfast," Bruce Pastor said, and laughed uproariously. Garraty chuckled and passed it back to McVries, who passed it to Olson. When the joke came back the second time, the Major was buggering his grandmother before breakfast. The third time he was buggering Sheila, the Bedlington terrier that appeared with him in so many of his press releases.

Garraty was still laughing over that one when he noticed that McVries's laughter had tapered off and disappeared. He was staring with an odd fixity at the wooden-faced soldiers atop the halftrack. They were staring back impassively.

"You think that's *funny*?" he yelled suddenly. The sound of his shout cut cleanly through the laughter and silenced it. McVries's face was dark with suffused blood. The scar stood out in dead white contrast, like a slashed exclamation mark, and for one fear-filled moment Garraty thought he was having a stroke.

"Major buggers *himself*, that's what I think!" McVries cried hoarsely. "You guys, you probably bugger each other. Pretty funny, huh? Pretty funny, you bunch of motherfuckers, right? Pretty goddam *FUNNY, am I right*?"

Other Walkers stared uneasily at McVries and then eased away.

McVries suddenly ran at the halftrack. Two of the three soldiers raised their guns to high port, ready, but McVries halted, halted dead, and raised his fists at them, shaking them above his head like a mad conductor.

"Come on down here! Put down those rifles and come on down here! I'll show you what's funny!"

"Warning," one of them said in a perfectly neutral voice. "Warning 61. Second warning."

Oh my God, Garraty thought numbly. He's going to get it and he's so close . . . so close to them . . . he'll fly through the air just like Freaky D'Allessio.

McVries broke into a run, caught up with the halftrack, stopped, and spat on the side of it. The spittle cut a clean streak through the dust on the side of the halftrack.

"*Come on!*" McVries screamed. "*Come on down here! One at a time or all at once, I don't give a shit!*"

"Warning! Third Warning, 61, final warning."

"*Fuck your warnings!*"

Suddenly, unaware he was going to do it, Garraty turned and ran back, drawing his own warning. He only heard it with some back part of his mind. The soldiers were drawing down on McVries now. Garraty grabbed McVries's arm. "Come on."

"*Get out of here, Ray, I'm gonna fight them!*"

Garraty put out his hands and gave McVries a hard, flat shove. "You're going to get shot, you asshole."

Stebbins passed them by.

McVries looked at Garraty, seeming to recognize him for the first time. A second later Garraty drew his own third warning, and he knew McVries could only be seconds away from his ticket.

"Go to hell," McVries said in a dead, washed-out voice. He began to walk again.

Garraty walked with him. "I thought you were going to buy it, that's all," he said.

"But I didn't, thanks to the musketeer," McVries said sullenly. His hand went to the scar. "Fuck, we're all going to buy it."

"Somebody wins. It might be one of us."

"It's a fake," McVries said, his voice trembling. "There's no winner, no Prize. They take the last guy out behind a barn somewhere and shoot him too."

"Don't be so fucking stupid!" Garraty yelled at him furiously. "You don't have the slightest idea what you're sa—"

"Everyone loses," McVries said. His eyes peered out of the dark cave of his sockets like baleful animals. They were walking by themselves. The other Walkers were keeping away, at least for the time being. McVries had shown red, and so had Garraty, in a way—he had gone against his own best interest when he ran back to McVries. In all probability he had kept McVries from being number twenty-eight.

"Everyone loses," McVries repeated. "You better believe it."

They walked over a railroad track. They walked under a cement bridge. On the other side they passed a boarded-up Dairy Queen with a sign that read: WILL REOPEN FOR SEASON JUNE 5.

Olson drew a warning.

Garraty felt a tap on his shoulder and turned around. It was Stebbins. He looked no better or worse than he had the night before. "Your friend there is jerked at the Major," he said.

McVries showed no sign of hearing.

"I guess so, yeah," Garraty said. "I myself have passed the point where I'd want to invite him home for tea."

"Look behind us."

Garraty did. A second halftrack had rolled up, and as he looked, a third fell in behind it, coming in off a side road.

"The Major's coming," Stebbins said, "and everybody will cheer." He smiled, and his smile was oddly lizardlike. "They don't really hate him yet. Not yet. They just think they do. They think they've been through hell. But wait until tonight. Wait until *tomorrow*."

Garraty looked at Stebbins uneasily. "What if they hiss and boo and throw canteens at him, or something?"

"Are you going to hiss and boo and throw your canteen?"

"No."

"Neither will anyone else. You'll see."

"Stebbins?"

Stebbins raised his eyebrows.

"You think you'll win, don't you?"

"Yes," Stebbins said calmly. "I'm quite sure of it." And he dropped back to his usual position.

At 5:25 Yannick bought his ticket. And at 5:30 AM, just as Stebbins had predicted, the Major came.

There was a winding, growling roar as his jeep bounced over the crest of the hill behind them. Then it was roaring past them, along the shoulder. The Major was standing at full attention. As before, he was holding a stiff, eyes-right salute. A funny chill of pride went through Garraty's chest.

Not all of them cheered. Collie Parker spat on the ground. Barkovitch thumbed his nose. And McVries only looked, his lips moving soundlessly. Olson appeared not to notice at all as the Major went by; he was back to looking at his feet.

Garraty cheered. So did Percy What's-His-Name and Harkness, who wanted to write a book, and

Wyman and Art Baker and Abraham and Sledge, who had just picked up his second warning.

Then the Major was gone, moving fast. Garraty felt a little ashamed of himself. He had, after all, wasted energy.

A short time later the road took them past a used car lot where they were given a twenty-one-horn salute. An amplified voice roaring out over double rows of fluttering plastic pennants told the Walkers—and the spectators—that no one out-traded McLaren's Dodge. Garraty found it all a little disheartening.

"You feel any better?" he asked McVries hesitantly.

"Sure," McVries said. "Great. I'm just going to walk along and watch them drop all around me. What fun it is. I just did all the division in my head—math was my good subject in school—and I figure we should be able to make at least three hundred and twenty miles at the rate we're going. That's not even a record distance."

"Why don't you just go and have it on some-place else if you're going to talk like that, Pete," Baker said. He sounded strained for the first time.

"Sorry, Mum," McVries said sullenly, but he shut up.

The day brightened. Garraty unzipped his fatigue jacket. He slung it over his shoulder. The road was level here. It was dotted with houses, small businesses, and occasional farms. The pines that had lined the road last night had given way to Dairy Queens and gas stations and little cracker-box ranchos. A great many of the ranchos were

FOR SALE. In two of the windows Garraty saw the familiar signs: MY SON GAVE HIS LIFE IN THE SQUADS.

"Where's the ocean?" Collie Parker asked Garraty. "Looks like I was back in Illy-noy."

"Just keep walking," Garraty said. He was thinking of Jan and Freeport again. Freeport was on the ocean. "It's there. About a hundred and eight miles south."

"Shit," said Collie Parker. "What a dipshit state this is."

Parker was a big-muscled blond in a polo shirt. He had an insolent look in his eye that not even a night on the road had been able to knock out. "Goddam trees everyplace! Is there a city in the whole damn place?"

"We're funny up here," Garraty said. "We think it's fun to breathe real air instead of smog."

"Ain't no smog in Joliet, you fucking hick," Collie Parker said furiously. "What are you laying on me?"

"No smog but a lot of hot air," Garraty said. He was angry.

"If we was home, I'd twist your balls for that."

"Now boys," McVries said. He had recovered and was his old sardonic self again. "Why don't you settle this like gentlemen? First one to get his head blown off has to buy the other one a beer."

"I hate beer," Garraty said automatically.

Parker cackled. "You fucking bumpkin," he said, and walked away.

"He's buggy," McVries said. "Everybody's buggy

this morning. Even me. And it's a beautiful day. Don't you agree, Olson?"

Olson said nothing.

"Olson's got bugs, too," McVries confided to Garraty. "Olson! Hey, Hank!"

"Why don't you leave him alone?" Baker asked.

"Hey *Hank!*" McVries shouted, ignoring Baker. "Wanna go for a walk?"

"Go to hell," Olson muttered.

"What?" McVries cried merrily, cupping a hand to his ear. "Wha choo say, bo?"

"Hell! *Hell!*" Olson screamed. "Go to hell!"

"Is *that* what you said." McVries nodded wisely.

Olson went back to looking at his feet, and McVries tired of baiting him . . . if that was what he was doing.

Garraty thought about what Parker had said. Parker was a bastard. Parker was a big drugstore cowboy and Saturday night tough guy. Parker was a leather jacket hero. What did he know about Maine? He had lived in Maine all his life, in a little town called Porterville, just west of Freeport. Population 970 and not so much as a blinker light and just what's so damn special about Joliet, Illynoy anyway?

Garraty's father used to say Porterville was the only town in the county with more graveyards than people. But it was a clean place. The unemployment was high, the cars were rusty, and there was plenty of screwing around going on, but it was a clean place. The only action was Wednesday Bingo at the grange hall (last game a coverall for a twenty-pound turkey and a twenty-dollar bill), but it was clean. And it was quiet. What was wrong with that?

He looked at Collie Parker's back resentfully. You missed out, buddy, that's all. You take Joliet and your candy-store ratpack and your mills and you jam them. Jam them crossways, if they'll fit.

He thought about Jan again. He needed her. I love you, Jan, he thought. He wasn't dumb, and he knew she had become more to him than she actually was. She had turned into a life-symbol. A shield against the sudden death that came from the halftrack. More and more he wanted her because she symbolized the time when he could have a piece of ass—his own.

It was quarter of six in the morning now. He stared at a clump of cheering housewives bundled together near an intersection, small nerve-center of some unknown village. One of them was wearing tight slacks and a tighter sweater. Her face was plain. She wore three gold bracelets on her right wrist that clinked as she waved. Garraty could hear them clink. He waved back, not really thinking about it. He was thinking about Jan, who had come up from Connecticut, who had seemed so smooth and self-confident, with her long blond hair and her flat shoes. She almost always wore flats because she was so tall. He met her at school. It went slow, but finally it clicked. God, had it clicked.

"Garraty?"

"Huh?"

It was Harkness. He looked concerned. "I got a cramp in my foot, man. I don't know if I can walk on it." Harkness's eyes seemed to be pleading for Garraty to do something.

Garraty didn't know what to say. Jan's voice, her laughter, the tawny caramel-colored sweater and her cranberry-red slacks, the time they took his little brother's sled and ended up making out in a snowbank (before she put snow down the back of his parka) . . . those things were life. Harkness was death. By now Garraty could smell it.

"I can't help you," Garraty said. "You have to do it yourself."

Harkness looked at him in panicked consternation, and then his face turned grim and he nodded. He stopped, kneeled, and fumbled off his loafer.

"Warning! Warning 49!"

He was massaging his foot now. Garraty had turned around and was walking backwards to watch him. Two small boys in Little League shirts with their baseball gloves hung from their bicycle handlebars were also watching him from the side of the road, their mouths hung open.

"Warning! Second warning, 49!"

Harkness got up and began to limp onward in his stocking foot, his good leg already trying to buckle with the extra weight it was bearing. He dropped his shoe, grabbed for it, got two fingers on it, juggled it, and lost it. He stopped to pick it up and got his third warning.

Harkness's normally florid face was now fire-

engine red. His mouth hung open in a wet, sloppy
O. Garraty found himself rooting for Harkness.
Come on, he thought, come on, catch up. Hark-
ness, you can.

Harkness limped faster. The Little League boys
began to pedal along, watching him. Garraty turned
around frontward, not wanting to watch Harkness anymore. He stared straight ahead, trying to
remember just how it had felt to kiss Jan, to touch
her swelling breast.

A Shell station came slowly up on the right.
There was a dusty, fender-dented pickup parked on
the tarmac, and two men in red-and-black-checked
hunting shirts sitting on the tailgate, drinking beer.
There was a mailbox at the end of a rutted dirt
driveway, its lid hanging open like a mouth. A dog
was barking hoarsely and endlessly somewhere
just out of sight.

The carbines came slowly down from high port
and found Harkness.

There was a long, terrible moment of silence,
and then they went back up again to high port, all
according to the rules, according to the book. Then
they came down again. Garraty could hear Harkness's hurried, wet breathing.

The guns went back up, then down, then slowly
back up to high port.

The two Little Leaguers were still keeping pace.
"Get outta here!" Baker said suddenly, hoarsely.
"You don't want to see this. Scat!"

They looked with flat curiosity at Baker and
kept on. They had looked at Baker as if he was some

kind of fish. One of them, a small, bulletheaded kid with a wiffle haircut and dish-sized eyes, blipped the horn bolted to his bike and grinned. He wore braces, and the sun made a savage metal glitter in his mouth.

The guns came back down. It was like some sort of dance movement, like a ritual. Harkness rode the edge. Read any good books lately? Garraty thought insanely. This time they're going to shoot you. Just one step too slow—

Eternity.

Everything frozen.

Then the guns went back up to high port.

Garraty looked at his watch. The second hand swung around once, twice, three times. Harkness caught up to him, passed him by. His face was set and rigid. His eyes looked straight ahead. His pupils were contracted to tiny points. His lips had a faint bluish cast, and his fiery complexion had faded to the color of cream, except for two garish spots of color, one on each cheek. But he was not favoring the bad foot anymore. The cramp had loosened. His stocking foot slapped the road rhythmically. How long can you walk without your shoes? Garraty wondered.

He felt a loosening in his chest all the same, and heard Baker let out his breath. It was stupid to feel that way. The sooner Harkness stopped walking, the sooner he could stop walking. That was the simple truth. That was logic. But something went deeper, a truer, more frightening logic. Harkness was a part of the group that Garraty was a part of, a segment of his subclan. Part of a magic circle that Garraty belonged to. And if one part of that circle could be broken, any part of it could be broken.

The Little Leaguers biked along with them for another two miles before losing interest and turning back. It was better, Garraty thought. It didn't matter if they had looked at Baker as though he were something in a zoo. It was better for them to be cheated of their death. He watched them out of sight.

Up ahead, Harkness had formed a new one-man vanguard, walking very rapidly, almost running. He looked neither right nor left. Garraty wondered what he was thinking.

Chapter 7

"I like to think I'm quite an engaging bloke, really.
People I meet consider I'm schizophrenic
just because I'm completely different offscreen
than I am before the cameras . . ."
—Nicholas Parsons
Sale of the Century
(British version)

Scramm, 85, did not fascinate Garraty because of his flashing intelligence, because Scramm wasn't all that bright. He didn't fascinate Garraty because of his moon face, his crew cut, or his build, which was mooselike. He fascinated Garraty because he was married.

"Really?" Garraty asked for the third time. He still wasn't convinced Scramm wasn't having him on. "You're really married?"

"Yeah." Scramm looked up at the early morning sun with real pleasure. "I dropped out of school when I was fourteen. There was no point to it, not for me. I wasn't no troublemaker, just not able to make grades. And our history teacher read us an article about how schools are over-populated. So I figured why not let somebody who can learn sit in, and I'll get down to business. I wanted to marry Cathy anyway."

"How old were you?" Garraty asked, more fascinated than ever. They were passing through another small town, and the sidewalks were lined with signs and spectators, but he hardly noticed. Already the watchers were in another world, not related to him in any way. They might have been behind a thick plate-glass shield.

"Fifteen," Scramm answered. He scratched his chin, which was blue with beard stubble.

"No one tried to talk you out of it?"

"There was a guidance counselor at school, he gave me a lot of shit about sticking with it and not being a ditch digger, but he had more important things to do besides keep me in school. I guess you could say he gave me the soft sell. Besides, somebody has to dig ditches, right?"

He waved enthusiastically at a group of little girls who were going through a spastic cheerleader routine, pleated skirts and scabbed knees flying.

"Anyhow, I never did dig no ditch. Never dug a one in my whole career. Went to work for a bedsheet factory out in Phoenix, three dollars an hour. Me and Cathy, we're happy people." Scramm smiled. "Sometimes we'll be watching TV and Cath will grab me and say, 'We're happy people, honey.' She's a peach."

"You got any kids?" Garraty asked, feeling more and more that this was an insane discussion.

"Well, Cathy's pregnant right now. She said we should wait until we had enough in the bank to pay for the delivery. When we got up to seven hundred, she said go, and we went. She caught pregnant in no time at all." Scramm looked sternly at Garraty. "My kid's going to college. They say dumb guys like me never have smart kids, but Cathy's smart enough for both of us. Cathy finished high school. I made her finish. Four night courses and then she took the H.S.E.T. My kid's going to as much college as he wants."

Garraty didn't say anything. He couldn't think of anything to say. McVries was off to the side, in close conversation with Olson. Baker and Abraham were playing a word game called Ghost. He wondered where Harkness was. Far out of sight, anyway. That was Scramm, too. Really out of sight. Hey Scramm, I think you made a bad mistake. Your wife, she's *pregnant*, Scramm, but that doesn't win you any special favors around here. Seven hundred in the bank? You don't spell *pregnant* with just three numbers, Scramm. And no insurance company in the world would touch a Long Walker.

Garraty stared at and through a man in a hound's tooth jacket who was deliriously waving a straw hat with a stringy brim.

"Scramm, what happens if you buy it?" he asked cautiously.

Scramm smiled gently. "Not me. I feel like I could walk forever. Say, I wanted to be in the Long Walk ever since I was old enough to want anything. I walked eighty miles just two weeks ago, no sweat."

"But suppose something should happen—"

But Scramm only chuckled.

"How old's Cathy?"

"About a year older than me. Almost eighteen. Her folks are with her now, there in Phoenix."

It sounded to Garraty as if Cathy Scramm's folks knew something Scramm himself did not.

"You must love her a lot," he said, a little wistfully.

Scramm smiled, showing the stubborn last survivors of his teeth. "I ain't looked at anyone else since I married her. Cathy's a peach."

"And you're doing this."

Scramm laughed. "Ain't it fun?"

"Not for Harkness," Garraty said sourly. "Go ask him if he thinks it's fun."

"You don't have any grasp of the consequences," Pearson said, falling in between Garraty and Scramm. "You *could* lose. You have to admit you *could* lose."

"Vegas odds made me the favorite just before the Walk started," Scramm said. "Odds-on."

"Sure," Pearson said glumly. "And you're in shape, too, anyone can see that." Pearson himself looked pale and peaked after the long night on the road. He glanced disinterestedly at the crowd gathered in a supermarket parking lot they were just passing. "Everyone who wasn't in shape is dead now, or almost dead. But there's still seventy-two of us left."

"Yeah, but . . ." A thinking frown spread over the broad circle of Scramm's face. Garraty could almost hear the machinery up there working: slow, ponderous, but in the end as sure as death and as inescapable as taxes. It was somehow awesome.

"I don't want to make you guys mad," Scramm said. "You're good guys. But you didn't get into this thinking of winning out and getting the Prize. Most of these guys don't know why they got into it. Look at that Barkovitch. He ain't in it to get no Prize. He's just walkin' to see other people die. He lives on it. When someone gets a ticket, he gets a little more go-power. It ain't enough. He'll dry up just like a leaf on a tree."

"And me?" Garraty asked.

Scramm looked troubled. "Aw, hell . . ."

"No, go on."

"Well, the way I see it, you don't know why you are walking, either. It's the same thing. You're going now because you're afraid, but . . . that's not enough. That wears out." Scramm looked down at the road and rubbed his hands together. "And when it wears out, I guess you'll buy a ticket like all the rest, Ray."

Garraty thought about McVries saying, *When I get tired . . . really tired . . . why, I guess I will sit down.*

"You'll have to walk a long time to walk me down," Garraty said, but Scramm's simple assessment of the situation had scared him badly.

"I," Scramm said, "am ready to walk a long time."

Their feet rose and fell on the asphalt, carrying them forward, around a curve, down into a dip and then over a railroad track that was metal grooves in the road. They passed a closed fried clam shack. Then they were out in the country again.

"I understand what it is to die, I think," Pearson said abruptly. "Now I do, anyway. Not death itself, I still can't comprehend that. But dying. If I stop walking, I'll come to an end." He swallowed, and there was a click in his throat. "Just like a record after the last groove." He looked at Scramm earnestly. "Maybe it's like you say. Maybe it's not enough. But . . . I don't want to die."

Scramm looked at him almost scornfully. "You think just knowing about death will keep you from dying?"

Pearson smiled a funny, sick little smile, like a businessman on a heaving boat trying to keep his dinner down. "Right now that's about all that's keeping me going." And Garraty felt a huge gratefulness, because his defenses had not been reduced to that. At least, not yet.

Up ahead, quite suddenly and as if to illustrate the subject they had been discussing, a boy in a black turtleneck sweater suddenly had a convulsion. He fell on the road and began to snap and sunfish and jackknife viciously. His limbs jerked and flopped. There was a funny gargling noise in his throat, *aaa-aaa-aaa*, a sheeplike sound that was entirely mindless. As Garraty hurried past, one of the fluttering hands bounced against his shoe and he felt a wave of frantic revulsion. The boy's eyes were rolled up to the whites. There were splotches of foam splattered on his lips and chin. He was being second-warned, but of course he was beyond hearing, and when his two minutes were up they shot him like a dog.

Not long after that they reached the top of a gentle grade and stared down into the green, unpopulated country ahead. Garraty was grateful for the cool morning breeze that slipped over his fast-perspiring body.

"That's some view," Scramm said.

The road could be seen for perhaps twelve miles ahead. It slid down the long slope, ran in flat zigzags through the woods, a blackish-gray charcoal mark across a green swatch of crepe paper. Far ahead it began to climb again, and faded into the rosy-pink haze of early morning light.

"This might be what they call the Hainesville Woods," Garraty said, not too sure. "Truckers' graveyard. Hell in the wintertime."

"I never seen nothing like it," Scramm said reverently. "There isn't this much green in the whole state of Arizona."

"Enjoy it while you can," Baker said, joining the group. "It's going to be a scorcher. It's hot already and it's only six-thirty in the morning."

"Think you'd get used to it, where you come from," Pearson said, almost resentfully.

"You don't get used to it," Baker said, slinging his light jacket over his arm. "You just learn to live with it."

"I'd like to build a house up here," Scramm said. He sneezed heartily, twice, sounding a little like a bull in heat. "Build it right up here with my own two hands, and look at the view every morning. Me and Cathy. Maybe I will someday, when this is all over."

Nobody said anything.

By 6:45 the ridge was above and behind them, the breeze mostly cut off, and the heat already walked among them. Garraty took off his own jacket, rolled it, and tied it securely about his waist. The road through the woods was no longer deserted. Here and there early risers had parked their cars off the road and stood or sat in clumps, cheering, waving, and holding signs.

Two girls stood beside a battered MG at the bottom of one dip. They were wearing tight summer shorts, middy blouses, and sandals. There were cheers and whistles. The faces of these girls were hot, flushed, and excited by something ancient, sinuous, and, to Garraty, erotic almost to the point of insanity. He felt animal lust rising in him, an aggressively alive thing that made his body shake with a palsied fever all its own.

It was Gribble, the radical among them, that suddenly dashed at them, his feet kicking up spurts of dust along the shoulder. One of them leaned back against the hood of the MG and spread her legs slightly, tilting her hips at him. Gribble put his hands over her breasts. She made no effort to stop him. He was warned, hesitated, and then plunged against her, a jamming, hurtling, frustrated, angry, frightened figure in a sweaty white shirt and cord pants. The girl hooked her ankles around Gribble's calves and put her arms lightly around his neck. They kissed.

Gribble took a second warning, then a third, and then, with perhaps fifteen seconds of grace left, he stumbled away and broke into a frantic, shambling run. He fell down, picked himself up, clutched at his crotch and staggered back onto the road. His tin face was hectically flushed.

"Couldn't," he was sobbing. "Wasn't enough time and she wanted me to and I couldn't . . . I . . ." He was weeping and staggering, his hands pressed against his crotch. His words were little more than indistinct wails.

"So you gave them their little thrill," Barkovitch said. "Something for them to talk about in Show and Tell tomorrow."

"Just shut up!" Gribble screamed. He dug at his crotch. "It hurts, I got a cramp—"

"Blue balls," Pearson said. "That's what he's got."

Gribble looked at him through the stringy bangs of black hair that had fallen over his eyes. He looked like a stunned weasel. "It hurts," he muttered again. He dropped slowly to his knees, hands pressed into his lower belly, head drooping, back bowed. He was shivering and snuffling and Garraty could see the beads of sweat on his neck, some of them caught in the fine hairs on the nape—what Garraty's own father had always called quackfuzz.

A moment later and he was dead.

Garraty turned his head to look at the girls, but

they had retreated inside their MG. They were nothing but shadow-shapes.

He made a determined effort to push them from his mind, but they kept creeping back in. How must it have been, dry-humping that warm, willing flesh? Her thighs had twitched, my God, they had *twitched*, in a kind of spasm, orgasm, oh God, the uncontrollable urge to squeeze and caress . . . and most of all to feel that heat . . . *that heat*.

He felt himself go. That warm, shooting flow of sensation, warming him. Wetting him. Oh Christ, it would soak through his pants and someone would notice. Notice and point a finger and ask him how he'd like to walk around the neighborhood with no clothes on, walk naked, walk . . . and walk . . . and walk . . .

Oh Jan I love you really I love you, he thought, but it was confused, all mixed up in something else.

He retied his jacket about his waist and then went on walking as before, and the memory dulled and browned very quickly, like a Polaroid negative left out in the sun.

The pace stepped up. They were on a steep downhill grade now, and it was hard to walk slowly. Muscles worked and pistoned and squeezed against each other. The sweat rolled freely. Incredibly, Garraty found himself wishing for night again. He looked over at Olson curiously, wondering how he was making it.

Olson was staring at his feet again. The cords in his neck were knotted and ridged. His lips were drawn back in a frozen grin.

"He's almost there now," McVries said at his elbow, startling him. "When they start half-hoping someone will shoot them so they can rest their feet, they're not far away."

"Is that right?" Garraty asked crossly. "How come everybody else around here knows so much more about it than me?"

"Because you're so sweet," McVries said tenderly, and then he sped up, letting his legs catch the downgrade, and passed Garraty by.

Stebbins. He hadn't thought about Stebbins in a long time. He turned his head to look for Stebbins. Stebbins was there. The pack had strung out coming down the long hill, and Stebbins was about a quarter of a mile back, but there was no mistaking those purple pants and that chambray workshirt. Stebbins was still tailing the pack like some thin vulture, just waiting for them to fall—

Garraty felt a wave of rage. He had a sudden urge to rush back and throttle Stebbins. There was no rhyme or reason to it, but he had to actively fight the compulsion down.

By the time they had reached the bottom of the grade, Garraty's legs felt rubbery and unsteady. The state of numb weariness his flesh had more or less settled into was broken by unexpected darning-needles of pain that drove through his feet and legs. threatening to make his muscles knot and cramp. And Jesus, he thought, why not? They had been on the road for twenty-two hours. Twenty-two hours of nonstop walking, it was unbelievable.

"How do you feel now?" he asked Scramm, as if

the last time he had asked him had been twelve hours ago.

"Fit and fine," Scramm said. He wiped the back of his hand across his nose, sniffed, and spat. "Just as fit and fine as can be."

"You sound like you're getting a cold."

"Naw, it's the pollen. Happens every spring. Hay fever. I even get it in Arizona. But I never catch colds."

Garraty opened his mouth to reply when a hollow, *poom-poom* sound echoed back from far ahead. It was rifle fire. The word came back. Harkness had burnt out.

There was an odd, elevatorish sensation in Garraty's stomach as he passed the word on back. The magic circle was broken. Harkness would never write his book about the Long Walk. Harkness was being dragged off the road someplace up ahead like a grain bag or was being tossed into a truck, wrapped securely in a canvas bodybag. For Harkness, the Long Walk was over.

"Harkness," McVries said. "Ol' Harkness bought a ticket to see the farm."

"Why don't you write him a poime?" Barkovitch called over.

"Shut up, killer," McVries answered absently. He shook his head. "Ol' Harkness, sonofabitch."

"I ain't no killer!" Barkovitch screamed. "I'll dance on your grave, scarface! I'll—"

A chorus of angry shouts silenced him. Muttering, Barkovitch glared at McVries. Then he began to stalk on a little faster, not looking around.

"You know what my uncle did?" Baker said suddenly. They were passing through a shady tunnel of overleafing trees, and Garraty was trying to forget about Harkness and Gribble and think only of the coolness.

"What?" Abraham asked.

"He was an undertaker," Baker said.

"Good deal," Abraham said disinterestedly.

"When I was a kid, I always used to wonder," Baker said vaguely. He seemed to lose track of his thought, then glanced at Garraty and smiled. It was a peculiar smile. "Who'd embalm him, I mean. Like you wonder who cuts the barber's hair or who operates on the doctor for gallstones. See?"

"It takes a lot of gall to be a doctor," McVries said solemnly.

"You know what I mean."

"So who got the call when the time came?" Abraham asked.

"Yeah," Scramm added. "Who did?"

Baker looked up at the twining, heavy branches under which they were passing, and Garraty noticed again that Baker now looked exhausted. Not that we don't all look that way, he added to himself.

"Come on," McVries said. "Don't keep us hanging. Who buried him?"

"This is the oldest joke in the world," Abraham said. "Baker says, whatever made you think he was dead?"

"He is, though," Baker said. "Lung cancer. Six years ago."

"Did he smoke?" Abraham asked, waving at a

family of four and their cat. The cat was on a leash. It was a Persian cat. It looked mean and pissed off.

"No, not even a pipe," Baker said. "He was afraid it would give him cancer."

"Oh, for Christ's sake," McVries said, "who *buried* him? Tell us so we can discuss world problems, or baseball, or birth control or something."

"I think birth control *is* a world problem," Garraty said seriously. "My girlfriend is a Catholic and—"

"*Come on!*" McVries bellowed. "Who the fuck buried your grandfather, Baker?"

"My uncle. He was my uncle. My grandfather was a lawyer in Shreveport. He—"

"I don't give a shit," McVries said. "I don't give a shit if the old gentleman had three cocks, I just want to know who buried him so we can get *on*."

"Actually, nobody buried him. He wanted to be cremated."

"Oh my aching balls," Abraham said, and then laughed a little.

"My aunt's got his ashes in a ceramic vase. At her house in Baton Rouge. She tried to keep the business going—the undertaking business—but nobody much seemed to cotton to a lady undertaker."

"I doubt if that was it," McVries said.

"No?"

"No. I think your uncle jinxed her."

"Jinx? How do you mean?" Baker was interested.

"Well, you have to admit it wasn't a very good advertisement for the business."

"What, dying?"

"No," McVries said. "Getting cremated."

Scramm chuckled stuffily through his plugged nose. "He's got you there, old buddy."

"I expect he might," Baker said. He and McVries beamed at each other.

"Your uncle," Abraham said heavily, "bores the tits off me. And might I also add that he—"

At that moment, Olson began begging one of the guards to let him rest.

He did not stop walking, or slow down enough to be warned, but his voice rose and fell in a begging, pleading, totally craven monotone that made Garraty crawl with embarrassment for him. Conversation lagged. Spectators watched Olson with horrified fascination. Garraty wished Olson would shut up before he gave the rest of them a black eye. He didn't want to die either, but if he had to he wanted to go out without people thinking he was a coward. The soldiers stared over Olson, through him, around him, wooden-faced, deaf and dumb. They gave an occasional warning, though, so Garraty supposed you couldn't call them dumb.

It got to be quarter to eight, and the word came back that they were just six miles short of one hundred miles. Garraty could remember reading that the largest number to ever complete the first hundred miles of a Long Walk was sixty-three. They looked a sure bet to crack that record; there were still sixty-nine in this group. Not that it mattered, one way or the other.

Olson's pleas rose in a constant, garbled litany to Garraty's left, somehow seeming to make the day hotter and more uncomfortable than it was. Several of the boys had shouted at Olson, but he seemed either not to hear or not to care.

They passed through a wooden covered bridge, the planks rumbling and bumping under their feet. Garraty could hear the secretive flap and swoop of the barn swallows that had made their homes among the rafters. It was refreshingly cool, and the sun seemed to drill down even hotter when they reached the other side. Wait till later if you think it's hot now, he told himself. Wait until you get back into open country. Boy howdy.

He yelled for a canteen, and a soldier trotted over with one. He handed it to Garraty wordlessly, then trotted back. Garraty's stomach was also growling for food. At nine o'clock, he thought. Have to keep walking until then. Be damned if I'm going to die on an empty stomach.

Baker cut past him suddenly, looked around for spectators, saw none, dropped his britches and squatted. He was warned. Garraty passed him, but heard the soldier warn him again. About twenty seconds after that he caught up with Garraty and McVries again, badly out of breath. He was cinching his pants.

"Fastest crap I *evah* took!" he said, badly out of breath.

"You should have brought a catalogue along," McVries said.

"I never could go very long without a crap," Baker said. "Some guys, hell, they crap once a week.

I'm a once-a-day man. If I don't crap once a day, I take a laxative."

"Those laxatives will ruin your intestines," Pearson said.

"Oh, shit," Baker scoffed.

McVries threw back his head and laughed.

Abraham twisted his head around to join the conversation. "My grandfather never used a laxative in his life and he lived to be—"

"You kept records, I presume," Pearson said.

"You wouldn't be doubting my grandfather's word, would you?"

"Heaven forbid." Pearson rolled his eyes.

"Okay. My grandfather—"

"Look," Garraty said softly. Not interested in either side of the laxative argument, he had been idly watching Percy What's-His-Name. Now he was watching him closely, hardly believing what his eyes were seeing. Percy had been edging closer and closer to the side of the road. Now he was walking on the sandy shoulder. Every now and then he snapped a tight, frightened glance at the soldiers on top of the halftrack, then to his right, at the thick screen of trees less than seven feet away.

"I think he's going to break for it," Garraty said.

"They'll shoot him sure as hell," Baker said. His voice had dropped to a whisper.

"Doesn't look like anyone's watching him," Pearson replied.

"Then for God's sake, don't tip them!" McVries said angrily. "You bunch of dummies! Christ!"

For the next ten minutes none of them said

anything sensible. They aped conversation and watched Percy watching the soldiers, watching and mentally gauging the short distance to the thick woods.

"He hasn't got the guts," Pearson muttered finally, and before any of them could answer, Percy began walking, slowly and unhurriedly, toward the woods. Two steps, then three. One more, two at the most, and he would be there. His jeans-clad legs moved unhurriedly. His sun-bleached blond hair ruffled just a little in a light puff of breeze. He might have been an Explorer Scout out for a day of bird-watching.

There were no warnings. Percy had forfeited his right to them when his right foot passed over the verge of the shoulder. Percy had left the road, and the soldiers had known all along. Old Percy What's-His-Name hadn't been fooling anybody. There was one sharp, clean report, and Garraty jerked his eyes from Percy to the soldier standing on the back deck of the halftrack. The soldier was a sculpture in clean, angular lines, the rifle nestled into the hollow of his shoulder, his head half-cocked along the barrel.

Then his head swiveled back to Percy again. Percy was the real show, wasn't he? Percy was standing with both his feet on the weedy border of the pine forest now. He was as frozen and as sculpted as the man who had shot him. The two of them together would have been a subject for Michelangelo, Garraty thought. Percy stood utterly still under a blue springtime sky. One hand was pressed to his chest, like a poet about to speak. His eyes were wide, and somehow ecstatic.

A bright seepage of blood ran through his fingers, shining in the sunlight. Old Percy What's-Your-Name. Hey Percy, your mother's calling. Hey Percy, does your mother know you're out? Hey Percy, what kind of silly sissy name is that, Percy, Percy, aren't you cute? Percy transformed into a bright, sunlit Adonis counterpointed by the savage, dun-colored huntsman. And one, two, three coin-shaped splatters of blood fell on Percy's travel-dusty black shoes, and all of it happened in a space of only three seconds. Garraty did not take even two full steps and he was not warned, and oh Percy, what *is* your mother going to say? Do you, tell me, *do* you really have the *nerve* to die?

Percy did. He pitched forward, struck a small, crooked sapling, rolled through a half-turn, and landed face-up to the sky. The grace, the frozen symmetry, they were gone now. Percy was just dead.

"Let this ground be seeded with salt," McVries said suddenly, very rapidly. "So that no stalk of corn or stalk of wheat shall ever grow. Cursed be the children of this ground and cursed be their loins. Also cursed be their hams and hocks. Hail Mary full of grace, let us blow this goddam place."

McVries began to laugh.

"Shut up," Abraham said hoarsely. "Stop talking like that."

"All the world is God," McVries said, and giggled hysterically. "We're *walking* on the Lord, and back there the flies are *crawling* on the Lord, in fact the flies are also the Lord, so blessed be the fruit of thy womb Percy. Amen, hallelujah, chunky peanut butter. Our father, which art in tinfoil, hallow'd be thy name."

"I'll hit you!" Abraham warned. His face was very pale. "I will, Pete!"

"A *praaayin'* man!" McVries gibed, and he giggled again. "Oh my suds and body! Oh my sainted *hat*!"

"I'll hit you if you don't shut up!" Abraham bellowed.

"Don't," Garraty said, frightened. "Please don't fight. Let's . . . be nice."

"Want a party favor?" Baker asked crazily.

"Who asked you, you goddam redneck?"

"He was awful young to be on this hike," Baker said sadly. "If he was fourteen, I'll smile 'n' kiss a pig."

"Mother spoiled him," Abraham said in a trembling voice. "You could tell." He looked around at Garraty and Pearson pleadingly. "You could tell, couldn't you?"

"She won't spoil him anymore," McVries said.

Olson suddenly began babbling at the soldiers again. The one who had shot Percy was now sitting down and eating a sandwich. They walked past eight o'clock. They passed a sunny gas station where a mechanic in greasy coveralls was hosing off the tarmac.

"Wish he'd spray us with some of that," Scramm said. "I'm as hot as a poker."

"We're all hot," Garraty said.

"I thought it never got hot in Maine," Pearson said. He sounded more tired than ever. "I thought Maine was s'posed to be cool."

"Well then, now you know different," Garraty said shortly.

"You're a lot of fun, Garraty," Pearson said. "You know that? You're really a lot of fun. Gee, I'm glad I met you."

McVries laughed.

"You know what?" Garraty replied.

"What?"

"You got skidmarks in your underwear," Garraty said. It was the wittiest thing he could think of at short notice.

They passed another truck stop. Two or three big rigs were pulled in, hauled off the highway no doubt to make room for the Long Walkers. One of the drivers was standing anxiously by his rig, a huge refrigerator truck, and feeling the side. Feeling the cold that was slipping away in the morning sun. Several of the waitresses cheered as the Walkers trudged by, and the trucker who had been feeling the side of his refrigerator compartment turned and gave them the finger. He was a huge man with a red neck bulling its way out of a dirty T-shirt.

"Now why'd he wanna do that?" Scramm cried. "Just a rotten old sport!"

McVries laughed. "That's the first honest citizen we've seen since this clambake got started, Scramm. Man, do I love him!"

"Probably he's loaded up with perishables

headed for Montreal," Garraty said. "All the way from Boston. We forced him off the road. He's probably afraid he'll lose his job—or his rig, if he's an independent."

"Isn't that tough?" Collie Parker brayed. "Isn't that too goddam tough? They only been tellin' people what the route was gonna be for two months or more. Just another goddam hick, that's all!"

"You seem to know a lot about it," Abraham said to Garraty.

"A little," Garraty said, staring at Parker. "My father drove a rig before he got . . . before he went away. It's a hard job to make a buck in. Probably that guy back there thought he had time to make it to the next cutoff. He wouldn't have come this way if there was a shorter route."

"He didn't have to give us the finger," Scramm insisted. "He didn't have to do that. By God, his rotten old tomatoes ain't life and death, like this is."

"Your father took off on your mother?" McVries asked Garraty.

"My dad was Squaded," Garraty said shortly. Silently he dared Parker—or anyone else—to open his mouth, but no one said anything.

Stebbins was still walking last. He had no more than passed the truck stop before the burly driver was swinging back up into the cab of his jimmy. Up ahead, the guns cracked out their single word. A body spun, flipped over, and lay still. Two soldiers dragged it over to the side of the road. A third tossed them a bodybag from the halftrack.

"I had an uncle that was Squaded," Wyman

said hesitantly. Garraty noticed that the tongue of Wyman's left shoe had worked out from beneath the lacings and was flapping obscenely.

"No one but goddam fools get Squaded," Collie Parker said clearly.

Garraty looked at him and wanted to feel angry, but he dropped his head and stared at the road. His father had been a goddam fool, all right. A goddam drunkard who could not keep two cents together in the same place for long no matter what he tried his hand at, a man without the sense to keep his political opinions to himself. Garraty felt old and sick.

"Shut your stinking trap," McVries said coldly.

"You want to try and make m—"

"No, I don't want to try and make you. Just shut up, you sonofabitch."

Collie Parker dropped back between Garraty and McVries. Pearson and Abraham moved away a little. Even the soldiers straightened, ready for trouble. Parker studied Garraty for a long moment. His face was broad and beaded with sweat, his eyes still arrogant. Then he clapped Garraty briefly on the arm.

"I got a loose lip sometimes. I didn't mean nothing by it. Okay?" Garraty nodded wearily, and Parker shifted his glance to McVries. "Piss on you, Jack," he said, and moved up again toward the vanguard.

"What an unreal bastard," McVries said glumly.

"No worse than Barkovitch," Abraham said. "Maybe even a little better."

"Besides," Pearson added, "what's getting Squaded? It beats the hell out of getting dead, am I right?"

"How would you know?" Garraty asked. "How would any of us know?"

His father had been a sandy-haired giant with a booming voice and a bellowing laugh that had sounded to Garraty's small ears like mountains cracking open. After he lost his own rig, he made a living driving Government trucks out of Brunswick. It would have been a good living if Jim Garraty could have kept his politics to himself. But when you work for the Government, the Government is twice as aware that you're alive, twice as ready to call in a Squad if things seem a little dicky around the edges. And Jim Garraty had not been much of a Long Walk booster. So one day he got a telegram and the next day two soldiers turned up on the doorstep and Jim Garraty had gone with them, blustering, and his wife had closed the door and her cheeks had been pale as milk and when Garraty asked his mother where Daddy was going with the soldier mens, she had slapped him hard enough to make his mouth bleed and told him to shut up, shut up. Garraty had never seen his father since. It had been eleven years. It had been a neat removal. Odorless, sanitized, pasteurized, sanforized, and dandruff-free.

"I had a brother that was in law trouble," Baker said. "Not the Government, just the law. He stole himself a car and drove all the way from our town to Hattiesburg, Mississippi. He got two years' suspended sentence. He's dead now."

"Dead?" The voice was a dried husk, wraithlike. Olson had joined them. His haggard face seemed to stick out a mile from his body.

"He had a heart attack," Baker said. "He was only three years older than me. Ma used to say he was her cross, but he only got into bad trouble that once. I did worse. I was a night rider for three years."

Garraty looked over at him. There was shame in Baker's tired face, but there was also dignity there, outlined against a dusky shaft of sunlight poking through the trees.

"That's a Squading offense, but I didn't care. I was only twelve when I got into it. Ain't hardly nothing but kids who go night-riding now, you know. Older heads are wiser heads. They'd tell us to go to it and pat our heads, but they weren't out to get Squaded, not them. I got out after we burnt a cross on some black man's lawn. I was scairt green. And ashamed, too. Why does anybody want to go burning a cross on some black man's lawn? Jesus Christ, that stuff's history, ain't it? Sure it is." Baker shook his head vaguely. "It wasn't right."

At that moment the rifles went again.

"There goes one more," Scramm said. His voice sounded clogged and nasal, and he wiped his nose with the back of his hand.

"Thirty-four," Pearson said. He took a penny out of one pocket and put it in the other. "I brought along ninety-nine pennies. Every time someone buys a ticket, I put one of 'em in the other pocket. And when—"

"That's gruesome!" Olson said. His haunted eyes stared balefully at Pearson. "Where's your death watch? Where's your voodoo dolls?"

Pearson didn't say anything. He studied the fallow field they were passing with anxious embarrassment. Finally he muttered, "I didn't mean to say anything about it. It was for good luck, that was all."

"It's dirty," Olson croaked. "It's *filthy.* It's—"

"Oh, quit it," Abraham said. "Quit getting on my nerves."

Garraty looked at his watch. It was twenty past eight. Forty minutes to food. He thought how nice it would be to go into one of those little roadside diners that dotted the road, snuggle his fanny against one of the padded counter stools, put his feet up on the rail (oh God, the relief of just that!) and order steak and fried onions, with a side of French fries and a big dish of vanilla ice cream with strawberry sauce for dessert. Or maybe a big plate of spaghetti and meatballs, with Italian bread and peas swimming in butter on the side. And milk. A whole pitcher of milk. To hell with the tubes and the canteens of distilled water. Milk and solid food and a place to sit and eat it in. Would that be fine?

Just ahead a family of five—mother, father, boy, girl, and white-haired grandmother—were spread beneath a large elm, eating a picnic breakfast of sandwiches and what looked like hot cocoa. They waved cheerily at the Walkers.

"Freaks," Garraty muttered.

"What was that?" McVries asked.

"I said I want to sit down and have something to eat. Look at those people. Fucking bunch of pigs."

"You'd be doing the same thing," McVries said. He waved and smiled, saving the biggest, flashiest part of the smile for the grandmother, who was waving back and chewing—well, gumming, was closer to the truth—what looked like an egg salad sandwich.

"The hell I would. Sit there and eat while a bunch of starving—"

"Hardly starving, Ray. It just feels that way."

"*Hungry*, then—"

"Mind over matter," McVries incanted. "Mind over matter, my young friend." The incantation had become a seamy imitation of W.C. Fields.

"To hell with you. You just don't want to admit it. Those people, they're animals. They want to see someone's brains on the road, that's why they turn out. They'd just as soon see yours."

"That isn't the point," McVries said calmly. "Didn't you say you went to see the Long Walk when you were younger?"

"Yes, when I didn't know any better!"

"Well, that makes it okay, doesn't it?" McVries uttered a short, ugly-sounding laugh. "Sure they're animals. You think you just found out a new principle? Sometimes I wonder just how naive you really are. The French lords and ladies used to screw after the guillotinings. The old Romans used to stuff each other during the gladiatorial matches. That's entertainment, Garraty. It's nothing new." He laughed again. Garraty stared at him, fascinated.

"Go on," someone said. "You're at second base, McVries. Want to try for third?"

Garraty didn't have to turn. It was Stebbins, of course. Stebbins the lean Buddha. His feet carried him along automatically, but he was dimly aware that they felt swollen and slippery, as if they were filling with pus.

"Death is great for the appetites," McVries said. "How about those two girls and Gribble? They wanted to see what screwing a dead man felt like. Now for Something Completely New and Different. I don't know if Gribble got much out of it, but they sure as shit did. It's the same with anybody. It doesn't matter if they're eating or drinking or sitting on their cans. They like it better, they feel it and taste it better because they're watching dead men.

"But even that's not the real point of this little expedition, Garraty. The point is, they're the smart ones. *They're* not getting thrown to the lions. *They're* not staggering along and hoping they won't have to take a shit with two warnings against them. You're dumb, Garraty. You and me and Pearson and Barkovitch and Stebbins, we're all dumb. Scramm's dumb because he thinks he understands and he doesn't. Olson's dumb because he understood too much too late. They're animals, all right. But why are you so goddam sure that makes us human beings?"

He paused, badly out of breath.

"There," he said. "You went and got me going. Sermonette No. 342 in a series of six thousand, et cetera, et cetera. Probably cut my lifespan by five hours or more."

"Then why are you doing it?" Garraty asked him. "If you know that much, and if you're that sure, why are you doing it?"

"The same reason we're all doing it," Stebbins said. He smiled gently, almost lovingly. His lips were a little sun-parched; otherwise, his face was still unlined and seemingly invincible. "We want to die, that's why we're doing it. Why else, Garraty? Why else?"

Chapter 8

"Three-six-nine, the goose drank wine
The monkey chewed tobacco on the streetcar line
The line broke
The monkey got choked
And they all went to heaven in a little rowboat . . . "
                                        —*Children's rhyme*

Ray Garraty cinched the concentrate belt tightly around his waist and firmly told himself he would eat absolutely nothing until nine-thirty at least. He could tell it was going to be a hard resolution to keep. His stomach gnawed and growled. All around him Walkers were compulsively celebrating the end of the first twenty-four hours on the road.

Scramm grinned at Garraty through a mouthful of cheese spread and said something pleasant but untranslatable. Baker had his vial of olives—real olives—and was popping them into his mouth with machine-gun regularity. Pearson was jamming crackers mounded high with tuna spread into his mouth, and McVries was slowly eating chicken spread. His eyes were half-lidded, and he might have been in extreme pain or at the pinnacle of pleasure.

Two more of them had gone down between

eight-thirty and nine; one of them had been the Wayne that the gas jockey had been cheering for a ways back. But they had come ninety-nine miles with just thirty-six gone. Isn't that wonderful, Garraty thought, feeling the saliva spurt in his mouth as McVries mopped the last of the chicken concentrate out of the tube and then cast the empty aside. Great. I hope they all drop dead right now.

A teenager in pegged jeans raced a middle-aged housewife for McVries's empty tube, which had stopped being something useful and had begun its new career as a souvenir. The housewife was closer but the kid was faster and he beat her by half a length. "Thanks!" he hollered to McVries, holding the bent and twisted tube aloft. He scampered back to his friends, still waving it. The housewife eyed him sourly.

"Aren't you eating anything?" McVries asked.

"I'm making myself wait."

"For what?"

"Nine-thirty."

McVries eyed him thoughtfully. "The old self-discipline bit?"

Garraty shrugged, ready for the backlash of sarcasm, but McVries only went on looking at him.

"You know something?" McVries said finally.

"What?"

"If I had a dollar . . . *just* a dollar, mind you . . . I think I'd put it on you, Garraty. I think you've got a chance to win this thing."

Garraty laughed self-consciously. "Putting the whammy on me?"

"The what?"

"The whammy. Like telling a pitcher he's got a no-hitter going."

"Maybe I am," McVries said. He put his hands out in front of him. They were shaking very slightly. McVries frowned at them in a distracted sort of concentration. It was a half-lunatic sort of gaze. "I hope Barkovitch buys out soon," he said.

"Pete?"

"What?"

"If you had it to do all over again ... if you knew you could get this far and still be walking ... would you do it?"

McVries put his hands down and stared at Garraty. "Are you kidding? You must be."

"No, I'm serious."

"Ray, I don't think I'd do it again if the Major put his pistol up against my nates. This is the next thing to suicide, except that a regular suicide is quicker."

"True," Olson said. "How true." He smiled a hollow, concentration-camp smile that made Garraty's belly crawl.

Ten minutes later they passed under a huge red-and-white banner that proclaimed: 100 MILES!! CONGRATULATIONS FROM THE JEFFERSON PLANTATION CHAMBER OF COMMERCE! CONGRATULATIONS TO THIS YEAR'S "CENTURY CLUB" LONG WALKERS!!

"I got a place where they can put their Century Club," Collie Parker said. "It's long and brown and the sun never shines there."

Suddenly the spotty stands of second-growth pine and spruce that had bordered the road in scruffy patches were gone, hidden by the first real crowd they had seen. A tremendous cheer went up, and that was followed by another and another. It was like surf hammering on rocks. Flashbulbs popped and dazzled. State police held the deep ranks of people back, and bright orange nylon restraining ropes were strung along the soft shoulders. A policeman struggled with a screaming little boy. The boy had a dirty face and a snotty nose. He was waving a toy glider in one hand and an autograph book in the other.

"Jeez!" Baker yelled. "Jeez, look at 'em, just look at 'em all!"

Collie Parker was waving and smiling, and it was not until Garraty closed up with him a little that he could hear him calling in his flat Midwestern accent: "Glad to seeya, ya goddam bunch of fools!" A grin and a wave. "Howaya, Mother Mc-Cree, you goddam bag. Your face and my ass, what a match. Howaya, howaya?"

Garraty clapped his hands over his mouth and giggled hysterically. A man in the first rank waving a sloppily lettered sign with Scramm's name on it had popped his fly. A row back a fat woman in a ridiculous yellow sunsuit was being ground between three college students who were drinking beer. Stone-ground fatty, Garraty thought, and laughed harder.

You're going to have hysterics, oh my God, don't

let it get you, think about Gribble . . . and don't . . . don't let . . . don't . . .

But it was happening. The laughter came roaring out of him until his stomach was knotted and cramped and he was walking bent-legged and somebody was hollering at him, screaming at him over the roar of the crowd. It was McVries. "Ray! *Ray!* What is it? You all right?"

"They're funny!" He was nearly weeping with laughter now. "Pete, Pete, they're so funny, it's just . . . just . . . that they're so *funny!*"

A hard-faced little girl in a dirty sundress sat on the ground, pouty-mouthed and frowning. She made a horrible face as they passed. Garraty nearly collapsed with laughter and drew a warning. It was strange—in spite of all the noise he could still hear the warnings clearly.

I could die, he thought. I could just die laughing, wouldn't that be a scream?

Collie was still smiling gaily and waving and cursing spectators and newsmen roundly, and that seemed funniest of all. Garraty fell to his knees and was warned again. He continued to laugh in short, barking spurts, which were all his laboring lungs would allow.

"He's gonna puke!" someone cried in an ecstasy of delight. "Watch 'im, Alice, he's gonna puke!"

"Garraty! Garraty for God's sake!" McVries was yelling. He got an arm around Garraty's back and hooked a hand into his armpit. Somehow he yanked him to his feet and Garraty stumbled on.

"Oh God," Garraty gasped. "Oh Jesus Christ

they're killing me. I . . . I can't . . ." He broke into loose, trickling laughter once more. His knees buckled. McVries ripped him to his feet once more. Garraty's collar tore. They were both warned. That's my last warning, Garraty thought dimly. I'm on my way to see that fabled farm. Sorry, Jan, I . . .

"Come on, you turkey, I can't lug you!" McVries hissed.

"I can't do it," Garraty gasped. "My wind's gone, I—"

McVries slapped him twice quickly, forehand on the right cheek, backhand on the left. Then he walked away quickly, not looking back.

The laughter had gone out of him now but his gut was jelly, his lungs empty and seemingly unable to refill. He staggered drunkenly along, weaving, trying to find his wind. Black spots danced in front of his eyes, and a part of him understood how close to fainting he was. His one foot fetched against his other foot, he stumbled, almost fell, and somehow kept his balance.

If I fall, I die. I'll never get up.

They were watching him. The crowd was watching him. The cheers had died away to a muted, almost sexual murmur. They were waiting for him to fall down.

He walked on, now concentrating only on putting one foot out in front of the other. Once, in the eighth grade, he had read a story by a man named Ray Bradbury, and this story was about the crowds that gather at the scenes of fatal accidents, about how these crowds always have the same faces, and about how they seem to know whether the wounded will live or die. I'm going to live a little longer, Garraty told them. I'm going to live. I'm going to live a little longer.

He made his feet rise and fall to the steady cadence in his head. He blotted everything else out, even Jan. He was not aware of the head, or of Collie Parker, or of Freaky D'Allessio. He was not even aware of the steady dull pain in his feet and the frozen stiffness of the hamstring muscles behind his knees. The thought pounded in his mind like a big kettledrum. Like a heartbeat. *Live a little longer. Live a little longer. Live a little longer.* Until the words themselves became meaningless and signified nothing.

It was the sound of the guns that brought him out of it.

In the crowd-hushed stillness the sound was shockingly loud and he could hear someone screaming. Now you know, he thought, you live long enough to hear the sound of the guns, long enough to hear yourself screaming—

But one of his feet kicked a small stone then and there was pain and it wasn't him that had bought it, it was 64, a pleasant, smiling boy named Frank Morgan. They were dragging Frank Morgan off the road. His glasses were dragging and bouncing on the pavement, still hooked stubbornly over one ear. The left lens had been shattered.

"I'm not dead," he said dazedly. Shock hit him in a warm blue wave, threatening to turn his legs to water again.

"Yeah, but you ought to be," McVries said.

"You saved him," Olson said, turning it into a curse. "Why did you do that? *Why did you do that?*" His eyes were as shiny and as blank as doorknobs. "I'd kill you if I could. I hate you. You're gonna die, McVries. You wait and see. God's gonna strike you dead for what you did. God's gonna strike you dead as dogshit." His voice was pallid and empty. Garraty could almost smell the shroud on him. He clapped his own hands over his mouth and moaned through them. The truth was that the smell of the shroud was on all of them.

"Piss on you," McVries said calmly. "I pay my debts, that's all." He looked at Garraty. "We're square, man. It's the end, right?" He walked away, not hurrying, and was soon only another colored shirt about twenty yards ahead.

Garraty's wind came back, but very slowly, and for a long time he was sure he could feel a stitch coming in his side . . . but at last that faded. McVries had saved his life. He had gone into hysterics, had a laughing jag, and McVries had saved him from going down. We're square, man. It's the end, right? All right.

"God will punish him," Hank Olson was blaring with dead and unearthly assurance. "God will strike him down."

"Shut up or I'll strike you down myself," Abraham said.

The day grew yet hotter, and small, quibbling arguments broke out like brushfires. The huge crowd dwindled a little as they walked out of the radius of TV cameras and microphones, but it did not disappear or even break up into isolated knots of spectators. The crowd had come now, and the crowd was here to stay. The people who made it up merged into one anonymous Crowd Face, a vapid, eager visage that duplicated itself mile by mile. It peopled doorsteps, lawns, driveways, picnic areas, gas station tarmacs (where enterprising owners had charged admission), and, in the next town they passed through, both sides of the street and the parking lot of the town's supermarket. The Crowd Face mugged and gibbered and cheered, but always remained essentially the same. It watched voraciously as Wyman squatted to make his bowels work. Men, women, and children, the Crowd Face was always the same, and Garraty tired of it quickly.

He wanted to thank McVries, but somehow doubted that McVries wanted to be thanked. He could see him up ahead, walking behind Barkovitch. McVries was staring intently at Barkovitch's neck.

Nine-thirty came and passed. The crowd seemed to intensify the heat, and Garraty unbuttoned his shirt to just above his belt buckle. He wondered if Freaky D'Allessio had known he was going to buy a ticket before he did. He supposed that knowing wouldn't have really changed things for him, one way or the other.

The road inclined steeply, and the crowd fell away momentarily as they climbed up and over four sets of east/west railroad tracks that ran below, glittering hotly in their bed of cinders. At the top, as they crossed the wooden bridge, Garraty could see another belt of woods ahead, and the built-up, almost suburban area through which they had just passed to the right and left.

A cool breeze played over his sweaty skin, making him shiver. Scramm sneezed sharply three times.

"I *am* getting a cold," he announced disgustedly.

"That'll take the starch right out of you," Pearson said. "That's a bitch."

"I'll just have to work harder," Scramm said.

"You must be made of steel," Pearson said. "If I had a cold I think I'd roll right over and die. That's how little energy I've got left."

"Roll over and die now!" Barkovitch yelled back. "Save some energy!"

"Shut up and keep walking, killer," McVries said immediately.

Barkovitch looked around at him. "Why don't you get off my back, McVries? Go walk somewhere else."

"It's a free road. I'll walk where I damn well please."

Barkovitch hawked, spat, and dismissed him.

Garraty opened one of his food containers and began to eat cream cheese on crackers. His stomach growled bitterly at the first bite, and he had to fight himself to keep from wolfing everything. He squeezed a tube of roast beef concentrate into his mouth, swallowing steadily. He washed it down with water and then made himself stop there.

They walked by a lumberyard where men stood atop stacks of planks, silhouetted against the sky like Indians, waving to them. Then they were in the woods again and silence seemed to fall with a crash. It was not silent, of course; Walkers talked, the halftrack ground along mechanically, somebody broke wind, somebody laughed, somebody behind Garraty made a hopeless little groaning sound. The sides of the road were still lined with spectators, but the great "Century Club" crowd had disappeared and it seemed quiet by comparison. Birds sang in the high-crowned trees, the furtive breeze now and then masked the heat for a moment or two, sounding like a lost soul as it soughed through the trees. A brown squirrel froze on a high branch, tail bushed out, black eyes brutally attentive, a nut caught between his ratlike front paws. He chittered at them, then scurried higher up and disappeared. A plane droned far away, like a giant fly.

To Garraty it seemed that everyone was deliberately giving him the silent treatment. McVries was still walking behind Barkovitch. Pearson and Baker were talking about chess. Abraham was eating noisily and wiping his hands on his shirt. Scramm had torn off a piece of his T-shirt and was using it as a hanky. Collie Parker was swapping girls with Wyman. And Olson . . . but he didn't even want to look at Olson, who seemed to want to implicate everyone else as an accessory in his own approaching death.

So he began to drop back, very carefully, just a little at a time (very mindful of his three warnings), until he was in step with Stebbins. The purple pants were dusty now. There were dark circles of sweat under the armpits of the chambray shirt. Whatever else Stebbins was, he wasn't Superman. He looked up at Garraty for a moment, lean face questioning, and then he dropped his gaze back to the road. The knob of spine at the back of his neck was very prominent.

"How come there aren't more people?" Garraty asked hesitantly. "Watching, I mean."

For a moment he didn't think Stebbins was going to answer. But finally he looked up again, brushed the hair off his forehead and replied, "There will be. Wait awhile. They'll be sitting on roofs three deep to look at you."

"But somebody said there was billions bet on this. You'd think they'd be lined up three deep the whole way. And that there'd be TV coverage—"

"It's discouraged."

"Why?"

"Why ask me?"

"Because you *know*," Garraty said, exasperated.

"How do you know?"

"Jesus, you remind me of the caterpillar in *Alice in Wonderland*, sometimes," Garraty said. "Don't you ever just talk?"

"How long would you last with people screaming at you from both sides? The body odor alone would be enough to drive you insane after a while. It would be like walking three hundred miles through Times Square on New Year's Eve."

"But they *do* let them watch, don't they? Someone said it was one big crowd from Oldtown on."

"I'm not the caterpillar, anyway," Stebbins said with a small, somehow secretive smile. "I'm more the white rabbit type, don't you think? Except I left my gold watch at home and no one has invited me to tea. At least, to the best of my knowledge, no one has. Maybe that's what I'll ask for when I win. When they ask me what I want for my prize, I'll say, 'Why, I want to be invited home for tea.' "

"Goddammit!"

Stebbins smiled more widely, but it was still only an exercise in lip-pulling. "Yeah, from Oldtown or thereabouts the damper is off. By then no one is thinking very much about mundane things like B.O. And there's continuous TV coverage from Augusta. The Long Walk is the national pastime, after all."

"Then why not here?"

"Too soon," Stebbins said. "Too soon."

From around the next curve the guns roared again, startling a pheasant that rose from the underbrush in an electric uprush of beating feathers. Garraty and Stebbins rounded the curve, but the bodybag was already being zipped up. Fast work. He couldn't see who it had been.

"You reach a certain point," Stebbins said, "when the crowd ceases to matter, either as an incentive or a drawback. It ceases to be there. Like a man on a scaffold, I think. You burrow away from the crowd."

"I think I understand that," Garraty said. He felt timid.

"If you understood it, you wouldn't have gone into hysterics back there and needed your friend to save your ass. But you will."

"How far do you burrow, I wonder?"

"How deep are you?"

"I don't know."

"Well, that's something you'll get to find out, too. Plumb the unplumbed depths of Garraty. Sounds almost like a travel ad, doesn't it? You burrow until you hit bedrock. Then you burrow *into* the bedrock. And finally you get to the bottom. And then you buy out. That's my idea. Let's hear yours."

Garraty said nothing. Right at present, he had no ideas.

The Walk went on. The heat went on. The sun hung suspended just above the line of trees the road cut its way through. Their shadows were stubby dwarves. Around ten o'clock, one of the soldiers disappeared through the back hatch of the half-track and reappeared with a long pole. The upper two thirds of the pole was shrouded in cloth. He closed the hatch and dropped the end of the pole into a slot in the metal. He reached under the cloth and did something . . . fiddled something, probably a stud. A moment later a large, dun-colored sun umbrella popped up. It shaded most of the halftrack's metal surface. He and the other two soldiers currently on duty sat cross-legged in the army-drab parasol's shade.

"You rotten sonsabitches!" somebody screamed. "My Prize is gonna be your public castration!"

The soldiers did not seem exactly struck to the heart with terror at the thought. They continued to scan the Walkers with their blank eyes, referring occasionally to their computerized console.

"They probably take this out on their wives," Garraty said. "When it's over."

"Oh, I'm sure they do," Stebbins said, and laughed.

Garraty didn't want to walk with Stebbins anymore, not right now. Stebbins made him uneasy. He could only take Stebbins in small doses. He walked faster, leaving Stebbins by himself again. 10:02. In twenty-three minutes he could drop a warning, but for now he was still walking with three. It didn't scare him the way he had thought it would. There was still the unshakable, blind assurances that this organism Ray Garraty could not die. The others could die, they were extras in the movie of his life, but not Ray Garraty, star of that long-running hit film, *The Ray Garraty Story*. Maybe he would eventually come to understand the untruth of that emotionally as well as intellectually . . . maybe that was the final depth of which Stebbins had spoken. It was a shivery, unwelcome thought.

Without realizing it, he had walked three quarters of the way through the pack. He was behind

McVries again. There were three of them in a fatigue-ridden conga line: Barkovitch at the front, still trying to look cocky but flaking a bit around the edges; McVries with his head slumped, hands half-clenched, favoring his left foot a little now; and, bringing up the rear, the star of *The Ray Garraty Story* himself. And how do I look? he wondered.

He rubbed a hand up the side of his cheek and listened to the rasp his hand made against his light beard-stubble. Probably he didn't look all that snappy himself.

He stepped up his pace a little more until he was walking abreast of McVries, who looked over briefly and then back at Barkovitch. His eyes were dark and hard to read.

They climbed a short, steep, and savagely sunny rise and then crossed another small bridge. Fifteen minutes went by, then twenty. McVries didn't say anything. Garraty cleared his throat twice but said nothing. He thought that the longer you went without speaking, the harder it gets to break the silence. Probably McVries was pissed that he had saved his ass now. Probably McVries had repented of it. That made Garraty's stomach quiver emptily. It was all hopeless and stupid and pointless, most of all that, so goddam pointless it was really pitiful. He opened his mouth to tell McVries that, but before he could, McVries spoke.

"Everything's all right." Barkovitch jumped at the sound of his voice and McVries added, "Not you, killer. Nothing's ever going to be all right for you. Just keep striding."

"Eat my meat," Barkovitch snarled.

"I guess I caused you some trouble," Garraty said in a low voice.

"I told you, fair is fair, square is square, and quits are quits," McVries said evenly. "I won't do it again. I want you to know that."

"I understand that," Garraty said. "I just—"

"Don't hurt me!" someone screamed. "Please don't hurt me!"

It was a redhead with a plaid shirt tied around his waist. He had stopped in the middle of the road and he was weeping. He was given first warning. And then he raced toward the halftrack, his tears cutting runnels through the sweaty dirt on his face, red hair glinting like a fire in the sun. "Don't ... I can't ... please ... my mother ... I can't ... don't ... no more ... my feet ..." He was trying to scale the side, and one of the soldiers brought the butt of his carbine down on his hands. The boy cried out and fell in a heap.

He screamed again, a high, incredibly thin note that seemed sharp enough to shatter glass and what he was screaming was:

"*My feeeeeeeeeeeeeeeeeeeeeeeeeeeeeeeeee—*"

"Jesus," Garraty muttered. "Why doesn't he stop that?" The screams went on and on.

"I doubt if he can," McVries said clinically. "The back treads of the halftrack ran over his legs."

Garraty looked and felt his stomach lurch into his throat. It was true. No wonder the redheaded kid was screaming about his feet. They had been obliterated.

"Warning! Warning 38!"

"—eeeeeeeeeeeeeeeeeeeeeeeeeee—"

"I want to go home," someone behind Garraty said very quietly. "Oh Christ, do I ever want to go home."

A moment later the redheaded boy's face was blown away.

"I'm gonna see my girl in Freeport," Garraty said rapidly. "And I'm not gonna have any warnings and I'm gonna kiss her, God I miss her, God, *Jesus*, did you see his *legs*? They were still warning him, Pete, like they thought he was gonna get up and *walk*—"

"Another boy has gone ober to dat Silver City, lawd, lawd," Barkovitch intoned.

"Shut up, killer," McVries said absently. "She pretty, Ray? Your girl?"

"She's beautiful. I love her."

McVries smiled. "Gonna marry her?"

"Yeah," Garraty babbled. "We're gonna be Mr. and Mrs. Norman Normal, four kids and a collie dog, his *legs*, he didn't have any *legs*, they ran over him, they can't run *over* a guy, that isn't in the rules, somebody ought to report that, somebody—"

"Two boys and two girls, that what you're gonna have?"

"Yeah, yeah, she's beautiful, I just wish I hadn't—"

"And the first kid will be Ray Junior and the dog'll have a dish with its name on it, right?"

Garraty raised his head slowly, like a punch-drunk fighter. "Are you making fun of me? Or what?"

"No!" Barkovitch exclaimed. "He's *shitting* on you, boy! And don't you forget it. But I'll dance on his grave for you, don't worry." He cackled briefly.

"Shut up, killer," McVries said. "I'm not dumping on you, Ray. Come on, let's get away from the killer, here."

"Shove it up your ass!" Barkovitch screamed after them.

"She love you? Your girl? Jan?"

"Yeah, I think so," Garraty said.

McVries shook his head slowly. "All of that romantic horseshit . . . you know, it's true. At least, for some people for some short time, it is. It was for me. I felt like you." He looked at Garraty. "You still want to hear about the scar?"

They rounded a bend and a camperload of children squealed and waved.

"Yes," Garraty said.

"Why?" He looked at Garraty, but his suddenly naked eyes might have been searching himself.

"I want to help you," Garraty said.

McVries looked down at his left foot. "Hurts. I can't wiggle the toes very much anymore. My neck is stiff and my kidneys ache. My girl turned out to be a bitch, Garraty. I got into this Long Walk shit the same way that guys used to get into the Foreign Legion. In the words of the great rock and roll poet, I gave her my heart, she tore it apart, and who gives a fart."

Garraty said nothing. It was 10:30. Freeport was still far.

"Her name was Priscilla," McVries said. "You

think you got a case? I was the original Korny Kid, Moon-June was my middle name. I used to kiss her fingers. I even took to reading Keats to her out in back of the house, when the wind was right. Her old man kept cows, and the smell of cowshit goes, to put it in the most delicate way, in a peculiar fashion with the works of John Keats. Maybe I should have read her Swinburne when the wind was wrong." McVries laughed.

"You're cheating what you felt," Garraty said.

"Ah, you're the one faking it, Ray, not that it matters. All you remember is the Great Romance, not all the times you went home and jerked your meat after whispering words of love in her shell-pink ear."

"You fake your way, I'll fake mine."

McVries seemed not to have heard. "These things, they don't even bear the weight of conversation," he said. "J. D. Salinger . . . John Knowles . . . even James Kirkwood and that guy Don Bredes . . . they've destroyed being an adolescent, Garraty. If you're a sixteen-year-old boy, you can't discuss the pains of adolescent love with any decency anymore. You just come off sounding like fucking Ron Howard with a hardon."

McVries laughed a little hysterically. Garraty had no idea what McVries was talking about. He was secure in his love for Jan, he didn't feel in the least self-conscious about it. Their feet scuffed on the road. Garraty could feel his right heel wobbling. Pretty soon the nails would let go, and he would shed the shoeheel like dead skin. Behind them, Scramm had a coughing fit. It was the Walk that bothered Garraty, not all this weird shit about romantic love.

"But that doesn't have anything to do with the story," McVries said, as if reading his mind. "About the scar. It was last summer. We both wanted to get away from home, away from our parents, and away from the smell of all that cowshit so the Great Romance could bloom in earnest. So we got jobs working for a pajama factory in New Jersey. How does that grab you, Garraty? A pj factory in New Jersey.

"We got separate apartments in Newark. Great town, Newark, on a given day you can smell all the cowshit in New Jersey in Newark. Our parents kicked a little, but with separate apartments and good summer jobs, they didn't kick too much. My place was with two other guys, and there were three girls in with Pris. We left on June the third in my car, and we stopped once around three in the afternoon at a motel and got rid of the virginity problem. I felt like a real crook. She didn't really want to screw, but she wanted to please me. That was the Shady Nook motel. When we were done I flushed that Trojan down the Shady Nook john and washed out my mouth with a Shady Nook paper cup. It was all very romantic, very ethereal.

"Then it was on to Newark, smelling the cowshit and being so sure it was *different* cowshit. I dropped her at her apartment and then went on to my own. The next Monday we started in at the Plymouth Sleepwear factory. It wasn't much like the movies, Garraty. It stank of raw cloth and my foreman was a bastard and during lunch break we used to throw baling hooks at the rats under the fabric bags. But I didn't mind because it was love. See? It was love."

He spat dryly into the dust, swallowed from his canteen, then yelled for another one. They were climbing a long, curve-banked hill now, and his words came in out-of-breath bursts.

"Pris was on the first floor, the showcase for all the idiot tourists who didn't have anything better to do than go on a guided tour of the place that made their jam-jams. It was nice down where Pris was. Pretty pastel walls, nice modern machinery, air conditioning. Pris sewed on buttons from seven till three. Just think, there are men all over the country wearing pj's held up by Priscilla's buttons. There is a thought to warm the coldest heart.

"I was on the fifth floor. I was a bagger. See, down in the basement they dyed the raw cloth and sent it up to the fifth floor in these warm-air tubes. They'd ring a bell when the whole lot was done, and I'd open my bin and there'd be a whole shitload of loose fiber, all the colors of the rainbow. I'd pitchfork it out, put it in two-hundred-pound sacks, and chain-hoist the sacks onto a big pile of other sacks for the picker machine. They'd separate it, the weaving machines wove it, some other guys cut it and sewed it into pajamas, and down there on that pretty pastel first floor Pris put on the buttons while the dumbass tourists watched her and the other girls through this glass wall . . . just like the people are watching us today. Am I getting through to you at all, Garraty?"

"The scar," Garraty reminded.

"I keep wandering away from that, don't I?" McVries wiped his forehead and unbuttoned his shirt as they breasted the hill. Waves of woods stretched away before them to a horizon poked with mountains. They met the sky like interlocking jigsaw pieces. Perhaps ten miles away, almost lost in the heat-haze, a fire tower jutted up through the green. The road cut through it all like a sliding gray serpent.

"At first, the joy and bliss was Keatsville all the way. I screwed her three more times, all at the drive-in with the smell of cowshit coming in through the car window from the next pasture. And I could never get all of the loose fabric out of my hair no matter how many times I shampooed it, and the worst thing was she was getting away from me, going beyond me; I loved her, I really did, I knew it and there was no way I could tell her anymore so she'd understand. I couldn't even screw it into her. There was always that smell of cowshit.

"The thing of it was, Garraty, the factory was on piecework. That means we got lousy wages, but a percentage for all we did over a certain minimum. I wasn't a very good bagger. I did about twenty-three bags a day, but the norm was usually right around thirty. And this did not endear me to the rest of the boys, because I was fucking them up. Harlan down in the dyehouse couldn't make piecework because I was tying up his blower with full

bins. Ralph on the picker couldn't make piecework because I wasn't shifting enough bags over
to him. It wasn't pleasant. They saw to it that it
wasn't pleasant. You understand?"

"Yeah," Garraty said. He wiped the back of his
hand across his neck and then wiped his hand on
his pants. It made a dark stain.

"Meanwhile, down in buttoning, Pris was keeping herself busy. Some nights she'd talk for hours
about her girlfriends, and it was usually the same
tune. How much this one was making. How
much that one was making. And most of all, how
much she was making. And she was making plenty.
So I got to find out how much fun it is to be in competition with the girl you want to marry. At the
end of the week I'd go home with a check for $64.40
and put some Cornhusker's Lotion on my blisters.
She was making something like ninety a week,
and socking it away as fast as she could run to
the bank. And when I suggested we go someplace
dutch, you would have thought I'd suggested ritual
murder.

"After a while I stopped screwing her. I'd like to
say I stopped going to bed with her, it's more pleasant, but we never had a bed to go to. I couldn't
take her to my apartment, there were usually about
sixteen guys there drinking beer, and there were
always people at her place—that's what she said,
anyway—and I couldn't afford another motel room
and I certainly wasn't going to suggest we go dutch
on *that*, so it was just screwing in the back seat at
the drive-in. And I could tell she was getting dis-

gusted. And since I knew it and since I had started to hate her even though I still loved her, I asked her to marry me. Right then. She started wriggling around, trying to put me off, but I made her come out with it, yes or no."

"And it was no."

"Sure it was no. 'Pete, we can't afford it. What would my mom say. Pete, we have to wait.' Pete this and Pete that and all the time the real reason was her money, the money she was making sewing on buttons."

"Well, you were damned unfair to ask her."

"Sure I was unfair!" McVries said savagely. "I knew that. I wanted to make her feel like a greedy, self-centered little bitch because she was making me feel like a failure."

His hand crept up to the scar.

"Only she didn't have to make me *feel* like a failure, because I *was* a failure. I didn't have anything in particular going for me except a cock to stick in her and she wouldn't even make me feel like a man by refusing that."

The guns roared behind them.

"Olson?" McVries asked.

"No. He's still back there."

"Oh . . ."

"The scar," Garraty reminded.

"Oh, why don't you let it alone?"

"You saved my life."

"Shit on you."

"The scar."

"I got into a fight," McVries said finally, after a

long pause. "With Ralph, the guy on the picker. He blacked both my eyes and told me I better take off or he'd break my arms as well. I turned in my time and told Pris that night that I'd quit. She could see what I looked like for herself. She understood. She said that was probably best. I told her I was going home and I asked her to come. She said she couldn't. I said she was nothing but a slave to her fucking buttons and that I wished I'd never seen her. There was just so much poison inside me, Garraty. I told her she was a fool and an unfeeling bitch that couldn't see any further than the goddam bank book she carried around in her purse. Nothing I said was fair, but . . . there was some truth in all of it, I guess. Enough. We were at her apartment. That was the first time I'd ever been there when all her roommates were out. They were at the movies. I tried to take her to bed and she cut my face open with a letter-opener. It was a gag letter-opener, some friend of hers sent it to her from England. It had Paddington Bear on it. She cut me like I was trying to rape her. Like I was germs and I'd infect her. Am I giving you the drift, Ray?"

"Yes, I'm getting it," Garraty said. Up ahead a white station wagon with the words WHGH NEWSMOBILE lettered on the side was pulled off the road. As they drew near, a balding man in a shiny suit began shooting them with a big newsreel ciné camera. Pearson, Abraham, and Jensen all clutched their crotches with their left hand and thumbed their noses with their right. There was a

Rockettelike precision about this little act of defiance that bemused Garraty.

"I cried," McVries said. "I cried like a baby. I got down on my knees and held her skirt and begged her to forgive me, and all the blood was getting on the floor, it was a basically disgusting scene, Garraty. She gagged and ran off into the bathroom. She threw up. I could hear her throwing up. When she came out, she had a towel for my face. She said she never wanted to see me again. She was crying. She asked me why I'd done that to her, hurt her like that. She said I had no right. There I was, Ray, with my face cut wide open and she's asking *me* why I hurt *her*."

"Yeah."

"I left with the towel still on my face. I had twelve stitches and that's the story of the fabulous scar and aren't you happy?"

"Have you ever seen her since?"

"No," McVries said. "And I have no real urge to. She seems very small to me now, very far away. Pris at this point in my life is no more than a speck on the horizon. She really was mental, Ray. Something . . . her mother, maybe, her mother was a lush . . . something had fixed her on the subject of money. She was a real miser. Distance lends perspective, they say. Yesterday morning Pris was still very important to me. Now she's nothing. That story I just told you, I thought that would hurt. It didn't hurt. Besides, I doubt if all that shit really has anything to do with why I'm here. It just made a handy excuse at the time."

"What do you mean?"

"Why are you here, Garraty?"

"I don't know." His voice was mechanical, doll-like. Freaky D'Allessio hadn't been able to see the ball coming—his eyes weren't right, his depth perception was screwed—it had hit him in the forehead, and branded him with stitches. And later (or earlier . . . all of his past was mixed up and fluid now) he had hit his best friend in the mouth with the barrel of an air rifle. Maybe he had a scar like McVries. Jimmy. He and Jimmy had been playing doctor.

"You don't know," McVries said. "You're dying and you don't know why."

"It's not important after you're dead."

"Yeah, maybe," McVries said, "but there's one thing you ought to know, Ray, so it won't be all so pointless."

"What's that?"

"Why, that you've been had. You mean you really didn't know that, Ray? You really didn't?"

Chapter 9

"Very good, Northwestern, now here is
your ten-point tossup question."
                                —Allen Ludden
                                College Bowl

At one o'clock, Garraty took inventory again.

One hundred and fifteen miles traveled. They were forty-five miles north of Oldtown, a hundred and twenty-five miles north of Augusta, the state capital, one hundred and fifty to Freeport (or more . . . he was terribly afraid there were more than twenty-five miles between Augusta and Freeport), probably two-thirty to the New Hampshire border. And the word was that this Walk was sure to go that far.

For a long while—ninety minutes or so—no one at all had been given a ticket. They walked, they half-listened to the cheers from the sidelines, and they stared at mile after monotonous mile of piney woods. Garraty discovered fresh twinges of pain in his left calf to go with the steady, wooden throbbing that lived in both of his legs, and the low-key agony that was his feet.

Then, around noon, as the day's heat mounted

toward its zenith, the guns began to make themselves heard again. A boy named Tressler, 92, had a sunstroke and was shot as he lay unconscious. Another boy suffered a convulsion and got a ticket as he crawdaddied on the road, making ugly noises around his swallowed tongue. Aaronson, I, cramped up in both feet and was shot on the white line, standing like a statue, his face turned up to the sun in neck-straining concentration. And at five minutes to one, another boy Garraty did not know had a sunstroke.

This is where I came in, Garraty thought, walking around the twitching, mumbling form on the road where the rifles sight in, seeing the jewels of sweat in the exhausted and soon-to-be-dead boy's hair. This is where I came in, can't I leave now?

The guns roared, and a covey of high school boys sitting in the scant shade of a Scout camper applauded briefly.

"I wish the Major would come through," Baker said pettishly. "I want to see the Major."

"What?" Abraham asked mechanically. He had grown gaunter in the last few hours. His eyes were sunk deeper in their sockets. The blue suggestion of a beard patched his face.

"So I can piss on him," Baker said.

"Relax," Garraty said. "Just relax." All three of his warnings were gone now.

"*You* relax," Baker said. "See what it gets you."

"You've got no right to hate the Major. He didn't *force* you."

"Force me? FORCE me? He's *KILLING* me, that's all!"

"It's still not—"

"Shut up," Baker said curtly, and Garraty shut. He rubbed the back of his neck briefly and stared up into the whitish-blue sky. His shadow was a deformed huddle almost beneath his feet. He turned up his third canteen of the day and drained it.

Baker said: "I'm sorry. I surely didn't mean to shout. My feet—"

"Sure," Garraty said.

"We're all getting this way," Baker said. "I sometimes think that's the worst part."

Garraty closed his eyes. He was very sleepy.

"You know what I'd like to do?" Pearson said. He was walking between Garraty and Baker.

"Piss on the Major," Garraty said. "Everybody wants to piss on the Major. When he comes through again we'll gang up on him and drag him down and all unzip and drown him in—"

"That isn't what I want to do." Pearson was walking like a man in the last stages of conscious drunkenness. His head made half-rolls on his neck. His eyelids snapped up and down like spastic windowblinds. "It's got nothin' to do with the Major. I just want to go into the next field and lay down and close my eyes. Just lay there on my back in the wheat—"

"They don't grow wheat in Maine," Garraty said. "It's hay."

"—in the hay, then. And compose myself a poem. While I go to sleep."

Garraty fumbled in his new foodbelt and found nothing in most of the pouches. Finally he happened on a waxpack of Saltines and began washing them down with water. "I feel like a sieve," he said. "I drink it and it pops out on my skin two minutes later."

The guns roared again and another figure collapsed gracelessly, like a tired jack-in-the-box.

"Fordy fibe," Scramm said, joining them. "I don't thing we'll even get to Pordland ad this rade."

"You don't sound so good," Pearson said, and there might have been careful optimism in his voice.

"Luggy for me I god a good codstitution," Scramm said cheerfully. "I thing I'be rudding a fever now."

"Jesus, how do you keep going?" Abraham asked, and there was a kind of religious fear in his voice.

"Me? Talk about *me*?" Scramm said. "Look at *hib*! How does he keep going? Thad's what I'd like to know!" And he cocked his thumb at Olson.

Olson had not spoken for two hours. He had not touched his newest canteen. Greedy glances were shot at his foodbelt, which was also almost untouched. His eyes, darkly obsidian, were fixed straight ahead. His face was speckled by two days of beard and it looked sickly vulpine. Even his hair, frizzed up in back and hanging across his forehead in front, added to the overall impression of ghoulishness. His lips were parched dry and blistering. His tongue hung over his bottom lip like a dead serpent on the lip of a cave. Its healthy pinkness had disappeared. It was dirty-gray now. Road-dust clung to it.

He's there, Garraty thought, sure he is. Where Stebbins said we'd all go if we stuck with it long enough. How deep inside himself is he? Fathoms? Miles? Light-years? How deep and how dark? And the answer came back to him: too deep to see out. He's hiding down there in the darkness and it's too deep to see out.

"Olson?" he said softly. "Olson?"

Olson didn't answer. Nothing moved but his feet.

"I wish he'd put his tongue in at least," Pearson whispered nervously.

The Walk went on.

The woods melted back and they were passing through another wide place in the road. The sidewalks were lined with cheering spectators. Garraty signs again predominated. Then the woods closed in again. But not even the woods could hold the spectators back now. They were beginning to line the soft shoulders. Pretty girls in shorts and halters. Boys in basketball shorts and muscle shirts.

Gay holiday, Garraty thought.

He could no longer wish he wasn't here; he was too tired and numb for retrospect. What was done was done. Nothing in the world would change it. Soon enough, he supposed, it would even become too much of an effort to talk to the others. He wished he could hide inside himself like a little boy rolled up inside a rug, with no more worries. Then everything would be much simpler.

He had wondered a great deal about what McVries had said. That they had all been swindled, rooked. But that couldn't be right, he insisted stubbornly to himself. One of them had not been swindled. One of them was going to swindle everyone else . . . wasn't that right?

He licked his lips and drank some water.

They passed a small green sign that informed them the Maine turnpike was forty-four miles hence.

"That's it," he said to no one in particular. "Forty-four miles to Oldtown."

No one replied and Garraty was just considering taking a walk back up to McVries when they came to another intersection and a woman began to scream. The traffic had been roped off, and the crowd pressed eagerly against the barriers and the cops manning them. They waved their hands, their signs, their bottles of suntan lotion.

The screaming woman was large and red-faced. She threw herself against one of the waist-high sawhorse barriers, toppling it and yanking a lot of the bright yellow guard-rope after it. Then she was fighting and clawing and screaming at the policemen who held her. The cops were grunting with effort.

I know her, Garraty thought. Don't I know her?

The blue kerchief. The belligerent, gleaming eyes. Even the navy dress with the crooked hem. They were all familiar. The woman's screams had become incoherent. One pinwheeling hand ripped stripes of blood across the face of one of the cops holding her—*trying* to hold her.

Garraty passed within ten feet of her. As he walked past, he knew where he had seen her before—she was Percy's mom, of course. Percy who had tried to sneak into the woods and had snuck right into the next world instead.

"I want m'boy!" she hollered. "I want m'boy!"

The crowd cheered her enthusiastically and impartially. A small boy behind her spat on her leg and then darted away.

Jan, Garraty thought. I'm walking to you, Jan, fuck this other shit, I swear to God I'm coming. But McVries had been right. Jan hadn't wanted him to come. She had cried. She had begged him to change his mind. They could wait, she didn't want to lose him, please Ray, don't be dumb, the Long Walk is nothing but murder—

They had been sitting on a bench beside the bandstand. It had been a month ago, April, and he had his arm around her. She had been wearing the perfume he had gotten her for her birthday. It seemed to bring out the secret girl-smell of her, a dark smell, fleshy and heady. I have to go, he had told her. I have to, don't you understand, I have to.

Ray, you don't understand what you're doing. Ray, please don't. I love you.

Well, he thought now, as he walked on down the road, she was right about that. I sure didn't understand what I was doing.

But I don't understand it even now. That's the hell of it. The pure and simple hell of it.

"Garraty?"

He jerked his head up, startled. He had been half-asleep again. It was McVries, walking beside him.

"How you feeling?"

"Feeling?" Garraty said cautiously. "All right, I guess. I guess I'm all right."

"Barkovitch is cracking," McVries said with quiet joy. "I'm sure of it. He's talking to himself. And he's limping."

"You're limping, too," Garraty said. "So's Pearson. So am I."

"My foot hurts, that's all. But Barkovitch . . . he keeps rubbing his leg. I think he's got a pulled muscle."

"Why do you hate him so much? Why not Collie Parker? Or Olson? Or all of us?"

"Because Barkovitch knows what he's doing."

"He plays to win, do you mean?"

"You don't know what I mean, Ray."

"I wonder if you do yourself," Garraty said. "Sure he's a bastard. Maybe it takes a bastard to win."

"Good guys finish last?"

"How the hell should I know?"

They passed a clapboard one-room schoolhouse. The children stood out in the play yard and waved. Several boys stood atop the jungle gym like sentries, and Garraty was reminded of the men in the lumberyard a ways back.

"Garraty!" One of them yelled. "Ray Garraty!

Gar-ra-*tee!*" A small boy with a tousled head of hair jumped up and down on the top level of the jungle gym, waving with both arms. Garraty waved back halfheartedly. The boy flipped over, hung upside down by the backs of his legs, and continued to wave. Garraty was a little relieved when he and the schoolyard were out of sight. That last had been a little too strenuous to bear thinking about for long.

Pearson joined them. "I've been thinking."

"Save your strength," McVries said.

"Feeble, man. That is feeble."

"What have you been thinking about?" Garraty asked.

"How tough it's going to be for the second-to-last guy."

"Why so tough?" McVries asked.

"Well . . ." Pearson rubbed his eyes, then squinted at a pine tree that had been struck by lightning some time in the past. "You know, to walk down everybody, absolutely *everybody* but that last guy. There ought to be a runner-up Prize, that's what I think."

"What?" McVries asked flatly.

"I dunno."

"How about his life?" Garraty asked.

"Who'd walk for that?"

"Nobody, before the Walk started, maybe. But right now I'd be happy enough with just that, the hell with the Prize, the hell with having my every heart's desire. How about you?"

Pearson thought about it for a long time. "I

just don't see the sense of it," he said at last, apologetically.

"You tell him, Pete," Garraty said.

"Tell him what? He's right. The whole banana or no banana at all."

"You're crazy," Garraty said, but without much conviction. He was very hot and very tired, and there were the remotest beginnings of a headache in back of his eyes. Maybe this is how sunstroke starts, he thought. Maybe that would be the best way, too. Just go down in a dreamy, slow-motion half-knowingness, and wake up dead.

"Sure," McVries said amiably. "We're all crazy or we wouldn't be here. I thought we'd thrashed that out a long time ago. We want to die, Ray. Haven't you got that through your sick, thick head yet? Look at Olson. A skull on top of a stick. Tell me he doesn't want to die. You can't. Second place? It's bad enough that even one of us has got to get gypped out of what he really wants."

"I don't know about all that fucking psycho-history," Pearson said finally. "I just don't think anyone should get to cop out second."

Garraty burst out laughing. "You're nuts," he said.

McVries also laughed. "Now you're starting to see it my way. Get a little more sun, stew your brain a little more, and we'll make a real believer out of you."

The Walk went on.

The sun seemed neatly poised on the roof of the world. The mercury reached seventy-nine degrees (one of the boys had a pocket thermometer) and eighty trembled in its grasp for a few broiling minutes. Eighty, Garraty thought. Eighty. Not that hot. In July the mercury would go ten degrees higher. Eighty. Just the right temperature to sit in the backyard under an elm tree eating a chicken salad on lettuce. Mighty. Just the ticket for belly-flopping into the nearest piece of the Royal River, oh Jesus, wouldn't that feel good. The water was warm on the top, but down by your feet it was cold and you could feel the current pull at you just a little and there were suckers by the rocks, but you could pick 'em off if you weren't a pussy. All that water, bathing your skin, your hair, your crotch. His hot flesh trembled as he thought about it. Eighty. Just right for shucking down to your swim trunks and laying up in the canvas hammock in the backyard with a good book. And maybe drowse off. Once he had pulled Jan into the hammock with him and they had lain there together, swinging and necking until his cock felt like a long hot stone against his lower belly. She hadn't seemed to mind. Eighty. Christ in a Chevrolet, eighty degrees.

Eighty. Eightyeightyeighty. Make it nonsense, make it gone.

"I'd never been so hod id by whole life," Scramm said through his plugged nose. His broad face was red and dripping sweat. He had stripped off his shirt and bared his shaggy torso. Sweat was running all over him like small creeks in spring flow.

"You better put your shirt back on," Baker said.

"You'll catch a chill when the sun starts to go down. Then you'll really be in trouble."

"This goddab code," Scramm said. "I'be burding ub."

"It'll rain," Baker said. His eyes searched the empty sky. "It has to rain."

"It doesn't have to do a goddam thing," Collie Parker said. "I never seen such a fucked-up state."

"If you don't like it, why don't you go on home?" Garraty asked, and giggled foolishly.

"Stuff it up your ass."

Garraty forced himself to drink just a little from his canteen. He didn't want water cramps. That would be a hell of a way to buy out. He'd had them once, and once had been enough. He had been helping their next-door neighbors, the Elwells, get in their hay. It was explosively hot in the loft of the Elwells' barn, and they had been throwing up the big seventy-pound bales in a fireman's relay. Garraty had made the tactical mistake of drinking three dipperfuls of the ice-cold water Mrs. Elwell had brought out. There had been sudden blinding pain in this chest and belly and head, he had slipped on some loose hay and had fallen bonelessly out of the loft and into the truck. Mr. Elwell held him around the middle with his work-callused hands while he threw up over the side, weak with pain and shame. They had sent him home, a boy who had flunked one of his first manhood tests, hay-rash on his arms and chaff in his hair. He had walked home, and the sun had beaten down on the back of his sunburned neck like a ten-pound hammer.

He shivered convulsively, and his body broke out momentarily in heat-bumps. The headache thumped sickishly behind his eyes . . . how easy it would be to let go of the rope.

He looked over at Olson. Olson was there. His tongue was turning blackish. His face was dirty. His eyes stared blindly. I'm not like him. Dear God, not like him. Please, I don't want to go out like Olson.

"This'll take the starch out," Baker said gloomily. "We won't make it into New Hampshire. I'd bet money on it."

"Two years ago they had sleet," Abraham said. "*They* made it over the border. Four of 'em did, anyway."

"Yeah, but the heat's different," Jensen said. "When you're cold you can walk faster and get warmed up. When you're hot you can walk slower . . . and get iced. What can you do?"

"No justice," Collie Parker said angrily. "Why couldn't they have the goddam Walk in Illinois, where the ground's flat?"

"I like Baine," Scramm said. "Why do you swear so buch, Parger?"

"Why do you have to wipe so much snot out of your nose?" Parker asked. "Because that's the way I am, that's why. Any objections?"

Garraty looked at his watch, but it was stopped at 10:16. He had forgotten to wind it. "Anybody got the time?" he asked.

"Lemme see." Pearson squinted at his watch. "Just happast an asshole, Garraty."

Everyone laughed. "Come on," he said. "My watch stopped."

Pearson looked again. "It's two after two." He looked up at the sky. "That sun isn't going to set for a long time."

The sun was poised malevolently over the fringe of woods. There was not enough angle on it yet to throw the road into the shade, and wouldn't be for another hour or two. Far off to the south, Garraty thought he could see purple smudges that might be thunderheads or only wishful thinking.

Abraham and Collie Parker were lackadaisically discussing the merits of four-barrel carbs. No one else seemed much disposed to talk, so Garraty wandered off by himself to the far side of the road, waving now and then to someone, but not bothering as a rule.

The Walkers were not spread out as much as they had been. The vanguard was in plain sight: two tall, tanned boys with black leather jackets tied around their waists. The word was that they were queer for each other, but Garraty believed that like he believed the moon was green cheese. They didn't look effeminate, and they seemed like nice enough guys . . . not that either one of those things had much to do with whether or not they were queer, he supposed. And not that it was any of his business if they were. But . . .

Barkovitch was behind the leather boys and McVries was behind him, staring intently at Barkovitch's back. The yellow rainhat still dangled out of Barkovitch's back pocket, and he didn't look like he was cracking to Garraty. In fact, he thought with a painful twinge, McVries was the one who looked bushed.

Behind McVries and Barkovitch was a loose knot of seven or eight boys, the kind of carelessly knit confederation that seemed to form and re-form during the course of the Walk, new and old members constantly coming and going. Behind them was a smaller group, and behind that group was Scramm, Pearson, Baker, Abraham, Parker, and Jensen. His group. There had been others with it near the start, and now he could barely remember their names.

There were two groups behind his, and scattered through the whole raggle-taggle column like pepper through salt were the loners. A few of them, like Olson, were withdrawn and catatonic. Others, like Stebbins, seemed to genuinely prefer their own company. And almost all of them had that intent, frightened look stamped on their faces. Garraty had come to know that look so well.

The guns came down and bore on one of the loners he had been looking at, a short, stoutish boy who was wearing a battered green silk vest. It seemed to Garraty that he had collected his final warning about half an hour ago. He threw a short, terrified glance at the guns and stepped up his pace. The guns lost their dreadful interest in him, at least for the time being.

Garraty felt a sudden incomprehensible rise in

spirits. They couldn't be much more than forty miles from Oldtown and civilization now—if you wanted to call a mill, shoe, and canoe town civilization. They'd pull in there sometime late tonight, and get on the turnpike. The turnpike would be smooth sailing, compared to this. On the turnpike you could walk on the grassy median strip with your shoes off if you wanted. Feel the cold dew. Good Christ, that would be great. He mopped his brow with his forearm. Maybe things were going to turn out okay after all. The purple smudges were a little closer, and they were definitely thunderheads.

The guns went off and he didn't even jump. The boy in the green silk vest had bought a ticket, and he was staring up at the sun. Not even death was that bad, maybe. Everybody, even the Major himself, had to face it sooner or later. So who was swindling who, when you came right down to it? He made a mental note to mention that to McVries the next time they spoke.

He picked up his heels a little and made up his mind to wave to the next pretty girl he saw. But before there was a pretty girl, there was the little Italian man.

He was a caricature Italian man, a small guy with a battered felt hat and a black mustache that curled up at the ends. He was beside an old station wagon with the back hatch standing open. He was waving and grinning with incredibly white, incredibly square teeth.

An insulating mat had been laid on the bottom

of the station wagon's cargo compartment. The mat had been piled high with crushed ice, and peeking through the ice in dozens of places, like wide pink peppermint grins, were wedges of watermelon.

Garraty felt his stomach flop over twice, exactly like a flip-rolling high diver. A sign on top of the station wagon read: DOM L'ANTIO LOVES ALL LONG WALKERS—FREE WATERMELON!!!

Several of the Walkers, Abraham and Collie Parker among them, broke for the shoulder at a dogtrot. All were warned. They were doing better than four an hour, but they were doing it in the wrong direction. Dom L'Antio saw them coming and laughed—a crystal, joyous, uncomplicated sound. He clapped his hands, dug into the ice, and came out with double handfuls of pink grinning watermelons. Garraty felt his mouth shrivel with want. But they won't let him, he thought. Just like they wouldn't let the storekeeper give the sodas. And then: But oh God, it'd taste good. Would it be too much, God, for them to be a little slow with the hook this time? Where did he get watermelon this time of year, anyway?

The Long Walkers milled outside the restraining ropes, the small crowd around Dom went mad with happiness, second warnings were parceled out, and three State Troopers appeared miraculously to restrain Dom, whose voice came loud and clear:

"Whatcha mean? Whatcha mean I can't? These my wat'amelon, you dumb cop! I wanna give, I gonna give, hey! what you t'ink? Get offa my case, you hardass!"

One of the Troopers made a grab for the watermelons Dom held in his hands. Another buttonhooked around him and slammed the cargo door of the wagon shut.

"You bastards!" Garraty screamed with all his force. His shriek sped through the bright day like a glass spear, and one of the Troopers looked around, startled and . . . well, almost hangdog.

"Stinking sonsofbitches!" Garraty shrieked at them. "I wish your mothers had miscarried you stinking *whoresons*!"

"You tell 'em Garraty!" someone else yelled, and it was Barkovitch, grinning like a mouthful of tenpenny nails and shaking both of his fists at the State Troopers. "You tell—"

But they were all screaming now, and the Troopers were not handpicked Long Walk soldiers fresh off the National Squads. Their faces were red and embarrassed, but all the same they were hustling Dom and his double handfuls of cool pink grins away from the sidelines at double time.

Dom either lost his English or gave it up. He began to yell fruity Italian curses. The crowd booed the State Troopers. A woman in a floppy straw sunhat threw a transistor radio at one of them. It hit him in the head and knocked off his cap. Garraty felt sorry for the Trooper but continued to scream curses. He couldn't seem to help it. That word "whoresons," he hadn't thought anybody ever used a word like that outside of books.

Just as it seemed that Dom L'Antio would be removed from their view for good, the little Italian slipped free and dashed back toward them, the crowd parting magically for him and closing—or trying to—against the police. One of the Troopers threw a flying tackle at him, caught him around the knees, and spilled him forward. At the last instant of balance Dom let his beautiful pink grins fly in a wide-swinging throw.

"DOM L'ANTIO LOVES YOU ALL!" he cried.

The crowd cheered hysterically. Dom landed headfirst in the dirt, and his hands were cuffed behind him in a trice. The watermelon slices arced and pinwheeled through the bright air, and Garraty laughed aloud and raised both hands to the sky and shook his fists triumphantly as he saw Abraham catch one with nonchalant deftness.

Others were third-warned for stopping to pick up chunks of watermelon, but amazingly, no one was shot and five—no, six, Garraty saw—of the boys had ended up with watermelon. The rest of them alternately cheered those who had managed to get some of it, or cursed the wooden-faced soldiers, whose expressions were now satisfyingly interpreted to hold subtle chagrin.

"I love everybody!" Abraham bellowed. His grinning face was streaked with pink watermelon juice. He spat three brown seeds into the air.

"Goddam," Collie Parker said happily. "I'm goddamned, goddam if I ain't." He drove his face into the watermelon, gobbled hungrily, then busted his piece in two. He threw half of it over to Garraty, who almost fumbled it in his surprise. "There ya go, hicksville!" Collie shouted. "Don't say I never gave ya nothin', ya goddam rube!"

Garraty laughed. "Go fuck yourself," he said. The watermelon was cold, cold. Some of the juice got up his nose, some more ran down his chin, and oh sweet heaven in his throat, running down his throat.

He only let himself eat half. "Pete!" he shouted, and tossed the remaining chunk to him.

McVries caught it with a flashy backhand, showing the sort of stuff that makes college shortstops and, maybe, major league ballplayers. He grinned at Garraty and ate the melon.

Garraty looked around and felt a crazy joy breaking through him, pumping at his heart, making him want to run around in circles on his hands. Almost everyone had gotten a scrap of the melon, even if it was no more than a scrap of the pink meat clinging to a seed.

Stebbins, as usual, was the exception. He was looking at the road. There was nothing in his hands, no smile on his face.

Screw him, Garraty thought. But a little of the joy went out of him nevertheless. His feet felt heavy again. He knew that it wasn't that Stebbins hadn't gotten any. Or that Stebbins didn't want any. Stebbins didn't need any.

2:30 PM. They had walked a hundred and twenty-one miles. The thunderheads drifted closer. A cool breeze sprang up, chill against Garraty's hot skin. It's going to rain again, he thought. Good.

The people at the sides of the road were rolling up blankets, catching flying bits of paper, reloading their picnic baskets. The storm came flying lazily at them, and all at once the temperature plummeted and it felt like autumn. Garraty buttoned his shirt quickly.

"Here it comes again," he told Scramm. "Better get your shirt on."

"Are you kidding?" Scramm grinned. "This is the besd I've feld all day!"

"It's gonna be a boomer!" Parker yelled gleefully.

They were on top of a gradually slanting plateau, and they could see the curtain of rain beating across the woods toward them below the purple thunderheads. Directly above them the sky had gone a sick yellow. A tornado sky, Garraty thought. Wouldn't that be the living end. What would they do if a tornado just came tearing ass down the road and carried them all off to Oz in a whirling cloud of dirt, flapping shoeleather, and whirling watermelon seeds?

He laughed. The wind ripped the laugh out of his mouth.

"McVries!"

McVries angled to meet him. He was bent into the wind, his clothes plastered against his body and streaming out behind him. The black hair and the white scar etched against his tanned face made him look like a weathered, slightly mad sea captain astride the bridge of his ship.

"What?" he bellowed.

"Is there a provision in the rules for an act of God?"

McVries considered. "No, I don't think so." He began buttoning his jacket.

"What happens if we get struck by lightning?"

McVries threw back his head and cackled. "We'll be dead!"

Garraty snorted and walked away. Some of the others were looking up into the sky anxiously. This was going to be no little shower, the kind that had cooled them off after yesterday's heat. What had Parker said? A boomer. Yes, it certainly was going to be a boomer.

A baseball cap went cartwheeling between his legs, and Garraty looked over his shoulder and saw a small boy looking after it longingly. Scramm grabbed it and tried to scale it back to the kid, but the wind took it in a big boomerang arc and it wound up in a wildly lashing tree.

Thunder whacked. A white-purple tine of lightning jabbed the horizon. The comforting sough of the wind in the pines had become a hundred mad ghosts, flapping and hooting.

The guns cracked, a small popgun sound almost lost in the thunder and the wind. Garraty jerked his head around, the premonition that Olson had finally bought his bullet strong upon him. But Olson was still there, his flapping clothes revealing how amazingly fast the weight had melted off him. Olson had lost his jacket somewhere; the arms that poked out of his short shirtsleeves were bony and as thin as pencils.

It was somebody else who was being dragged off. The face was small and exhausted and very dead beneath the whipping mane of his hair.

"If it was a tailwind we could be in Oldtown by four-thirty!" Barkovitch said gleefully. He had his rainhat jammed down over his ears, and his sharp face was joyful and demented. Garraty suddenly understood. He reminded himself to tell McVries. Barkovitch was crazy.

A few minutes later the wind suddenly dropped off. The thunder faded to a series of thick mutters. The heat sucked back at them, clammy and nearly unbearable after the rushy coolness of the wind.

"What happened to it?" Collie Parker brayed. "Garraty! Does this goddam state punk out on its rainstorms, too?"

"I think you'll get what you want," Garraty said. "I don't know if you'll want it when you get it, though."

"Yoo-hoo! Raymond! Raymond Garraty!"

Garraty's head jerked up. For one awful moment he thought it was his mother, and visions of Percy danced through his head. But it was only an elderly, sweet-faced lady peeping at him from beneath a *Vogue* magazine she was using as a rainhat.

"Old bag," Art Baker muttered at his elbow.

"She looks sweet enough to me. Do you know her?"

"I know the type," Baker said balefully. "She looks just like my Aunt Hattie. She used to like to go to funerals, listen to the weeping and wailing and carrying-ons with just that same smile. Like a cat that got into the aigs."

"She's probably the Major's mother," Garraty said. It was supposed to be funny, but it fell flat. Baker's face was strained and pallid under the fading light in the rushing sky.

"My Aunt Hattie had nine kids. Nine, Garraty. She buried four of 'em with just that same look. Her own young. Some folks like to see other folks die. I can't understand that, can you?"

"No," Garraty said. Baker was making him uneasy. The thunder had begun to roll its wagons across the sky again. "Your Aunt Hattie, is she dead now?"

"No." Baker looked up at the sky. "She's down home. Probably out on the front porch in her rockin' chair. She can't walk much anymore. Just sittin' and rockin' and listenin' to the bulletins on the radio. And smilin' each time she hears the new figures." Baker rubbed his elbows with his palms. "You ever see a cat eat its own kittens, Garraty?"

Garraty didn't reply. There was an electric tension in the air now, something about the storm poised above them, and something more. Garraty could not fathom it. When he blinked his eyes he seemed to see the out-of-kilter eyes of Freaky D'Allessio looking back at him from the darkness.

Finally he said to Baker: "Does everybody in your family study up on dying?"

Baker smiled pallidly. "Well, I was turnin' over the idea of going to mortician's school in a few years. Good job. Morticians go on eating even in a depression."

"I always thought I'd get into urinal manufacture," Garraty said. "Get contracts with cinemas and bowling alleys and things. Sure-fire. How many urinal factories can there be in the country?"

"I don't think I'd still want to be a mortician," Baker said. "Not that it matters."

A huge flash of lightning tore across the sky. A gargantuan clap of thunder followed. The wind picked up in jerky gusts. Clouds raced across the sky like crazed privateers across an ebony nightmare sea.

"It's coming," Garraty said. "It's coming, Art."

"Some people say they don't care," Baker said suddenly. " 'Something simple, that's all I want when I go, Don.' That's what they'd tell him. My uncle. But most of 'em care plenty. That's what he always told me. They say, 'Just a pine box will do me fine.' But they end up having a big one . . . with a lead sleeve if they can afford it. Lots of them even write the model number in their wills."

"Why?" Garraty asked.

"Down home, most of them want to be buried in mausoleums. Aboveground. They don't want to be underground 'cause the water table's so high where I come from. Things rot quick in the damp. But if you're buried aboveground, you got the rats to worry about. Big Louisiana bayou rats. Graveyard rats. They'd gnaw through one of them pine boxes in zip flat."

The wind pulled at them with invisible hands.

Garraty wished the storm would come on and come. It was like an insane merry-go-round. No matter who you talked to, you came around to this damned subject again.

"Be fucked if I'd do it," Garraty said. "Lay out fifteen hundred dollars or something just to keep the rats away after I was dead."

"I dunno," Baker said. His eyes were half-lidded, sleepy. "They go for the soft parts, that's what troubles my mind. I could see 'em worryin' a hole in my own coffin, then makin' it bigger, finally wrigglin' through. And goin' right for my eyes like they was jujubes. They'd eat my eyes and then I'd be part of that rat. Ain't that right?"

"I don't know," Garraty said sickly.

"No thanks. I'll take that coffin with the lead sleeve. Every time."

"Although you'd only actually need it the once," Garraty said with a horrified little giggle.

"That *is* true," Baker agreed solemnly.

Lightning forked again, an almost pink streak that left the air smelling of ozone. A moment later the storm smote them again. But it wasn't rain this time. It was hail.

In a space of five seconds they were being pelted by hailstones the size of small pebbles. Several of the boys cried out, and Garraty shielded his eyes with one hand. The wind rose to a shriek. Hailstones bounced and smashed against the road, against faces and bodies.

Jensen ran in a huge, rambling circle, eyes covered, feet stumbling and rebounding against each other, in a total panic. He finally blundered off the shoulder, and the soldiers on the halftrack pumped half a dozen rounds into the undulating curtain of hail before they could be sure. Goodbye, Jensen, Garraty thought. Sorry, man.

Then rain began to fall through the hail, sluicing down the hill they were climbing, melting the hail scattered around their feet. Another wave of stones hit them, more rain, another splatter of hail, and then the rain was falling in steady sheets, punctuated by loud claps of thunder.

"Goddam!" Parker yelled, striding up to Garraty. His face was covered with red blotches, and he looked like a drowned water rat. "Garraty, this is without a doubt—"

"—yeah, the most fucked-up state in the fifty-one," Garraty finished. "Go soak your head."

Parker threw his head back, opened his mouth, and let the cold rain patter in. "I am, goddammit, I am!"

Garraty bent himself into the wind and caught up with McVries. "How does this grab you?" he asked.

McVries clutched himself and shivered. "You can't win. Now I wish the sun was out."

"It won't last long," Garraty said, but he was wrong. As they walked into four o'clock, it was still raining.

Chapter 10

"Do you know *why* they call me the Count?
Because I love to count! Ah-hah-hah."
—The Count
Sesame Street

There was no sunset as they walked into their second night on the road. The rainstorm gave way to a light, chilling drizzle around four-thirty. The drizzle continued on until almost eight o'clock. Then the clouds began to break up and show bright, coldly flickering stars.

Garraty pulled himself closer together inside his damp clothes and did not need a weatherman to know which way the wind blew. Fickle spring had pulled the balmy warmth that had come with them this far from beneath them like an old rug.

Maybe the crowds provided some warmth. Radiant heat, or something. More and more of them lined the road. They were huddled together for warmth but were undemonstrative. They watched the Walkers go past and then went home or hurried on to the next vantage point. If it was blood the crowds were looking for, they hadn't gotten much of it. They had lost only two since Jensen, both of them younger boys who had simply fainted dead away. That put them exactly halfway. No . . . really more than half. Fifty down, forty-nine to go.

Garraty was walking by himself. He was too cold to be sleepy. His lips were pressed together to keep the tremble out of them. Olson was still back there; halfhearted bets had gone round to the effect that Olson would be the fiftieth to buy a ticket, the halfway boy. But he hadn't. That signal honor had gone to 13, Roger Fenum. Unlucky old 13. Garraty was beginning to think that Olson would go on indefinitely. Maybe until he starved to death. He had locked himself safely away in a place beyond pain. In a way he supposed it would be poetic justice if Olson won. He could see the headlines: LONG WALK WON BY DEAD MAN.

Garraty's toes were numb. He wiggled them against the shredded inner linings of his shoes and could feel nothing. The real pain was not in his toes now. It was in his arches. A sharp, blatting pain that knifed up into his calves each time he took a step. It made him think of a story his mother had read him when he was small. It was about a mermaid who wanted to be a woman. Only she had a tail and a good fairy or someone said she could have legs if she wanted them badly enough. Every step she took on dry land would be like walking on knives, but she could have them if she wanted them, and she said yeah, okay, and that was the Long Walk. In a nutshell—

"Warning! Warning 47!"

"I hear you," Garraty snapped crossly, and picked up his feet.

The woods were thinner. The real northern part of the state was behind them. They had gone through two quietly residential towns, the road cutting them lengthwise and the sidewalks packed with people that were little more than shadows beneath the drizzle-diffused streetlamps. No one cheered much. It was too cold, he supposed. Too cold and too dark and Jesus Christ now he had another warning to walk off and if that wasn't a royal pisser, nothing was.

His feet were slowing again and he forced himself to pick them up. Somewhere quite far up ahead Barkovitch said something and followed it up with a short burst of his unpleasant laughter. He could hear McVries's response clearly: "Shut up, killer." Barkovitch told McVries to go to hell, and now he seemed quite upset by the whole thing. Garraty smiled wanly in the darkness.

He had dropped back almost to the tail of the column and reluctantly realized he was angling toward Stebbins again. Something about Stebbins fascinated him. But he decided he didn't particularly care what that something was. It was time to give up wondering about things. There was no percentage in it. It was just another royal pisser.

There was a huge, luminescent arrow ahead in the dark. It glowed like an evil spirit. Suddenly a brass band struck up a march. A good-sized band, by the sound. There were louder cheers. The air was full of drifting fragments, and for a crazy moment Garraty thought it was snowing. But it wasn't snow. It was confetti. They were changing roads. The old one met the new one at a right angle and another Maine Turnpike sign announced that Oldtown was now a mere sixteen miles away. Garraty felt a tentative feeler of excitement, maybe even pride. After Oldtown he knew the route. He could have traced it on the palm of his hand.

"Maybe it's your edge. I don't think so, but maybe it is."

Garraty jumped. It was as if Stebbins had pried the lid of his mind and peeked down inside.

"What?"

"It's your country, isn't it?"

"Not up here. I've never been north of Greenbush in my life, except when we drove up to the marker. And we didn't come this way." They left the brass band behind them, its tubas and clarinets glistening softly in the moist night.

"But we go through your hometown, don't we?"

"No, but close by it."

Stebbins grunted. Garraty looked down at Stebbins's feet and saw with surprise that Stebbins had removed his tennis shoes and was wearing a pair of soft-looking moccasins. His shoes were tucked into his chambray shirt.

"I'm saving the tennis shoes," Stebbins said, "just in case. But I think the mocs will finish it."

"Oh."

They passed a radio tower standing skeletal in an empty field. A red light pulsed as regular as a heartbeat at its tip.

"Looking forward to seeing your loved ones?"

"Yes, I am," Garraty said.

"What happens after that?"

"Happens?" Garraty shrugged. "Keep on walking down the road, I guess. Unless you are all considerate enough to buy out by then."

"Oh, I don't think so," Stebbins said, smiling remotely. "Are you sure you won't be walked out? After you see them?"

"Man, I'm not sure of anything," Garraty said. "I didn't know much when I started, and I know less now."

"You think you have a chance?"

"I don't know that either. I don't even know why I bother talking to you. It's like talking to smoke."

Far ahead, police sirens howled and gobbled in the night.

"Somebody broke through to the road up ahead where the police are spread thinner," Stebbins said. "The natives are getting restless, Garraty. Just think of all the people diligently making way for you up ahead."

"For you too."

"Me too," Stebbins agreed, then didn't say anything for a long time. The collar of his chambray workshirt flapped vacuously against his neck. "It's amazing how the mind operates the body," he said at last. "It's amazing how it can take over and dictate to the body. Your average housewife may walk up to sixteen miles a day, from icebox to ironing board to clothesline. She's ready to put her feet up at the end of the day but she's not exhausted. A door-to-door salesman might do twenty. A high school kid in training for football walks twenty-five to twenty-eight . . . that's in one day from getting up in the morning to going to bed at night. All of them get tired, but none of them get exhausted."

"Yeah."

"But suppose you told the housewife: today you must walk sixteen miles before you can have your supper."

Garraty nodded. "She'd be exhausted instead of tired."

Stebbins said nothing. Garraty had the perverse feeling that Stebbins was disappointed in him.

"Well . . . wouldn't she?"

"Don't you think she'd have her sixteen miles in by noon so she could kick off her shoes and spend the afternoon watching the soaps? I do. Are you tired, Garraty?"

"Yeah," Garraty said shortly. "I'm tired."

"Exhausted?"

"Well, I'm getting there."

"No, you're not getting exhausted yet, Garraty." He jerked a thumb at Olson's silhouette. "*That's* exhausted. He's almost through now."

Garraty watched Olson, fascinated, almost expecting him to drop at Stebbins's word. "What are you driving at?"

"Ask your cracker friend, Art Baker. A mule doesn't like to plow. But he likes carrots. So you hang a carrot in front of his eyes. A mule without a carrot gets exhausted. A mule with a carrot spends a long time being tired. You get it?"

"No."

Stebbins smiled again. "You will. Watch Olson. He's lost his appetite for the carrot. He doesn't quite know it yet, but he has. Watch Olson, Garraty. You can learn from Olson."

Garraty looked at Stebbins closely, not sure how seriously to take him. Stebbins laughed aloud. His laugh was rich and full—a startling sound that made other Walkers turn their heads. "Go on. Go talk to him, Garraty. And if he won't talk, just get up close and have a good look. It's never too late to learn."

Garraty swallowed. "Is it a very important lesson, would you say?"

Stebbins stopped laughing. He caught Garraty's wrist in a strong grip. "The most important lesson you'll ever learn, maybe. The secret of life over death. Reduce that equation and you can afford to die, Garraty. You can spend your life like a drunkard on a spree."

Stebbins dropped his hand. Garraty massaged his wrist slowly. Stebbins seemed to have dismissed him again. Nervously, Garraty walked away from him, and toward Olson.

It seemed to Garraty that he was drawn toward Olson on an invisible wire. He flanked him at four o'clock. He tried to fathom Olson's face.

Once, a long time ago, he had been frightened into a long night of wakefulness by a movie starring—who? It had been Robert Mitchum, hadn't it? He had been playing the role of an implacable Southern revival minister who had also been a compulsive murderer. In silhouette, Olson looked a little bit like him now. His form had seemed to elongate as the weight sloughed off him. His skin had gone scaly with dehydration. His eyes had sunk into hollowed sockets. His hair flew aimlessly on his skull like wind-driven cornsilk.

Why, he's nothing but a robot, nothing but an automation, really. Can there still be an Olson in there hiding? No. He's gone. I am quite sure that the Olson who sat on the grass and joked and told about the kid who froze on the starting line and bought his ticket right there, that Olson is gone. This is a dead clay thing.

"Olson?" he whispered.

Olson walked on. He was a shambling haunted house on legs. Olson had fouled himself. Olson smelled bad.

"Olson, can you talk?"

Olson swept onward. His face was turned into the darkness, and he *was* moving, yes he *was* moving. Something was going on here, something was still ticking over, but—

Something, yes, there was *something*, but what?

They breasted another rise. The breath came shorter and shorter in Garraty's lungs until he was panting like a dog. Tiny vapors of steam rose from his wet clothes. There was a river below them, lying in the dark like a silver snake. The Stillwater, he imagined. The Stillwater passed near Oldtown. A few halfhearted cheers went up, but not many.

Further on, nestled against the far side of the river's dogleg (maybe it was the Penobscot, after all), was a nestle of lights. Oldtown. A smaller nestle of light on the other side would be Milford and Bradley. Oldtown. They had made it to Oldtown.

"Olson," he said. "That's Oldtown. Those lights are Oldtown. We're getting there, fellow."

Olson made no answer. And now he could remember what had been eluding him and it was nothing so vital after all. Just that Olson reminded him of the Flying Dutchman, sailing on and on after the whole crew had disappeared.

They walked rapidly down a long hill, passed through an S-curve, and crossed a bridge that spanned, according to the sign, Meadow Brook. On the far side of this bridge was another STEEP HILL TRUCKS USE LOW GEAR sign. There were groans from some of the Walkers.

It was indeed a steep hill. It seemed to rise above them like a toboggan slide. It was not long; even in the dark they could see the summit. But it was steep, all right. Plenty steep.

They started up.

Garraty leaned into the slope, feeling his grip on his respiration start to trickle away almost at once. Be panting like a dog at the top, he thought . . . and then thought, if I *get* to the top. There was a protesting clamor rising in both legs. It started in his thighs and worked its way down. His legs were screaming at him that they simply weren't going to do this shit any longer.

But you will, Garraty told them. You will or you'll die.

I don't care, his legs answered back. Don't care if I do die, do die, do die.

The muscles seemed to be softening, melting like Jell-O left out in a hot sun. They trembled almost helplessly. They twitched like badly controlled puppets.

Warnings cracked out right and left, and Garraty realized he would be getting one for his very own soon enough. He kept his eyes fixed on Olson, forcing himself to match his pace to Olson's. They would make it together, up over the top of this killer hill, and then he would get Olson to tell him his secret. Then everything would be jake and he wouldn't have to worry about Stebbins or McVries or Jan or his father, no, not even about Freaky D'Allessio, who had spread his head on a stone wall beside U.S. 1 like a dollop of glue.

What was it, a hundred feet on? Fifty? What?

Now he was panting.

The first gunshots rang out. There was a loud, yipping scream that was drowned by more gunshots. And at the brow of the hill they got one more. Garraty could see nothing in the dark. His tortured pulse hammered in his temples. He found that he didn't give a fuck who had bought it this time. It didn't matter. Only the pain mattered, the tearing pain in his legs and lungs.

The hill rounded, flattened, and rounded still more on the downslope. The far side was gently sloping, perfect for regaining wind. But that soft

jelly feeling in his muscles didn't want to leave.
My legs are going to collapse, Garraty thought
calmly. They'll never take me as far as Freeport. I
don't think I can make it to Oldtown. I'm dying, I
think.

A sound began to beat its way into the night
then, savage and orgiastic. It was a voice, it was
many voices, and it was repeating the same thing
over and over.

*Garraty! Garraty! GARRATY! GARRATY!
GARRATY!*

It was God or his father, about to cut the legs out
from under him before he could learn the secret,
the secret, the secret of—

Like thunder: *GARRATY! GARRATY! GARRATY!*

It wasn't his father and it wasn't God. It was
what appeared to be the entire student body of
Oldtown High School, chanting his name in unison. As they caught sight of his white, weary, and
strained face, the steady beating cry dissolved into
wild cheering. Cheerleaders fluttered pompoms.
Boys whistled shrilly and kissed their girls. Garraty waved back, smiled, nodded, and craftily crept
closer to Olson.

"Olson," he whispered. "Olson."

Olson's eyes might have flickered a tiny bit. A
spark of life like the single turn of an old starter in
a junked automobile.

"Tell me how, Olson," he whispered. "Tell me
what to do."

The high school girls and boys (did I once go to

high school? Garraty wondered, was that a dream?) were behind them now, still cheering rapturously.

Olson's eyes moved jerkily in their sockets, as if long rusted and in need of oil. His mouth fell open with a nearly audible clunk.

"That's it," Garraty whispered eagerly. "Talk. Talk to me, Olson. Tell me. Tell me."

"Ah," Olson said. "Ah. Ah."

Garraty moved even closer. He put a hand on Olson's shoulder and leaned into an evil nimbus of sweat, halitosis, and urine.

"Please," Garraty said. "Try hard."

"Ga. Go. God. God's garden—"

"God's garden," Garraty repeated doubtfully. "What about God's garden, Olson?"

"It's full. Of. Weeds," Olson said sadly. His head bounced against his chest. "I."

Garraty said nothing. He could not. They were going up another hill now and he was panting again. Olson did not seem to be out of breath at all.

"I don't. Want. To die," Olson finished.

Garraty's eyes were soldered to the shadowed ruin that was Olson's face. Olson turned creakily toward him.

"Ah?" Olson raised his lolling head slowly. "Ga. Ga. Garraty?"

"Yes, it's me."

"What time is it?"

Garraty had rewound and reset his watch earlier. God knew why. "It's quarter of nine."

"No. No later. Than that?" Mild surprise washed over Olson's shattered old man's face.

"Olson—" He shook Olson's shoulder gently and Olson's whole frame seemed to tremble, like a gantry in a high wind. "What's it all about?" Suddenly Garraty cackled madly. "What's it all about, Alfie?"

Olson looked at Garraty with calculated shrewdness.

"Garraty," he whispered. His breath was like a sewer-draught.

"What?"

"What time is it?"

"Dammit!" Garraty shouted at him. He turned his head quickly, but Stebbins was staring down at the road. If he was laughing at Garraty, it was too dark to see.

"Garraty?"

"What?" Garraty said more quietly.

"Je. Jesus will save you."

Olson's head came up all the way. He began to walk off the road. He was walking at the halftrack.

"Warning. Warning 70!"

Olson never slowed. There was a ruinous dignity about him. The gabble of the crowd quieted. They watched, wide-eyed.

Olson never hesitated. He reached the soft shoulder. He put his hands over the side of the halftrack. He began to clamber painfully up the side.

"Olson!" Abraham yelled, startled. "Hey, that's Hank Olson!"

The soldiers brought their guns around in perfect four-part harmony. Olson grabbed the barrel of the closest and yanked it out of the hands that held it as if it had been an ice-cream stick. It clattered off into the crowd. They shrank from it, screaming, as if it had been a live adder.

Then one of the other three guns went off. Garraty saw the flash at the end of the barrel quite clearly. He saw the jerky ripple of Olson's shirt as the bullet entered his belly and then punched out the back.

Olson did not stop. He gained the top of the halftrack and grabbed the barrel of the gun that had just shot him. He levered it up into the air as it went off again.

"Get 'em!" McVries was screaming savagely up ahead. "Get 'em, Olson! Kill 'em! Kill 'em!"

The other two guns roared in unison and the impact of the heavy-caliber slugs sent Olson flying off the halftrack. He landed spread-eagled on his back like a man nailed to a cross. One side of his belly was a black and shredded ruin. Three more bullets were pumped into him. The guard Olson had disarmed had produced another carbine (effortlessly) from inside the halftrack.

Olson sat up. He put his hands against his belly and stared calmly at the poised soldiers on the deck of the squat vehicle. The soldiers stared back.

"You bastards!" McVries sobbed. "You bloody bastards!"

Olson began to get up. Another volley of bullets drove him flat again.

Now there was a sound from behind Garraty. He didn't have to turn his head to know it was Stebbins. Stebbins was laughing softly.

Olson sat up again. The guns were still trained on him, but the soldiers did not shoot. Their silhouettes on the halftrack seemed almost to indicate curiosity.

Slowly, reflectively, Olson gained his feet, hands crossed on his belly. He seemed to sniff the air for direction, turned slowly in the direction of the Walk, and began to stagger along.

"Put him out of it!" a shocked voice screamed hoarsely. "For Christ's sake put him out of it!"

The blue snakes of Olson's intestines were slowly slipping through his fingers. They dropped like link sausages against his groin, where they flapped obscenely. He stopped, bent over as if to retrieve them (*retrieve* them, Garraty thought in a near ecstasy of wonder and horror), and threw up a huge glut of blood and bile. He began to walk again, bent over. His face was sweetly calm.

"Oh my God," Abraham said, and turned to Garraty with his hands cupped over his mouth. Abraham's face was white and cheesy. His eyes were bulging. His eyes were frantic with terror. "Oh my God, Ray, what a fucking gross-out, oh Jesus!" Abraham vomited. Puke sprayed through his fingers.

Well, old Abe has tossed his cookies, Garraty thought remotely. That's no way to observe Hint 13, Abe.

"They gut-shot him," Stebbins said from behind Garraty. "They'll do that. It's deliberate. To discourage anybody else from trying the old Charge of the Light Brigade number."

"Get away from me," Garraty hissed. "Or I'll knock your block off!"

Stebbins dropped back quickly.

"Warning! Warning 88!"

Stebbins laugh drifted softly to him.

Olson went to his knees. His head hung between his arms, which were propped on the road.

One of the rifles roared, and a bullet clipped asphalt beside Olson's left hand and whined away. He began to climb slowly, wearily, to his feet again. They're playing with him, Garraty thought. All of this must be terribly boring for them, so they are playing with Olson. Is Olson fun, boys? Is Olson keeping you amused?

Garraty began to cry. He ran over to Olson and fell on his knees beside him and held the tired, hectically hot face against his chest. He sobbed into the dry, bad-smelling hair.

"Warning! Warning 47!"

"Warning! Warning 61!"

McVries was pulling at him. It was McVries again. "Get up, Ray, get up, you can't help him, for God's sake get up!"

"Its not *fair*!" Garraty wept. There was a sticky smear of Olson's blood on his cheekbone. "It's just not fair!"

"I know. Come on. Come on."

Garraty stood up. He and McVries began walking backward rapidly, watching Olson, who was on his knees. Olson got to his feet. He stood astride the white line. He raised both hands up into the sky. The crowd sighed softly.

"I DID IT *WRONG!*" Olson shouted tremblingly, and then fell flat and dead.

The soldiers on the halftrack put another two bullets in him and then dragged him busily off the road.

"Yes, that's that."

They walked quietly for ten minutes or so, Garraty drawing a low-key comfort just from McVries's presence. "I'm starting to see something in it, Pete," he said at last. "There's a pattern. It isn't all senseless."

"Yeah? Don't count on it."

"He talked to me, Pete. He wasn't dead until they shot him. He was *alive.*" Now it seemed that was the most important thing about the Olson experience. He repeated it. "*Alive.*"

"I don't think it makes any difference," McVries said with a tired sigh. "He's just a number. Part of the body count. Number fifty-three. It means we're a little closer and that's all it means."

"You don't really think that."

"Don't tell me what I think and what I don't!" McVries said crossly. "Leave it alone, can't you?"

"I put us about thirteen miles outside of Old-town," Garraty said.

"Well hot shit!"

"Do you know how Scramm is?"

"I'm not his doctor. Why don't you scram yourself?"

"What the hell's eating you?"

McVries laughed wildly. "Here we are, here we are and you want to know what's *eating* me! I'm worried about next year's income taxes, that's what's eating me. I'm worried about the price of grain in South Dakota, that's what's eating me. Olson, his *guts* were falling out, Garraty, at the end he was walking with his *guts falling out*, and that's eating me, that's *eating* me—" He broke off and Garraty watched him struggle to keep from vomiting. Abruptly McVries said, "Scramm's poor."

"Is he?"

"Collie Parker felt his forehead and said he was burning up. He's talking funny. About his wife, about Phoenix, Flagstaff, weird stuff about the Hopis and the Navajos and kachina dolls . . . it's hard to make out."

"How much longer can he go?"

"Who can say. He still might outlast us all. He's built like a buffalo and he's trying awful hard. Jesus, am I tired."

"What about Barkovitch?"

"He's wising up. He knows a lot of us'll be glad to see him buy a ticket to see the farm. He's made up his mind to outlast me, the nasty little fucker. He doesn't like me nagging him. Tough shit, right, I know." McVries uttered his wild laugh again. Garraty didn't like the sound of it. "He's scared, though. He's easing up on the lung-power and going to leg-power."

"We all are."

"Yeah. Oldtown coming up. Thirteen miles?"

"That's right."

"Can I say something to you, Garraty?"

"Sure. I'll carry it with me to the grave."

"I suppose that's true."

Someone near the front of the crowd set off a firecracker, and both Garraty and McVries jumped. Several women screeched. A burly man in the front row said "Goddammit!" through a mouthful of popcorn.

"The reason all of this is so horrible," McVries said, "is because it's just trivial. You know? We've sold ourselves and traded our souls on trivialities. Olson, he was trivial. He was magnificent, too, but those things aren't mutually exclusive. He was magnificent and trivial. Either way, or both, he died like a bug under a microscope."

"You're as bad as Stebbins," Garraty said resentfully.

"I wish Priscilla had killed me," McVries said. "At least that wouldn't have been—"

"Trivial," Garraty finished.

"Yes. I think—"

"Look, I want to doze a little if I can. You mind?"

"No. I'm sorry." McVries sounded stiff and offended.

"*I'm* sorry," Garraty said. "Look, don't take it to heart. It's really—"

"Trivial," McVries finished. He laughed his wild laugh for the third time and walked away. Garraty wished—not for the first time—that he had made no friends on the Long Walk. It was going to make it hard. In fact, it was already hard.

There was a sluggish stirring in his bowels. Soon they would have to be emptied. The thought made him grind his mental teeth. People would point and laugh. He would drop his shit in the street like a mongrel hound and afterward people would gather it up in paper napkins and put it in bottles for souvenirs. It seemed impossible that people would do such things, but he knew it happened.

Olson with his guts falling out.

McVries and Priscilla and the pajama factory.

Scramm, glowing fever-bright.

Abraham . . . what price stovepipe hat, audience?

Garraty's head dropped. He dozed. The Walk went on.

Over hill, over dale, over stile and mountain. Over ridge and under bridge and past my lady's fountain. Garraty giggled in the dimming recesses of his brain. His feet pounded the pavement and the loose heel flapped looser, like an old shutter on a dead house.

I think, therefore I am. First-year Latin class. Old tunes in a dead language. Ding-dong-bell-pussy's-down-the-well. Who pushed her in? Little Jackie Flynn.

I *exist*, therefore I am.

Another firecracker went off. There were whoops and cheers. The halftrack ground and clattered and Garraty listened for the sound of his number in a warning and dozed deeper.

Daddy, I wasn't glad when you had to go, but I never really missed you when you were gone. Sorry. But that's not the reason I'm here. I have no subconscious urge to kill myself, sorry Stebbins. So sorry but—

The guns again, startling him awake, and there was the familiar mailsack thud of another boy going home to Jesus. The crowd screamed its horror and roared its approval.

"Garraty!" a woman squealed. "Ray *Garraty*!" Her voice was harsh and scabbed. "We're *with* you, boy!" *We're with you Ray!*"

Her voice cut through the crowd and heads turned, necks craned, so that they could get a better look at Maine's Own. There were scattered boos drowned in a rising cheer.

The crowd took up the chant again. Garraty heard his name until it was reduced to a jumble of nonsense syllables that had nothing to do with him.

He waved briefly and dozed again.

Chapter II

"Come on, assholes! You want to live forever?"
—Unknown World War I
Top Sergeant

They passed into Oldtown around midnight. They switched through two feeder roads, joined Route 2, and went through the center of town.

For Ray Garraty the entire passage was a blurred, sleep-hazed nightmare. The cheering rose and swelled until it seemed to cut off any possibility of thought or reason. Night was turned into glaring, shadowless day by flaring arc-sodium lamps that threw a strange orange light. In such a light even the most friendly face looked like something from a crypt. Confetti, newspaper, shredded pieces of telephone book, and long streamers of toilet paper floated and soared from second- and third-story windows. It was a New York tickertape parade in Bush League U.S.A.

No one died in Oldtown. The orange arc-lamps faded and the crowd depleted a little as they walked along the Stillwater River in the trench of morning. It was May 3rd now. The ripe smell of paper mill smote them. A juicy smell of chemicals, wood-smoke, polluted river, and stomach cancer waiting to happen. There were conical piles of sawdust higher than the buildings downtown. Heaped stacks of pulpwood stood to the sky like monoliths. Garraty dozed and dreamed his shadowy dreams of relief and redemption and after what seemed to be an eternity, someone began jabbing him in the ribs. It was McVries.

"Wassamatter?"

"We're going on the turnpike," McVries said. He was excited. "The word's back. They got a whole sonofabitchin' color guard on the entrance ramp. We're gonna get a four-hundred-gun salute!"

"Into the valley of death rode the four hundred," Garraty muttered, rubbing the sleepy-seeds out of his eyes. "I've heard too many three-gun salutes tonight. Not interested. Lemme sleep."

"That isn't the point. After *they* get done, we're gonna give *them* a salute."

"We are?"

"Yeah. A forty-six-man raspberry."

Garraty grinned a little. It felt stiff and uncertain on his lips. "That right?"

"It certainly is. Well . . . a forty-man raspberry. A few of the guys are pretty far gone now."

Garraty had a brief vision of Olson, the human Flying Dutchman.

"Well, count me in," he said.

"Bunch up with us a little, then."

Garraty picked it up. He and McVries moved in tighter with Pearson, Abraham, Baker and

Scramm. The leather boys had further shortened their vanguard.

"Barkovitch in on it?" Garraty asked.

McVries snorted. "He thinks it's the greatest idea since pay toilets."

Garraty clutched his cold body a little tighter to himself and let out a humorless little giggle. "I bet he's got a hell of a wicked raspberry."

They were paralleling the turnpike now. Garraty could see the steep embankment to his right, and the fuzzy glow of more arc-sodiums—bone-white this time—above. A distance ahead, perhaps half a mile, the entrance ramp split off and climbed.

"Here we come," McVries said.

"Cathy!" Scramm yelled suddenly, making Garraty start. "I ain't gave up yet, Cathy!" He turned his blank, fever-glittering eyes on Garraty. There was no recognition in them. His cheeks were flushed, his lips cracked with fever blisters.

"He ain't so good," Baker said apologetically, as if he had caused it. "We been givin' him water every now and again, also sort of pourin' it over his head. But his canteen's almost empty, and if he wants another one, he'll have to holler for it himself. It's the rules."

"Scramm," Garraty said.

"Who's that?" Scramm's eyes rolled wildly in their sockets.

"Me. Garraty."

"Oh. You seen Cathy?"

"No," Garraty said uncomfortably. "I—"

"Here we come," McVries said. The crowd's cheers rose in volume again, and a ghostly green sign came out of the darkness: INTERSTATE 95 AUGUSTA PORTLAND PORTSMOUTH POINTS SOUTH.

"That's us," Abraham whispered. "God help us an' points south."

The exit ramp tilted up under their feet. They passed into the first splash of light from the over-head arcs. The new paving was smoother beneath their feet, and Garraty felt a familiar lift-drop of excitement.

The soldiers of the color guard had displaced the crowd along the upward spiral of the ramp. They silently held their rifles to high port. Their dress uniforms gleamed resplendently; their own soldiers in their dusty halftrack looked shabby by comparison.

It was like rising above a huge and restless sea of noise and into the calm air. The only sound was their footfalls and the hurried pace of their breath-ing. The entrance ramp seemed to go on forever, and always the way was fringed by soldiers in scarlet uniforms, their arms held in high-port salute.

And then, from the darkness somewhere, came the Major's electronically amplified voice: "Pre-*sent* harms!"

Weapons slapped flesh.

"Salute *ready*!"

Guns to shoulders, pointed skyward above them in a steely arch. Everyone instinctively huddled together against the crash which meant death—it had been Pavloved into them.

"*Fire!*"

Four hundred guns in the night, stupendous, ear-shattering. Garraty fought down the urge to put his hands to his head.

"*Fire!*"

Again the smell of powder smoke, acrid, heavy with cordite. In what book did they fire guns over the water to bring the body of a drowned man to the surface?

"My head," Scramm moaned. "Oh Jesus my head aches."

"*Fire!*"

The guns exploded for the third and last time.

McVries immediately turned around and walked backward, his face going a spotty red with the effort it cost him to shout. "Pre-*sent* harms!"

Forty tongues pursed forty sets of lips.

"Salute ready!"

Garraty drew breath into his lungs and fought to hold it.

"*Fire!*"

It was pitiful, really. A pitiful little noise of defiance in the big dark. It was not repeated. The wooden faces of their color guard did not change, but seemed all the same to indicate a subtle reproach.

"Oh, screw it," said McVries. He turned around and began to walk frontwards again, with his head down.

The pavement leveled off. They were on the

turnpike. There was a brief vision of the Major's jeep spurting away to the south, a flicker of cold fluorescent light against black sunglasses, and then the crowd closed in again, but farther from them now, for the highway was four lanes wide, five if you counted the grassy median strip.

Garraty angled to the median quickly, and walked in the close-cropped grass, feeling the dew seep through his cracked shoes and paint his ankles. Someone was warned. The turnpike stretched ahead, flat and monotonous, stretches of concrete tubing divided by this green inset, all of it banded together by strips of white light from the arc-sodiums above. Their shadows were sharp and clear and long, as if thrown by a summer moon.

Garraty tipped his canteen up, swigged deep, recapped it, and began to doze again. Eighty, maybe eighty-four miles to Augusta. The feel of the wet grass was soothing . . .

He stumbled, almost fell, and came awake with a jerk. Some fool had planted pines on the median strip. He knew it was the state tree, but wasn't that taking it a little far? How could they expect you to walk on the grass when there were—

They didn't of course.

Garraty moved over to the left lane, where most of them were walking. Two more halftracks had rattled onto the turnpike at the Orono entrance to fully cover the forty-six Walkers now left. They didn't expect you to walk on the grass. Another joke on you, Garraty old sport. Nothing vital, just another little disappointment. Trivial, really. Just . . .

don't dare wish for anything, and don't count on anything. The doors are closing. One by one, they're closing.

"They'll drop out tonight," he said. "They'll go like bugs on a wall tonight."

"I wouldn't count on it," Collie Parker said, and now he sounded worn and tired—subdued at last.

"Why not?"

"It's like shaking a box of crackers through a sieve, Garraty. The crumbs fall through pretty fast. Then the little pieces break up and they go, too. But the big crackers"—Parker's grin was a crescent flash of saliva-coated teeth in the darkness—"the *whole* crackers have to bust off a crumb at a time."

"But such a long way to walk . . . still . . ."

"I still want to live," Parker said roughly. "So do you, don't shit me, Garraty. You and that guy McVries can walk down the road and bullshit the universe and each other, so what, it's all a bunch of phony crap but it passes the time. But don't shit me. The bottom line is you still want to live. So do most of the others. They'll die slow. They'll die one piece at a time. I may get it, but right now I feel like I could walk all the way to New Orleans before I fell down on my knees for those wet ends in their kiddy car."

"Really?" He felt a wave of despair wash over him. "Really?"

"Yeah, really. Settle down, Garraty. We still got a long way to go." He strode away, up to where the leather boys, Mike and Joe, were pacing the group. Garraty's head dropped and he dozed again.

His mind began to drift clear of his body, a huge sightless camera full of unexposed film snapping shuttershots of everything and anything, running freely, painlessly, without friction. He thought of his father striding off big in green rubber boots. He thought of Jimmy Owens, he had hit Jimmy with the barrel of his air rifle, and yes he had meant to, because it had been Jimmy's idea, taking off their clothes and touching each other had been Jimmy's idea, it had been Jimmy's idea. The gun swinging in a glittering arc, a glittering *purposeful* arc, the splash of blood ("I'm sorry Jim oh jeez you need a bandaid") across Jimmy's chin, helping him into the house . . . Jimmy hollering . . . hollering.

Garraty looked up, half-stupefied and a little sweaty in spite of the night chill. Someone had hollered. The guns were centered on a small, nearly portly figure. It looked like Barkovitch. They fired in neat unison, and the small, nearly portly figure was thrown across two lanes like a limp laundry sack. The bepimpled moon face was not Barkovitch's. To Garraty the face looked rested, at peace.

He found himself wondering if they wouldn't all be better off dead, and shied away from the thought skittishly. But wasn't it true? The thought was inexorable. The pain in his feet would double, perhaps treble before the end came, and the pain seemed insupportable now. And it was not even pain that was the worst. It was the death, the constant death, the stink of carrion that had settled into his nostrils. The crowd's cheers were a constant background to his thoughts. The sound lulled him. He began to doze again, and this time it was the image of Jan that came. For a while he had forgotten all about her. In a way, he thought disjointedly, it was better to doze than to sleep. The pain in his feet and his legs seemed to belong to someone else to whom he was tethered only loosely, and with just a little effort he could regulate his thoughts. Put them to work for him.

He built her image slowly in his mind. Her small feet. Her sturdy but completely feminine legs— small calves swelling to full earthy peasant thighs. Her waist was small, her breasts full and proud. The intelligent, rounded planes of her face. Her long blond hair. Whore's hair he thought it for some reason. Once he had told her that—it had simply slipped out and he thought she would be angry, but she had not replied at all. He thought she had been secretly pleased . . .

It was the steady, reluctant contraction in his bowels that raised him this time. He had to grit his teeth to keep walking at speed until the sensation had passed. The fluorescent dial on his watch said it was almost one o'clock.

Oh God, please don't make me have to take a crap in front of all these people. Please God. I'll give You half of everything I get if I win, only please constipate me. Please. Please. Pl—

His bowels contracted again, strongly and hurtfully, perhaps affirming the fact that he was still essentially healthy in spite of the pounding his body had taken. He forced himself to go on until he had passed out of the merciless glare of the nearest overhead. He nervously unbuckled his belt, paused, then, grimacing, shoved his pants down with one hand held protectively across his genitals, and squatted. His knees popped explosively. The muscles in his thighs and calves protested screamingly and threatened to knot as they were bullied unwillingly in a new direction.

"Warning! Warning 47!"

"John! Hey Johnny, look at that poor bastard over there."

Pointing fingers, half-seen and half-imagined in the darkness. Flashbulbs popped and Garraty turned his head away miserably. Nothing could be worse than this. Nothing.

He almost fell on his back and managed to prop himself up with one arm.

A squealing girlish voice: "I *see* it! I see his *thing*!"

Baker passed him without a glance.

For a terrifying moment he thought it was all going to be for nothing anyway—a false alarm—but then it was all right. He was able to take care of business. Then, with a grunting half-sob, he rose to his feet and stumbled into a half-walk, half-run, cinching his pants tight again, leaving part of him behind to steam in the dark, eyed avidly by a thousand people—bottle it! put it on your mantel! The shit of a man with his life laid straight out in the line! *This is it, Betty, I told you we had something special in the game room ... right up here, over the stereo. He was shot twenty minutes later ...*

He caught up with McVries and walked beside him, head down.

"Tough?" McVries asked. There was unmistakable admiration in his voice.

"Real tough," Garraty said, and let out a shivery, loosening sigh. "I knew I forgot something."

"What?"

"I left my toilet paper home."

McVries cackled. "As my old granny used to say, if you ain't got a cob, then just let your hips slide a little freer."

Garraty burst out laughing, a clear, hearty laugh with no hysteria in it. He felt lighter, looser. No matter how things turned out, he wouldn't have to go through *that* again.

"Well, you made it," Baker said, falling in step.

"Jesus," Garraty said, surprised. "Why don't all you guys just send me a get-well card, or something?"

"It's no fun, with all those people staring at you," Baker said soberly. "Listen, I just heard something. I don't know if I believe it. I don't know if I even *want* to believe it."

"What is it?" Garraty asked.

"Joe and Mike? The leather-jacket guys everybody thought was queer for each other? They're Hopis. I think that was what Scramm was trying to tell us before, and we weren't gettin' him. But . . . see . . . what I hear is that they're brothers."

Garraty's jaw dropped.

"I walked up and took a good look at 'em,"

Baker was going on. "And I'll be goddamned if they don't *look* like brothers."

"That's twisted," McVries said angrily. "That's fucking twisted! Their folks ought to be Squaded for allowing something like that!"

"You ever know any Indians?" Baker asked quietly.

"Not unless they came from Passaic," McVries said. He still sounded angry.

"There's a Seminole reservation down home, across the state line," Baker said. "They're funny people. They don't think of things like 'responsibility' the same way we do. They're proud. And poor. I guess those things are the same for the Hopis as they are for the Seminoles. And they know how to die."

"None of that makes it right," McVries said.

"They come from New Mexico," Baker said.

"It's an abortion," McVries said with finality, and Garraty tended to agree.

Talk flagged all up and down the line, partially because of the noise from the crowd, but more, Garraty suspected, because of the very monotony of the turnpike itself. The hills were long and gradual, barely seeming like hills. Walkers dozed, snorted fitfully, and seemed to pull their belts tighter and resign themselves to a long, barely understood bitterness ahead. The little clots of society dissolved into threes, twos, solitary islands.

The crowd knew no fatigue. They cheered steadily with one hoarse voice, they waved unreadable placards. Garraty's name was shouted with monotonous frequency, but blocs of out-of-staters cheered briefly for Barkovitch, Pearson, Wyman. Other names blipped past and were gone with the speeding velocity of snow across a television screen.

Firecrackers popped and spluttered in strings. Someone threw a burning road flare into the cold sky and the crowd scattered, screaming, as it pinwheeled down to hiss its glaring purple light into the dirt of a gravel shoulder beyond the breakdown lane. There were other crowd standouts. A man with an electric bullhorn who alternately praised Garraty and advertised his own candidacy to represent the second district; a woman with a big crow in a small cage which she hugged jealously to her giant bosom; a human pyramid made out of college boys in University of New Hampshire sweatshirts; a hollow-cheeked man with no teeth in an Uncle Sam suit wearing a sign which said: WE GAVE AWAY THE PANAMA CANAL TO THE COMMUNIST NIGGERS. But otherwise the crowd seemed as dull and bland as the turnpike itself.

Garraty dozed on fitfully, and the visions in his head were alternately of love and horror. In one of the dreams a low and droning voice asked over and over again: *Are you experienced? Are you experienced? Are you experienced?* and he could not tell if it was the voice of Stebbins or of the Major.

Chapter 12

"I went down the road, the road was muddy.
I stubbed my toe, my toe was bloody.
You all here?"
—Child's hide-and-seek rhyme

Somehow it had got around to nine in the morning again.

Ray Garraty turned his canteen over his head, leaning back until his neck popped. It had only just warmed up enough so you could no longer see your breath, and the water was frigid, driving back the constant drowsiness a little.

He looked his traveling companions over. McVries had a heavy scrub of beard now, as black as his hair. Collie Parker looked haggard but tougher than ever. Baker seemed almost ethereal. Scramm was not so flushed, but he was coughing steadily—a deep, thundering cough that reminded Garraty of himself, long ago. He had had pneumonia when he was five.

The night had passed in a dream-sequence of odd names on the reflectorized overhead signs. Veazie. Bangor. Hermon. Jampden. Winterport. The soldiers had made only two kills, and Garraty was beginning to accept the truth of Parker's cracker analogy.

And now bright daylight had come again. The little protective groups had re-formed, Walkers joking about beards but not about feet . . . never about feet. Garraty had felt several small blisters break on his right heel during the night, but the soft, absorbent sock had buffered the raw flesh somewhat. Now they had just passed a sign that read AUGUSTA 48 PORTLAND 117.

"It's further than you said," Pearson told him reproachfully. He was horribly haggard, his hair hanging lifelessly about his cheeks.

"I'm not a walking roadmap," Garraty said.

"Still . . . it's your state."

"Tough."

"Yeah, I suppose so." There was no rancor in Pearson's tired voice. "Boy, I'd never do this again in a hundred thousand years."

"You should live so long."

"Yeah." Pearson's voice dropped. "I've made up my mind, though. If I get so tired and I can't go on, I'm gonna run over there and dive into the crowd. They won't dare shoot. Maybe I can get away."

"It'd be like hitting a trampoline," Garraty said. "They'll bounce you right back onto the pavement so they can watch you bleed. Don't you remember Percy?"

"Percy wasn't thinkin'. Just trying to walk off into the woods. They beat the dog out of Percy, all right." He looked curiously at Garraty. "Aren't you tired, Ray?"

"Shit, no." Garraty flapped his thin arms with mock grandeur. "I'm coasting, couldn't you tell?"

"I'm in bad shape," Pearson said, and licked his lips. "I'm havin' a hard job just thinking straight. And my legs feel like they got harpoons in them all the way up to—"

McVries came up behind them. "Scramm's dying," he said bluntly.

Garraty and Pearson said "Huh?" in unison.

"He's got pneumonia," McVries said.

Garraty nodded. "I was afraid it might be that."

"You can hear his lungs five feet away. It sounds like somebody pumped the Gulf Stream through them. If it gets hot again today, he'll just burn up."

"Poor bastard," Pearson said, and the tone of relief in his voice was both unconscious and unmistakable. "He could have taken us all, I think. And he's married. What's his wife gonna do?"

"What *can* she do?" Garraty asked.

They were walking fairly close to the crowd, no longer noticing the outstretched hands that strove to touch them—you got to know your distance after fingernails had taken skin off your arm once or twice. A small boy whined that he wanted to go home.

"I've been talking to everybody," McVries said. "Well, just about everybody. I think the winner should do something for her."

"Like what?" Garraty asked.

"That'll have to be between the winner and Scramm's wife. And if the bastard welshes, we can all come back and haunt him."

"Okay," Pearson said. "What's to lose?"

"Ray?"

"All right. Sure. Have you talked to Gary Barkovitch?"

"That prick? He wouldn't give his mother artificial respiration if she was drowning."

"I'll talk to him," Garraty said.

"You won't get anywhere."

"Just the same. I'll do it now."

"Ray, why don't you talk to Stebbins, too? You seem to be the only one he talks to."

Garraty snorted. "I can tell you what he'll say in advance."

"No?"

"He'll say why. And by the time he gets done, I won't have any idea."

"Skip him then."

"Can't." Garraty began angling toward the small, slumped figure of Barkovitch. "He's the only guy that still thinks he's going to win."

Barkovitch was in a doze. With his eyes nearly closed and the faint peachfuzz that coated his olive cheeks, he looked like a put-upon and badly used teddy bear. He had either lost his rainhat or thrown it away.

"Barkovitch."

Barkovitch snapped awake. "Wassamatter? Whozat? Garraty?"

"Yes. Listen, Scramm's dying."

"Who? Oh, right. Beaver-brains over there. Good for him."

"He's got pneumonia. He probably won't last until noon."

Barkovitch looked slowly around at Garraty with his bright black shoebutton eyes. Yes, he looked remarkably like some destructive child's teddy bear this morning.

"Look at you there with your big earnest face hanging out, Garraty. What's your pitch?"

"Well, if you didn't know, he's married, and—"

Barkovitch's eyes widened until it seemed they were in danger of falling out. *"Married! MARRIED? ARE YOU TELLING ME THAT NUMBSKULL IS—"*

"Shut up, you asshole! He'll hear you!"

"I don't give a sweet fuck! He's crazy!" Barkovitch looked over at Scramm, outraged. *"WHAT DID YOU THINK YOU WERE DOING, NUMBNUTS, PLAYING GIN RUMMY?"* he screamed at the top of his lungs. Scramm looked around blearily at Barkovitch, and then raised his hand in a half-hearted wave. He apparently thought Barkovitch was a spectator. Abraham, who was walking near Scramm, gave Barkovitch the finger. Barkovitch gave it right back, and then turned to Garraty. Suddenly he smiled.

"Aw, goodness," he said. "It shines from your dumb hick face, Garraty. Passing the hat for the dying guy's wifey, right? Ain't that cute."

"Count you out, huh?" Garraty said stiffly. "Okay." He started to walk away.

Barkovitch's smile wobbled at the edges. He grabbed Garraty's sleeve. "Hold on, hold on. I didn't say no, did I? Did you hear me say no?"

"No—"

"No, course I didn't." Barkovitch's smile reappeared, but now there was something desperate in it. The cockiness was gone. "Listen, I got off on the wrong foot with you guys. I didn't mean to. Shit, I'm a good enough guy when you get to know me, I'm always gettin' off on the wrong foot, I never had much of a crowd back home. In my school, I mean. Christ, I don't know why. I'm a good enough guy when you get to know me, as good as anyone else, but I always just, you know, seem to get off on the wrong foot. I mean a guy's got to have a couple of friends on a thing like this. It's no good to be alone, right? Jesus *Christ*, Garraty, you know that. That Rank. He started it, Garraty. He wanted to tear my ass. Guys, they always want to tear my ass. I used to carry a switchblade back at my high school on account of guys wanting to tear my ass. That Rank. I didn't mean for him to *croak*, that wasn't the idea at all. I mean, it wasn't my fault. You guys just saw the end of it, not the way he was . . . ripping my ass, you know . . ." Barkovitch trailed off.

"Yeah, I guess so," Garraty said, feeling like a hypocrite. Maybe Barkovitch could rewrite history for himself, but Garraty remembered the Rank incident too clearly. "Well, what do you want to do, anyway? You want to go along with the deal?"

"Sure, sure." Barkovitch's hand tightened convulsively on Garraty's sleeve, pulling it like the emergency-stop cord on a bus. "I'll send her enough bread to keep her in clover the rest of her life. I just wanted to tell you . . . make you see . . . a guy's got to have some friends . . . a guy's got to have a crowd, you know? Who wants to die hated, if you got to die, that's the way I look at it. I . . . I . . ."

"Sure, right." Garraty began to drop back, feeling like a coward, still hating Barkovitch but somehow feeling sorry for him at the same time. "Thanks a lot." It was the touch of human in Barkovitch that scared him. For some reason it scared him. He didn't know why.

He dropped back too fast, got a warning, and spent the next ten minutes working back to where Stebbins was ambling along.

"Ray Garraty," Stebbins said. "Happy May 3rd, Garraty."

Garraty nodded cautiously. "Same goes both ways."

"I was counting my toes," Stebbins said companionably. "They are fabulously good company because they always add up the same way. What's on your mind?"

So Garraty went through the business about Scramm and Scramm's wife for the second time, and halfway through another boy got his ticket (HELL'S ANGELS ON WHEELS stenciled on the back of his battered jeans jacket) and made it all seem rather meaningless and trite. Finished, he waited tensely for Stebbins to start anatomizing the idea.

"Why not?" Stebbins said amiably. He looked up at Garraty and smiled. Garraty could see that fatigue was finally making its inroads, even in Stebbins.

"You sound like you've got nothing to lose," he said.

"That's right," Stebbins said jovially. "None of us really has anything to lose. That makes it easier to give away."

Garraty looked at Stebbins, depressed. There was too much truth in what he said. It made their gesture toward Scramm look small.

"Don't get me wrong, Garraty old chum. I'm a bit weird, but I'm no old meanie. If I could make Scramm croak any faster by withholding my promise, I would. But I can't. I don't know for sure, but I'll bet every Long Walk finds some poor dog like Scramm and makes a gesture like this, Garraty, and I'll further bet it always comes at just about this time in the Walk, when the old realities and mortalities are starting to sink in. In the old days, before the Change and the Squads, when there was still millionaires, they used to set up foundations and build libraries and all that good shit. Everyone wants a bulwark against mortality, Garraty. Some people can kid themselves that it's their kids. But none of those poor lost children"—Stebbins swung one thin arm to indicate the other Walkers and laughed, but Garraty thought he sounded sad—"they're never even going to leave any bastards." He winked at Garrity. "Shock you?"

"I . . . I guess not."

"You and your friend McVries stand out in this

motley crew, Garraty. I don't understand how either of you got here. I'm willing to bet it runs deeper than you think, though. You took me seriously last night, didn't you? About Olson."

"I suppose so," Garraty said slowly.

Stebbins laughed delightedly. "You're the bee's knees, Ray. Olson had no secrets."

"I don't think you were ribbing last night."

"Oh, yes. I was."

Garraty smiled tightly. "You know what I think? I think you had some sort of insight and now you want to deny it. Maybe it scared you."

Stebbins's eyes went gray. "Have it how you like it, Garraty. It's your funeral. Now what say you flake off? You got your promise."

"You want to cheat it. Maybe that's your trouble. You like to think the game is rigged. But maybe it's a straight game. That scare you, Stebbins?"

"Take off."

"Go on, admit it."

"I admit nothing, except your own basic foolishness. Go ahead and tell yourself it's a straight game." Thin color had come into Stebbins's cheeks. "Any game looks straight if everyone is being cheated at once."

"You're all wet," Garraty said, but now his voice lacked conviction. Stebbins smiled briefly and looked back down at his feet.

They were climbing out of a long, swaybacked dip, and Garraty felt sweat pop out on him as he hurried back up through the line to where McVries, Pearson, Abraham, Baker, and Scramm were bundled up together—or, more exactly, the others were bundled around Scramm. They looked like worried seconds around a punchy fighter.

"How is he?" Garraty asked.

"Why ask them?" Scramm demanded. His former husky voice had been reduced to a mere whisper. The fever had broken, leaving his face pallid and waxy.

"Okay, I'll ask you."

"Aw, not bad," Scramm said. He coughed. It was a raspy, bubbling sound that seemed to come from underwater. "I'm not so bad. It's nice, what you guys are doing for Cathy. A man likes to take care of his own, but I guess I wouldn't be doing right to stand on my pride. Not the way things are now."

"Don't talk so much," Pearson said, "you'll wear yourself out."

"What's the difference? Now or later, what's the difference?" Scramm looked at them dumbly, then shook his head slowly from side to side. "Why'd I have to get sick? I was going good, I really was. Odds-on favorite. Even when I'm tired I like to walk. Look at folks, smell the air . . . why? Is it God? Did God do it to me?"

"I don't know," Abraham said.

Garraty felt the death-fascination coming over him again, and was repulsed. He tried to shake it off. It wasn't fair. Not when it was a friend.

"What time is it?" Scramm asked suddenly, and Garraty was eerily reminded of Olson.

"Ten past ten," Baker said.

"Just about two hundred miles down the road," McVries added.

"My feet ain't tired," Scramm said. "That's something."

A little boy was screaming lustily on the sidelines. His voice rose above the low crowd rumble by virtue of pure shrillness. "Hey Ma! Look at the big guy! Look at that moose, Ma! Hey Ma! Look!"

Garraty's eyes swept the crowd briefly and picked out the boy in the first row. He was wearing a Randy the Robot T-shirt and goggling around a half-eaten jam sandwich. Scramm waved at him.

"Kids're nice," he said. "Yeah. I hope Cathy has a boy. We both wanted a boy. A girl would be all right, but you guys know . . . a boy . . . he keeps your name and passes it on. Not that Scramm's such a great name." He laughed, and Garraty thought of what Stebbins had said, about bulwarks against mortality.

An apple-cheeked Walker in a droopy blue sweater dropped through them, bringing the word back. Mike, of Mike and Joe, the leather boys, had been struck suddenly with gut cramps.

Scramm passed a hand across his forehead. His chest rose and fell in a spasm of heavy coughing that he somehow walked through. "Those boys are from my neck of the woods," he said. "We all coulda come together if I'd known. They're Hopis."

"Yeah," Pearson said. "You told us."

Scramm looked puzzled. "Did I? Well, it don't matter. Seems like I won't be making the trip alone, anyway. I wonder—"

An expression of determination settled over Scramm's face. He began to step up his pace. Then he slowed again for a moment and turned around to face them. It seemed calm now, settled. Garraty looked at him, fascinated in spite of himself.

"I don't guess I'll be seeing you guys again." There was nothing in Scramm's voice but simple dignity. "Goodbye."

McVries was the first to respond. "Goodbye, man," he said hoarsely. "Good trip."

"Yeah, good luck," Pearson said, and then looked away.

Abraham tried to speak and couldn't. He turned away, pale, his lips writhing.

"Take it easy," Baker said. His face was solemn.

"Goodbye," Garraty said through frozen lips. "Goodbye, Scramm, good trip, good rest."

"Good rest?" Scramm smiled a little. "The real Walk may still be coming."

He sped up until he had caught up with Mike and Joe, with their impassive faces and their worn leather jackets. Mike had not allowed the cramps to bow him over. He was walking with both hands pressed against his lower belly. His speed was constant.

Scramm talked with them.

They all watched. It seemed that the three of them conferred for a very long time.

"Now what the hell are they up to?" Pearson whispered fearfully to himself.

Suddenly the conference was over. Scramm

walked a ways distant from Mike and Joe. Even from back here Garraty could hear the ragged bite of his cough. The soldiers were watching all three of them carefully. Joe put a hand on his brother's shoulder and squeezed it hard. They looked at each other. Garraty could discern no emotion on their bronzed faces. Then Mike hurried a little and caught up with Scramm.

A moment later Mike and Scramm did an abrupt about-face and began to walk toward the crowd, which, sensing the sharp tang of fatality about them, shrieked, unclotted, and backed away from them as if they had the plague.

Garraty looked at Pearson and saw his lips tighten.

The two boys were warned, and as they reached the guardrails that bordered the road, they about-faced smartly and faced the oncoming halftrack. Two middle fingers stabbed the air in unison.

"I fucked your mother and she sure was fine!" Scramm cried.

Mike said something in his own language.

A tremendous cheer went up from the Walkers, and Garraty felt weak tears beneath his eyelids. The crowd was silent. The spot behind Mike and Scramm was barren and empty. They took second warning, then sat down together, crosslegged, and began to talk together calmly. And that was pretty goddamned strange, Garraty thought as they passed by, because Scramm and Mike did not seem to be talking in the same language.

He did not look back. None of them looked back, not even after it was over.

"Whoever wins better keep his word," McVries said suddenly. "He just better."

No one said anything.

Chapter 13

"Joanie Greenblum, *come on down!*"
—Johnny Olsen
The New Price Is Right

Two in the afternoon.

"You're cheating, you fuck!" Abraham shouted.

"I'm not cheating," Baker said calmly. "That's a dollar forty you owe me, turkey."

"I don't pay cheaters." Abraham clutched the dime he had been flipping tightly in his hand.

"And I usually don't match dimes with guys that call me that," Baker said grimly, and then smiled. "But in your case, Abe, I'll make an exception. You have so many winning ways I just can't help myself."

"Shut up and flip," Abraham said.

"Oh please don't take that tone of voice to me," Baker said abjectly, rolling his eyes. "I might fall over in a dead faint!" Garraty laughed.

Abraham snorted and flicked his dime, caught it, and slapped it down on his wrist. "You match me."

"Okay." Baker flipped his dime higher, caught

it more deftly and, Garraty was sure, palmed it on edge.

"You show first this time," Baker said.

"Nuh-uh. I showed first last time."

"Oh shit, Abe, I showed first three times in a row before *that*. Maybe you're the one cheating."

Abraham muttered, considered, and then revealed his dime. It was tails, showing the Potomac River framed in laurel leaves.

Baker raised his hand, peeked under it, and smiled. His dime also showed tails. "That's a dollar *fifty* you owe me."

"My *God* you must think I'm dumb!" Abraham hollered. "You think I'm some kind of idiot, right? Go on and admit it! Just taking the rube to the cleaners, right?"

Baker appeared to consider.

"Go on, go on!" Abraham bellowed. "I can take it!"

"Now that you put it to me," Baker said, "whether or not you're a rube never entered my mind. That you're an ijit is pretty well established. As far as taking you to the cleaners"—he put a hand on Abraham's shoulder—"that, my friend, is a certainty."

"Come on," Abraham said craftily. "Double or nothing for the whole bundle. And this time *you* show first."

Baker considered. He looked at Garraty. "Ray, would you?"

"Would I what?" Garraty had lost track of the

conversation. His left leg had begun to feel decidedly strange.

"Would you go double or nothing against this here fella?"

"Why not? After all, he's too dumb to cheat *you*."

"Garraty, I thought you were my friend," Abraham said coldly.

"Okay, dollar fifty, double or nothing," Baker said, and that was when the monstrous pain bolted up Garraty's left leg, making all the pain of the last thirty hours seem like a mere whisper in comparison.

"*My leg, my leg, my leg!*" he screamed, unable to help himself.

"Oh, Jesus, Garraty," Baker had time to say— nothing in his voice but mild surprise, and then they had passed beyond him, it seemed that they were all passing him as he stood here with his left leg turned to clenched and agonizing marble, passing him, leaving him behind.

"Warning! Warning 47!"

Don't panic. If you panic now you've had the course.

He sat down on the pavement, his left leg stuck out woodenly in front of him. He began to massage the big muscles. He tried to knead them. It was like trying to knead ivory.

"Garraty?" It was McVries. He sounded scared . . . surely that was only an illusion? "What is it? Charley horse?"

"Yeah, I guess so. Keep going. It'll be all right."

Time. Time was speeding up for him, but everyone else seemed to have slowed to a crawl, to the speed of an instant replay on a close play at first base. McVries was picking up his pace slowly, one heel showing, then the other, a glint from the worn nails, a glimpse of cracked and tissue-thin shoe-leather. Barkovitch was passing by slowly, a little grin on his face, a wave of tense quiet came over the crowd slowly, moving outward in both directions from where he had sat down, like great glassy combers headed for the beach. My second warning, Garraty thought, my second warning's coming up, come on leg, come on goddam leg. I don't want to buy a ticket, what do you say, come on gimme a break.

"Warning! Second warning, 47!"

Yeah, I know, you think I can't keep score, you think I'm sitting here trying to get a suntan?

The knowledge of death, as true and unarguable as a photograph, was trying to get in and swamp him. Trying to paralyze him. He shut it out with a desperate coldness. His thigh was excruciating agony, but in his concentration he barely felt it. A minute left. No, fifty seconds now, no, forty-five, it's dribbling away, my time's going.

With an abstract, almost professorly expression on his face, Garraty dug his fingers into the frozen straps and harnesses of muscle. He kneaded. He flexed. He talked to his leg in his head. Come on, come on, come on, goddam thing. His fingers began to ache and he did not notice that much either. Stebbins passed him and murmured something. Garraty did not catch what it was. It might have been good luck. Then he was alone, sitting on the broken white line between the travel lane and the passing lane.

All gone. The carny just left town, pulled stakes in the middle of everything and blew town, no one left but this here kid Garraty to face the emptiness of flattened candy wrappers and squashed cigarette butts and discarded junk prizes.

All gone except one soldier, young and blond and handsome in a remote sort of way. His silver chronometer was in one hand, his rifle in the other. No mercy in that face.

"Warning! Warning 47! Third warning, 47!"

The muscle was not loosening at all. He was going to die. After all this, after ripping his guts out, that was the fact, after all.

He let go of his leg and stared calmly at the soldier. He wondered who was going to win. He wondered if McVries would outlast Barkovitch. He wondered what a bullet in the head felt like, if it would just be sudden darkness or if he would actually feel his thoughts being ripped apart.

The last few seconds began to drain away.

The cramp loosened. Blood flowed back into the muscle, making it tingle with needles and pins, making it warm. The blond soldier with the remotely handsome face put away the pocket chronometer. His lips moved soundlessly as he counted down the last few seconds.

But I can't get up, Garraty thought. It's too good just to sit. Just sit and let the phone ring, the hell with it, why didn't I take the phone off the hook?

Garraty let his head fall back. The soldier seemed to be looking down at him, as if from the mouth of a tunnel or over the lip of a deep well. In slow motion he transferred the gun to both hands and his right forefinger kissed over the trigger, then curled around it and the barrel started to come around. The soldier's left hand was solid on the stock. A wedding band caught a glimmer of sun. Everything was slow. So slow. Just . . . hold the phone.

This, Garraty thought.

"This is what it's like. To die.

The soldier's right thumb was rotating the safety catch to the off position with exquisite slowness. Three scrawny women were directly behind him, three weird sisters, hold the phone. Just hold the phone a minute longer, I've got something to die here. Sunshine, shadow, blue sky. Clouds rushing up the highway. Stebbins was just a back now, just a blue workshirt with a sweatstain running up between the shoulder blades, goodbye, Stebbins.

Sounds thundered in on him. He had no idea if it was his imagination, or heightened sensibility, or simply the fact of death reaching out for him. The safety catch snapped off with a sound like a breaking branch. The rush of indrawn air between his teeth was the sound of a wind tunnel. His heartbeat was a drum. And there was a high singing, not in his ears but between them, spiraling up and up, and he was crazily sure that it was the actual sound of brainwaves—

He scrambled to his feet in a convulsive flying

jerk, screaming. He threw himself into an accelerating, gliding run. His feet were made of feathers. The finger of the soldier tightened on the trigger and whitened. He glanced down at the solid-state computer on his waist, a gadget that included a tiny but sophisticated sonar device. Garraty had once read an article about them in *Popular Mechanix*. They could read out a single Walker's speed as exactly as you would have wanted, to four numbers to the right of the decimal point.

The soldier's finger loosened.

Garraty slowed to a very fast walk, his mouth cottony dry, his heart pounding at triphammer speed. Irregular white flashes pulsed in front of his eyes, and for a sick moment he was sure he was going to faint. It passed. His feet, seemingly furious at being denied their rightful rest, screamed at him rawly. He gritted his teeth and bore the pain. The big muscle in his left leg was still twitching alarmingly, but he wasn't limping. So far.

He looked at his watch. It was 2:17 PM. For the next hour he would be less than two seconds from death.

"Back to the land of the living," Stebbins said as he caught up.

"Sure," Garraty said numbly. He felt a sudden wave of resentment. They would have gone on walking even if he had bought his ticket. No tears shed for him. Just a name and number to be entered in the official records—GARRATY, RAYMOND, #47, ELIMINATED 218th MILE. And a human-interest story in the state newspapers for a couple of days. GARRATY DEAD; "MAINE'S OWN" BECOMES 61ST TO FALL!

"I hope I win," Garraty muttered.

"Think you will?"

Garraty thought of the blond soldier's face. It had shown as much emotion as a plate of potatoes.

"I doubt it," he said. "I've already got three strikes against me. That means you're out, doesn't it?"

"Call the last one a foul tip," Stebbins said. He was regarding his feet again.

Garraty picked his own feet up, his two-second margin like a stone in his head. There would be no warning this time. Not even time for someone to say, you better pick it up, Garraty, you're going to draw one.

He caught up with McVries, who glanced around. "I thought you were out of it, kiddo," McVries said.

"So did I."

"That close?"

"About two seconds, I think."

McVries pursed a silent whistle. "I don't think I'd like to be in your shoes right now. How's the leg?"

"Better. Listen, I can't talk. I'm going up front for a while."

"It didn't help Harkness any."

Garraty shook his head. "I have to make sure I'm topping the speed."

"All right. You want company?"

"If you've got the energy."

McVries laughed. "I got the time if you got the money, honey."

"Come on, then. Let's pick it up while I've still got the sack for it."

Garraty stepped up his pace until his legs were at the point of rebellion, and he and McVries moved quickly through the front-runners. There was a space between the boy who had been walking second, a gangling, evil-faced boy named Harold Quince, and the survivor of the two leather boys. Joe. Closer to, his complexion was startlingly bronzed. His eyes stared steadily at the horizon, and his features were expressionless. The many zippers on his jacket jingled, like the sound of faraway music.

"Hello, Joe," McVries said, and Garraty had an hysterical urge to add, whaddaya know?

"Howdy," Joe said curtly.

They passed him and then the road was theirs, a wide double-barreled strip of composition concrete stained with oil and broken by the grassy median strip, bordered on both sides by a steady wall of people.

"Onward, ever onward," McVries said. "Christian soldiers, marching as to war. Ever hear that one, Ray?"

"What time is it?"

McVries glanced at his watch. "2:20, Look, Ray, if you're going to—"

"God, is that all? I thought—" He felt panic rising in his throat, greasy and thick. He wasn't going to be able to do it. The margin was just too tight.

"Look, if you keep thinking about the time, you're gonna go nuts and try to run into the crowd and they'll shoot you dog-dead. They'll shoot you with your tongue hanging out and spit running down your chin. Try to forget about it."

"I can't." Everything was bottling up inside him, making him feel jerky and hot and sick. "Olson . . . Scramm . . . they died. Davidson died. I can die too, Pete! I believe it now. It's breathing down my fucking back!"

"Think about your girl. Jan, what's-her-face. Or your mother. Or your goddam kitty-cat. Or don't think about anything. Just pick 'em up and put 'em down. Just keep on walking down the road. Concentrate on that."

Garraty fought for control of himself. Maybe he even got a little. But he was unraveling just the same. His legs didn't want to respond smoothly to his mind's commands anymore, they seemed as old and as flickery as ancient lightbulbs.

"He won't last much longer," a woman in the front row said quite audibly.

"Your tits won't last much longer!" Garraty snapped at her, and the crowd cheered him.

"They're screwed up," Garraty muttered. "They're really screwed up. Perverted. What time is it, McVries?"

"What was the first thing you did when you got your letter of confirmation?" McVries asked softly.

"What did you do when you knew you were really in?"

Garraty frowned, wiped his forearm quickly across his forehead, and then let his mind free of the sweaty, terrifying present to that sudden, flashing moment.

"I was by myself. My mother works. It was a Friday afternoon. The letter was in the mailbox and it had a Wilmington, Delaware, postmark, so I knew that had to be it. But I was sure it said I'd flunked the physical or the mental or both. I had to read it twice. I didn't go into any fits of joy, but I was pleased. Real pleased. And confident. My feet didn't hurt then and my back didn't feel like somebody had shoved a rake with a busted handle into it. I was one in a million. I wasn't bright enough to realize the circus fat lady is, too."

He broke off for a moment, thinking, smelling early April.

"I couldn't back down. There were too many people watching. I think it must work the same with just about everyone. It's one of the ways they tip the game, you know. I let the April 15th back-out date go by and the day after that they had a big testimonial dinner for me at the town hall—all my friends were there and after dessert everyone started yelling Speech! Speech! And I got out and mumbled something down at my hands about how I was gonna do the best I could if I got in, and everyone applauded like mad. It was like I'd laid the fucking Gettysburg Address on their heads. You know what I mean?"

"Yes, I know," McVries said, and laughed—but his eyes were dark.

Behind them the guns thunderclapped suddenly. Garraty jumped convulsively and nearly froze in his tracks. Somehow he kept walking. Blind instinct this time, he thought. What about next time?

"Son of a bitch," McVries said softly. "It was Joe."

"What time is it?" Garraty asked, and before McVries could answer he remembered that he was wearing a watch of his own. It was 2:38. Christ. His two-second margin was like an iron dumbbell on his back.

"No one tried to talk you out of it?" McVries asked. They were far out beyond the rest now, better than a hundred yards beyond Harold Quince. A soldier had been dispatched to keep tabs on them. Garraty was very glad it wasn't the blond guy. "No one tried to talk you into using the April 31st blackout?"

"Not at first. My mother and Jan and Dr. Patterson—he's my mother's special friend, you know, they've been keeping company for the last five years or so—they just kind of soft-pedaled it at first. They were pleased and proud because most of the kids in the country over twelve take the tests but only one in fifty passes. And that still leaves thousands of kids and they can use two hundred—one hundred Walkers and a hundred backups. And there's no skill in getting picked, you know that."

"Sure, they draw the names out of that cock-sucking drum. Big TV spectacular." McVries's voice cracked a little.

"Yeah. The Major draws the two hundred names, but the names're all they announce. You don't know if you're a Walker or just a backup."

"And no notification of which you are until the final backout date itself," McVries agreed, speaking of it as if the final backout date had been years ago instead of only four days. "Yeah, they like to stack the deck their way."

Somebody in the crowd had just released a flotilla of balloons. They floated up to the sky in a dissolving arc of reds, blues, greens, yellows. The steady south wind carried them away with taunting, easy speed.

"I guess so," Garraty said. "We were watching the TV when the Major drew the names, I was number seventy-three out of the drum. I fell right out of my chair. I just couldn't believe it."

"No, it can't be *you*," McVries agreed. "Things like that always happen to the other guy."

"Yeah, that's the feeling. That's when everybody started in on me. It wasn't like the first backout date when it was all speeches and pie in the sky by-and-by. Jan . . ."

He broke off. Why not? He'd told everything else. It didn't matter. Either he or McVries was going to be dead before it was over. Probably both of them. "Jan said she'd go all the way with me, any time, any way, as often as I wanted if I'd take the April 31st backout. I told her that would make me feel like an opportunist and a heel, and she got mad at me and said it was better than feeling dead, and then she cried a lot. And begged me." Garraty looked up at McVries. "I don't know. Anything else she could have asked me, I would have tried to do it. But this one thing . . . I couldn't. It was like there was a stone caught in my throat. After a while she knew I couldn't say Yes, okay, I'll call the 800 number. I think she started to understand. Maybe as well as I did myself, which God knows wasn't—isn't—very well.

"Then Dr. Patterson started in. He's a diagnostician, and he's got a wicked logical mind. He said, 'Look here, Ray. Figuring in the Prime group and the backups, your chance of survival is fifty-to-one. Don't do this to your mother, Ray.' I was polite with him for as long as I could, but finally I told him to just kiss off. I said I figured the odds on him ever marrying my mother were pretty long, but I never noticed him backing off because of that."

Garraty ran both hands through the straw-thatch of his hair. He had forgotten about the two-second margin.

"God, didn't he get mad. He ranted and raved and told me if I wanted to break my mother's heart to just go ahead. He said I was as insensitive as a . . . a wood tick, I think that's what he said, insensitive as a wood tick, maybe it's a family saying of his or something, I don't know. He asked me how it felt to be doing the number on my mom and on a nice girl like Janice. So I countered with my own unarguable logic."

"Did you," McVries said, smiling. "What was that?"

"I told him if he didn't get out I was going to hit him."

"What about your mother?"

"She didn't say much at all. I don't think she could believe it. And the thought of what I'd get if I won. The Prize—everything you want for the rest of your life—that sort of blinded her, I think. I had a brother, Jeff. He died of pneumonia when he was six, and—it's cruel—but I don't know how we'd've gotten along if he'd've lived. And . . . I guess she just kept thinking I'd be able to back out of it if I did turn out to be Prime. The Major is a nice man. That's what she said. I'm sure he'd let you out of it if he understood the circumstances. But they Squad them just as fast for trying to back out of a Long Walk as they do for talking against it. And then I got the call and I knew I was a Walker. I was Prime."

"I wasn't."

"No?"

"No. Twelve of the original Walkers used the April 31st backout. I was number twelve, backup. I got the call just past 11 PM four days ago."

"Jesus! Is that so?"

"Uh-huh. That close."

"Doesn't it make you . . . bitter?"

McVries only shrugged.

Garraty looked at his watch. It was 3:02. It was

going to be all right. His shadow, lengthening in the afternoon sun, seemed to move a little more confidently. It was a pleasant, brisk spring day. His leg felt okay now.

"Do you still think you might just . . . sit down?" he asked McVries. "You've outlasted most of them. Sixty-one of them."

"How many you or I have outlasted doesn't matter, I think. There comes a time when the will just runs out. Doesn't matter what I *think*, see? I used to have a good time smearing away with oil paints. I wasn't too bad, either. Then one day—bingo. I didn't taper off, I just stopped. Bingo. There was no urge to go on even another minute. I went to bed one night liking to paint and when I woke up it was nowhere."

"Staying alive hardly qualifies as a hobby."

"I don't know about that. How about skin divers? Big-game hunters? Mountain climbers? Or even some half-witted millworker whose idea of a good time is picking fights on Saturday night? All of those things reduce staying alive to a hobby. Part of the game."

Garraty said nothing.

"Better pick it up some," McVries said gently. "We're losing speed. Can't have that."

Garraty picked it up.

"My dad has a half-ownership in a drive-in movie theater," McVries said. "He was going to tie me and gag me down in the cellar under the snack concession to keep me from coming, Squads or no Squads."

"What did you do? Just wear him down?"

"There was no time for that. When the call came, I had just ten hours. They laid on an airplane and a rental car at the Presque Isle airport. He ranted and raved and I just sat there and nodded and agreed and pretty soon there was a knock on the door and when my mom opened it, two of the biggest, meanest-looking soldiers you ever saw were standing on the porch. Man, they were so ugly they could have stopped clocks. My dad took one look at them and said, 'Petie, you better go upstairs and get your Boy Scout pack.'" McVries jolted the pack up and down on his shoulders and laughed at the memory. "And just about the next thing any of us knew, we were on that plane, even my little sister Katrina. She's only four. We landed at three in the morning and drove up to the marker. And I think Katrina was the only who really understood. She kept saying 'Petie's going on an adventure.'" McVries flapped his hands in an oddly uncompleted way. "They're staying at a motel in Presque Isle. They didn't want to go home until it was over. One way or the other."

Garraty looked at his watch. It was 3:20.

"Thanks," he said.

"For saving your life again?" McVries laughed merrily.

"Yes, that's just right."

"Are you sure that would be any kind of a favor?"

"I don't know." Garraty paused. "I'll tell you something though. It's never going to be the same for me. The time limit thing. Even when you're walking with no warnings, there's only two minutes between you and the inside of a cemetery fence. That's not much time."

As if on cue, the guns roared. The holed Walker made a high, gobbling sound, like a turkey grabbed suddenly by a silent-stepping farmer. The crowd made a low sound that might have been a sigh or a groan or an almost sexual outletting of pleasure.

"No time at all," McVries agreed.

They walked. The shadows got longer. Jackets appeared in the crowd as if a magician had conjured them out of a silk hat. Once Garraty caught a warm whiff of pipesmoke that brought back a hidden, bittersweet memory of his father. A pet dog escaped from someone's grasp and ran out into the road, red plastic leash dragging, tongue lolling out pinkly, foam flecked on its jaws. It yipped, chased drunkenly after its stubby tail, and was shot when it charged drunkenly at Pearson, who swore bitterly at the soldier who had shot it. The force of the heavy-caliber bullet drove it to the edge of the crowd where it lay dull-eyed, panting, and shivering. No one seemed anxious to claim it. A small boy got past the police, wandered out into the left lane of the road, and stood there, weeping. A soldier advanced on him. A mother screamed shrilly from the crowd. For one horrified moment Garraty thought the soldier was going to shoot the kid as the dog had been shot, but the soldier merely swept the little boy indifferently back into the crowd.

At 6:00 PM the sun touched the horizon and turned the western sky orange. The air turned cold. Collars were turned up. Spectators stamped their feet and rubbed their hands together.

Collie Parker registered his usual complaint about the goddam Maine weather.

By quarter of nine we'll be in Augusta, Garraty thought. Just a hop, skip, and a jump from there to Freeport. Depression dropped over him. What then? Two minutes you'll have to see her, unless you should miss her in the crowd—God forbid. Then what? Fold up?

He was suddenly sure Jan and his mother wouldn't be there anyway. Just the kids he had gone to school with, anxious to see the suicidal freak they had unknowingly nurtured among them. And the Ladies' Aid. They would be there. The Ladies' Aid had given him a tea two nights before the Walk started. In that antique time.

"Let's start dropping back," McVries said. "We'll do it slow. Get together with Baker. We'll walk into Augusta together. The original Three Musketeers. What do you say, Garraty?"

"All right," Garraty said. It sounded good.

They dropped back a little at a time, eventually leaving the sinister-faced Harold Quince to lead the parade. They knew they were back with their own people when Abraham, out of the gathering gloom, asked: "You finally decide to come back and visit the po' folks?"

"Je-sus, he really does look like him," McVries

said, staring at Abraham's weary, three-day-bearded face. "Especially in this light."

"Fourscore and seven years ago," Abraham intoned, and for an eerie moment it was as if a spirit had inhabited seventeen-year-old Abraham. "Our fathers set forth on this continent . . . ah, bullshit. I forget the rest. We had to learn it in eighth grade history if we wanted an A."

"The face of a founding father and the mentality of a syphilitic donkey," McVries said sadly. "Abraham, how did you get into a balls-up like this?"

"Bragged my way in," Abraham said promptly. He started to go on and the guns interrupted him. There was the familiar mailsack thud.

"That was Gallant," Baker said, looking back. "He's been walking dead all day."

"Bragged his way into it," Garraty mused, and then laughed.

"Sure." Abraham ran a hand up one cheek and scratched the cavernous hollow under one eye. "You know the essay test?"

They all nodded. An essay, *Why Do You Feel Qualified to Participate in the Long Walk?*, was a standard part of the Mentals section of the exam. Garraty felt a warm trickle on his right heel and wondered if it was blood, pus, sweat, or all of the above. There seemed to be no pain, although his sock felt ragged back there.

"Well, the thing was," Abraham said, "I didn't feel particularly qualified to participate in anything. I took the exam completely on the spur of the moment. I was on my way to the movies and I just happened past the gym where they were having the test. You have to show your Work Permit card to get in, you know. I just happened to have mine with me that day. If I hadn't, I wouldn't have bothered to go home and get it. I just would have gone on to the movies and I wouldn't be here right now, dying in such jolly company."

They considered this silently.

"I took the physical and then I zipped through the objective stuff and then I see this three-page blank at the end of the folder. 'Please answer this question as objectively and honestly as you can, using not more than 1500 words,' oh holy shit, I think. The rest of it was sort of fun. What a bunch of fucked-up questions."

"Yeah, how often do you have a bowel movement?" Baker said dryly. "Have you ever used snuff?"

"Yeah, yeah, stuff like that," Abraham agreed. "I'd forgotten all about that stupid snuff question. I just zipped along, bullshitting in good order, you know, and I come to this essay about why I feel qualified to participate. I couldn't think of a thing. So finally some bastard in an army coat strolls by and says, 'Five minutes. Will everyone finish up, please?' So I just put down, 'I feel qualified to participate in the Long Walk because I am one useless S.O.B. and the world would be better off without me, unless I happened to win and get rich in which case I would buy a Van Go to put in every room of my manshun and order up sixty high-class horrs and not bother anybody.' I thought about that for about a minute, and then I put in parenthesis: '(I would give all my sixty high-class horrs old-age pensions, too.)' I thought that would really screw 'em up. So a month later—I'd forgotten all about the whole thing—I get a letter saying I qualified. I damn near creamed my jeans."

"And you went through with it?" Collie Parker demanded.

"Yeah, it's hard to explain. The thing was, everybody thought it was a big joke. My girlfriend wanted to have the letter photographed and get it turned into a T-shirt down at the Shirt Shack, like she thought I'd pulled the biggest practical joke of the century. It was like that with everybody. I'd get the big glad hand and somebody was always saying something like, 'Hey, Abe, you really tweaked the Major's balls, din'tchoo?' It was so funny I just kept on going. I tell you," Abraham said, smiling morbidly, "it got to be a real laff riot. Everybody thought I was just gonna go on tweaking the Major's balls to the very end. Which was what I did. Then one morning I woke up and I was in. I was a Prime Walker, sixteenth out of the drum, as a matter of fact. So I guess it turned out the Major was tweaking *my* balls."

An abortive little cheer went through the Walkers, and Garraty glanced up. A huge reflector sign overhead informed them: AUGUSTA 10.

"You could just die laughing, right?" Collie said.

Abraham looked at Parker for a long time. "The Founding Father is not amused," he said hollowly.

Chapter 14

"And remember, if you use your hands,
   or gesture with any part of your body,
   or use any part of the word, you will forfeit
   your chance for the ten thousand dollars.
   Just give a list. Good luck."
            —Dick Clark
            The Ten Thousand Dollar Pyramid

They had all pretty much agreed that there was little emotional stretch or recoil left in them. But apparently, Garraty thought tiredly as they walked into the roaring darkness along U.S. 202 with Augusta a mile behind them, it was not so. Like a badly treated guitar that has been knocked about by an unfeeling musician, the strings were not broken but only out of tune, discordant, chaotic.

Augusta hadn't been like Oldtown. Oldtown had been a phony hick New York. Augusta was some new city, a once-a-year city of crazy revelers, a party-down city full of a million boogying drunks and cuckoo birds and out-and-out maniacs.

They had heard Augusta and seen Augusta long before they had reached Augusta. The image of waves beating on a distant shore recurred to Garraty again and again. They heard the crowd five miles out. The lights filled the sky with a bubble-like pastel glow that was frightening and apocalyptic, reminding Garraty of pictures he had seen in the history books of the German air-blitz of the American East Coast during the last days of World War II.

They stared at each other uneasily and bunched closer together like small boys in a lightning storm or cows in a blizzard. There was a raw redness in that swelling sound of Crowd. A hunger that was numbing. Garraty had a vivid and scary image of the great god Crowd clawing its way out of the Augusta basin on scarlet spider-legs and devouring them all alive.

The town itself had been swallowed, strangled, and buried. In a very real sense there was no Augusta, and there were no more fat ladies, or pretty girls, or pompous men, or wet-crotched children waving puffy clouds of cotton candy. There was no bustling Italian man here to throw slices of watermelon. Only Crowd, a creature with no body, no head, no mind. Crowd was nothing but a Voice and an Eye, and it was not surprising that Crowd was both God and Mammon. Garraty felt it. He knew the others were feeling it. It was like walking between giant electrical pylons, feeling the tingles and shocks stand every hair on end, making the tongue jitter nuttily in the mouth, making the eyes seem to crackle and shoot off sparks as they rolled in their beds of moisture. Crowd was to be pleased. Crowd was to be worshiped and feared. Ultimately, Crowd was to be made sacrifice unto.

They plowed through ankle-deep drifts of confetti. They lost each other and found each other in a sheeting blizzard of magazine streamers. Garraty snatched a paper out of the dark and crazy air at random and found himself looking at a Charles Atlas body-building ad. He grabbed another one and was brought face-to-face with John Travolta.

And at the height of the excitement, at the top of the first hill on 202, overlooking the mobbed turnpike behind and the gorged and glutted town at their feet, two huge purple-white spotlights split the air ahead of them and the Major was there, drawing away from them in his jeep like an hallucination, holding his salute ramrod stiff, incredibly, fantastically oblivious of the crowd in the gigantic throes of its labor all around him.

And the Walkers—the strings were not broken on their emotions, only badly out-of-tune. They had cheered wildly with hoarse and totally unheard voices, the thirty-seven of them that were left. The crowd could not know they were cheering but somehow they did, somehow they understood that the circle between death-worship and death-wish had been completed for another year and the crowd went completely loopy, convulsing itself in greater and greater paroxysms. Garraty felt a stabbing, needling pain in the left side of his chest and was still unable to stop cheering, even though he understood he was driving at the very brink of disaster.

A shifty-eyed Walker named Milligan saved them all by falling to his knees, his eyes squeezed shut and his hands pressed to his temples, as if he were trying to hold his brains in. He slid forward on the end of his nose, abrading the tip of it on the road like soft chalk on a rough blackboard—how amazing, Garraty thought, that kid's wearing his nose away on the road—and then Milligan was mercifully blasted. After that the Walkers stopped cheering. Garraty was badly scared by the pain in his chest that was subsiding only partially. He promised that was the end of the craziness.

"We getting close to your girl?" Parker asked. He had not weakened, but he had mellowed. Garraty liked him okay now.

"About fifty miles. Maybe sixty. Give or take."

"You're one lucky sonofabitch, Garraty," Parker said wistfully.

"I am?" He was surprised. He turned to see if Parker was laughing at him. Parker wasn't.

"You're gonna see your girl and your mother. Who the hell am I going to see between now and the end? No one but these pigs." He gestured with his middle finger at the crowd, which seemed to take the gesture as a salute and cheered him deliriously. "I'm homesick," he said. "And scared." Suddenly he screamed at the crowd: *"Pigs! You pigs!"* They cheered him more loudly than ever.

"I'm scared, too. And homesick. I . . . I mean *we* . . ." He groped. "We're all too far away from home. The road keeps us away. I may see them, but I won't be able to touch them."

"The rules say—"

"I know what the rules say. Bodily contact with anyone I wish, as long as I don't leave the road. But it's not the same. There's a wall."

"Fuckin' easy for you to talk. You're going to see them, just the same."

"Maybe that'll only make it worse," McVries said. He had come quietly up behind them. They had just passed under a blinking yellow warning flasher at the Winthrop intersection. Garraty could see it waxing and waning on the pavement after they had passed it, a fearful yellow eye, opening and closing.

"You're all crazy," Parker said amiably. "I'm getting out of here." He put on a little speed and had soon nearly disappeared into the blinking shadows.

"He thinks we're queer for each other," McVries said, amused.

"He *what*?" Garraty's head snapped up.

"He's not such a bad guy," McVries said thoughtfully. He cocked a humorous eye at Garraty. "Maybe he's even half-right. Maybe that's why I saved your ass. Maybe I'm queer for you."

"With a face like mine? I thought you perverts liked the willowy type." Still, he was suddenly uneasy.

Suddenly, shockingly, McVries said: "Would you let me jerk you off?"

Garraty hissed in breath. "What the hell—"

"Oh, shut up," McVries said crossly. "Where do you get off with all this self-righteous shit? I'm not even going to make it any easier by letting you know if I'm joking. What say?"

Garraty felt a sticky dryness in his throat. The thing was, he wanted to be touched. Queer, not queer, that didn't seem to matter now that they were all busy dying. All that mattered was McVries. He didn't want McVries to touch him, not that way.

"Well, I suppose you did save my life—" Garraty let it hang.

McVries laughed. "I'm supposed to feel like a heel because you owe me something and I'm taking advantage? Is that it?"

"Do what you want," Garraty said shortly. "But quit playing games."

"Does that mean yes?"

"Whatever you want!" Garraty yelled. Pearson, who had been staring, nearly hypnotized, at his feet, looked up, startled. "Whatever you goddam want!" Garraty yelled.

McVries laughed again. "You're all right, Ray. Never doubt it." He clapped Garraty's shoulder and dropped back.

Garraty stared after him, mystified.

"He just can't get enough," Pearson said tiredly.

"Huh?"

"Almost two hundred and fifty miles," Pearson groaned. "My feet are like lead with poison inside them. My back's burning. And that screwed-up McVries doesn't have enough yet. He's like a starving man gobbling up laxatives."

"He wants to be hurt, do you think?"

"Jesus, what do you think? He ought to be wearing a BEAT ME HARD sign. I wonder what he's trying to make up for."

"I don't know," Garraty said. He was going to

add something else, but saw Pearson wasn't listening anymore. He was watching his feet again, his weary features drawn in lines of horror. He had lost his shoes. The dirty white athletic socks on his feet made gray-white arcs in the darkness.

They passed a sign that said LEWISTON 32 and a mile beyond that an arched electric sign that proclaimed GARRATY 47 in lightbulb lettering.

Garraty wanted to doze but was unable. He knew what Pearson meant about his back. His own spine felt like a blue rod of fire. The muscles at the backs of his legs were open, flaming sores. The numbness in his feet was being replaced by an agony much more sharp and defined than any that had gone before. He was no longer hungry, but he ate a few concentrates anyway. Several Walkers were nothing but flesh-covered skeletons—concentration-camp horrors. Garraty didn't want to get like that . . . but of course he was, anyway. He ran a hand up his side and played the xylophone on his ribs.

"I haven't heard from Barkovitch lately," he said in an effort to raise Pearson from his dreadful concentration—it was altogether too much like Olson reincarnated.

"No. Somebody said one of his legs went stiff on him coming through Augusta."

"That right?"

"That's what they said."

Garraty felt a sudden urge to drop back and look at Barkovitch. He was hard to find in the dark and Garraty drew a warning, but finally he spotted Barkovitch, now back in the rear echelon. Barkovitch was scurrying gimpily along, his face set in strained lines of concentration. His eyes were slitted down to a point where they looked like dimes seen edge-on. His jacket was gone. He was talking to himself in a low, strained monotone.

"Hello, Barkovitch," Garraty said.

Barkovitch twitched, stumbled, and was warned his third warning. "There!" Barkovitch screamed shrewishly. "There, see what you did? Are you and your hotshit friends satisfied?"

"You don't look so good," Garraty said.

Barkovitch smiled cunningly. "It's all a part of the Plan. You remember when I told you about the Plan? Didn't believe me. Olson didn't. Davidson neither. Gribble neither." Barkovitch's voice dropped to a succulent whisper, pregnant with spit. "Garraty, I daaanced on their graves!"

"Your leg hurt?" Garraty asked softly. "Say, isn't that awful."

"Just thirty-five left to walk down. They're all going to fall apart tonight. You'll see. There won't be a dozen left on the road when the sun comes up. You'll see. You and your diddy-bop friends, Garraty. All dead by morning. Dead by *midnight*."

Garraty felt suddenly very strong. He knew that Barkovitch would go soon now. He wanted to break into a run, bruised kidneys and aching spine and screaming feet and all, run and tell McVries he was going to be able to keep his promise.

"What will you ask for?" Garraty said aloud. "When you win?"

Barkovitch grinned gleefully as if he had been waiting for the question. In the uncertain light his face seemed to crumple and squeeze as if pushed and pummeled by giant hands. "Plastic feet," he whispered. "Plaaastic feet, Garraty. I'm just gonna have these ones cut off, fuck 'em if they can't take a joke. I'll have new plastic feet put on and put these ones in a laundromat washing machine and watch them go around and around and around—"

"I thought maybe you'd wish for friends," Garraty said sadly. A heady sense of triumph, suffocating and enthralling, roared through him.

"Friends?"

"Because you don't have any," Garraty said pityingly. "We'll all be glad to see you die. No one's going to miss *you*, Gary. Maybe I'll walk behind you and spit on your brains after they blow them all over the road. Maybe I'll do that. Maybe we all will." It was crazy, crazy, as if his whole head was flying off, it was like when he had swung the barrel of the air rifle at Jimmy, the blood . . . Jimmy screamed . . . his whole head had gone heat-hazy with the savage, primitive justice of it.

"Don't hate me," Barkovitch was whining, "why do you want to hate me? I don't want to die any more than you do. What do you want? Do you want me to be sorry? I'll be sorry! I . . . I . . ."

"We'll all spit in your brains," Garraty said crazily. "Do you want to touch me too?"

Barkovitch looked at him palely, his eyes confused and vacant.

"I . . . I'm sorry," Garraty whispered. He felt degraded and dirty. He hurried away from Barkovitch. Damn you McVries, he thought, why? Why?

All at once the guns roared, and there were two of them falling down dead at once and one of them *had* to be Barkovitch, *had* to be. And this time it was his fault, he was the murderer.

Then Barkovitch was laughing. Barkovitch was cackling, higher and madder and even more audible than the madness of the crowd. "Garraty! Gaaarrratee! I'll dance on your grave, Garraty! I'll *daaaance*—"

"Shut up!" Abraham yelled. "Shut up, you little prick!"

Barkovitch stopped, then began to sob.

"Go to hell," Abraham muttered.

"Now you did it," Collie Parker said reproachfully. "You made him cry, Abe, you bad boy. He's gonna go home and tell his mommy."

Barkovitch continued to sob. It was an empty, ashy sound that made Garraty's skin crawl. There was no hope in it.

"Is little uggy-wuggy gonna tell Mommy?" Quince called back. "Ahhhh, Barkovitch, ain't that too *bad*?"

Leave him alone, Garraty screamed out in his mind, leave him alone, you have no idea how bad he's hurting. But what kind of lousy hypocritical thought was that? He wanted Barkovitch to die. Might as well admit it. He wanted Barkovitch to crack up and croak off.

And Stebbins was probably back there in the dark laughing at them all.

He hurried, caught up with McVries, who was ambling along and staring idly at the crowd. The crowd was staring back at him avidly.

"Why don't you help me decide?" McVries said.

"Sure. What's the topic for decision?"

"Who's in the cage. Us or them."

Garraty laughed with genuine pleasure. "All of us. And the cage is in the Major's monkey house."

McVries didn't join in Garraty's laughter. "Barkovitch is going over the high side, isn't he?"

"Yes, I think so."

"I don't want to see it anymore. It's lousy. And it's a cheat. You build it all around something . . . set yourself on something . . . and then you don't want it. Isn't it too bad the great truths are all such lies?"

"I never thought much about it. Do you realize it's almost ten o'clock?"

"It's like practicing pole-vaulting all your life and then getting to the Olympics and saying, 'What the hell do I want to jump over that stupid bar for?' "

"Yeah."

"You almost could care, right?" McVries said, nettled.

"It's getting harder to work me up," Garraty admitted. He paused. Something had been troubling him badly for some time now. Baker had joined them. Garraty looked from Baker to McVries and then back again. "Did you see Olson's . . . did you see his hair? Before he bought it?"

"What about his hair?" Baker asked.

"It was going gray."

"No, that's crazy," McVries said, but he suddenly sounded very scared. "No, it was dust or something."

"It was gray," Garraty said. "It seems like we've been on this road forever. It was Olson's hair getting . . . getting that way that made me think of it first, but . . . maybe this is some crazy kind of immortality." The thought was terribly depressing. He stared straight ahead into the darkness, feeling the soft wind against his face.

"I walk, I did walk, I will walk, I will have walked," McVries chanted. "Shall I translate into Latin?"

We're suspended in time, Garraty thought.

Their feet moved but they did not. The cherry cigarette glows in the crowd, the occasional flashlight or flaring sparkler might have been stars, weird low constellations that marked their existence ahead and behind, narrowing into nothing both ways.

"Bruh," Garraty said, shivering. "A guy could go crazy."

"That's right," Pearson agreed, and then laughed nervously. They were starting up a long, twisting hill. The road was now expansion-jointed concrete, hard on the feet. It seemed to Garraty that he felt every pebble through the paper-thinness of his shoes. The frisky wind had scattered shallow drifts of candy wrappers, popcorn boxes, and other assorted muck in their way. At some places they almost had to fight their way through. It's not fair, Garraty thought self-pityingly.

"What's the layout up ahead?" McVries asked him apologetically.

Garraty closed his eyes and tried to make a map in his head. "I can't remember all the little towns. We come to Lewiston, that's the second-biggest city in the state, bigger than Augusta. We go right down the main drag. It used to be Lisbon Street, but now it's Cotter Memorial Avenue. Reggie Cotter was the only guy from Maine to ever win the Long Walk. It happened a long time ago."

"He died, didn't he?" Baker said.

"Yeah. He hemorrhaged in one eye and finished the Walk half-blind. It turned out he had a blood clot on his brain. He died a week or so after the Walk." And in a feeble effort to remove the onus, Garraty repeated: "It was a long time ago."

No one spoke for a while. Candy wrappers crackled under their feet like the sound of a faraway forest fire. A cherry bomb went off in the crowd. Garraty could see a faint lightness on the horizon that was probably the twin cities of Lewiston and Auburn, the land of Dussettes and Aubuchons and Lavesques, the land of *Nous parlons francais ici*. Suddenly Garraty had a nearly obsessive craving for a stick of gum.

"What's after Lewiston?"

"We go down Route 196, then along 126 to Freeport, where I'm going to see my mom and my girl. That's also where we get on U.S. 1. And that's where we stay until it's over."

"The big highway," McVries muttered.

"Sure."

The guns blasted and they all jumped.

"It was Barkovitch or Quince," Pearson said. "I can't tell . . . one of them's still walking . . . it's—"

Barkovitch laughed out of the darkness, a high, gobbling sound, thin and terrifying. "Not yet, you whores! I ain't gone yet! Not *yeeeeeettttt* . . ."

His voice kept climbing and climbing. It was like a fire whistle gone insane. And Barkovitch's hands suddenly went up like startled doves taking flight and Barkovitch ripped out his own throat.

"My *Jesus*!" Parson wailed, and threw up over himself.

They fled from him, fled and scattered ahead and behind, and Barkovitch went on screaming and gobbling and clawing and walking, his feral face turned up to the sky, his mouth a twisted curve of darkness.

Then the fire-whistle sound began to fail, and Barkovitch failed with it. He fell down and they shot him, dead or alive.

Garraty turned around and walked forward again. He was dimly grateful that he hadn't been warned. He saw a carbon copy of his horror on the faces of all about him. The Barkovitch part of it was over. Garraty thought it did not bode well for the rest of them, for their future on this dark and bloody road.

"I don't feel good," Pearson said. His voice was flat. He dry-retched and walked doubled over for a moment. "Oh. Not so good. Oh God. I don't. Feel. So good. Oh."

McVries looked straight ahead. "I think ... I wish I were insane," he said thoughtfully.

Only Baker said nothing. And that was odd, because Garraty suddenly got a whiff of Louisiana honeysuckle. He could hear the croak of the frogs in the bottoms. He could feel the sweaty, lazy hum of cicadas digging into the tough cypress bark for their dreamless seventeen-year sleep. And he could see Baker's aunt rocking back and forth, her eyes dreamy and smiley and vacant, sitting on her porch and listening to the static and hum and faraway voices on an old Philco radio with a chipped and cracked mahogany cabinet. Rocking and rocking and rocking. Smiling, sleepy. Like a cat that has been into the cream and is well satisfied.

Chapter 15

"I don't care if you win or lose, just
as long as you win."
—Vince Lombardi
Ex–Green Bay Packers Head Coach

Daylight came in creeping through a white, muted
world of fog. Garraty was walking by himself again.
He no longer even knew how many had bought it
in the night. Five, maybe. His feet had headaches.
Terrible migraines. He could feel them swelling
each time he put his weight on them. His buttocks
hurt. His spine was icy fire. But his feet had headaches and the blood was coagulating in them and
swelling them and turning the veins to *al dente*
spaghetti.

And still there was a worm of excitement growing in his guts: they were now only thirteen miles
out of Freeport. They were in Porterville now, and
the crowd could barely see them through the dense
fog, but they had been chanting his name rhythmically since Lewiston. It was like the pulse of a
giant heart.

Freeport and Jan, he thought.

"Garraty?" The voice was familiar but washed

out. It was McVries. His face was a furry skull. His eyes were glittering feverishly. "Good morning," McVries croaked. "We live to fight another day."

"Yeah. How many got it last night, McVries?"

"Six." McVries dug a jar of bacon spread out of his belt and began to finger it into his mouth. His hands were shaking badly. "Six since Barkovitch." He put the jar back with an old man's palsied care. "Pearson bought it."

"Yeah?"

"There's not many of us left, Garraty. Only twenty-six."

"No, not many." Walking through the fog was like walking through weightless clouds of mothdust.

"Not many of *us*, either. The Musketeers. You and me and Baker and Abraham. Collie Parker. And Stebbins. If you want to count him in. Why not? Why the fuck not? Let's count Stebbins in, Garraty. Six Musketeers and twenty spear-carriers."

"Do you still think I'll win?"

"Does it always get this foggy up here in the spring?"

"What's that mean?"

"No, I don't think you'll win. It's Stebbins, Ray. Nothing can wear him down, he's like diamonds. The word is Vegas likes him nine-to-one now that Scramm's out of it. Christ, he looks almost the same now as when we started."

Garraty nodded as if expecting this. He found his tube of beef concentrate and began to eat it.

What he wouldn't have given for some of McVries's long-gone raw hamburger.

McVries snuffled a little and wiped a hand across his nose. "Doesn't it seem strange to you? Being back on your home stomping grounds after all of this?"

Garraty felt the worm of excitement wriggle and turn again. "No," he said. "It seems like the most natural thing in the world."

They walked down a long hill, and McVries glanced up into white drive-in screen nothing. "The fog's getting worse."

"It's not fog," Garraty said. "It's rain now."

The rain fell softly, as if it had no intention of stopping for a very long time.

"Where's Baker?"

"Back there someplace," McVries said.

Without a word—words were almost unnecessary now—Garraty began dropping back. The road took them past a traffic island, past the rickety Porterville Rec Center with its five lanes of candlepins, past a dead black Government Sales building with a large MAY IS CONFIRM-YOUR-SEX MONTH sign in the window.

In the fog Garraty missed Baker and ended up walking beside Stebbins. Hard like diamonds, McVries had said. But this diamond was showing some small flaws, he thought. Now they were walking parallel to the mighty and dead-polluted Androscoggin River. On the other side the Porterville Weaving Company, a textile mill, reared its turrets into the fog like a filthy medieval castle.

Stebbins didn't look up, but Garraty knew Stebbins knew he was there. He said nothing, foolishly determined to make Stebbins say the first word. The road curved again. For a moment the crowd was gone as they crossed the bridge spanning the Androscoggin. Beneath them the water boiled along, sullen and salty, dressed with cheesy yellow foam.

"Well?"

"Save your breath for a minute," Garraty said. "You'll need it."

They came to the end of the bridge and the crowd was with them again as they swung left and started up the Brickyard Hill. It was long, steep, and banked. The river was dropping away below them on the left, and on their right was an almost perpendicular upslope. Spectators clung to trees, to bushes, to each other, and chanted Garraty's name. Once he had dated a girl who lived on Brickyard Hill, a girl named Carolyn. She was married now. Had a kid. She might have let him, but he was young and pretty dumb.

From up ahead Parker was giving a whispery, out-of-breath *goddam!* that was barely audible over the crowd. Garraty's legs quivered and threatened to go to jelly, but this was the last big hill before Freeport. After that it didn't matter. If he went to hell he went to hell. Finally they breasted it (Carolyn had nice breasts, she often wore cashmere sweaters) and Stebbins, panting just a little, repeated: "Well?"

The guns roared. A boy named Charlie Field bowed out of the Walk.

"Well, nothing," Garraty said. "I was looking for Baker and found you instead. McVries says he thinks you'll win."

"McVries is an idiot," Stebbins said casually. "You really think you'll see your girl, Garraty? In all these people?"

"She'll be in the front," Garraty said. "She's got a pass."

"The cops'll be too busy holding everybody back to get her through to the front."

"That isn't true," Garraty said. He spoke sharply because Stebbins had articulated his own deep fear. "Why do you want to say a thing like that?"

"It's really your mother you want to see anyway."

Garraty recoiled sharply. "What?"

"Aren't you going to marry her when you grow up, Garraty? That's what most little boys want."

"You're crazy!"

"Am I?"

"Yes!"

"What makes you think you deserve to win, Garraty? You're a second-class intellect, a second-class physical specimen, and probably a second-class libido. Garraty, I'd bet my dog and lot you never slipped it to that girl of yours."

"Shut your goddam mouth!"

"Virgin, aren't you? Maybe a little bit queer in the bargain? Touch of the lavender? Don't be afraid. You can talk to Papa Stebbins."

"I'll walk you down if I have to walk to Virginia,

you cheap fuck!" Garraty was shaking with anger. He could not remember being so angry in his whole life.

"That's okay," Stebbins said soothingly. "I understand."

"Motherfucker! You!—"

"Now *there's* an interesting word. What made you use *that* word?"

For a moment Garraty was sure he must throw himself on Stebbins or faint with rage, yet he did neither. "If I have to walk to Virginia," he repeated. "If I have to walk all the way to Virginia."

Stebbins stretched up on his toes and grinned sleepily. "*I* feel like I could walk all the way to Florida, Garraty."

Garraty lunged away from him, hunting for Baker, feeling the anger and rage die into a throbbing kind of shame. He supposed Stebbins thought he was an easy mark. He supposed he was.

Baker was walking beside a boy Garraty didn't know. His head was down, his lips moving a little.

"Hey, Baker," Garraty said.

Baker started, then seemed to shake himself all over, like a dog. "Garraty," he said. "You."

"Yea, me."

"I was having a dream—an awful real one. What time?"

Garraty checked. "Almost twenty to seven."

"Will it rain all day, you think?"

"I . . . *uh!*" Garraty lurched forward, momentarily off balance. "My damn shoeheel came off," he said.

"Get rid of 'em both," Baker advised. "The nails will get to pokin' through. And you have to work harder when you're off balance."

Garraty kicked off one shoe and it went end over end almost to the edge of the crowd, where it lay like a small crippled puppy. The hands of Crowd groped for it eagerly. One snared it, another took it away, and there was a violent, knotted struggle over it. His other shoe would not kick off; his foot had swelled tight inside it. He knelt, took his warning, untied it, and took it off. He considered throwing it to the crowd and then left it lying on the road instead. A great and irrational wave of despair suddenly washed over him and he thought: *I have lost my shoes. I have lost my shoes.*

The pavement was cold against his feet. The ripped remains of his stockings were soon soaked. Both feet looked strange, oddly lumpish. Garraty felt despair turn to pity for his feet. He caught up quickly with Baker, who was also walking shoeless. "I'm about done in," Baker said simply.

"We all are."

"I get to remembering all the nice things that ever happened to me. The first time I took a girl to a dance and there was this big ole drunk fella that kep tryin' to cut in and I took him outside and whipped his ass for him. I was only able to because he was so drunk. And that girl looked at me like I was the greatest thing since the internal combustion engine. My first bike. The first time I read *The Woman in White,* by Wilkie Collins . . . that's my favorite book, Garraty, should anyone ever ask you. Sittin' half asleep by some mudhole with a fishin' line and catchin' crawdaddies by the thousands. Layin' in the backyard and sleepin' with a *Popeye* funnybook over my face. I think about those things, Garraty. Just lately. Like I was old and gettin' senile."

The early morning rain fell silverly around them. Even the crowd seemed quieter, more withdrawn. Faces could be seen again, blurrily, like faces behind rainy panes of glass. They were pale, sloe-eyed faces with brooding expressions under dripping hats and umbrellas and spread newspaper tents. Garraty felt a deep ache inside him and it seemed it would be better if he could cry out, but he could not, any more than he could comfort Baker and tell him it was all right to die. It might be, but then again, it might not.

"I hope it won't be dark," Baker said. "That's all I hope. If there is an ... an after, I hope it's not dark. And I hope you can *remember*. I'd hate to wander around in the dark forever, not knowing who I was or what I was doin' there, or not even knowing that I'd ever had anything different."

Garraty began to speak, and then the gunshots silenced him. Business was picking up again. The hiatus Parker had so accurately predicted was almost over. Baker's lips drew up in a grimace.

"That's what I'm most afraid of. That sound. Why did we do it, Garraty? We must have been insane."

"I don't think there was any good reason."

"All we are is mice in a trap."

The Walk went on. Rain fell. They walked past the places that Garraty knew—tumbledown shanties where no one lived, an abandoned one-room schoolhouse that had been replaced by the new Consolidated building, chicken houses, old trucks up on blocks, newly harrowed fields. He seemed to remember each field, each house. Now he tingled with excitement. The road seemed to fly by. His legs seemed to gain a new and spurious springiness. But maybe Stebbins was right—maybe she wouldn't be there. It had to be considered and prepared for, at least.

The word came back through the thinned ranks that there was a boy near the front who believed he had appendicitis.

Garraty would have boggled at this earlier, but now he couldn't seem to care about anything except Jan and Freeport. The hands on his watch were racing along with a devilish life of their own. Only five miles out now. They had passed the Freeport town line. Somewhere up ahead Jan and his mother were already standing in front of Woolman's Free Trade Center Market, as they had arranged it.

The sky brightened somewhat but remained overcast. The rain turned to a stubborn drizzle. The road was now a dark mirror, black ice in which Garraty could almost see the twisted reflection of his own face. He passed a hand across his forehead. It felt hot and feverish. Jan, oh Jan. You must know I—

The boy with the hurting side was 59, Klinger-man. He began to scream. His screams quickly be-came monotonous. Garraty thought back to the one Long Walk he had seen—also in Freeport—and the boy who had been monotonously chant-ing *I can't. I can't. I can't.*

Klingerman, he thought, shut ya trap.

But Klingerman kept on walking, and he kept on screaming, hands laced over his side, and Gar-raty's watch hands kept on racing. It was eight-fifteen now. You'll be there, Jan, right? Right. Okay. I don't know what you mean anymore, but I know I'm still alive and that I need you to be there, to give me a sign, maybe. Just be there. Be there.

Eight-thirty.

"We gettin' close to this goddam town, Garraty?" Parker hollered.

"What do *you* care?" McVries jeered. "You sure don't have a girl waiting for you."

"I got girls everywhere, you dumb hump," Parker said. "They take one look at this face and cream in their silks." The face to which he referred was now haggard and gaunt, just a shadow of what it had been.

Eighty forty-five.

"Slow down, fella," McVries said as Garraty caught up with him and started to pass by. "Save a little for tonight."

"I can't. Stebbins said she wouldn't be there. That they wouldn't have a man to spare to help her through. I have to find out. I have to—"

"Just take it easy is all I'm saying. Stebbins would

get his own mother to drink a Lysol cocktail if it would help him win. Don't listen to him. She'll be there. It makes great PR, for one thing."

"But—"

"But me no buts, Ray. Slow down and live."

"You can just cram your fucking platitudes!" Garraty shouted. He licked his lips and put a shaky hand to his face. "I . . . I'm sorry. That was uncalled for. Stebbins also said I really only wanted to see my mother anyway."

"Don't you want to see her?"

"Of course I want to see her! What the hell do you think I—no—yes—I don't know. I had a friend once. And he and I—we—we took off our clothes— and she—she—"

"Garraty," McVries said, and put a hand to touch his shoulder. Klingerman was screaming very loudly now. Somebody near the front lines asked him if he wanted an Alka-Seltzer. This sally brought general laughter. "You're falling apart, Garraty. Settle down. Don't blow it."

"*Get off my back!*" Garraty screamed. He crammed one fist against his lips and bit down on it. After a second he said, "Just get off me."

"Okay. Sure."

McVries strode away. Garraty wanted to call him back but couldn't.

Then, for the fourth time, it was nine o'clock in the morning. They turned left and the crowd was again below the twenty-four of them as they crossed the 295 overpass and into the town of Freeport. Up

ahead was the Dairy Joy where he and Jan sometimes used to stop after the movies. They turned
right and were on U.S. 1, what somebody had
called the big highway. Big or small, it was the last
highway. The hands on Garraty's watch seemed to
jump out at him. Downtown was straight ahead.
Woolman's was on the right. He could just see it, a
squat and ugly building hiding behind a false front.
The tickertape was starting to fall again. The rain
made it sodden and sticky, lifeless. The crowd was
swelling. Someone turned on the town fire siren,
and its wails mixed and blended with Klingerman's. Klingerman and the Freeport fire siren sang
a nightmarish duet.

Tension filled Garraty's veins, stuffed them full
of copper wire. He could hear his heart thudding,
now in his guts, now in his throat, now right between the eyes. Two hundred yards. They were
screaming his name again (*RAY-RAY-ALL-THE-
WAY!*) but he had not seen a familiar face in the
crowd yet.

He drifted over to the right until the clutching
hands of Crowd were inches from him—one long
and brawny arm actually twitched the cloth of his
shirt, and he jumped back as if he had almost been
drawn into a threshing machine—and the soldiers
had their guns on him, ready to let fly if he tried to
disappear into the surge of humanity. Only a hundred yards to go now. He could see the big brown
Woolman's sign, but no sign of his mother or of
Jan. God, oh God God, Stebbins had been right . . .

and even if they were here, how was he going to see them in this shifting, clutching mass?

A shaky groan seeped out of him, like a disgorged strand of flesh. He stumbled and almost fell over his own loose legs. Stebbins had been right. He wanted to stop here, to not go any further. The disappointment, the sense of loss, was so staggering it was hollow. What was the point? What was the point now?

Fire siren blasting, Crowd screaming, Klingerman shrieking, rain falling, and his own little tortured soul, flapping through his head and crashing blindly off its walls.

I can't go on. Can't, can't, can't. But his feet stumbled on. *Where am I? Jan? Jan? . . . JAN!*

He saw her. She was waving the blue silk scarf he had gotten her for her birthday, and the rain shimmered in her hair like gems. His mother was beside her, wearing her plain black coat. They had been jammed together by the mob and were being swayed helplessly back and forth. Over Jan's shoulder a TV camera poked its idiot snout.

A great sore somewhere in his body seemed to burst. The infection ran out of him in a green flood. He burst into a shambling, pigeon-toed run. His ripped socks flapped and slapped his swollen feet.

"Jan! Jan!"

He could hear the thought but not the words in his mouth. The TV camera tracked him enthusiastically. The din was tremendous. He could see her lips form his name, and he had to reach her, had to—

An arm brought him up short. It was McVries. A

soldier speaking through a sexless bullhorn was giving them both first warning.

"Not into the crowd!" McVries's lips were against Garraty's ear and he was shouting. A lancet of pain pierced into Garraty's head.

"Let me go!"

"I won't let you kill yourself, Ray!"

"Let me go goddammit!"

"Do you want to die in her arms? Is that it?"

The time was fleeting. She was crying. He could see the tears on her cheeks. He wrenched free of McVries. He started for her again. He felt hard, angry sobs coming up from inside him. He wanted sleep. He would find it in her arms. He loved her.

Ray, I love you.

He could see the words on her lips.

McVries was still beside him. The TV camera glared down. Now, peripherally, he could see his high school class, and they were unfurling a huge banner and somehow it was his own face, his yearbook photo, blown up to Godzilla size, he was grinning down at himself as he cried and struggled to reach her.

Second warning, blared from the loudhailer like the voice of God.

Jan—

She was reaching out to him. Hands touching. Her cool hand. Her tears—

His mother. Her hands, reaching—

He grasped them. In one hand he held Jan's hand, in the other his mother's hand. He touched them. It was done.

It was done until McVries's arm came down around his shoulder again, cruel McVries.

"Let me *go*! Let me *go*!"

"Man, you must really hate her!" McVries screamed in his ear. "What do you want? To die knowing they're both stinking with your blood? Is that what you want? For Christ's sake, come on!"

He struggled, but McVries was strong. Maybe McVries was even right. He looked at Jan and now her eyes were wide with alarm. His mother made shooing gestures. And on Jan's lips he could read the words like a damnation: *Go on! Go on!*

Of course I must go on, he thought dully. I am Maine's Own. And in that second he hated her, although if he had done anything, it was no more than to catch her—and his mother—in the snare he had laid for himself.

Third warning for him and McVries, rolling majestically like thunder; the crowd hushed a little and looked on with wet-eyed eagerness. Now there was panic written on the faces of Jan and his mother. His mother's hands flew to her face, and he thought of Barkovitch's hands flying up to his neck and startled doves and ripping out his own throat.

"If you've got to do it, do it around the next corner, you cheap shit!" McVries cried.

He began to whimper. McVries had beaten him again. McVries was very strong. "All right," he said, not knowing if McVries could hear him or not. He began to walk. "All right, all right, let me loose before you break my collarbone." He sobbed, hiccuped, wiped his nose.

McVries let go of him warily, ready to grab him again.

Almost as an afterthought, Garraty turned and looked back, but they were already lost in the crowd again. He thought he would never forget that look of panic rising in their eyes, that feeling of trust and sureness finally kicked brutally away. He got nothing but half a glimpse of a waving blue scarf.

He turned around and faced forward again, not looking at McVries, and his stumbling, traitorous feet carried him on and they walked out of town.

Chapter 16

"The blood has begun to flow! Liston is staggering!
Clay is rocking him with combinations! . . .
boring in! Clay is killing him! Clay is killing him!
Ladies and gentlemen, Liston is down!
Sonny Liston is down! Clay is dancing . . .
waving . . . yelling into the crowd!
Oh, ladies and gentlemen, I don't know how
to describe this scene!"

—Radio Commentator
Second Clay-Liston Fight

Tubbins had gone insane.

Tubbins was a short boy with glasses and a face-ful of freckles. He wore hip-hanging bluejeans that he had been constantly hitching up. He hadn't said much, but he had been a nice enough sort before he went insane.

"WHORE!" Tubbins babbled to the rain. He had turned his face up into it, and the rain dripped off his specs onto his cheeks and over his lips and down off the end of his blunted chin. "THE WHORE OF BABYLON HAS COME AMONG US! SHE LIES IN THE STREETS AND SPREADS HER LEGS ON THE FILTH OF COBBLESTONES! VILE! VILE! BEWARE THE WHORE OF BABYLON! HER LIPS DRIP HONEY BUT HER HEART IS GALL AND WORMWOOD—"

"And she's got the clap," Collie Parker added

tiredly. "Jeezus, he's worse than Klingerman." He raised his voice. "Drop down dead, Tubby!"

"WHOREMONGER AND WHOREMASTER!" shrieked Tubbins. "VILE! UNCLEAN!"

"Piss on him," Parker muttered. "I'll kill him myself if he don't shut up." He passed trembling skeletal fingers across his lips, dropped them to his belt, and spent thirty seconds making them undo the clip that held his canteen to his belt. He almost dropped it getting it to his mouth, and then spilled half of it. He began to weep weakly.

It was three in the afternoon. Portland and South Portland were behind them. About fifteen minutes ago they had passed under a wet and flapping banner that proclaimed that the New Hampshire border was only 44 miles away.

Only, Garraty thought. *Only*, what a stupid little word that is. Who was the idiot who took it into his head that we needed a stupid little word like that?

He was walking next to McVries, but McVries had spoken only in monosyllables since Freeport. Garraty hardly dared speak to him. He was indebted again, and it shamed him. It shamed him because he knew he would not help McVries if the chance came. Now Jan was gone, his mother was gone. Irrevocably and for eternity. Unless he won. And now he wanted to win very badly.

It was odd. This was the first time he could remember wanting to win. Not even at the start, when he had been fresh (back when dinosaurs walked the earth), had he consciously *wanted* to win. There had only been the challenge. But the guns didn't produce little red flags with BANG written on them. It wasn't baseball or Giant Step; it was all real.

Or had he known it all along?

His feet seemed to hurt twice as badly since he had decided he wanted to win, and there were stabbing pains in his chest when he drew long breaths. The sensation of fever was growing—perhaps he had picked something up from Scramm.

He wanted to win, but not even McVries could carry him over the invisible finish line. He didn't think he was going to win. In the sixth grade he had won his school's spelling bee and had gone on to the district spelldown, but the district spellmaster wasn't Miss Petrie, who let you take it back. Softhearted Miss Petrie. He had stood there, hurt, unbelieving, sure there must have been some mistake, but there had been none. He just hadn't been good enough to make the cut then, and he wasn't going to be good enough now. Good enough to walk most of them down, but not all. His feet and legs had gone beyond numb and angry rebellion, and now mutiny was just a step away.

Only three had gone down since they left Freeport. One of them had been the unfortunate Klingerman. Garraty knew what the rest of them were thinking. It was too many tickets issued for them to just quit, any of them. Not with only twenty left to walk over. They would walk now until their bodies or minds shook apart.

They passed over a bridge spanning a placid little brook, its surface lightly pocked by the rain. The guns roared, the crowd cheered, and Garraty felt the stubborn cranny of hope in the back of his brain open an infinitesimal bit more.

"Did your girl look good to you?"

It was Abraham, looking like a victim of the Bataan March. For some inconceivable reason he had shucked both his jacket and his shirt, leaving his bony chest and stacked ribcage bare.

"Yeah," Garraty said. "I hope I can make it back to her."

Abraham smiled. "Hope? Yeah, I'm beginning to remember how to spell that word, too." It was like a mild threat. "Was that Tubbins?"

Garraty listened. He heard nothing but the steady roar of the crowd. "Yeah, by God it was. Parker put the hex on him, I guess."

"I keep telling myself," Abraham said, "that all I got to do is to continue putting one foot in front of the other."

"Yeah."

Abraham looked distressed. "Garraty . . . this is a bitch to say . . ."

"What's that?"

Abraham was quiet for a long time. His shoes were big heavy Oxfords that looked horrendously heavy to Garraty (whose own feet were now bare, cold, and scraping raw). They clopped and dragged on the pavement, which had now expanded to three lanes. The crowd did not seem so loud or quite so terrifyingly close as it had ever since Augusta.

Abraham looked more distressed than ever. "It's a bitch. I just don't know how to say it."

Garraty shrugged, bewildered. "I guess you just say it."

"Well, look. We're getting together on something. All of us that are left."

"Scrabble, maybe?"

"It's a kind of a . . . a promise."

"Oh yeah?"

"No help for anybody. Do it on your own or don't do it."

Garraty looked at his feet. He wondered how long it had been since he was hungry, and he wondered how long it would be before he fainted if he didn't eat something. He thought that Abraham's Oxfords were like Stebbins—those shoes could carry him from here to the Golden Gate Bridge without so much as a busted shoelace . . . at least they looked that way.

"That sounds pretty heartless," he said finally.

"It's gotten to be a pretty heartless situation." Abraham wouldn't look at him.

"Have you talked to all the others about this?"

"Not yet. About a dozen."

"Yeah, it's a real bitch. I can see how hard it is for you to talk about."

"It seems to get harder rather than easier."

"What did they say?" He knew what they said, what were they supposed to say?

"They're for it."

Garraty opened his mouth, then shut it. He looked at Baker up ahead. Bake was wearing his jacket, and it was soaked. His head was bent. One hip swayed and jutted awkwardly. His left leg had stiffened up quite badly.

"Why'd you take off your shirt?" he asked Abraham suddenly.

"It was making my skin itch. It was raising hives or something. It was a synthetic, maybe I have an allergy to synthetic fibers, how the hell should I know? What do you say, Ray?"

"You look like a religious penitent or something."

"What do you say? Yes or no?"

"Maybe I owe McVries a couple." McVries was still close by, but it was impossible to tell if he could hear their conversation over the din of the crowd. Come on, McVries, he thought. Tell him I don't owe you anything. Come on, you son of a bitch. But McVries said nothing.

"All right, count me in," Garraty said.

"Cool."

Now I'm an animal, nothing but a dirty, tired, stupid animal. You did it. You sold it out.

"If you try to help anybody, we can't hold you back. That's against the rules. But we'll shut you out. And you'll have broken your promise."

"I won't try."

"Same goes for anyone who tries to help you."

"Yuh."

"It's nothing personal. You know that, Ray. But we're down against it now."

"Root hog or die."

"That's it."

"Nothing personal. Just back to the jungle."

For a second he thought Abraham was going to

get pissed, but his quickly drawn-in breath came out in a harmless sigh. Maybe he was too tired to get pissed. "You agreed. I'll hold you to that, Ray."

"Maybe I should get all high-flown and say I'll keep my promise because my word is my bond," Garraty said. "But I'll be honest. I want to see you get that ticket, Abraham. The sooner the better."

Abraham licked his lips. "Yeah."

"Those look like good shoes, Abe."

"Yeah. But they're too goddam heavy. You buy for distance, you gain the weight."

"Just ain't no cure for the summertime blues, is there?"

Abraham laughed. Garraty watched McVries. His face was unreadable. He might have heard. He might not have. The rain fell in steady straight lines, heavier now, colder. Abraham's skin was fish-belly white. Abraham looked more like a convict with his shirt off. Garraty wondered if anyone had told Abraham he didn't stand a dog's chance of lasting the night with his shirt off. Twilight already seemed to be creeping in. McVries? Did you hear us? I sold you down, McVries. Musketeers forever.

"Ah, I don't want to die this way," Abraham said. He was crying. "Not in public with people rooting for you to get up and walk another few miles. It's so fucking mindless. Just fucking *mindless*. This has about as much dignity as a mongoloid idiot strangling on his own tongue and shitting his pants at the same time."

It was quarter past three when Garraty gave his no help promise. By six that evening, only one more had gotten a ticket. No one talked. There seemed to be an uncomfortable conspiracy afoot to ignore the last fraying inches of their lives, Garraty thought, to just pretend it wasn't happening. The groups—what pitiful little remained of them—had broken down completely. Everyone had agreed to Abraham's proposal. McVries had. Baker had. Stebbins had laughed and asked Abraham if he wanted to prick his finger so he could sign in blood.

It was growing very cold. Garraty began to wonder if there really was such a thing as a sun, or if he had dreamed it. Even Jan was a dream to him now—a summer dream of a summer that never was.

Yet he seemed to see his father ever more clearly. His father with the heavy shock of hair he himself had inherited, and the big, meaty truck-driver's shoulders. His father had been built like a fullback. He could remember his father picking him up, swinging him dizzyingly, rumpling his hair, kissing him. Loving him.

He hadn't really seen his mother back there in Freeport at all, he realized sadly, but she had been there—in her shabby black coat, "for best," the one that showed the white snowfall of dandruff on the collar no matter how often she shampooed. He had probably hurt her deeply by ignoring her in favor of Jan. Perhaps he had even meant to hurt her. But that didn't matter now. It was past. It was the future that was unraveling, even before it was knit.

You get in deeper, he thought. It never gets shallower, just deeper, until you're out of the bay and swimming into the ocean. Once all of this had looked simple. Pretty funny, all right. He had talked to McVries and McVries had told him the first time he had saved him out of pure reflex. Then, in Freeport, it had been to prevent an ugliness in front of a pretty girl he would never know. Just as he would never know Scramm's wife, heavy with child. Garraty had felt a pang at the thought, and sudden sorrow. He had not thought of Scramm in such a long time. He thought McVries was quite grownup, really. He wondered why *he* hadn't managed to grow up any.

The Walk went on. Towns marched by.

He fell into a melancholy, oddly satisfying mood that was shattered quite suddenly by an irregular rattle of gunfire and hoarse screams from the crowd. When he looked around he was stunned to see Collie Parker standing on top of the halftrack with a rifle in his hands.

One of the soldiers had fallen off and lay staring up at the sky with empty, expressionless eyes. There was a neat blue hole surrounded by a corona of powder burns in the center of his forehead.

"Goddam bastards!" Parker was screaming. The other soldiers had jumped from the halftrack. Parker looked out over the stunned Walkers. "Come on, you guys! Come on! We can—"

The Walkers, Garraty included, stared at Parker as if he had begun to speak in a foreign language. And now one of the soldiers who had jumped when Parker swarmed up the side of the 'track now carefully shot Collie Parker in the back.

"Parker!" McVries screamed. It was as if he alone

understood what had happened, and a chance that might have been missed. "Oh, no! *Parker!*"

Parker grunted as if someone had hit him in the back with a padded Indian club. The bullet mushroomed and there was Collie Parker, standing on top of the halftrack with his guts all over his torn khaki shirt and blue jeans. One hand was frozen in the middle of a wide, sweeping gesture, as if he was about to deliver an angry philippic.

"God.

"Damn," Parker said.

He fired the rifle he had wrenched away from the dead soldier twice into the road. The slugs snapped and whined, and Garraty felt one of them tug air in front of his face. Someone in the crowd screamed in pain. Then the gun slid from Parker's hands. He made an almost military half-turn and then fell to the road where he lay on his side, panting rapidly like a dog that has been struck and mortally wounded by a passing car. His eyes blazed. He opened his mouth and struggled through blood for some coda.

"You. Ba. Bas. Bast. Ba." He died, staring viciously at them as they passed by.

"What happened?" Garraty cried out to no one in particular. "What *happened* to him?"

"He snuck up on 'em," McVries said. "That's what happened. He must have known he couldn't make it. He snuck right up behind 'em and caught 'em sleep at the switch." McVries's voice hoarsened. "He wanted us all up there with him, Garraty. And I think we could have done it."

"What are you talking about?" Garraty asked, suddenly terrified.

"You don't know?" McVries asked. "You don't *know*?"

"Up there with him? . . . What? . . ."

"Forget it. Just forget it."

McVries walked away. Garraty had a sudden attack of the shivers. He couldn't stop them. He didn't know what McVries was talking about. He didn't want to know what McVries was talking about. Or even think about it.

The Walk went on.

By nine o'clock that night the rain had stopped, but the sky was starless. No one else had gone down, but Abraham had begun to moan inarticulately. It was very cold, but no one offered to give Abraham something to wear. Garraty tried to think of it as poetic justice, but it only made him feel sick. The pain within him had turned into a sickness, a rotten sick feeling that seemed to be growing in the hollows of his body like a green fungus. His concentrate belt was nearly full, but it was all he could do to eat a small tube of tuna paste without gagging.

Baker, Abraham, and McVries. His circle of friends had come down to those three. And Stebbins, if he was anyone's friend. Acquaintance, then. Or demigod. Or devil. Or whatever. He wondered if any of them would be here by morning, and if he would be alive to know.

Thinking such things, he almost ran into Baker in the dark. Something clinked in Baker's hands.

"What you doing?" Garraty asked.

"Huh?" Baker looked up blankly.

"What're you doing?" Garraty repeated patiently.

"Counting my change."

"How much you got?"

Baker clinked the money in his cupped hands and smiled. "Dollar twenty-two," he said.

Garraty grinned. "A fortune. What you going to do with it?"

Baker didn't smile back. He looked into the cold darkness dreamily. "Git me one of the big ones," he said. His light Southern drawl had thickened appreciably. "Git me a lead-lined one with pink silk insides and a white satin headpillow." He blinked his empty doorknob eyes. "Wouldn't never rot then, not till Judgment Trump, when we are as we were. Clothed in flesh incorruptible."

Garraty felt a warm trickle of horror. "Baker? Have you gone nuts, Baker?"

"You cain't beat it. We-uns was all crazy to try. You cain't beat the rottenness of it. Not in this world. Lead-lined, that's the ticket . . ."

"If you don't get hold of yourself, you'll be dead by morning."

Baker nodded. His skin was drawn tight over his cheekbones, giving him the aspect of a skull. "That's the ticket. I wanted to die. Didn't you? Isn't that why?"

"Shut up!" Garraty yelled. He had the shakes again.

The road sloped sharply up then, cutting off their talk. Garraty leaned into the hill, cold and hot, his spine hurting, his chest hurting. He was sure his muscles would flatly refuse to support him much longer. He thought of Baker's lead-lined box, sealed against the dark millennia, and wondered if it would be the last thing he ever thought of. He hoped not, and struggled for some other mental track.

Warnings cracked out sporadically. The soldiers on the halftrack were back up to the mark; the one Parker had killed had been unobtrusively replaced. The crowd cheered monotonously. Garraty wondered how it would be, to lie in the biggest, dustiest library silence of all, dreaming endless, thoughtless dreams behind gummed-down eyelids, dressed forever in your Sunday suit. No worries about money, success, fear, joy, pain, sorrow, sex, or love. Absolute zero. No father, mother, girlfriend, lover. The dead are orphans. No company but the silence like a moth's wing. An end to the agony of movement, to the long nightmare of going down the road. The body in peace, stillness, and order. The perfect darkness of death.

How would that be? Just how would that be?

And suddenly his roiling, agonized muscles, the sweat running down his face, even the pain itself— seemed very sweet and real. Garraty tried harder. He struggled to the top of the hill and gasped raggedly all the way down the far side.

At 11:40 Marty Wyman bought his hole. Garraty had forgotten all about Wyman, who hadn't spoken or gestured for the last twenty-four hours. He didn't die spectacularly. He just lay down and got shot. And someone whispered, that was Wyman.

And someone else whispered, that's eighty-three, isn't it? And that was all.

By midnight they were only eight miles from the New Hampshire border. They passed a drive-in theater, a huge white oblong in the darkness. A single slide blazed from the screen: THE MANAGEMENT OF THIS THEATRE SALUTES THIS YEAR'S LONG WALKERS! At 12:20 in the morning it began to rain again, and Abraham began to cough—the same kind of wet, ragged cough that had gotten Scramm not long before he bought out. By one o'clock the rain had become a hard, steady downpour that stung Garraty's eyes and made his body ache with a kind of internal ague. The wind drove at their backs.

At quarter past the hour, Bobby Sledge tried to scutter quietly into the crowd under the cover of the dark and the driving rain. He was holed quickly and efficiently. Garraty wondered if the blond soldier who had almost sold him his ticket had done it. He knew the blond was on duty; he had seen his face clearly in the glare from the drive-in spotlights. He wished heartily that the blond had been the one Parker had ticketed.

At twenty of two Baker fell down and hit his head on the paving. Garraty started to go to him without even thinking. A hand, still strong, clamped on his arm. It was McVries. Of course it would have to be McVries.

"No," he said. "No more musketeers. And now it's real."

They walked on without looking back.

Baker collected three warnings, and then the silence stretched out interminably. Garraty waited for the guns to come down, and when they didn't, he checked his watch. Over four minutes had passed. Not long after, Baker walked past him and McVries, not looking at anything. There was an ugly, trickling wound on his forehead, but his eyes looked saner. The vacuous, dazed look was gone.

A little before two AM they crossed into New Hampshire amid the greatest pandemonium yet. Cannons went off. Fireworks burst in the rainy sky, lighting a multitude that stretched away as far as the eye could see in a crazy feverlight. Competing brass bands played martial airs. The cheers were thunder. A great overhead airburst traced the Major's face in fire, making Garraty think numbly of God. This was followed by the face of the New Hampshire Provo Governor, a man known for having stormed the German nuclear base in Santiago nearly single-handed back in 1953. He had lost a leg to radiation poisoning.

Garraty dozed again. His thoughts grew incoherent. Freaky D'Allessio was crouched beneath the rocking chair of Baker's aunt, curled in a tiny coffin. His body was that of a plump Cheshire cat. He was grinning toothily. Faintly, in the fur between his slightly off-center green eyes, were the healed brand-marks of an old baseball wound. They were watching Garraty's father being led to an unmarked black van. One of the soldiers flanking Garraty's father was the blond soldier. Garraty's father was wearing only undershorts.

The other soldier looked back over his shoulder and for a moment Garraty thought it was the Major. Then he saw it was Stebbins. He looked back and the Cheshire cat with Freaky's head had disappeared—all but the grin, which hung crescently in the air under the rocker like the outside edge of a watermelon . . .

The guns were shooting again, God, they were shooting at him now, he felt the air from that one, it was over, all over—

He snapped full awake and took two running steps, sending jolts of pain all the way up from his feet to his groin before he realized they had been shooting at someone else, and the someone else was dead, facedown in the rain.

"Hail Mary," McVries muttered.

"Full of grace," Stebbins said from behind them. He had moved up, moved up for the kill, and he was grinning like the Cheshire cat in Garraty's dream. "Help me win this stock-car race."

"Come on," McVries said. "Don't be a wise-ass."

"My ass is no wiser than your ass," Stebbins said solemnly.

McVries and Garraty laughed—a little uneasily.

"Well," Stebbins said, "maybe a little."

"Pick 'em up, put 'em down, shut your mouth," McVries chanted. He passed a shaky hand across his face and walked on, eyes straight ahead, his shoulders like a broken bow.

One more bought out before three o'clock—shot down in the rain and windy darkness as he went to his knees somewhere near Portsmouth. Abraham, coughing steadily, walked in a hopeless glitter of fever, a kind of death-glow, a brightness that made Garraty think of streaking meteorites. He was going to burn up instead of burning out—that was how tight it had gotten now.

Baker walked with steady, grim determination, trying to get rid of his warnings before they got rid of him. Garraty could just make him out through the slashing rain, limping along with his hands clenched at his sides.

And McVries was caving in. Garraty was not sure when it had begun; it might have happened in a second, while his back was turned. At one moment he had still been strong (Garraty remembered the clamp of McVries's fingers on his lower arm when Baker had fallen), and now he was like an old man. It was unnerving.

Stebbins was Stebbins. He went on and on, like Abraham's shoes. He seemed to be favoring one leg slightly, but it could have been Garraty's imagination.

Of the other ten, five seemed to have drawn into that special netherworld that Olson had discovered—one step beyond pain and the comprehension of what was coming to them. They walked through the rainy dark like gaunt ghosts, and Garraty didn't like to look at them. They were the walking dead.

Just before dawn, three of them went down at once. The mouth of the crowd roared and belched anew with enthusiasm as the bodies spun and thumped like chunks of cut cordwood. To Garraty it seemed the beginning of a dreadful chain reaction that might sweep through them and finish them all. But it ended. It ended with Abraham crawling on his knees, eyes turned blindly up to the halftrack and the crowd beyond, mindless and filled with confused pain. They were the eyes of a sheep caught in a barbed wire fence. Then he fell on his face. His heavy Oxfords drummed fitfully against the wet road and then stopped.

Shortly after, the aqueous symphony of dawn began. The last day of the Walk came up wet and overcast. The wind howled down the almost-empty alley of the road like a lost dog being whipped through a strange and terrible place.

Part Three

THE RABBIT

Chapter 17

"Mother! Mother! Mother! Mother!"
—The Reverend Jim Jones,
    at the moment of his apostasy

The concentrates were being passed out for the fifth and last time. It took only one of the soldiers to pass them out now. There were only nine Walkers left. Some of them looked at the belts dully, as if they had never seen such things, and let them slide out of their hands like slippery snakes. It took Garraty what seemed like hours to make his hands go through the complicated ritual of snapping the belt closed around his waist, and the thought of eating made his cramped and shriveled stomach feel ugly and nauseated.

Stebbins was now walking beside him. My guardian angel, Garraty thought wryly. As Garraty watched, Stebbins smiled widely and crammed two crackers smeared with peanut butter into his mouth. He ate noisily. Garraty felt sick.

"Wassa matter?" Stebbins asked around his sticky mouthful. "Can't take it?"

"What business is it of yours?"

Stebbins swallowed with what looked to Garraty like real effort. "None. If you faint from malnutrition, all the better for me."

"We're going to make it into Massachusetts, I think," McVries said sickly.

Stebbins nodded. "The first Walk to do it in seventeen years. They'll go crazy."

"How do you know so much about the Long Walk?" Garraty asked abruptly.

Stebbins shrugged. "It's all on record. They don't have anything to be ashamed of. Now do they?"

"What'll you do if you win, Stebbins?" McVries asked.

Stebbins laughed. In the rain, his thin, fuzzed face, lined with fatigue, looked lionlike. "What do *you* think? Get a big yella Cadillac with a purple top and a color TV with stereo speakers for every room of the house?"

"I'd expect," McVries said, "that you'd donate two or three hundred grand to the Society for Intensifying Cruelty to Animals."

"Abraham looked like a sheep," Garraty said abruptly. "Like a sheep caught on barbed wire. That's what I thought."

They passed under a huge banner that proclaimed they were now only fifteen miles from the Massachusetts border—there was really not much of New Hampshire along U.S. 1, only a narrow neck of land separating Maine and Massachusetts.

"Garraty," Stebbins said amiably, "why don't you go have sex with your mother?"

"Sorry, you're not pushing the right button anymore." He deliberately selected a bar of chocolate from his belt and crammed it whole into his mouth. His stomach knotted furiously, but he swallowed the chocolate. And after a short, tense struggle with his own insides, he knew he was going to keep it down. "I figure I can walk another full day if I have to," he said casually, "and another two if I need to. Resign yourself to it, Stebbins. Give up the old psy-war. It doesn't work. Have some more crackers and peanut butter."

Stebbins's mouth pursed tightly—just for a moment, but Garraty saw it. He had gotten under Stebbins's skin. He felt an incredible surge of elation. The mother lode at last.

"Come on, Stebbins," he said. "Tell us why *you're* here. Seeing as how we won't be together much longer. Tell us. Just between the three of us, now that we know you're not Superman."

Stebbins opened his mouth and with shocking abruptness he threw up the crackers and peanut butter he had eaten, almost whole and seemingly untouched by digestive juices. He staggered, and for only the second time since the Walk began, he was warned.

Garraty felt hard blood drumming in his head. "Come on, Stebbins. You've thrown up. Now own up. Tell us."

Stebbins's face had gone the color of old cheese-cloth, but he had his composure back. "Why am I here? You want to know?"

McVries was looking at him curiously. No one

was near; the closest was Baker, who was wandering along the edge of the crowd, looking intently into its mass face.

"Why am I here or why do I walk? Which do you want to know?"

"I want to know everything," Garraty said. It was only the truth.

"I'm the rabbit," Stebbins said. The rain fell steadily, dripping off their noses, hanging in droplets on their earlobes like earrings. Up ahead a barefoot boy, his feet purple patchworks of burst veins, went to his knees, crawled along with his head bobbing madly up and down, tried to get up, fell, and finally made it. He plunged onward. It was Pastor, Garraty noted with some amazement. Still with us.

"I'm the rabbit," Stebbins repeated. "You've seen them, Garraty. The little gray mechanical rabbits that the greyhounds chase at the dog races. No matter how fast the dogs run, they can never quite catch the rabbit. Because the rabbit isn't flesh and blood and they are. The rabbit, he's just a cutout on a stick attached to a bunch of cogs and wheels. In the old days, in England, they used to use a real rabbit, but sometimes the dogs caught it. More reliable the new way.

"He fooled me."

Stebbins's pale blue eyes stared into the falling rain.

"Maybe you could even say . . . he conjured me. He changed me into a rabbit. Remember, the one in *Alice in Wonderland*? But maybe you're right,

Garraty. Time to stop being rabbits and grunting pigs and sheep and to be people . . . even if we can only rise to the level of whoremasters and the perverts in the balconies of the theaters on 42nd Street." Stebbins's eyes grew wild and gleeful, and now he looked at Garraty and McVries—and they flinched away from that stare. Stebbins was crazy. In that instant there could be no doubt of it. Stebbins was totally mad.

His low-pitched voice rose to a pulpit shout.

"How come I know so much about the Long Walk? I know all about the Long Walk! I ought to! *The Major is my father, Garraty! He's my father!*"

The crowd's voice rose in a mindless cheer that was mountainous and mindless in its intensity; they might have been cheering what Stebbins had said, if they could have heard it. The guns blasted. That was what the crowd was cheering. The guns blasted and Pastor rolled over dead.

Garraty felt a crawling in his guts and scrotum.

"Oh my God," McVries said. "Is it true?" He ran his tongue over his cracked lips.

"It's true," Stebbins said, almost genially, "I'm his bastard. You see . . . I didn't think he knew. I didn't think he knew I was his son. That was where I made my mistake. He's a randy old sonofabitch, is the Major. I understand he's got dozens of little bastards. What I wanted was to spring it on him—spring it on the world. Surprise, surprise. And when I won, the Prize I was going to ask for was to be taken into my father's house."

"But he knew *everything*?" McVries whispered.

"He made me his rabbit. A little gray rabbit to make the rest of the dogs run faster . . . and further. And I guess it worked. We're going to make it into Massachusetts."

"And now?" Garraty asked.

Stebbins shrugged. "The rabbit turns out to be flesh and blood after all. I walk. I talk. And I suppose if all this doesn't end soon, I'll be crawling on my belly like a reptile."

They passed under a heavy brace of power lines. A number of men in climbing boots clung to the support posts, above the crowd, like grotesque praying mantises.

"What time is it?" Stebbins asked. His face seemed to have melted in the rain. It had become Olson's face, Abraham's face, Barkovitch's face . . . then, terribly, Garraty's own face, hopeless and drained, sunken and crenellated in on itself, the face of a rotten scarecrow in a long-since-harvested field.

"It's twenty until ten," McVries said. He grinned—a ghostly imitation of his old cynical grin. "Happy day five to you, suckers."

Stebbins nodded. "Will it rain all day, Garraty?"

"Yeah, I think so. It looks that way."

Stebbins nodded slowly. "I think so, too."

"Well, come on in out of the rain," McVries said suddenly.

"All right. Thanks."

They walked on, somehow in step, although all three of them were bent forever in different shapes by the pains that pulled them.

* * *

When they crossed into Massachusetts, they were seven: Garraty, Baker, McVries, a struggling, hollow-eyed skeleton named George Fielder, Bill Hough ("pronounce that Huff," he had told Garraty much earlier on), a tallish, muscular fellow named Rattigan who did not seem to be in really serious shape yet, and Stebbins.

The pomp and thunder of the border crossing slowly passed behind them. The rain continued, constant and monotonous. The wind howled and ripped with all the young, unknowing cruelty of spring. It lifted caps from the crowd and whirled them, saucerlike, in brief and violent arcs across the whitewash-colored sky.

A very short while ago—just after Stebbins had made his confession—Garraty had experienced an odd, light lifting of his entire being. His feet seemed to remember what they had once been. There was a kind of frozen cessation to the blinding pains in his back and neck. It was like climbing up a final sheer rock face and coming out on the peak—out of the shifting mist of clouds and into the cold sunshine and the bracing, undernourished air . . . with noplace to go but down, and that at flying speed.

The halftrack was a little ahead of them. Garraty looked at the blond soldier crouched under the big canvas umbrella on the back deck. He tried to project all the ache, all the rainsoaked misery out of himself and into the Major's man. The blond stared back at him indifferently.

Garraty glanced over at Baker and saw that his nose was bleeding badly. Blood painted his cheeks and dripped from the line of his jaw.

"He's going to die, isn't he?" Stebbins said.

"Sure," McVries answered. "They've all been dying, didn't you know?"

A hard gust of wind sheeted rain across them, and McVries staggered. He drew a warning. The crowd cheered on, unaffected and seemingly impervious. At least there had been fewer firecrackers today. The rain had put a stop to that happy bullshit.

The road took them around a big, banked curve, and Garraty felt his heart lurch. Faintly he heard Rattigan mutter, "Good Jesus!"

The road was sunk between two sloping hills. The road was like a cleft between two rising breasts. The hills were black with people. The people seemed to rise above them and around them like the living walls of a huge dark slough.

George Fielder came abruptly to life. His skullhead turned slowly this way and that on his pipestem neck. "They're going to eat us up," he muttered. "They're gonna fall in on us and eat us up."

"I think not," Stebbins said shortly. "There has never been a—"

"They're gonna eat us up! Eat us up! Eatusup! Up! Up! Eatusupeatusup—" George Fielder whirled around in a huge, rambling circle, his arms flapping madly. His eyes blazed with mousetrap terror. To Garraty he looked like one of those video games gone crazy.

"Eatusupeatusupeatusup—"

He was screeching at the top of his voice, but Garraty could barely hear him. The waves of sound from the hills beat down on them like hammers. Garraty could not even hear the gunshots when Fielder bought out; only the savage scream from the throat of Crowd. Fielder's body did a gangling but strangely graceful rhumba in the center of the road, feet kicking, body twitching, shoulders jerking. Then, apparently too tired to dance anymore, he sat down, legs spread wide, and he died that way, sitting up, his chin tucked down on his chest like a tired little boy caught by the sandman at playtime.

"Garraty," Baker said. "Garraty, I'm bleeding." The hills were behind them now and Garraty could hear him—badly.

"Yeah," he said. It was a struggle to keep his voice level. Something inside Art Baker had hemorrhaged. His nose was gushing blood. His cheeks and neck were lathered with gore. His shirt collar was soaked with it.

"It's not bad, is it?" Baker asked him. He was crying with fear. He knew it was bad.

"No, not too bad," Garraty said.

"The rain feels so warm," Baker said. "I know it's only rain, though. It's only rain, right, Garraty?"

"Right," Garraty said sickly.

"I wish I had some ice to put on it," Baker said, and walked away. Garraty watched him go.

Bill Hough ("you pronounce that Huff") bought

a ticket at quarter of eleven, and Rattigan at eleven-thirty, just after the Flying Deuces precision-flying team rocketed overhead in six electric blue F-111s. Garraty had expected Baker to go before either of them. But Baker continued on, although now the whole top half of his shirt was soaked through.

Garraty's head seemed to be playing jazz. Dave Brubeck, Thelonius Monk, Cannonball Adderly—the Banned Noisemakers that everybody kept under the table and played when the party got noisy and drunk.

It seemed that he had once been loved, once he himself had loved. But now it was just jazz and the rising drumbeat in his head and his mother had only been stuffed straw in a fur coat, Jan nothing but a department store dummy. It was over. Even if he won, if he managed to outlast McVries and Stebbins and Baker, it was over. He was never going home again.

He began to cry a little bit. His vision blurred and his feet tangled up and he fell down. The pavement was hard and shockingly cold and unbelievably restful. He was warned twice before he managed to pick himself up, using a series of drunken, crab-like motions. He got his feet to work again. He broke wind—a long, sterile rattle that seemed to bear no relationship at all to an honest fart.

Baker was zigging and zagging drunkenly across the road and back. McVries and Stebbins had their heads together. Garraty was suddenly very sure they were plotting to kill him, the way someone named Barkovitch had once killed a faceless number named Rank.

He made himself walk fast and caught up with them. They made room for him wordlessly. (You've stopped talking about me, haven't you? But you were. Do you think I don't know? Do you think I am nuts?), but there was a comfort. He wanted to be with them, stay with them, until he died.

They passed a sign now which seemed to summarize to Garraty's dumbly wondering eyes all the screaming insanity there might be in the universe, all the idiot whistling laughter of the spheres, and this sign read: 49 MILES TO BOSTON! WALKERS YOU CAN MAKE IT! He would have shrieked with laughter if he had been able. Boston! The very sound was mythic, rich with unbelievability.

Baker was beside him again. "Garraty?"

"What?"

"Are we in?"

"Huh?"

"In, are we in? Garraty, *please*."

Baker's eyes pleaded. He was an abattoir, a raw-blood machine.

"Yeah. We're in. We're in, Art." He had no idea what Baker was talking about.

"I'm going to die now, Garraty."

"All right."

"If you win, will you do something for me? I'm scairt to ask anyone else." And Baker made a sweeping gesture at the deserted road as if the Walk was still rich with its dozens. For a chilling moment

Garraty wondered if maybe they were all there still, walking ghosts that Baker could now see in his moment of extremis.

"Anything."

Baker put a hand on Garraty's shoulder, and Garraty began weeping uncontrollably. It seemed that his heart would burst out of his chest and weep its own tears.

Baker said, "Lead-lined."

"Walk a little bit longer," Garraty said through his tears. "Walk a little longer, Art."

"No—I can't."

"All right."

"Maybe I'll see you, man," Baker said, and wiped slick blood from his face absently.

Garraty lowered his head and wept.

"Don't watch 'em do it," Baker said. "Promise me that, too."

Garraty nodded, beyond speech.

"Thanks. You've been my friend, Garraty." Baker tried to smile. He stuck his hand blindly out, and Garraty shook it with both of his.

"Another time, another place," Baker said.

Garraty put his hands over his face and had to bend over to keep walking. The sobs ripped out of him and made him ache with a pain that was far beyond anything the Walk had been able to inflict.

He hoped he wouldn't hear the shots. But he did.

Chapter 18

"I proclaim this year's Long Walk at an end.
Ladies and gentlemen—citizens—behold
your winner!"

—The Major

They were forty miles from Boston.

"Tell us a story, Garraty," Stebbins said abruptly.
"Tell us a story that will take our minds off our
troubles." He had aged unbelievably; Stebbins was
an old man.

"Yeah," McVries said. He also looked ancient
and wizened. "A story, Garraty."

Garraty looked from one to the other dully, but
he could see no duplicity in their faces, only the
bone-weariness. He was falling off his own peak
now; all the ugly, dragging pains were rushing
back in.

He closed his eyes for a long moment. When he
opened them, the world had doubled and came
only reluctantly back into focus. "All right," he said.

McVries clapped his hands solemnly, three times.
He was walking with three warnings; Garraty had
one; Stebbins, none.

"Once upon a time—"

"Oh, who wants to hear a fucking fairy story?" Stebbins asked.

McVries giggled a little.

"You'll hear what I want to tell you!" Garraty said shrewishly. "You want to hear it or not?"

Stebbins stumbled against Garraty. Both he and Stebbins were warned. "I s'pose a fairy story's better than no story at all."

"It's not a fairy story, anyway. Just because it's in a world that never was doesn't mean it's a fairy story. It doesn't mean—"

"Are you gonna tell it or not?" McVries asked pettishly.

"Once upon a time," Garraty began, "there was a white knight that went out into the world on a Sacred Quest. He left his castle and walked through the Enchanted Forest—"

"Knights ride," Stebbins objected.

"Rode through the Enchanted Forest, then. *Rode.* And he had many strange adventures. He fought off thousands of trolls and goblins and a whole shitload of wolves. All right? And he finally got to the king's castle and asked permission to take Gwendolyn, the famous Lady Fair, out walking."

McVries cackled.

"The king wasn't digging it, thinking no one was good enough for his daughter Gwen, the world-famous Lady Fair, but the Lady Fair loved the White Knight so much that she threatened to run away into the Wildwoods if . . . if . . ." A wave of dizziness rode over him darkly, making him feel as if he were floating. The roar of the crowd came to him like the boom of the sea down a long, cone-shaped tunnel. Then it passed, but slowly.

He looked around. McVries's head had dropped, and he was walking at the crowd, fast asleep.

"Hey!" Garraty shouted. "Hey, Pete! *Pete!*"

"Let him alone," Stebbins said. "You made the promise like the rest of us."

"Fuck you," Garraty said distinctly, and darted to McVries's side. He touched McVries's shoulders, setting him straight again. McVries looked up at him sleepily and smiled. "No, Ray. It's time to sit down."

Terror pounded Garraty's chest. "No! No way!"

McVries looked at him for a moment, then smiled again and shook his head. He sat down, cross-legged on the pavement. He looked like a world-beaten monk. The scar on his cheek was a white slash in the rainy gloom.

"*No!*" Garraty screamed.

He tried to pick McVries up, but, thin as he was, McVries was much too heavy. McVries wouldn't even look at him. His eyes were shut. And suddenly two of the soldiers were wrenching McVries away from him. They were putting their guns to McVries's head.

"*No!*" Garraty screamed again. "*Me! Me! Shoot me!*"

But instead, they gave him his third warning.

McVries opened his eyes and smiled again. The next instant, he was gone.

Garraty walked unknowingly now. He stared

blankly at Stebbins, who stared back at him curiously. Garraty was filled with a strange, roaring emptiness.

"Finish the story," Stebbins said. "Finish the story, Garraty."

"No," Garraty said. "I don't think so."

"Let it go, then," Stebbins said, and smiled winningly. "If there are such things as souls, his is still close. You could catch up."

Garraty looked at Stebbins and said, "I'm going to walk you into the ground."

Oh, Pete, he thought. He didn't even have any tears left to cry.

"Are you?" Stebbins said. "We'll see."

By eight that evening they were walking through Danvers, and Garraty finally knew. It was almost done, because Stebbins could not be beaten.

I spent too much time thinking about it. McVries, Baker, Abraham . . . they didn't think about it, they just did it. As if it were natural. And it *is* natural. In a way, it's the most natural thing in the world.

He shambled along, bulge-eyed, jaw hanging agape, rain swishing in. For a misty, shutterlike moment he thought he saw someone he knew, knew as well as himself, weeping and beckoning in the dark ahead, but it was no use. He couldn't go on.

He would just tell Stebbins. He was up ahead a little, limping quite a bit now, and looking emaciated. Garraty was very tired, but he was no longer afraid. He felt calm. He felt okay. He made himself go faster until he could put a hand on Stebbins's shoulder. "Stebbins," he said.

Stebbins turned and looked at Garraty with huge, floating eyes that saw nothing for a moment. Then recognition came and he reached out and clawed at Garraty's shirt, pulling it open. The crowd screamed its anger at this interference, but only Garraty was close enough to see the horror in Stebbins's eyes, the horror, the darkness, and only Garraty knew that Stebbins's grip was a last despairing reach for rescue.

"Oh Garraty!" he cried, and fell down.

Now the sound of the crowd was apocalyptic. It was the sound of mountains falling and breaking, the earth shattering. The sound crushed Garraty easily beneath it. It would have killed him if he had heard it. But he heard nothing but his own voice.

"Stebbins?" he said curiously. He bent and somehow managed to turn Stebbins over. Stebbins still stared at him, but the despair had already skimmed over. His head rolled bonelessly on his neck.

He put a cupped hand in front of Stebbins's mouth. "Stebbins?" he said again.

But Stebbins was dead.

Garraty lost interest. He got to his feet and began to walk. Now the cheers filled the earth and fireworks filled the sky. Up ahead, a jeep roared toward him.

No vehicles on the road, you damn fool. That's a capital offense, they can shoot you for that.

The Major stood in the jeep. He held a stiff salute.

Ready to grant first wish, every wish, any wish, death wish. The Prize.

Behind him, they finished by shooting the already-dead Stebbins, and now there was only him, alone on the road, walking toward where the Major's jeep had stopped diagonally across the white line, and the Major was getting out, coming to him, his face kind and unreadable behind the mirror sunglasses.

Garraty stepped aside. He was not alone. The dark figure was back, up ahead, not far, beckoning. He knew that figure. If he could get a little closer, he could make out the features. Which one hadn't he walked down? Was it Barkovitch? Collie Parker? Percy What'shisname? Who was it?

"GARRATY!" the crowd screamed deliriously. "GARRATY, GARRATY, GARRATY!"

Was it Scramm? Gribble? Davidson?

A hand on his shoulder. Garraty shook it off impatiently. The dark figure beckoned, beckoned in the rain, beckoned for him to come and walk, to come and play the game. And it was time to get started. There was still so far to walk.

Eyes blind, supplicating hands held out before him as if for alms, Garraty walked toward the dark figure.

And when the hand touched his shoulder again, he somehow found the strength to run.